DATE

UN CHANGED

By JESSICA BRODY

JESSICA BRODY

THE UNREMEMBERED TRILOGY:
BOOK 3

UN CHANGED

FARRAR STRAUS GIROUX
New York

Farrar Straus Giroux Books for Young Readers
175 Fifth Avenue, New York 10010

Printed in the United States of America
First edition, 2015
10 9 8 7 6 5 4 3 2 1

macteenbooks.com

Library of Congress Cataloging-in-Publication Data
Brody, Jessica.
    Unchanged / Jessica Brody. — First edition.
       pages cm. — (The Unremembered trilogy ; book 3)
    Summary: "As more secrets are revealed, more enemies are uncovered, and the
reality of a Diotech-controlled world grows closer every day, Sera will have to choose
where her true loyalties lie, but it's a choice that may cost her everything she's ever
loved"—Provided by publisher.
    ISBN 978-0-374-37989-6 (hardcover)
    ISBN 978-1-250-07359-4 (trade pbk.)
    ISBN 978-0-374-30178-1 (e-book)
    [1. Amnesia—Fiction.   2. Genetic engineering—Fiction.   3. Space and time—Fiction.
4. Love—Fiction.   5. Science fiction.]   I. Title.

PZ7.B786157Um 2015
[Fic]—dc23

2014040382

Farrar Straus Giroux Books for Young Readers may be purchased for business
or promotional use. For information on bulk purchases please contact Macmillan
Corporate and Premium Sales Department at (800) 221-7945 x5442 or by email
at specialmarkets@macmillan.com.

To my readers,

For believing anything is possible.
Even the crazy stories I make up in my head.

Faith is the strength by which
a shattered world shall emerge
into the light.

—Helen Keller

CONTENTS

0

BEFORE

The girl didn't fight. She knew it was pointless. She watched
the doctor prepare the needle, drawing up the Cv9 into the reservoir and inserting it directly into her vein.

Of course, there were more modern ways to inject sedatives
but he preferred the tactile feel of the needle. The small popping
sound it made as it penetrated the skin. The pressure of manually compelling the drug into the bloodstream.

He could trust his own fingers.

He couldn't say the same for much else.

"Don't worry," he told her. "This won't hurt. And you won't remember a thing."

The serum worked fast. The dose was significant. As she drifted
to sleep, she held one face in her mind. The face she longed to
remember. And also longed to forget.

She would wake up chained. She would wake up changed.

She knew this.

The smile on her lips as her mind slipped into darkness was
her last act of rebellion.

The doctor watched her vitals on a monitor. When she was fully under, he sent for the president.

The slender blond man entered the room ten minutes later, limping against a cane. It was a vast improvement over the mechanical chair that carried him only yesterday.

"She's ready," the doctor informed him.

The president walked unsteadily around the edge of the hovering metal slab that held the unconscious girl. Without uttering a word, he gazed down upon her. An ignorant bystander might even describe the look in his eyes as adoring, particularly as he reached down to brush a strand of golden-brown hair from her face.

But the longer he watched her, the less innocuous his stare became. Hardening with each passing second. Until icy blue stones glared out from the sockets where his eyes had once been.

She had betrayed him for the last time. He would not make the same mistakes again.

"I have a Memory Coder standing by," the doctor informed him. "I've ordered a full wipe to be initiated on your command."

"No." The president's response was swift and stern.

The doctor was certain he had misunderstood. "No?"

"We've tried that before. Countless times. And it always leads us right back here."

"But surely this time the Coders can—"

The president silenced him with a shaky raise of his hand. "She keeps her memories. *All* of them. Restore everything we have in the server bunker."

"Everything?"

"Guilt is a powerful weapon. Her memories will be a constant reminder of her disloyalty. Every time she thinks of him, I want her to *feel* that betrayal. Tell the Coder we're going to implement the new procedure."

The doctor squirmed. "Sir, with all due respect, that procedure hasn't been fully tested and—"

"That will be all."

The doctor stood in stunned silence until he finally managed to utter an acknowledgment of the order.

The president returned his gaze to the girl, reaching out to gently stroke her silken cheek. Then, so the doctor couldn't hear, he bent down and whispered in her ear, "This time you won't be given the luxury of forgetting."

PART 1

THE UNKNOWING

1

UPDATED

ONE YEAR LATER . . .

The air is harsh and blistering, whipping around me as I cross the barren field. There are no buildings to thwart the desert wind, and today it seems angrier than most. I could outrun it. I'm certainly capable. But I keep my current pace.

I'm in no rush to get there.

The compound is almost unrecognizable out here. The landscaped pathways ended a half mile back. The sleek, reflective surfaces of the Aerospace Sector were the last signs of civilization.

Now it's just . . .

Nothingness.

But I feel reassured knowing the fortifications that mark the boundaries lie beyond the hill to my left.

There used to be a time when the walls of the compound kept me in—when I thought of them as prison walls and tried to escape. Now, it's as though someone has lifted a veil of deception from my eyes and I can finally see the truth.

The walls are there to keep others out.

Those who don't understand me. Those who want to hurt me. Those who are unlike me.

Of course, there are plenty of people on this side of the wall who are unlike me, too, but they can be trusted. Their bodies and minds may not be as strong as mine, but they still think like me. They still serve the Objective.

The dry shrubs crunch beneath my feet as I approach the cottage. The ten-foot wall around the perimeter remains standing but the gate is no longer locked.

I run my fingertips along the warm unyielding surface of the concrete, feeling the rough edges prickle my skin.

He used to climb these walls.

The boy from my memories.

That's how he got to me. How he broke into my world and corrupted my brain with impossible notions. Impossible dreams. Promises of a life outside these barriers.

As if I could ever live anywhere else.

This is where I belong. Where I've always belonged. And now that my memories have been restored and the truth has been revealed to me, my brain is stronger, my goals refortified. I am no longer susceptible to bewitching lies.

I can no longer be swayed.

They fixed me. They introduced me to my true purpose. And I am grateful.

I push open the heavy steel gate of what was once the Restricted Sector and slip inside. The white cottage is smaller than I remember. As though it's physically shrinking day by day, its importance diminishing in my mind. This is the first time I've visited in over a year. The first time I've been able to gather the strength to.

I'm hoping that today it will remind me of where I started. Who I was. How far I've come.

I'm no longer the vulnerable, naïve little girl who had to be locked in a cage for her own protection.

I am strong now. A fully functioning member of the Objective. A soldier.

Even if he were here, even if he had found his way back, it wouldn't matter. I would be able to resist him now. I will never fall prey to his charms again.

That stupid girl is gone.

I am the better version.

The grass surrounding the cottage is overgrown and burnt to a brown crisp by the desert sun. No one comes here anymore. There is no reason to. The Restricted Sector of the compound was originally built to shield me from the world. But ever since the announcement of the Unveiling three months ago, I no longer have to be shielded.

I exist.

And the world knows.

Now the sector remains abandoned. All of my training, testing, and recreation takes place in the other sectors.

When I step through the front door of the house, I find the rooms barren. They must have emptied them, redistributing the furniture to other parts of the compound. What few possessions I had were undoubtedly thrown away. Which is for the best. That was the darkest time in my life. I don't want mementos.

I walk from room to room, my legs wobbly and unreliable beneath me. I may collapse at any minute from the sheer heaviness of this place. But I push myself to keep going.

I stand in the middle of what used to be the living room and close my eyes. I can smell the scent of my own betrayal. My weakness is steeped in these walls. It makes me gag, but I force myself to breathe it in, allow it to settle in my lungs. The shame trickles through my body like a cold insect. I hate how ugly it feels inside of me but I don't fight it. I don't push it out. I only draw it in deeper. Letting it saturate me.

This is exactly what I need to make sure I stay strong. Focused. Committed. This is an important time for the Objective. And I won't allow myself to falter again.

Outside, the sun is already setting, the bright gold orb kissing the pink horizon. As I step onto the porch, my gaze is pulled toward a patch of indented grass on the far side of the lawn. I know from accessing the memories of my life before my rehabilitation that there used to be a white marble bench there.

The boy and I used to hide things under it before we escaped. It was our way of communicating with each other without the scientists knowing.

Another method of flagrant rebellion on my part.

A new onslaught of guilt punches me in the chest. I clench my fists and grit my teeth, soaking in the sensation, letting it fuel the fire of determination I keep lit inside me at all times.

The bench is long gone, but something is strangely drawing me to the spot where it once stood. Like a magnetic force field pulling me in, rendering me helpless in its grasp.

Could something still be buried there after all this time?

The thought enters my mind before I can stop it and I feel my feet drag as I approach, my mind and body at war.

A small object in the grass where the bench once stood catches my eye. I walk over and bend down, plucking the small blossom from the ground and holding it up. The white feathery surface sparkles as the vanishing sunlight shines through it.

"Dandelion," I say, accessing the correct name from my mind.

I smile at how easily the word comes to me. The uploads I receive weekly provide me with more data than I'll ever need. Now that I am trustworthy, I have been given full clearance to all the knowledge I desire. My access to data is no longer limited.

I search for more information, quickly discovering that a

dandelion is a weed that was eradicated thanks to advances made in Diotech's Agricultural Sector.

But evidently they weren't able to eliminate all of them.

"Weed," I say curiously, rolling the thick, rough stem between my thumb and forefinger.

The memory of the first time I saw one explodes into my mind. I was with him. The boy called Lyzender. The day we met. Right here in this yard.

He told me to wish on it.

He told me a lot of things.

"It's more beautiful than other plants," I remark, clutching the stem.

His eyes find mine. Endless brown eyes. "It most certainly is."

I wrap my palm around the downy white flower and squeeze, crushing the soft fibers against my hand. When I unfurl my fingers, there's nothing but a sickly grayish pulp left.

"I wish I had never fallen," I announce to the empty yard, wiping my hand against my pant leg and dropping the barren stem to the ground. There's a satisfying *squish* as my shoe lands on top of it. "I wish we had never met."

2

AMISS

I take the long route back to the Residential Sector, weaving through the glinting Aerospace hangars whose surfaces always distort my reflection in unsettling ways. Turning me into a disfigured monster with one giant eye and no neck.

I'm one of the few people who walk around the compound. Most people prefer to travel by hovercart, due to the heat and distance between sectors, but I actually enjoy walking. The distances don't bother me and my body was designed to withstand severe climates.

I used to like to walk the perimeters, alongside the VersaScreens so I could see the world on the other side. But ever since the announcement of the upcoming Unveiling, the world on the other side is populated with news crews and protesters and people wanting to steal a peek inside our walls.

Even though I know they can't see through—the screens are programmed for one-way visibility—it still frightens me to walk past them. I can feel their energy in the air like buzzing flies around a dead carcass. There's a franticness about their desperation that unnerves me.

Dr. A says that's normal. I'm allowed to be afraid.

"Fear doesn't equate with weakness," he told me. "It equates with obedience. You want to be obedient, don't you?"

I nodded. "I want to serve the Objective."

He smiled. "We all do. And your distrust of strangers will keep you safe."

I know I won't be able to stay hidden behind those walls for much longer, though. The Unveiling is in two days. Then they will see my face. Then they will know me.

And that is the part that frightens me most of all.

I cut across the Agricultural Sector, making a wide arc around the cottonwood tree in the corner. I've never liked that tree. It looks like a pudgy old ogre with too many twisted limbs. And when the sun splinters through the branches at just the right angle, I swear I can hear it screaming. A shadowy, piercing sound that vanishes the second I turn around. Like the ghost of an echo.

The delicious scents of the freshly grown herbs waft from the vents of the hydroponic dome as I walk. Dr. A says one day we won't need to grow food at all. Computers will be able to engineer molecules from raw materials and shape them into anything we want to eat.

"Kind of like we did with you," he likes to say, as though I'm a hot plate of superberry flatcakes, molecularly processed to order.

I like when Dr. A talks about the future. It implies that the Objective will be a success. And really, we're not that far off. Diotech already mastered the engineering of synthetic meat after the government outlawed the breeding of livestock for food seven years ago. I learned about it from one of my uploads on agricultural history.

From here, with my enhanced vision, I can see all the way

to the northwest gate, the main entrance of the compound, where the majority of the media crews have gathered. They're all hoping to gain access or corner someone for an interview to put on the Feed. I know they will never be allowed inside. Director Raze's security force is top-notch.

"They'll have to step over my dead body before I let them get near you, princess," he says to me. Always with a wink.

As I exit the Agricultural Sector and near the polished metallic archway of the Medical Sector, I stop when a familiar nagging sensation starts to tickle the pit of my stomach. I turn around, almost expecting to find someone standing behind me, but there's no one there.

Yet the feeling persists.

I spin in a slow circle, letting my flawless eyes zero in on every planted flower, every curved ceiling of every building, each individual blade of grass along the pathway. I can feel my shoulders tighten, my body clench.

What are you looking for? I silently ask myself.

But there is no reply. I can't answer the question.

I can never answer the question.

All I know is that almost every day something compels me to look.

I once asked Dr. A about holes.

He thought I was referring to the holes that the rodents dig in the desert floor outside the compound and offered me an upload about animal habitats, but I shook my head. "No. I mean, holes inside of me."

"There are no holes inside of you, Sera," he replied sharply. "I made you perfect, remember?"

I was frustrated that I couldn't make him understand. "Something is missing," was the only way I could think to explain it.

"Nothing is missing," he snapped, anger unexpectedly flashing in his eyes. "I've given you everything you could ever ask for. Are you ungrateful for all the luxuries you have here?"

I knew instantly that I had said the wrong thing. I often do. "I'm sorry," I offered, desperate to reverse the distress I had caused him. "You're right. Nothing is missing. I am very grateful."

I never asked him about holes again.

I jog down the pathway through the Medical Sector, keeping careful watch on my pace. Dr. A says when I'm walking around the compound, it's important for me to hide my enhancements as much as possible so I don't make anyone else uncomfortable.

On my left is the grand, ornate building that houses the memory labs. It's by far the largest, most well-appointed structure in the sector. If appearances are any indication of funding allocation, memories are definitely high on Dr. A's priority list.

And I know why.

So much goes on within these compound walls that the outside world can never know about. So many secrets are buried inside the sleek surfaces of the labs, you'd need more than just a mini-military to keep them guarded.

I used to be one of those secrets.

Director Raze's team is tasked with preventing breaches. But what happens when those preventative measures fail?

That's when the Memory Coders step in.

As I pass, I peer through the synthoglass walls at the pristine white entry hallway that leads to the labs where Sevan Sidler and his team of Memory Coders work to keep Diotech's secrets safe. The synthetic tile floors are so clean the pillars on either side are reflected in their surface, making the tall posts appear as though they plunge deep into the ground below.

A shiver runs through me and I pick up my pace until I've put a considerable distance between me and the building. It always feels so sinister to me. Thinking of all the memories that enter those doors and never come out. Innumerable bytes of data removed from people's minds and stored in a pod somewhere.

How many dreams were forgotten in that place?

How many kisses stolen? Loves removed?

It's almost as though every time I enter those labs, I can feel the memories clinging to the walls, trying so desperately to stay remembered.

Every once in a while I have to go inside. When Dr. A orders a random memory scan. Other than that, I try to stay clear of it.

I hang a left toward the entrance to the gardens, but before I reach it, I hear the distinct sound of footsteps behind me.

I slow to a stop and turn around, looking for the source, but once again, there is no one there. The path is empty. Most of the scientists are still at work.

"Hello?" I call out.

No one replies.

My first thought is that one of the media crew from outside the gates somehow bypassed Director Raze's security team and is hoping to get a glimpse of me.

But if that were the case, why would they hide from me?

I wait, watching for flickers of movement, but the compound is still.

Feeling uneasy, I spin, focusing on every detail around me. I can hear someone breathing. Maybe fifty feet away. A hundred at most.

I start moving again. This time, I don't limit my pace. I run. As fast as my genetically enhanced legs will go.

But I don't get very far. The second I set foot in the gardens, someone tackles me to the ground.

3

MATED

The attacker moves so quickly I barely have time to process what is happening. One minute I'm standing upright and the next I'm lying on my back, a massive body pressing down on me. I grunt at the impact of my head slamming against the ground.

I open my eyes and blink. A face comes into focus. Oval shaped, framed by a fringe of silky dark blond hair that falls across his forehead, veiling his vibrant aquamarine eyes. An impish grin curves his perfect pale pink lips.

"Kaelen," I say, relieved, releasing a nervous giggle.

"*Jouw reflexen zijn traag.*"

Translation: Your reflexes are slow.

So he's switched to Dutch. This morning it was Arabic.

"I wasn't prepared to be attacked in the middle of the garden." I defend myself in the same tongue without missing a beat. Kaelen thinks he can trick me, switching languages throughout the day. He hasn't succeeded once.

"Exactly my point. You should always be prepared."

I groan and plant two hands on his chest, attempting to

shove him off me, but he doesn't budge. He's stronger than me. He always has been. He's the second generation ExGen, while I'm the first.

He likes to joke that he's an improved version of me.

I like to joke that he's just a watered-down copy of an original masterpiece.

He smirks at my effort, enjoying watching me struggle. Then he grabs each of my hands in his and pins them down next to my shoulders.

"What are you going to do now?" he goads, keeping with the smooth Dutch.

I puff out a breath, pretending to resign myself, letting my muscles and limbs slacken under him, before launching another escape attempt.

Kaelen only laughs as he continues to restrain me without much effort. "Pitiful."

"You're stronger than I am!" I cry. "There's nothing I can do."

"You can kiss me back."

"Wha—?"

And then his lips are on mine, stopping the word from ever being completed. His kiss isn't soft or tentative. Kaelen doesn't do soft or tentative. Kaelen does fierce. He does eager. He does commanding. His lips part mine as he releases some of his body weight against me.

He lets go of my wrists and I immediately reach for his hair, loving the way it feels between my fingers. Softer than human hair is supposed to be. I pull him closer to me and he responds instantly by deepening the kiss, reading my body language perfectly, the way only he can do.

The way he's always been able to do.

We are fluent in every spoken language on earth. But it's the silent language between us that we speak best.

That's what happens when you're Print Mates—created from

18

two complementary genetic blueprints. You can almost feel what the other person is going to do before they do it.

Dr. A says it's like soul mates but without the heartache. Print Mates are scientifically proven to be compatible matches, while the concept of "soul mates" is just an idea invented by humans a long time ago in an effort to explain the unexplainable.

There's not much in today's world that is unexplainable.

Dr. A has made sure of that.

Taking advantage of Kaelen's distraction, in one swift motion I pull away from him and roll myself to the left. He collapses into the space I just vacated, landing on his stomach with an *oomph*. Before he has time to process it, I'm on my feet, flashing him a teasing smile.

He grins at the challenge, leaps up, and chases after me. But this time, I have a head start. And I need it. Kaelen is not only stronger than I am, but faster, too.

We weave deftly through the meticulously trimmed hedges and immaculate flower beds of the garden, two blurs of color and laughter. The flowers are in bloom yearlong on the compound, despite the heat and inhospitable growing conditions of the desert. The Agricultural Sector is to thank for that. As well as for the life span of the blossoms once they're cut. Flowers used to die within days. Now they can brighten someone's home for months without showing signs of withering.

It's one of the few advancements made by Diotech I can truly appreciate. Hovercarts and DigiSlates and long-range mutation lasers can certainly make life easier, sometimes even safer. But they don't do anything to make the world more beautiful.

Eventually Kaelen catches up to me by bounding effortlessly over a hedge taller than both of us. He seizes me around the waist and pulls me back to him, wrapping his strong, chiseled arms around me so I can't break free. When his lips find mine again, my knees nearly give out.

He presses his hands into the small of my back, sending

tingles up my spine. I squeal and press my tongue into his mouth, tangling it around his. I can feel him smiling against me as he pushes back, playfully jockeying for control of the kiss.

"Hello, Sera. Hello, Kaelen," a voice says, startling us out of our embrace.

I open my eyes and turn my head away from Kaelen's searching lips. When I see who's standing there, a glacial chill runs through my veins, erasing all evidence of Kaelen's warmth.

I was so consumed by our kiss, I didn't even hear him approach. And apparently neither did Kaelen. So much for *his* reflexes.

"Hello," Kaelen replies cordially, smiling toward the man who stands next to a nearby shrub with a pair of red trimming shears dangling from one hand while the other waves wildly in our direction.

Uncomfortable, I quickly fight to disentangle myself from Kaelen's grasp. He tries to draw me back toward him, murmuring in silky Italian, "*Tranquilla. Stai calma.*"

He always shifts to Italian when he's trying to calm me. Or when he's trying to sweeten his words. He knows the soft vowel sounds help soothe me.

But I can't. I can't be in Kaelen's arms with him standing there.

I can't even bear to look at the slack-jawed man in the yard with his ill-fitting clothes, unkempt auburn beard, and dust-covered shoes.

"He doesn't understand what he just saw," Kaelen assures me.

He thinks this is about the kiss. He thinks I'm embarrassed by our public display of affection. If only it were that simple.

"It's a nice evening, isn't it?" the man says in his clumsy, awkward cadence, oblivious to our struggle. "Not too hot for May."

I brave a glance in his direction but his vacant stare sends a shudder through me and I have to avert my gaze again.

Kaelen steps in front of me, offering his body as a shield. "It's almost dark," he tells the man. "You should head home." The way he addresses him is the way everyone on this compound addresses him. Like they're communicating with a small child who was born without the ability to comprehend the world.

When the man speaks again, he fumbles with the shapes of the letters, as though he's forming them for the first time. "I just thought I'd get a head start on tomorrow's work. There are a lot of hedges around this place."

"There are," Kaelen agrees gently. "But maybe it's time to call it a day. It's getting late."

The man stands eerily still as he stares back at Kaelen. It's almost a full ten seconds before he responds. "Is it now?"

"It is."

I eye the entrance to the Residential Sector, not too far from here. I could run. Keep running until I'm home. I could slam the door, push against it with all my strength.

"*Tranquilla*," Kaelen repeats. "He won't hurt you."

Of course, I know he's not going to hurt me. The poor man couldn't hurt a fly. It's not pain that I'm afraid of. It's looking into his eyes. It's seeing the emptiness that stares back. It's knowing what brilliance used to be there.

It's knowing that he's a traitor. Like me.

Just not as lucky.

I got a second chance.

He got . . . this.

An artificial brain cobbled together with nanoprocessors and synthetic metal. A new life that is insulting in comparison to the one he used to have.

"We have to punish our enemies," Dr. A once told me. "Otherwise, how will we stop more people from betraying us?"

"What time is it?" the man asks, gazing up at the few stars that have started to appear, as though they might provide the answer.

"It's almost eight," Kaelen says.

The man's mouth hangs slightly ajar as he lets this sink in. "Is it now?"

"It is," Kaelen confirms. "So you should probably get some rest, right?"

I bury my face in Kaelen's muscular back, silently willing the man to obey. To leave. His warped face is already going to haunt my dreams tonight. I don't need that nightmare spilling over into my last few waking hours, too.

"I think you're right," the man eventually agrees. "I should probably go home."

Yes. Go. Please.

"Good night, then."

"Good night," Kaelen echoes.

I can't bring myself to talk.

Because I'm a glitching coward.

I steal a peek through the crook of Kaelen's elbow and watch the man drop his trimming shears at his feet before turning to walk away. They embed themselves in the grass, red handles up. I finally emerge from behind Kaelen.

Just as the man turns back around.

"Sera," he says, staring right at me with his dead eyes.

I freeze on the spot. Swallow. Force myself to breathe. Kaelen bumps me on the shoulder, urging me to respond.

I clear my throat and coerce my tongue into motion. "Yes?"

The man smiles. It's a disconcerting facial contortion that never reaches his eyes. "It's nice to see you."

I can feel Kaelen watching me. I can feel the stars watching me. Waiting for my reaction. Waiting to judge me for it.

Dr. A wouldn't be happy if he knew how much this upsets me. He would call my queasiness weak. He would say I still have the blood of a traitor running through my veins.

I have to prove him wrong.

I stand up straighter, puff out my chest, and in my most affable, detached tone, I say, "It's nice to see you, too, Rio."

4

REMINDERS

They have landscaping bots on the compound. They've had them for years. And they're much more efficient and productive than any human gardener. But Dr. A wanted to make an example of his former business partner, previously one of the most gifted scientists on the Diotech compound. He wanted everyone to see what happens when you cross him.

No one is safe from punishment. Not even the cofounder of the company.

I doubt anyone is as disturbed by the sight of him as I am though.

Dr. Havin Rio was the lead scientist of the Genesis Project, the official launch of the Objective, and the project that brought me to life on June 27, 2114. And later Kaelen, on December 19, 2115. But Dr. Rio was long gone by the time Kaelen was created.

He was more than just my creator, though. He lived with me in the cottage for the first months of my life. At one point, I even referred to him as my father.

Then he committed the ultimate betrayal.

He helped set me free.

Just like Lyzender, the boy in my memories, he developed feelings for me. As though I were his real daughter. And he put those feelings before the Objective.

Now he pays the price every day.

The memory starts to billow inside of me. Like a tropical storm brewing, bending the trees until they look like they're about to snap.

"You saved my life," I whisper in his ear as I hold the tiny vial in my hands. The transession gene that would allow me to travel through time. The key to my escape.

I feel his body sag. He wraps his arms tightly around me. "It was the least I could do."

The recollection of our mutually treasonous words makes my stomach twist. Every time I see him wandering around the compound with those trimming shears, I'm reminded of our mistakes. At least he can't remember his part. At least he doesn't have to marinate in the guilt every morning when he wakes up. Like a dirty, lukewarm bath.

But I'm grateful for the mercy Dr. A took on me. I was swayed by temptation—corrupted by a boy with maple eyes and a crooked smile—and Dr. A saved me. He gave me a second chance.

Kaelen guides me to a nearby bench and I collapse onto it, my body a trembling, shaking mess.

I shouldn't react to reminders of my old life this way.

I should be able to shut that part of me down. Put the Objective before everything else.

I should be more like Kaelen.

And I try. I swear I try. But somehow I'm still flawed. Even after my rehabilitation. I just can't seem to shut it off.

"Hey, hey, hey." Kaelen is crouched at my feet, his hands on my knees. *"Guardami."* The soft Italian returns as he commands me to look at him.

I am shaking so hard, I can't hold my gaze steady. Everything is convulsing. Inside I'm screaming.

Pull yourself together!

Stop this NOW!

You are no longer weak!

But it's as though I'm screaming in an empty room and no one is listening.

Where are these emotions coming from?

"Look at me," Kaelen commands again. This time he grabs my chin and holds it steady. It might be the only part of me not trembling.

"He's nothing. He doesn't matter anymore. What is this about? Why are you reacting this way?"

"I . . . I . . . don't know." My voice is shattered. Barely recognizable.

It's the truth, though. I don't know. I don't understand why his mere presence turns me into this quivering mess. It's like every time I see him, I open up some kind of poorly covered chasm inside of me. Some tunnel to the past that I can't disconnect myself from. He's not my father. He never was. He's just a scientist who got too close. Who broke his vows to the Objective.

"He's . . . he's . . ." I go on.

"He's irrelevant. He's a traitor."

I nod.

"And you are not."

"I . . . *was*."

"Not anymore."

I nod again.

"Dr. A fixed you. He gave you another chance. You should be grateful."

I try to keep my teeth from clattering. "I . . . I . . . am."

"Good. Now use that. Use whatever you're feeling right now to reconfirm your commitment to the Objective. You are not the person you used to be. You are not a traitor like him."

The way he says "him" I'm not sure if he's referring to Rio or to the boy from my memories. The one who helped me escape. But I know better than to ask. It doesn't matter anyway.

I'm not like either of them.

"Okay?" he asks me.

I take in a shuddering breath. "Okay."

He leans in and places a gentle kiss on my lips. "Good." He wraps his fingers around mine and gives me a tug. "C'mon. Let's get back. Evening meal starts in a few minutes."

5

WATCHFUL

The Residential Sector is large and well landscaped. It's where most of the compound employees spend their free time. In the center there is a complex of five tall apartment buildings connected to the rest of the sector with landscaped pathways. These are the housing units for the scientists, employees, and their families.

Kaelen and I live in the Owner's Estate with Dr. A and his staff. It's a beautiful house at the back of the sector that was modeled after a pre–Civil War Southern plantation.

I've heard some people complain about how out of place it looks among the ultramodern architecture of the rest of the compound, but Dr. A doesn't seem to mind. Plus, he's placed VersaScreens in every window, so when you peer out from within, it looks like the house is surrounded by green meadows and cherry blossoms.

When we reach the entrance to the sector, a MagBall game has commenced on the Rec Field. The few teenagers who live on the compound—children of Diotech employees—like to play it in the evenings, after the weather has cooled down.

They all stop and stare at us as we pass, letting the silver oblong ball linger in the air, untouched and unguarded. A few of them whisper to each other.

I have grown accustomed to this reaction. It's become an everyday occurrence.

It doesn't bother me.

"You and Kaelen are so special," Dr. A likes to tell me. "You will elicit awe and envy everywhere you go. You were kept a secret for so many years. Give the Normates time to get used to the idea of your existence."

That's what Dr. A calls them. Normates. An amalgamation of *normal* and *primate*. It amuses me that he uses the word so loosely, when he himself is plagued by the same limitations they are.

I stop walking and stare back at them. I don't mean it to be a challenge, but they appear to take it that way, because they all look away and return to their game, pretending that they don't notice me. I watch the action for a minute. I know the rules of MagBall from an upload. When I asked Dr. A if I could join in one time, he told me that it would be unfair. Their strength and speed would be no match for mine.

The team in red sends the MagBall into the goal at the other end of the field, eliciting an eruption of cheers. I'm about to turn and leave when I notice one boy has not returned to the game. He's tall and lanky with electric-blue hair that's been fashioned into slopes atop his head. He's standing at the edge of the synthograss, watching me. Our gazes connect and, unlike the other players on the field, he doesn't turn away. He's not afraid of me. In fact, he almost looks like he wants to say something to me.

I send a query through my DigiLenses, capturing his face with a blink and running it through the Diotech personnel database to find a name.

The result appears across my vision a moment later.

Klo Raze

Raze?

Like Director Raze? Is this boy Director Raze's son? I didn't even know Raze had any family members on the compound. Why has he never mentioned Klo before?

He takes a hesitant step in my direction but freezes, his body visibly tensing. Like a deer caught in the beam of a hovercopter. His eyes dart to something behind me and I turn to see Dr. A strolling down the path from the Owner's Estate to greet Kaelen, who I now notice is a good ten yards ahead of me.

"Sera?" Kaelen calls back. "What are you doing?"

I hurry to catch up with him, offering Dr. A a smile that I pray looks genuine. "Good evening."

"It most certainly *was*," Dr. A replies, a tad too sharply for my comfort. He gives me a once-over and I'm suddenly extremely self-conscious about my windswept hair. "Now it's practically night."

"Sorry, Dr. A," Kaelen is quick to reply. "We were kissing in the gardens and lost track of time."

I wince inwardly at Kaelen's brutal honesty. Does he have to tell Dr. A *everything* we do?

I guess I should be grateful that he hasn't mentioned Rio. Or at least not yet. But it doesn't really matter. My memories will give me away eventually. That moment is bound to show up on my next random scan. And I'm bound to be reprimanded for it.

Dr. A cocks an eyebrow. "In the gardens, you say? Interesting venue. Then again, I created you two with the inability to resist each other. So how could I ever fault you for what's in your DNA?"

Dr. A guffaws as he reaches out to ruffle Kaelen's hair before throwing an arm around his shoulders and guiding him toward the Estate. "Join me for a drink, my dear boy. We have much to discuss about tomorrow." He pauses long enough to glance back at me with disapproval. "Sera, gem. Why don't you change into something more suitable for evening meal? And fix your hair. You're looking a bit . . . rumpled."

I nod obligingly and follow them. As we reach the end of the tree-lined pathway that leads to the Owner's Estate, I brave a glance back at the MagBall field.

The boy is still there. Still watching. Even though the game has gone on without him.

6

FORTUNATE

I watch stony-faced in the ReflectoGlass as the nanopin disappears against the silky golden-brown fibers of my hair.

"There," Crest says, stepping back to admire her handiwork. "All finished."

As usual, her efforts are more impressive than the final result. The elaborate half updo she has attempted sits slightly off center on my head. As Dr. A's personal assistant, fixing my "rumpled" hair is not necessarily in Crest's job description, but she seems to enjoy helping, even if she's not very good at it. I don't complain though. It saves me the trouble of doing my own hair. A task I despise, even though I've received multiple uploads that have made me a rather accomplished hairstylist.

"It's a bit warped," she says, frowning at her creation. "But I majored in business. Not beautification." She sighs. "Next time you want to prance around in thirty-mile-per-hour winds, how about wearing a hat?"

"Sorry," I say, my vibrant purple eyes still staring at my reflection.

The Feed has been minimized to a small window in the corner of the ReflectoGlass, pulling my focus away from the shimmery blue dress that I haphazardly picked out of my closet. A reporter is talking about the highest-performing stocks of the day. Of course, Diotech Corporation is at the top of the list. The stock has been soaring ever since the announcement of the Unveiling. And Dr. A predicts this rise is only the beginning. Once the first product line of the Objective has been released into the marketplace in a few months, Diotech will be untouchable.

Crest's jubilant face appears next to mine. She gives my head a light bump with her own. "Why so sad, my pearl? Is it really that horrible?"

She's referring to my hair and I immediately feel bad. I always try my best to praise Crest for anything she does for me. Especially since I've never heard Dr. A offer her a single compliment, or even so much as a thank-you. And Crest works so hard for him.

"No. I love it. It's beautiful. Your best work yet."

She laughs, her dark eyes dancing. "You should probably request an upload on the art of lying. You're dreadful at it. Now, tell me. What's wrong?"

"I ran into Dr. Rio again," I tell her, cringing as soon as I realize my mistake.

It's just Rio now.

His brain isn't capable of advanced science anymore. His title and accolades have been stripped away. He's no longer himself. He only looks the same. Apart from the creepy eyes and permanently ajar mouth.

"And?" Crest prompts.

"And I completely warped out."

I can always confide in Crest. She's the only one who doesn't judge me for the reactions I can't seem to control, no matter how hard I try. Kaelen doesn't understand my anxiety about disappointing Dr. A. He's always been his favorite. If anyone can understand the pressures of pleasing the president of Diotech, it's Crest.

She sits down next to me on the small velvet bench, but keeps speaking to my reflection. "So?"

"So," I echo. "That means I failed him. What if Dr. A sees that memory in my next scan? What if he thinks it means I'm still the girl who betrayed the Objective?"

"Don't be silly. That was over two years ago."

How could I forget? That date has been seared into my memory like an engraving in stone. I know it better than I know my own birthday.

January 9, 2115.

The day I left the compound. With him.

"Dr. Alixter has forgiven you," Crest assures me, referring to him by his full name. Kaelen and I are the only ones who call him Dr. A. He told us to. He thought it sounded less formal. But hardly anyone calls him by his first name, Jans. "He's fixed you."

I nod. I want to believe this, but I'm not sure I can. There's an iciness when Dr. A addresses me. A distance. One that doesn't exist between him and Kaelen. Just further evidence that I have to keep trying. I have to keep proving myself.

I study Crest's face in the glass. Her sleek curtain of jet-black hair is cut in choppy, uneven layers. A chunk of longer strands falls to the bridge of her nose, splitting her short bangs in half. I can never look at Crest for too long. She has more nanotats on her body than anyone I've ever seen. And sometimes staring at them makes me dizzy. She says she's addicted to them. That they give her a sense of control.

I point to the one on her cheek, which she's reprogrammed since yesterday. Now it's displaying a loop of two people kissing in slow motion. "Who are they?" I ask.

She gives me a surprised look. "You've never seen *The Rifters*? It's only the best show on the Feed."

"Fictional shows don't interest me. I can never believe the stories."

She shakes her head in disappointment. "Dr. A made you too logical for your own good." She points at the moving graphic on her cheek. "You see, that's Ashander and that's Glia. They are hopelessly in love but they can never be together because their blood is incompatible due to the alien experiments. But that's a whole other plotline. Anyway, in this scene Ashander braves death and the destruction of their two worlds just to steal *one* kiss from her. It was the most thermal, romantic thing *ever*."

Crest's eyes close and for a moment I wonder if she's fallen asleep. But then she snaps to and beams at me. I can tell she's waiting for a reaction so I force a smile and say, "Wow."

I expect that's what she wants from me. Some kind of mutual enthusiasm for what she's explained.

She chuckles and stands up from the bench, giving my cheek a light tap with the comb in her hand. "*Dreadful liar*."

"You told the story well," I offer as consolation. "You were very passionate."

"Well, it's about as much passion in my life as I can hope for right now. Once again, I've proven disastrous in the love department. Jin still hasn't returned any of my pings."

Jin is a lab assistant Crest has been pining after for months. She calls him her "Dark Matter." Partly because he works in the Aerospace Sector, but mostly because she says there's a darkness around his heart, like a semipermanent storm cloud. That's why she's obsessed with him.

Crest sighs and her thoughts disappear into another place for a moment. A sad place. When they return, she says, "You know how lucky you are, right? You and Kaelen. To have someone *created* just for you. Your perfect soul mate. It's something out of a fairy tale."

I want to remind her that Kaelen and I are *Print Mates*, not soul mates, but something tells me to simply reply with, "Yes. I know."

She is visibly relieved. "That's good."

Something on the glass catches her eye and she grimaces and expands the Feed window until it's taking up almost the entire wall. "Oh flux, not this idiot again." She turns up the volume and a silky charismatic voice floods my bathroom.

"The time to act is now. Before Diotech unleashes these monstrosities into the world. Is that what we want? Synthetically engineered *humans* walking among us?"

From his inflection on the word *human*, he could easily have replaced it with *rodent* and no one would have noticed.

"As if those horrible labor robots they shoved upon us weren't disturbing enough, are we going to let this godless company take over our country with synthetic beings?"

Shouts of opposition follow his question and the cams zoom out to reveal a giant crowd gathered around the speaker at the podium. His dark, graying hair is concealed beneath a Western-style, wide-brimmed hat, and the whites of his eyes are tinted blue by the prescription glasses he's wearing. He clearly doesn't believe in corrective eye surgery. The strip of text at the bottom of the Feed window reads: *Pastor Peder: Church of Eternal Light.*

Crest groans. "Godless," she echoes with disgust at the man's face. "Well, *you're* heartless!"

"We must band together," he goes on, eliciting cheers from his spectators. "God has tasked us with this tiresome challenge. Are we going to turn down God's request?"

A resounding "No!" shakes the ReflectoGlass.

"Then help me!" Peder pleads to his audience. "Join me in opposing this disgraceful corporation and all that they are attempting to do to corrupt us."

"Oh, shut it," Crest grumbles, and deactivates the Feed. Peder's face vanishes and I'm grateful for the silence.

Dr. A says I'm not supposed to worry about Pastor Peder. He's not a threat to us. He just enjoys hearing himself talk. But it still doesn't mean I like having that man in my bathroom. And it doesn't help that nearly every time I turn on the Feed someone is talking about him.

A ping flashes across the glass a moment later. It's for Crest, from Dr. A. He's reprimanding her for not correctly packing his hover-case for tomorrow's departure.

She paints on a grin. I can tell she's trying to renew the same enthusiasm she came in here with, but she's struggling to find it. "Well, duty calls. You should really get down to the dining room."

I turn toward the door, but stop when I feel Crest's hand around my arm, squeezing just a little too tight. When I look back at her, the sparkle in her eyes is gone.

"Life is messy for the rest of us. You have it really good here, you know? Promise me you won't forget that."

Her intensity unnerves me but I manage a smile. "I won't forget."

7

MORE

By the time I get downstairs, it's after nine and Dr. A, Director Raze, and Dane, the head of Diotech publicity, are already deep in discussion about the next steps in the Objective. I find them in the living room, sipping a deep brown liqueur out of what look like real crystal glasses. Crystal is now manufactured synthetically but Dr. A has an obsession with old-fashioned things that were built before Diotech mastered synthetics.

"It's not as valuable if you can just whip it up in a lab in a matter of minutes," he's been known to say. "But it is nice to be able to offer a cheaper version to the masses, isn't it?"

Every time he says something like this I wonder about my own value. And Kaelen's. We were, as he said, "whipped up in a lab." Perhaps it wasn't in a matter of minutes, but isn't the concept the same?

Kaelen does not have a drink in his hand. He says he doesn't like the way it dulls his senses. I've never tried it. Not that Dr. A has ever offered.

All four men stand when they see me. Kaelen has changed into a dark gray suit with red trim. He looks striking.

Dr. A's gaze dips over my dress, a full-length shimmering blue evening gown with swirling silver and gold nanostitching embroidered into the hem. I watch his reaction diligently. It's the only one I care about. After all, it's Dr. A who insists we dress up for evening meal.

His lips split into a grin. "Gorgeous as always, my gem," he says, and I feel my shoulders relax. Even though my various uploads have given me an impeccable fashion sense, the hundreds of stunning garments in my closet still make me feel awkward and slightly off balance. As if they were meant for someone else.

Kaelen walks over to me, kisses me on the cheek, and whispers one word into my ear. "Luminous."

I can't help but smile. "You have to say that."

"No, I don't."

"It's in your DNA."

"To love you? Yes. To think you look especially beautiful right this second? Not that I'm aware of."

"Don't be so sure of that."

"Excellent timing," Dane chirps. "I was just about to show everyone the final edit of our new Feed ad."

He commands the wall screen to activate and selects a file from a pod on the internal network. The familiar Diotech logo covers the entire wall, eventually bleeding into fast, stylized cuts of a girl's full, pink mouth, a man's tanned, toned biceps, a slender feminine leg, a pair of dazzling iridescent eyes, hair that sparkles in the light.

"This will stream directly after the Unveiling," Dane explains. "You won't be able to turn on the Feed without seeing it."

The ad continues with two bodies in motion. Running, punching, kicking, leaping. The slow-capture effect almost makes it look like they're flying. We never see either of their faces, but it's obvious from their agile turns and soaring heights, these are not Normates. Normates don't move like that. Only ExGens move like that.

It doesn't take me long to recognize that the two people in the footage are Kaelen and me. I remember when they captured it a few months ago. We stood in front of a green screen in the publicity building for nearly a day while Dane told us what to do, how to pose, where to look, how high to jump.

A voice booms over the imagery. A deep, clear voice that demands attention. Demands to be heard.

"Be stronger. Be faster. Be smarter. Be *more*."

The Diotech logo appears again, this time with two lines of text beneath it.

**The ExGen Collection
Coming Soon**

The screen fades to black.

"What do you think?" Dane asks, his face radiating with pride.

Everyone in the room breaks into applause. I hastily join in, desperate to hide my real reaction.

In truth, I'm torn. The advertisement does exactly what it's supposed to do: promote Diotech's newest product line. Make people want to improve themselves. But everything about it is misleading. Normates won't be able to actually become ExGens like me and Kaelen. They will only be able to purchase a handful of self-administered genetic modifications that will each enhance one specific attribute. Like eye color, skin tone, muscle capacity, hair sheen, brain function, body shape.

"Absolutely splendid," Dr. A commends. "They will be lining up outside every drugstore in the country! Well done, Dane."

Dane grins, basking in the compliment. We all know how rarely Dr. A dishes them out.

Dr. A puts his arm around Kaelen's shoulder and leads him toward the dining room. "Let's eat. It's quite late and I'm starving." He flashes a glance back at me and I know what he's thinking. It's my fault we're eating late.

I bow my head, accepting the blame.

Dane comes up behind me and pinches my waist. "Don't worry. I kept him distracted. It's part of the job."

I give him a grateful smile.

"Now," he whispers to me, checking to make sure Dr. A is out of earshot, "what did you really think of the ad?"

"I loved it." My response is quick. Maybe too quick.

Dane scowls in disbelief. "C'mon. It's me. You can be honest."

"I'm just confused," I concede.

He nods. "Okay. About?"

"The ad, the Unveiling, the name of the collection. It makes it seem like people can pay to be exactly like Kaelen and me, but they can't. With the number of enhancements being offered they'll never even come close. Isn't that . . . lying?"

Dane laughs a little. "No, it's marketing. You never give them *exactly* what they want. Otherwise you lose all your power. Ad firms have been doing it for years with strategic lighting and airbrushing and digital models. You show them what they can't have, then you turn around and sell them the next best thing."

I struggle to follow his logic. "And you're sure that's what people want? To be more like Kaelen and me?"

Dane places a warm hand on my cheek and offers me a mirthless smile. "The truth is, Sera, people want what Diotech tells them to want."

8

THREATS

We take our usual seats in the formal dining room. Dr. A at the head of the long rectangular table, Kaelen and I seated to his left, and Dane and Raze on his right. Crest is never invited to dine with us. She says it doesn't bother her, that she's far too busy managing Dr. A's schedule to sit down to a meal, but it bothers me. I've just never articulated it.

Luly, the kitchen maid, delivers our customized meal choices and Dr. A turns his attention to Kaelen and me. "Dane and I have some excellent news about the Unveiling."

My whole body tenses and I remind myself to take deep breaths. Stay calm. If the nanosensors running through my veins right now detect any abnormal rise in my heartbeat, Dr. A will know. An alert will go off on a screen somewhere in the Medical Sector. He'll get a report on his Slate later tonight and he'll match the time stamp with the hour this conversation took place.

This is what I'm here for. This is my role in the Objective. To show the world how Diotech products can improve their lives.

He can't know that the very thought of fulfilling my duty makes my system go into hyperdrive.

I start to count by 89s, opting for a prime number to keep my mind engaged.

89, 178, 267, 356, 445 . . .

"What's the news?" I force myself to ask, cringing at how strangled my voice sounds.

Dane grins wildly. "Take a look."

He turns to the wall screen behind him and gives it the command to resume playback. Suddenly, Mosima Chan, the most famous Feed journalist in the country, is in the room with us, her hologram springing to life as she begins speaking in great earnest.

"This is Mosima Chan, bringing you this breaking-news stream. I can now officially announce that on May 8, 2117, AFC Streamwork will be feedcasting the first exclusive live interview with the offspring of Diotech's revolutionary scientific breakthrough, dubbed the Genesis Project."

I choke on the small piece of synthetic steak that I just popped into my mouth, causing Dr. A to shoot me a venomous look.

"Excuse me," I say as I swallow water from my goblet.

"Eighteen-year-olds Sera and Kaelen, referred to as 'ExGens' in an official Diotech digital press release, will be right here in this studio in only two days. Up until this point, neither Sera nor Kaelen has been seen by anyone outside of the highly restricted Diotech headquarters located in the east Nevada desert. Diotech has been keeping a close wrap on the project, refusing to release even a single still capture of their faces."

The comment bar on the side of the screen is going absolutely warped. I want to issue the command to slow it down so I can catch a glimpse of one of the viewer comments but I'm afraid of what it might say.

Dane deactivates the screen a moment later. "Mosima Chan is

going to kick off our publicity tour!" he announces, the goofy grin still plastered to his face.

Suddenly I have trouble breathing. The thought of being in her studio, our faces feedcasted to the world, paralyzes me. I remember watching her live interview with Eean Glick after he returned from Neptune. The viewer counter was at over eight billion. I feel my pulse start to race.

534, 623, 712, 801, 890 . . .

"Isn't that amazing?" Kaelen asks.

"Amazing," I manage to echo. But the room has already started to spin. It's becoming too real. Too fast. Mosima Chan. A twenty-eight-city publicity tour. Billions of eyes trained on us. Judging us. "Are you sure we're ready for all that?"

I suck in a surprised breath when I realize I said that aloud. I had intended it to stay in my head. But now my uncertainty is in the open and I immediately regret it.

Dr. A's hand slams down on the table, startling everyone, and sending his liqueur glass flying over the edge. It crashes a few feet away and shatters into pieces. That's when I know for sure it's real crystal. The synthetic kind never would have even cracked.

"Of course, you're ready." His icy blue eyes narrow in my direction. "Do you really think I would send you out into the world before you're ready? Do you still doubt me so much?"

"No," I'm quick to say while internally berating myself for my stupidity. "I don't doubt you at all."

Luly is back, having heard the commotion. She eyes the mess. "I'll call a bot." And then she's gone again.

"We have pushed this back long enough," Dr. A continues. "We have spent the last year preparing you for this. Giving you access to countless uploads. Teaching you the popular slang and euphemisms. Training you to behave more like normal human beings so you wouldn't come off as creepy robots in the public eye." He turns to Dane. "That's what *you* said they needed. This was *your* idea."

Dane has always been better at appeasing Dr. A than any of us have. Especially me. "They've come a *long* way," he assures him gleefully, resting a gentle hand on Dr. A's arm. "If it weren't for those exquisite faces, I would believe they were just Normate teenagers off the street. I definitely think they're ready."

"I am very confident we can do this," I rush to say, still trying to cover for my horrendous misstep. "I want to serve the Objective."

Kaelen squeezes my hand. "We both do."

I flinch when out of the corner of my eye I see the cleaning bot silently enter the room. Those things always unnerve me with their humanlike top half and wheeled bottom. This one is designed to look like a man. They're tasked with various chores around the compound. All the things real people don't want to do. Mostly janitorial work. Cleaning. Basic maintenance. And of course, there are the med bots, who help around the labs. The faces of the bots are so convincing, so flawless, you'd almost believe they were real. That is, until you look into their eyes. No matter how advanced Diotech's technology is, they can never quite perfect the eyes. There's always a void there. A soullessness that strikes you deep in your gut.

Looking a labor bot in the eye is a mistake you only make once.

I focus on my plate as the bot clears away the broken glass, sucking it up into its base, mopping the spilled liquid with an extension that protrudes from the bottom, and then giving the wood floors a shiny polish to finish the job.

Director Raze, who up until this point has been silently enjoying his synthetic pork chop, swallows and says, "You do realize, Dr. Alixter, that the added media attention will give Peder and his people more fodder. He's not simply going to go away."

I wince at the brazenness of his comment. Particularly so close on the heels of Dr. A's last reaction to skepticism. But Dr. A simply waves his hand at this, as though it's hardly a concern worth talking about. "Peder is a raving lunatic with no real claims. He's crazy. No one takes him seriously."

"If he manages to get enough support in the public eye or—"

Dr. A stands up, pushing his chair back and tossing his napkin down on the table. "That'll be all for now, Director. Thank you." He turns to Dane. "Ping Crest with the final tour schedule." Then he stalks out of the room, leaving a plate of barely touched food behind.

Dane gets up a moment later and follows him, leaving the three of us to finish our meal in awkward silence. I've never had much to say to Director Raze. The truth is, he scares me a little, with his tall build and domineering stance. The way he sometimes looks at me like I'm a piece of synthetic meat he'd like to devour. But I assume those same intimidating qualities also help to keep the compound safe. So maybe I'm *supposed* to be afraid of him.

It's only after Luly has cleared the plates that I have the nerve to ask, "Director, do you really think Peder is a threat to us?"

He stands up, dabs his mouth with his napkin, and winks. "Don't worry, princess. You know I'd never let anything happen to you."

"But you said—"

"Just let me do my job and you'll be safe." There's an edge to his tone that makes me feel the opposite of safe.

Once he's gone, Kaelen, seemingly unfazed by the previous confrontations, stands up and grabs my hand, pulling me out of my seat.

"Feeling better?" he asks, clearly referring to the meltdown I had in the gardens earlier.

I nod. "Much."

"Good." He cups my face with his hands and draws me to him.

Our lips crush together and suddenly I can no longer remember what I was worried about two seconds ago.

"What do you want to do now?" I ask.

His lips burrow against my neck. "I have something in mind."

I giggle. "What's that?"

"Something you won't be able to do in that dress." Then he intertwines his fingers with mine and pulls me urgently toward the door.

9

SENSE

Kaelen gives me a head start. We both know I need it. I bow my head and run straight into the night. The wind tangles my hair, destroying Crest's updo in a matter of seconds. But she won't care. Evening meal is over. Dr. A has retired to his rooms. We are alone.

The compound is quiet, everyone tucked into their respective corners of the Residential Sector. This is the only time Kaelen and I can really stretch our legs. I head east, cutting across the center of the Agricultural Sector and into the barren field that lies beyond it. If I were to turn right, I would end up back at the cottage. But right now that's the last place I want to be. Even the thought of it sitting out there, empty yet full of memories, reminds me of all the things I don't want to think about. Like Rio and his vacuous eyes. Like the boy and his stupid dandelions.

Like me and my weaknesses.

So I continue straight, plunging deeper into untamed pasture, the wild shrubbery scratching my ankles. Leaving my wearisome thoughts farther and farther behind with every lightning-fast step I take.

I can hear Kaelen's nimble footsteps close behind me. He's gaining. I push harder. Faster. My muscles never tire. My lungs never burn. This is what being an ExGen is all about. The speed. The stamina. The unparalleled senses.

I sniff the air, breathing in the tangy desert. But there's another scent that catches me off guard—a sickly, putrid odor. It causes me to slow, gradually at first, then slamming to a stop as I catch a stronger whiff. Kaelen pulls up next to me. I watch his reaction. Judging by the confusion on his face, he smells it, too.

"We should go back," he says after a moment, and I swear I see comprehension flash in his eyes.

I take a step, inhaling deeply. "What is that? It's almost like . . . like . . ." My body grows cold when the recognition hits. I remember that scent. It rose up from my own limbs as the fire consumed me. That was in another world. Another time. But the smell hasn't changed.

". . . burning flesh." I finish the thought, all emotion drained from my voice.

Kaelen gives my arm a tug. "C'mon. Let's go. We shouldn't be here."

But I brush him away and stride purposefully forward, letting my nose guide me until I find the source. I stop dead in my tracks and stare at the spectacle laid out before us, no more than a hundred yards in the distance.

A large transparent structure has been erected in the middle of the field. A freestanding glass cube with no ceiling. Inside, a deadly fire roars.

I watch in horror as a scientist in a white lab coat guides a blindfolded woman toward the entrance of the chamber. Another scientist standing nearby presses a button on his Slate and a door in the glass wall slides opens. The fire doesn't try to escape. It's being controlled. Limited to the boundaries of the small room.

The first scientist removes the blindfold from the woman. She stares blankly into the flames. Not a drop of fear registers on her face. The second scientist presses another button on his Slate and the woman advances toward the open chamber.

Without a flicker of hesitation or even a flinch of concern, she walks straight into the fire. It consumes her instantly, the blistering flames wrapping around her slender body and yielding her motionless and silent in a matter of seconds.

I open my mouth to scream but nothing comes out. That's when I realize Kaelen's hand is clamped over my lips, blocking the sound.

"Sera," he whispers urgently. "We have to go. Now."

I try to speak, but he won't allow it. In a blur, he lifts me with one arm, his other hand still firmly secured over my mouth. I don't struggle. I let him carry me away. As we vanish into the darkness, I hear a voice behind us. It's coming from the nightmare we just witnessed.

"Excellent work," it commends the scientists. "I believe we are ready."

There's no doubt in my mind that the voice belongs to Dr. A.

10

GAPS

I wake up in a chair. My hands are shackled to the armrests, my brain is fuzzy. It feels like my head has been stuffed with cotton. I blink and look around. It takes me a moment to recognize where I am. The VersaScreens that surround me are powered down, leaving the four walls a muted black.

I'm inside the memory labs.

Sevan Sidler's familiar voice comes through a small speaker by my ear. "Hi, Sera. How are you feeling?"

"Fine," I mumble groggily.

I do what I always do when I wake up in this room: struggle to conjure the last thing I remember.

Crest did my hair. I went to evening meal. Dr. A got angry and smashed a crystal glass. Dane told us about our upcoming appearance on Mosima's show. Kaelen and I went running. And then . . .

Then there is nothing.

Then I woke up here.

I know exactly what this means. One of my memories has been altered. Probably erased. It's not an uncommon occurrence.

It happens fairly often, actually. Often enough that it doesn't warp me out like it used to. Over the past year, I've come to terms with the fact that memory modifications are in the best interest of everyone, and, above all else, in the best interest of the Objective. I trust Dr. A's judgment. That's why, with me, they no longer go through the trouble of coding artificial memories to replace the ones they remove. I've accepted the fact that there are some things I just don't need to know.

But tonight, after everything else that's happened, I feel curiosity trickling its way into my thoughts.

The time flashes across my Lenses: 01:42 a.m. When Kaelen and I left the house after evening meal it was after ten. What happened in those three hours? What did I see?

The restraints holding my wrists release and I stand up and flex my fingers. One of the VersaScreens splits open and I walk into the hallway where Kaelen is waiting, a beatific smile on his face.

"Ça va?" He asks me if I'm doing okay in French.

"Oui," I respond. The fog in my brain has already started to lift. In a few minutes, I will be sharp and alert again.

Sevan pops his head through the doorway that leads to the control room. That's where he sits at a computer all day as the cryptic code of Revisual+, the language of memories, streams across his screen.

"Have a good night, you two," he says, his usual cheerfulness not at all affected by whatever memory he took, or the fact that it's now the middle of the night and he was most likely woken from sleep to perform my alteration.

"You, too," I reply, and follow Kaelen outside.

We walk back to the Residential Sector in silence. I want to ask so many questions. I want to ask what happened. What they stole. Did they alter his memories, too? Or was it just mine? But I know that I can't. It goes against all the rules. All the protocols. And even if Kaelen does know the answers, he's not allowed to tell me.

We are so close in so many ways—bonded by the very life that runs in our veins—but Diotech always comes first.

The Objective always comes first.

I fight to draw out even the smallest strand of what was removed from my mind. What I might have seen. How it might have made me feel. Hoping, beyond reason, that some remnant of the past few hours might still be lingering. Hiding somewhere in the back corners of my brain.

But Sevan is good at his job. There is nothing left.

I don't even notice that Kaelen has stopped walking until I feel a rough tug on my arm and I'm suddenly spun around. He brings me crushing against his chest as he urgently captures my mouth with his. His kiss is hungry. Desperately redemptive. For what, I don't know. But like always, I lose everything that once stood guard in my mind. My knees start to buckle.

Kaelen has a way of consuming me with his kisses. Rendering me useless. Stealing everything from me. Almost as effectively as a Memory Coder.

When he pulls away, I'm wobbly, leaning against him for balance.

"Can I come to your room tonight?" he whispers into the skin behind my ear.

All I can do is nod against his lingering lips.

We run. Hand in hand. Up the manicured pathway of the house. With nothing at our backs but desert wind and lost memories. This is us. This has always been us. An undeniable pull toward each other. An invisible force field that pulses in the spaces between us, holding us together, connecting us with the same heartbeat.

A thrill of nervous energy fuels my legs as we spring up the porch steps. A fierce longing to be close to him thrums through me as he pauses before the front door, wrapping his strong, chiseled arms around my waist and pulling me into him.

His scent is intoxicating.

His mouth is debilitating.

His touch makes me forget.

He looks at me, his eyes wild and unfocused. "You completely warp me."

I flash him a coy smirk. "You have to say that. It's in your DNA."

"And what glitching good DNA it is."

This makes me laugh. Kaelen opens the front door and starts up the stairs, keeping his hand firmly secured around mine. I stay close to him, hoping the anguish of the day will gradually fade with every step.

But as we reach the landing of the second floor, I begin to realize, with a profound disappointment, that it will take more than a flight of stairs to erase the demons inside of me. I could climb to the moon and I would still feel my fears following right behind me like a dark shadow.

An unwanted passenger who was never invited. And never leaves.

11

RELEASED

That night, I dream of Rio countless times. I watch his skull being sawed open over and over again. I'm trapped behind thick synthoglass, high above the sterile white surgical room. I stand idle and motionless as they carve out his brain, which has turned black and rotten, and replace it with a sleek and shimmering artificial substitute.

In the last dream, I finally fight back. I bang against the glass but no one even bothers to look up. They work tirelessly, replacing the top of his skull, sealing his skin around the incision with flesh-colored nanopatches.

I yell and cry and bang harder.

"They can't hear you," a voice says behind me. I whip around and he is there. The boy from my memories. The one I've tried so hard to forget. His dark eyes are cold and untrusting.

"Zen." I murmur his name softly. So no one else can hear.

"They'll never be able to hear you."

I wake up screaming.

A body is there to calm me. Lips whispering soothing words

into my ear. A hand brushing back my damp hair. The only time I sweat is when I'm trapped in a nightmare.

I blink against the darkness and the lingering images in my mind.

"Shhh, it was just a dream." Crest sits on the edge of my bed, continuing to stroke my hair.

Her presence calms me. It always does.

It's not part of her job—chasing away nightmares. But she knows I have trouble sleeping. And her room is, unfortunately for her, next to mine, so she can hear the screams.

My ragged breathing gradually begins to subside. I turn my head to see the empty space next to me. Kaelen left a while ago. Not long after we entered my room, he kissed me like he wanted more, but I told him I couldn't give him more. Not tonight. I told him I was anxious about our departure this morning and needed to be alone. He tried to hide his disappointment but I read it on his slightly downturned lips, in the subtle wilt of his shoulders as he left.

"There you go, my sweet pearl," Crest encourages. "It's okay. Just a dream."

I sink down under the covers as she opens the top drawer of my nightstand. She riffles around until she finds the injector she keeps there. "Just one dose," she tells me as she clicks a vial of pale blue liquid into place. "To help you fall back asleep. You need your beauty rest."

I smile at her joke. I would look the same no matter how much sleep I got. But Crest likes to say it's why she comes in here. Why she cares so much about whether or not I'm sleeping. I secretly think she likes taking care of me. I think this semiregular nightly routine is one of the ways she combats her loneliness.

She places the tip of the injector against my arm. I feel a slight pinch of pressure as the Releaser enters my system. The drug usually works fast and I pray that tonight will be no exception.

Crest pulls the blanket up to my chin. "Have I told you about Jin's eyelashes?"

I shake my head.

It's a lie and we both know it. She's told me about every part of his body so many times even I've lost count. But it makes her happy to talk about him so I let her. Tonight, apparently it's his eyelashes that are monopolizing her thoughts. Two nights ago, it was his wrists.

"They are the most thermal shade of dark green," she begins dreamily. Her gaze drifts to that place on the wall just above my bed. Always the same spot. As though his capture is playing on a constant loop on the wall screen behind me. "Don't ever let him look at you from beneath them. If you do? Flux, it's all over. I've broken promises because of those lashes. They can turn a good girl bad in three seconds flat."

I giggle as my eyes start to close.

Crest bends down and kisses my forehead. "Don't let those nightmares frighten you, pearl. You're stronger than you give yourself credit for."

The sleep is coming on fast. I hear the drawer of my nightstand opening and closing as Crest replaces the injector. She stands up and walks quietly toward the door.

"And if you ever realized how strong you really are," she whispers to the darkness, "we'd all be in trouble."

12

UNEARTHED

The Releaser wears off in a few hours, like it always does. My system is too strong for the injector's maximum dose. When I wake the next morning, the sun hasn't yet risen. The clock on my wall screen reads 5:07 a.m.

The night shield on my windows is active and I give the command for transparency so I can see outside. The real one. Not the simulated plantation backyard that Dr. A programmed as a default.

The dark façade lifts and I see the back of the Transportation Sector hangars, where they make prototypes for the next generation of hovers and repair all the carts that roam the compound. I admit it's not the nicest of views. It's no wonder Dr. A chose the digital veneer that he did. But the sight of it grounds me.

So many aspects of our lives are artificial. Holograms are projected onto our screens. Fictional stories are streamed onto the Feed. Our DigiLenses transform the world around us with virtual programs and apps. Every once in a while, it's nice to get fleeting glimpses of the real world.

From here, I can barely see the edge of the vast field that

separates the rest of the compound from what used to be the Restricted Sector and I'm instantly reminded of my run with Kaelen last night.

Something happened in that field, I know it.

Something they don't want me to remember.

I climb out of bed and quietly dress, careful not to wake the rest of the house.

I hurry down the tree-lined path. My speed is somewhere between human and ExGen. Not quite a blur, but definitely a pace that would draw attention. Good thing no one is around to notice.

It isn't until I'm halfway through the curved, polished buildings of the Aerospace Sector that I realize where I'm going. It's almost as though I didn't even have a choice in the matter. As though some invisible force was pulling me back here all along.

The small white cottage looks exactly the same as when I left it yesterday evening.

How can I feel so different when nothing has changed? When the grass is still overgrown? When the gate is still unlocked? When this sector that used to be restricted—that once held a foolish, disobedient girl—is still abandoned?

Soon the sun will rise. The compound will wake up. The hovercopters will arrive to take us from the compound. Tomorrow Kaelen and I will be introduced to the world for the first time. We will be on display, like merchandise. We will show the people what they want.

"As soon as they see you and everything that you can do," Dr. A once said to me, "they'll be lining up at the doors to pay for whatever it is you have. They'll be begging to be more like you. *That's* how you save a species."

For the past few months, Dane has been extensively preparing us for our interviews and public appearances. We've received countless uploads on effective media strategies, body language, the art of conversation, and social etiquette. Not to mention a full pod's worth of archived press interviews with important people.

I can now speak with eloquence, walk with poise, and make witty banter for hours on end. But it doesn't mean I don't feel like a fraud when I do it. And it doesn't mean I'm actually *ready* for the entire world to know my face.

My feet feel heavy and uncooperative as I walk the perimeter of the empty cottage. My eyes don't want to follow my path around the house. They drift. They are drawn to one place.

To the empty patch of dirt where the bench used to be.

Where the boy and I used to leave each other messages.

In just one night, a new dandelion has managed to sprout up in place of the one I destroyed. It's a strong weed. A rebellious fighter. Despite all of Diotech's advances in horticulture—despite all of Dr. A's attempts to squash it from existence—it still grows.

A memory instantly wells up inside me, too strong to hold back, too powerful to control. The anguished guilt that accompanies it nearly doubles me over. There's nothing left to do but close my eyes and let the memory overtake me.

"Did I ever tell you about our bench?" Lyzender says, trying to squeeze my hand. The sickness in his veins reduces his efforts to a meager muscle spasm. "It was made of white marble. In your front yard."

His body is racked by a cough that leaves a smear of blood on his lips. I pluck a tissue and dab at the crimson droplets.

"Every morning when you woke up, you were supposed to bury something under the bench. It was your signal to me that you remembered."

"Remembered what?" I ask.

"Me."

I press my lips together, stifling a shudder. "How did you find the strength to do it so many times?" I ask. "Why did you keep coming back when you knew I'd look at you like you were a stranger?"

He closes his eyes and then whispers, "You never looked at me like I was a stranger. That's how I knew they could never win."

My eyes snap open and I look toward the open gate. I should leave. I should walk away and never look back.

That is, after all, the real reason I returned here today, isn't it? Because I was hoping the walls of my former prison—the remembrance of my former crimes—would motivate me to do the right thing. To *be* the right person.

But now that I'm here, every dark corner of my mind is lit with curiosity. Every part of my body is drawn to the spot on the desert floor that represents my treasonous acts. As though my old self is calling to me, inviting me back.

I fight it, but not hard enough. The *want* is too powerful. It overpowers the *should*. The defect buried deep within me is strong today. Stronger than I've ever felt it.

I have to know.

I can't leave here not knowing.

My feet find their own way. My waning resolve pulls me to my knees. And before I can give my mind the opportunity to dissent, I am digging.

I am digging.

I am digging.

The dirt is hard and tough and cakes painfully under my nails as I claw and scrape at the ground. The earth is so compacted, I find it hard to believe that anyone has buried anything here recently.

So why are you digging? a voice somewhere inside me asks.

But I don't have an answer.

Something simply compels me to dig.

Dr. A doesn't believe in hunches. He says they are for unscientific people who would rather trust in nonsense than learn how the world works.

But I don't know how else to explain the sensation that's coursing through me. The certainty overtakes me like programming overtakes a drone.

There is something here. I know it.

Yet the hole is now more than a foot deep and I have come up with nothing. I glance at the sun rising in the sky. They will come looking for me soon.

What will Dr. A think if he finds me here, literally digging up a past that I'm supposed to forget?

But I can't stop now.

Not when this conviction is pulsing through me like sweet fire. Not when I've never felt so alive.

My fingertips are bleeding but I keep going. Any wounds I inflict on myself will be healed by the time I return to the Owner's Estate. I feel like one of the wild dogs I sometimes see roaming outside the compound walls, ripping at the dirt in hopes of finding food.

Then my hand hits something. Something solid.

I dig faster until I've completely excavated the buried object. It's a small wooden box. I hastily brush the remaining dirt away and gasp when I see what's carved into the top.

Like a memory etched in wood.

The symbol.

Our symbol.

"It means eternity. It means forever."

I remember how I always liked it. The endless loop of the eternal knot. The way it almost looks like two inverted hearts, crisscrossing at their cores.

My fingers are thick with numbness as I feel for a latch and pop open the box.

A single object is housed inside. I recognize it immediately. The smooth sides, the clean, precise edges of the metal, the way it glows green when I swipe my fingertip across it, activating whatever is inside.

It's a cube drive. Exactly like the one Lyzender stored my stolen memories on when we ran away.

Exactly like the one Kaelen had when he came to bring me back.

But how did it get here? Buried more than a foot below the earth?

Drives aren't normally used on the compound. Not when the Diotech network allows us to wirelessly transfer data between devices and server pods.

I remember the last time I saw one like this. It was in the year 2032. I had taken it from Kaelen. I had used it to show my foster brother, Cody, all my memories. So that he could see for himself what my past was like.

This was when I still believed Diotech was the enemy. When I was still firmly under Lyzender's spell.

And then what?

What happened to that drive after Cody accessed my memories? I don't remember seeing it again. Kaelen and I left. Did we bring the drive with us? I certainly didn't. And I don't recall Kaelen having it.

It must have been left behind in Cody's house. In the guest room where Lyzender lay sick and dying. Where Kaelen administered the Repressor that disabled Lyzender's transession gene, cured his illness, and trapped him in time forever.

That was over eighty years ago.

Which means . . .

A ping flashes across my vision, disrupting my thoughts. It's a message from Kaelen, asking where I am.

I return the now-empty wooden box to the hole and shove the pile of dirt on top of it. I do my best to smooth out the small mound that I've formed, even attempting to resurrect the fragile dandelion that was tossed aside during my excavation. It looks lopsided and sad when I'm finished.

I push myself to my feet and slip the drive into my pocket.

I take off at a run, leaping effortlessly over the concrete wall that used to hold me in. That used to protect me from my own rebellious spirit.

The entire time I run, I think about the small cube banging gently against my hip. A hard drive that once held all of my memories.

Does it still? Or is there something new stored inside its sturdy metal walls?

Something that someone wanted me to find?

That has been buried for nearly a century.

13

LEAVES

I sprint across the empty field and cut through the Agricultural Sector. Normally I try to steer clear of the creepy cottonwood tree in the corner for fear that its gnarled, twisted limbs will reach out and grab me. But today, I don't have time to make my usual wide arc around it. I still duck my head and avert my eyes as I pass it, but just as I'm about to clear its last outstretched branch, I hear the far-off sound of a little girl screaming.

I slow and turn around, the piercing noise coming to a halt as soon as I do. That's when I see the man standing beneath the tree, his red-handled shears dangling from his limp hand, as if he had been in the process of trimming the tree but then simply stopped mid-snip. My rib cage tightens around my heart, threatening to squash it like a bug.

Rio.

My eyes dart back in the direction I was running. I could keep going. Pretend I didn't see him. But he's already staring at me with those stony eyes. Like he's expecting me to say something. I consider pinging Kaelen and asking him to come help me. He's always so good with Rio. So composed. Unlike me, who turns into a useless mess in his presence. I know Kaelen would only be disappointed if I summoned him, though. He thinks I should be able to handle this. And he's right. I should. But now my hands are shaking and my mouth has gone bone dry and Rio is still just standing there, mouth slack, arms at his sides.

I steel myself and take a few steps toward him and the unnerving tree, holding my breath while I walk, fidgeting with my fingers. I do exactly what Kaelen would do. I force a smile that I hope looks genuine and I say, "Good morning, Rio."

But something is wrong. He doesn't answer. He always answers Kaelen. He always returns the salutation and mutters something about how many hedges there are around the compound. Not today, though. In fact, he doesn't even move. His eyes are still fixed forward. Not on me anymore, but on something in the distance behind me. I steal a glance over my shoulder but see nothing of interest. When I turn my attention back to him, his trimming sheers drop from his hand, clattering to the ground.

"Rio?" I can hear the quiver in my voice.

When he still doesn't respond, I wave my hand in front of his face.

Nothing. Not even a flinch.

Is he alive?

If it weren't for the fact that he's standing up, I would safely assume he's not. He looks like a bot who simply ran out of power halfway between locations, waiting for someone to come by and juice him up.

I step in front of him and suck in my breath as I brave a glimpse directly into his eyes. He doesn't register my existence with so much as a blink. I can feel my stomach tumbling as I search for something. Anything. A flicker of recognition. A gleam of the man who used to be there. Who risked everything to help me escape with Lyzender. Who came to find me in the past. Who betrayed Dr. A at the price of his mind. His faculties. His life.

But I don't see any of that. I only see a shell of a person. A man who's been replaced by a hollow void.

I shudder and step back, bowing my head once more and returning to the path. But a hand on my arm makes me shriek. It's squeezing so tight, the blood flow is stanched.

With horror, I look up to see Rio's face inches from mine. The emptiness in his eyes is gone. Replaced with something intense. Something crazed. A determined wildness that reveals too much of the whites around his irises.

"Sariana," he says, his voice tight and full of warning.

Sariana?

I glance around. Who is he talking to? I'm the only one here.

I try to pull away but his grip is strong. I could rip through it and break his hand but his mouth starts to move again, stopping me. His lips flutter without making a sound.

It takes me a moment before I realize what's happening.

He's trying to tell me something.

"L-l-l-l-l—" More saliva comes out than actual noise. It drips down his jaw.

"Rio?"

"L-l-l-l-l—" I can almost see the struggle on his face. I can almost hear his mind screaming in frustration.

I gently pry his fingers from my arm, shaking it out to restart the blood flow.

I move away, but he reaches out and grabs me again. This time by the wrist. My gaze lifts to meet his just as the word comes spilling out of his mouth. "Leave."

14

SEQUENCED

When I arrive home, two hovercopters are parked outside the Owner's Estate. Crest is ordering around a harried team of valets and housemaids who are loading the luggage and boxes for our tour.

Crest stops to give me a wave and then notices my hands. They're caked in dirt. "What on earth have you been doing?"

"Digging," I say, knowing I can't lie to Crest. It's no use even trying.

I fear she's about to ask why and I won't have an answer to give her, but fortunately, one of the valets trips over a floating hovercase, kicking it open and spilling garments onto the grass. Crest groans and looks to the sky, as if asking it for help.

I use this distraction as my chance to get away, bounding up the porch steps.

"Clean yourself up!" she calls after me, not even bothering to turn around. "And change into the travel clothes I laid out for you."

I sigh and mutter my assent. Even my travel clothes are co-ordinated. Crest says once I leave the compound, I will be in the public eye. Everywhere I go, I have to look breathtaking, be on my best behavior, and never appear bored. "ExGens are the epitome of a sparkling, charmed life. You must look vivacious at all times."

I was tempted to joke that I think Dr. A omitted the "vivacious" gene when he created me but I didn't think anyone would appreciate the humor except me.

As promised, when I reach my bedroom, I find a shimmering black bodysuit waiting for me on the bed.

I remove the cube drive from my pocket and place it on my bedside table. I don't have time to shower or bathe, so I simply scrub the dirt off my hands and arms, watching it wash down the drain in a light brown swirl of soap bubbles and mud. I find myself hoping that the extra-strength Diotech cleanser will wash away more than just the dirt on my skin. Maybe some of the dirt on my conscience as well.

I pull off my regular clothes, toss them down the laundry chute in my closet, and put on the bodysuit. The material is soft and pliable but the fit is much tighter than I would have preferred.

Gotta show off that trillion-dollar body, Crest would say. Otherwise, what would the rest of us have to be jealous of?

I stand in front of the ReflectoGlass, trying to find a hint of recognition in my own purple eyes. Who is this person staring back at me with her caramel skin and dark golden hair? A girl who digs holes in the ground and hides what she finds? A girl who can't seem to escape her past no matter how fast she's engineered to run?

Rio's solitary word echoes in my mind like a phantom warning. *"Leave."*

Clearly, that was just the rambling of a madman. Some kind of negative reaction to his procedure.

This is the man who betrayed the Objective. Who betrayed Dr. A.

Even if that was an unusual remnant of the man he used to be, he's not to be trusted. He's an enemy.

Like me?

Or like I *used* to be?

And who is Sariana? He was looking at me when he said it. As if he believed that was my name. I suppose this is only further confirmation that his brain is warped beyond repair. Beyond sense.

The glint off the metal cube drive sparkles in the glass and I turn around and pick it up. I sit down on the edge of the bed and turn the small object over and over in my palm, studying its smooth, shiny surface, wondering what could possibly be stored on it. Some kind of message left for me to find?

"Sync to device," I command my Lenses. Instantly in my vision, I see a list of all the devices that are within range. My wall screen, my ceiling screen, the ReflectoGlass, the Slate lying on my bed.

Then finally, the last item to appear on the list: the drive.

It flashes green, waiting for me to access its contents. It almost seems to be shouting at me to select it. To give it permission to infiltrate my brain. Sour my thoughts. Mangle my certainties.

Nothing I stream to my Lenses is private. Everything can be tracked.

Even though I know the security team is probably too preoccupied with preparations for our tour to be monitoring Lens streams right now, the history will still be stored on a log somewhere. Accessible anytime suspicion is aroused.

I can't take the risk.

And what if it really was Lyzender who left it? What would he have stored inside for me to find?

Nothing that can do any good.

A knock on the door makes me jump. My bodysuit doesn't have pockets so I drop the cube into the toe of my shoe and jam my foot in behind it. The cold metal sends a chill all the way to the tip of my skull.

"Open," I command the door, and a second later Kaelen enters the room. His face is as bright and eager as the sun making its first appearance in the morning. Apparently *he* received the vivacious gene.

"Everything okay?" he asks. "You seem, I don't know, frazzled."

I know I should tell him. Tell him everything. About the cottage. About the drive. About Rio's wild, terrifying eyes as he called me by a different name and told me to leave. I don't know what is stopping me from opening my mouth and revealing everything. But something holds my tongue hostage in that moment.

"Yes," I tell him. "I'm fine."

I'm grateful when Kaelen leans in to kiss me. It means he trusts my answer. I'm eager for his kiss to erase the past few hours. The way it always manages to do. But when he starts to pull away a moment later, I feel the uneasiness lingering inside me like dust settling back into place.

I grab his face with both of my hands and pull him back to me, seizing his mouth with my own, trying to draw from his lips whatever magic vanquishing power he seems to possess.

"Are you ready?" he asks when we break apart. "The hyperloop leaves in an hour."

I'm not ready. I'm not sure I'll ever be ready, but I don't tell him this. I won't tell anyone.

I am an ExGen. This is my purpose. My part in the Objective. Director Raze is tasked with keeping us safe. Crest is tasked with keeping us on schedule. Everyone has a role to play. All I have to do is not look bored. You would think I could handle such a small responsibility. You would think I could embrace my part—maybe even enjoy it—the way Kaelen seems to do so effortlessly.

I paint on my best smile, the one I've been rehearsing for the past year, waiting for the day when it won't feel rehearsed.

Apparently today is not that day. With the drive digging into my toes, I feel more like a fraud than ever.

"Yes. I'll be right down. Just give me a minute?"

"Of course." He slips back out the door and it seals shut behind him.

I roll up my Slate and place it in a small travel pouch that Crest has hung on my bedpost. It's filled with superfood snacks for the road. I swing the strap over my shoulder, take one final look around my bedroom, and head out the door.

In the hallway, I pause at the gold DigiPlaque on the wall and watch as it completes a rotation through the history of the Genesis Project.

Sequence: D / Recombination: W – October 25, 2113
Sequence: D / Recombination: X – December 19, 2113
Sequence: D / Recombination: Y – March 19, 2114
Sequence: D / Recombination: Z – April 23, 2114

One hundred and four failed DNA sequences until mine was a success.

Sequence: E / Recombination: A – June 27, 2114

The day I was "born."

As far as I know, the giant artificial womb where I gestated is still sitting untouched, collecting dust in Rio's old lab in the Medical Sector. No one goes in there anymore. The door has been locked for over a year. There were a few times, after I returned to the compound, when I was intrigued by the thought of returning to the lab where Rio spent so many long, sleepless nights trying to bring me to life, but my fingerprints and retinas would never open the door. Eventually I gave up.

I often stand here in this hallway, watching the revolving text of the DigiPlaque and wondering what happened to all those other failed attempts. Why didn't they work? What was so special about S:E/R:A?

Why *me*?

Then I wonder if any of the other sequences would have been better suited for this role. Would S:D/R:E have been a traitor like me, too? Would S:A/R:U have been as big a disappointment to the Objective? Or would she have been brave and obedient like Dr. A wanted her to be?

The DigiPlaque holds the final date for thirty seconds before starting over again with Sequence: A / Recombination: A. I let myself drift away and continue down the stairs, where Crest and Kaelen are waiting for me.

Crest looks me over and I expect her to tell me to go back upstairs and try again. Surely I've done something wrong. Put my shoes on the wrong feet. Mistaken a neck hole for a sleeve. But she purses her lips and says, "Perfect."

Kaelen kisses my temple, right next to my hairline, and I suddenly panic, thinking he's going to come away with dirt on his lips. "Perfect," he echoes softly into my ear.

Right now, it feels like the most inaccurate word in the English language.

Kaelen, Crest, and I board the first hovercopter. Dr. A is already seated in the front row. He gives me an approving nod. Apparently the bodysuit is going over well. Kaelen sits next to him and I take the row behind them with Crest. Director Raze sits in the front seat, next to the pilot. The role of pilot is pretty obsolete. The hovercopters can fly themselves, but someone has to be there to make sure nothing goes wrong.

I find it amusing that with all this technology Diotech has developed, we still need human beings to supervise.

Outside my window people have gathered to send us off. Scientists, lab assistants, and children. They wave and cheer as the hovercopter lifts off the ground. A crop of blue hair catches my eye. Klo Raze—the boy I saw on the Rec Field yesterday—stares back at me with an unsettling intensity.

He's the only one not waving.

Our ascent into the sky is smooth and fast. I watch through my window as the compound becomes smaller and smaller, less and less recognizable, until it's just a tiny toy city made of disposable plastic and doll-sized people. The mass of media crews and onlookers outside the walls are now nothing more than mismatched freckles on the earth.

The walls are there to keep me safe. That's what I've been told.

But as we float high in the sky, leaving my protected little world behind in a stream of invisible vapor, I wonder who will keep me safe out here. From those who don't understand me. From those who want to hurt me.

From myself.

PART 2

THE UNVEILING

15

ENCAPSULATE

The skin of my cheek tugs and ripples after Crest injects me.
I let out a sharp cry as the drug in my veins goes to work, recoding my DNA, reshaping my face. My lips tingle as they swell and discolor and I reach up to brush my fingers against them. Crest pulls my hand away.

"I wouldn't. It'll only warp you out more."

She injects Kaelen next and I watch his head bow as he endures the pain in stoic silence. He won't turn around so I can't see how different he appears. But I know no matter what he looks like now, I'll still love him and he'll still love me.

That's the beauty of being Print Mates. There is no doubt. There is no insecurity. There is only certainty.

I close my eyes against the sting of my forehead stretching.

"It's just a precaution, pearl," Crest tells me, rubbing my back. "The effects will be gone by tomorrow morning and you'll be back to your stunning self."

Genetic disguises have been around for more than half a decade. Not many people have access to them, though, or even know of their existence. They're mostly used for government work. Undercover operations and the like.

I first heard of them when I was trapped in Dr. Maxxer's submarine in 2032. When she tried to feed me lies about the Objective and what its true purpose was. One of the men she was working with, Trestin, had been genetically disguised when I first met him. He was made to look older and heavier.

Dr. Rylan Maxxer was the woman who invented the transession gene that allowed me to travel back in time. It's since been discontinued and banned after it was discovered to cause negative side effects in Normates. The most dire being death.

Even though the gene didn't affect Kaelen and me in the same way, as a precaution ours were deactivated, too.

After I found the Repressor that Dr. Maxxer had manufactured as an antidote to the transession gene, Dr. A had it reverse engineered and synthesized in bulk so that he could cure every sick person on the compound who'd been implanted with the gene in the past.

Those who weren't already dead, that is.

Dr. A says Maxxer was once a very fine scientist. One of the best on the compound. But she was too passionate for her own good. She would test her experiments on herself, including the transession gene, and eventually the damaging consequences caught up to her. She became overly paranoid. Delusional. Eventually Dr. A had to dismiss her from Diotech service. She wasn't mentally fit for research anymore.

This made her angry and she started trying to spread malicious false rumors about Diotech, Dr. A, and even the Objective itself. Rumors about a secret organization called the Providence, which was trying to control the world.

"If that's not a paranoid delusion," Dr. A told me, "then I don't know what is."

She even tried to recruit me. Tried to feed me her vicious fabrications. Thankfully, I was smart enough to decline.

The one and only redeeming act of my past.

When Dr. A explained all of this to me, I asked him if she was a threat to the Objective.

"She's too crazy to be a threat," he assured me. "And besides, she's not much of a danger to us, being trapped in the year 2032."

That's where I left her. By now, she's most likely dead.

The closest hyperloop station to the compound is in Las Vegas. The station is deserted when we arrive. Dane says all departing and arriving capsules were canceled today to allow us to travel without being seen. The cost of such an expensive endeavor was apparently covered by AFC Streamwork, where Mosima's show airs, as was the cost of our genetic disguises—in order to protect the exclusive reveal they paid for. If one person managed to capture an image of us, it would be uploaded to the Feed in a matter of seconds and the streamwork's exclusive would be ruined.

We are escorted through the station by Director Raze's security team—twenty guards dressed in black with mutation lasers strapped to their belts.

We're positioned in a sea of clacking shoes, blocked from every side in case any onlookers manage to steal a peek through the darkened synthoglass of the station windows. A precaution taken on top of all the others.

Our departure date and time were not released to the public so there shouldn't be anyone lurking, but Director Raze says you can never be too careful. Any company can have a mole.

Crest also had us don dark, large, old-fashioned sunglasses and MagBall caps. I notice that the logo flashing in the nanostitching of Kaelen's cap belongs to the Denver team, which is currently in first place, while mine is the Detroit team, currently in last place. Even if that was a coincidence, I find it terribly fitting.

As we pass through the massive hyperloop station with its domed ceilings and modern light fixtures, I take in the closed shops that normally sell snacks and motion sickness meds for passengers who can't handle the pressure of the vacuum. A few even advertise varieties of alcohol for those who just want to make it all fade into the background.

"Don't worry," Killy, a female security agent, says to me, clearly reading the trepidation on my face. "It only feels warped the first time. You'll get used to it."

I nod to one of the darkened shops. An ad for meds is playing on the window screen, despite the store being closed. "Do you ever need those?"

She follows my gaze. "Never." She pats her stomach. "Gut of steel."

I tilt my head curiously, which seems to make her laugh.

"It's an old phrase. It means nothing makes me feel sick. Kind of like you."

I want to tell her she's wrong. So much makes me feel sick.

The memory of Lyzender's face.

The small cube drive chafing my toe at the tip of my shoe.

The hollowness of Rio's eyes.

The way Dr. A regards me as though I really am diseased. Diseased in the mind.

I don't say any of this, though. I keep walking with my head up and my gaze forward. We reach a bank of lifts and split into groups to ride them to the fifth floor of the station. The voice in the lift tells me it's the embarkation level.

I'm not sure what will await me when the door opens. I've seen hyperloops on the Feed and, of course, in my uploads, but I've learned that things tend to feel very different when you're standing right in front of them.

The first thing I notice when we exit the lifts and I see the open capsules awaiting us is the smell. It must be the gases they use to seal the vacuum tubes at the end of the loading track. Or maybe it's my own fear that I smell. A mix of metal and singed air. Like something burning.

Burning.

I stop walking, suddenly overtaken by the recollection of scent.

Burning.

Burning what? Wood?

No. Flesh.

The thought makes my stomach roll. Why would I think of burning flesh?

The memory of my witchcraft trial in the year 1609 flickers to my mind but it doesn't match. It feels more immediate than that. More recent.

"Everything okay?" Killy asks, coming up beside me.

I blink rapidly and force myself to smile. "Yes. It was just . . . the smell. It caught me off guard."

She nods understandingly. "It gets me every time, too. It's nothing like watching it on the Feed, huh?"

The streamworks have tried to emulate the fourth sense. The screens will sometimes emit the delectable scent of baking bread when a character is in the kitchen, or the perfume of flowers when someone is running through a meadow, but it's never quite real. The sweet smells are too sugary, the scent of rain too sharp. Whatever they do, they can't seem to match the real thing.

Each capsule holds six people so our group is split into five parties. Kaelen and I are separated. Dr. A, Dane, Director Raze, and two other agents are assigned to the first capsule with Kaelen and I'm assigned to the last one along with Crest, Killy, and Agent Thatch, Raze's second-in-command.

Before Kaelen boards the capsule, he stands before me, studying my disguised face. For the first time, I take a moment to study his, too. His straight nose is now slightly crooked, his vibrant aquamarine eyes have dampened to a dull, Normate green. There are tiers of wrinkles under his eyes like he hasn't slept in days. His high cheekbones have sagged down his face, and his strong, squared chin is now cone shaped and tilted upward. Even his lustrous dark blond hair seems like it was washed with filthy water.

But I can still see him behind the disguise.

He's still there. My beautiful Kaelen.

He traces the outline of my temporary cheek with his fingertip, as though he's trying to memorize it.

"Not so perfect now," I joke.

Kaelen's lips crack into a smile. "So that's how you'd look as a Normate."

I strike a pose similar to those I've seen countless times on the fashion streams. "What do you think?"

Despite how Kaelen responds, I know exactly what I think. Even though I haven't seen my own reflection, I finally look how I feel.

Flawed. Crooked. Blemished.

Without answering, he bends down to kiss me. His misshapen mouth feels foreign against mine. We are two strangers kissing for the thousandth time. But the tingle of warmth he leaves on my lips is one hundred percent Kaelen.

"I'll see you in less than thirty minutes," he murmurs. Then he climbs into the capsule, taking the third seat of the six-row passenger arrangement. As soon as his weight is registered on the seat, the triple-crossing metal restraints secure around his upper body, prohibiting him from even waving goodbye to me.

I watch the door seal shut and the surface darken. It's for the passengers' own safety. And sanity. Evidently, if you were able to see how fast you were traveling, you might warp out and try to break free, which would surely kill you.

Moving around too much while you're in the loop, especially going around the turns, can also be dangerous. The restraints are there not only to keep you from getting jostled, but also to keep you from injuring yourself by trying to rotate your body.

I can see why some people opt for the alcohol.

I watch Kaelen's capsule glide slowly toward the tube entrance, stopping to await its departure window.

The next part happens almost too fast for even me to register.

The tube opening unseals, the vacuum takes hold, and the capsule blasts inside, shooting off like a bullet before the tube is shut again, a mist of gas swirling behind it.

If you blink, you'll surely miss it.

I watch in a panicked daze as three more capsules shoot off into the loop before a tap on my shoulder jolts me back to the present. I turn to see Killy pointing toward the next capsule, which has just appeared on the loading track. "We're up."

Bracing myself with a deep breath, I step into the vehicle, taking the third row just as Kaelen did. Crest bounces into the seat behind me. "How thermal is this? I have the best job in the world!"

The restraints extend from both sides, pinning me to the seat. I know I should be used to being confined by now, but the thought of being trapped inside this capsule for the next 27.2 minutes is making me hyperventilate.

I start to recite the square root of pi.

1.77245385091 . . .

"How are you feeling, Sera?" Killy calls out.

"Fine," I say, and then quickly amend my answer to "Great."

But I find it impossible to inflate the word with any enthusiasm.

The door seals and I watch the station disappear as the glass dims to black. I can feel the loading track vibrating under my seat as we move toward the tube entrance. Soon there will be nothing beneath us but air.

Only twenty-eight tour stops to go, I think as the capsule slows to a heart-pounding pause.

Then I'm thrust against the back of my seat with the force of the earth falling.

16

REACTIVE

I'm grateful when we finally begin to decelerate less than thirty minutes later and our capsule connects with the loading track that brings us into the Los Angeles hyperloop station. It feels good to have something sturdy and metal underneath me again. As opposed to the rush of unreliable air.

We pull up to the disembarkation platform and the black tint of the synthoglass dissolves, allowing me to view the inside of the station. As I struggle to turn my head to peer out, I expect to see Kaelen waiting for me on the platform, his genetically disguised face greeting me with a crooked smile. But I'm met with a far more disturbing reality.

A man I've never seen before is lying unconscious on the ground, his body contorted in the most unnatural way. He's not moving. I don't think he's even breathing. A pile of shattered Digi-Cams lie in pieces next to his head.

Five people—more unrecognizable faces—are gathered around him. Someone kneels down to check his pulse. Another—a stocky man with longish hair—shouts something I can't hear through the thick glass of the capsule. I follow his feverish gaze across the platform and suck in a breath when I see his angry bellows are directed at Kaelen.

At least I think it's Kaelen. He's still disguised by the injection and his face is twisted in such rage, he barely even looks human. He's being held back by four of Raze's burly security agents and I immediately understand why. He looks like he wants to kill someone. My gaze darts back to the man lying motionless on the platform.

Or perhaps he *already* has.

Did Kaelen do that?

The minute the question pops into my head, I have my answer. Kaelen wrestles free from the agents' grasp and lunges himself forward so fast, I doubt anyone can follow the trajectory of his movement except me.

He clobbers the shouting man, knocking him hard onto his back. His head crunches against the unyielding surface of the platform. Kaelen thrusts a fist into the man's face. Blood splatters Kaelen's disfigured cheeks and the surrounding floor.

"Oh, flux," I hear Crest swear behind me. "This is bad."

My mind finally reacts to what I'm seeing and I struggle against my restraints, wedging my hands between my body and the metal bars pinning me to the seat, but it's no use. I can't force them to budge even an inch.

Synthosteel.

I twist my head again, straining to see what's happening on the platform. My heart thuds violently in my chest as I watch Kaelen continue to pound the man's face. But the man is no longer fighting back. His arms have fallen limp at his sides.

I catch a glimpse of the four agents who were restraining Kaelen. They're all itching to reach for their mutation lasers, but a definitive shake of the head from Raze changes their minds. Instead, they storm toward him, trying to pull him off the man. Kaelen's mouth stretches in what I can only assume is a roar and he quickly thrusts each of them back, sending them flying through the air. One of them slams into our capsule. His frozen, terrified face presses against the side of the glass before he slides slowly to the ground.

I let out a desperate cry as I, once again, thrash under my restraints. "Crest!" I yell. "Get me out!"

Whatever happened in the three-minute gap between Kaelen's arrival and mine, I'm the only one who can stop it.

"I know, pearl," Crest soothes. "I know." But the misery in her voice tells me she hasn't a clue what to do, or how to release us.

"We have to wait for the capsule to engage the sensors," Killy says.

With my back still pinned to the seat, I try my best to bang on the glass of the capsule, hoping it may give way, but at this awkward angle, my fist is only capable of making a weak plunk against the synthetic surface.

"Who are they?" I ask Crest, peering at the strangers who have scattered to opposite ends of the platform in an attempt to escape Kaelen's wrath.

"Paparazzi probably."

"How did they know we'd be here?"

There's only silence behind me and I know that Crest is shaking her head in stunned disbelief, words escaping her.

When I peer out at Kaelen again, his hair is tousled, his clothes are slightly askew on his large, muscular frame, but it's his face that's the least recognizable of all. Stretched in unbridled rage. His eyes are wild, revealing too much white as he searches for more challengers. But there are none to be found. The rest of the crowd—including Raze's remaining agents—have backed away, pressing themselves against the perimeters of the platform.

I can tell from the hunger in Kaelen's eyes that he wants more. He's a monster looking for prey. His eyes land on one of the cowering paparazzi in the corner and my chest starts to constrict.

No, I silently plead. *Don't do it.*

But telepathy has never been one of the languages Kaelen and I are fluent in. He starts to move toward his next victim. Slowly and purposefully. I bang on the glass. "No!" This time I shout it. It's no use, though. I can't hear him and he can't hear me. Not that the sound of my voice would do anything to stop him now. He's too far gone. I can see that.

Finally, a whoosh echoes like music in my ears and I feel my restraints loosen. I shove them away from me and bolt through the capsule door the instant it unseals. I'm in front of Kaelen in a nanosecond, positioning myself between him and the man he's set on destroying. Blocking his path, I place my palm flat on his chest. To my surprise, he stops at my touch. But he doesn't look at me. His eyes are fixed on his destination.

The familiarity of his intense gaze crashes into me as I realize I've seen this reaction from him before. In a New York City subway station in the year 2032. Kaelen attacked a man he believed was a threat to me. One minute he was perfectly fine, and the next minute he wasn't. He just kind of . . . *snapped.*

Back then, I didn't know what to do about it. Fortunately, now I do.

I press against his shirt with my thumb, fourth finger, and pinkie, like a pianist playing a chord.

Then I lift all five fingers up and bring down only my thumb.

Next, I press fingers one, two, four, and five into his chest, followed by two, four, and five.

In less than a few seconds, I've played out two four-letter words. CALM DOWN.

He blinks, his heavy breathing gradually returning to normal, but the fury on his face doesn't dim. His eyes dart wildly around the station, nostrils flaring, pupils dilated, teeth clenched.

I keep going. My fingers move fast but methodically, the letters flowing out of me one tap at a time.

Thumb, index, fourth, pinkie = L.
Thumb, index, middle = O.
Thumb, index, middle = O.
Thumb, fourth, pinkie = K.
I pause, indicating a new word.
A.
T.
Pause. New word.
M.
E.

Kaelen obeys and turns his hungry eyes to me. He's caught on to what I'm doing. It's a code we invented to keep our minds sharp and to be able to communicate with each other without speaking. Each combination of fingers corresponds to a letter in the alphabet. Like a piano concerto of words.

The foreign languages are fun but anyone with a Slate can run our sentences through a translator and understand. This is a language only for us.

The energy of my fingers moving against his chest is enough to distract him and pull him out of his state. I smile at him but he's still too riled up to return the gesture.

The hush on the platform is palpable. No one even dares to breathe. All eyes are on us.

I gently wrap my hand around Kaelen's and give it a tug, pulling him behind a VersaScreen programmed to display the list of arrivals and departures. It gives us a little privacy.

I hear footsteps approaching and I turn to see Raze coming over to us. I hold up my hand, warning him not to come any closer. "What happened?" I ask Raze.

He shakes his head, visibly dazed. "I-I-I'm not sure." I don't think I've ever heard Raze stammer before. "We disembarked and they jumped at us with their cams and Kaelen just warped out."

I nod. "Give us a minute."

Raze obliges, backtracking and calling orders to his agents to start the damage control. Something has to be done to cover this up.

Once we're alone and the rest of the team is busy cleaning up the mess Kaelen made, my brain finally has a chance to make sense of what has happened.

Kaelen attacked someone. *Multiple* someones. Each of them clearly unable to compete with his strength, speed, and reflexes.

I think back to his face—the rash, unseeing eyes, the agape mouth, the red irritated skin. It's like he turned into someone else. *Something* else. And now that it's over and I'm able to sort through my thoughts, I can finally identify how it made me feel.

Terrified.

The realization seizes my breath.

Where did he learn that?

I never would have reacted that way. If we're made from complementary genetic blueprints shouldn't we have similar responses to situations?

I think about the proud look on Dr. A's face as he watched Kaelen's reaction.

Is this what Dr. A wants of us?

Is this what makes Kaelen a better ExGen? A better soldier for the Objective?

"Normally I'm pretty good at reading you." Kaelen's voice interrupts my thoughts. "But right now I'm at a loss."

I peer up at him, relieved to see his features have lost that frightening rigidity and, aside from his genetic disguise, he's almost back to his normal self.

"What are you thinking?" he asks.

I want to tell him the truth about what I'm feeling, about the disturbing thoughts streaming through my mind. But I'm not sure how he'll react. So I make something up.

"I was thinking of an upload I received about fish."

He breaks into laughter. It's a beautiful sound. "Has anyone ever told you you're a horrible liar?"

I smile. "Actually, yes."

"Do I need to put my nanoscanners on and steal the thoughts right out of your brain?"

I smile. I know he's joking. He hasn't used the nanoscanners on me since my escape, when he needed to access my memories so that he could fulfill his mission. Back then, my loyalties were so distorted, I tried to keep things from him. Things that would help the Objective.

Thankfully, now I know better.

"I was thinking about what happened," I finally admit. "Back there."

"I know that. But *what* are you thinking about it?"

I look directly into his eyes. I need to see his reaction when I say this. "I'm thinking that I don't understand it. I'm thinking that it scared me. I'm wondering why you felt the need to attack those people."

Kaelen's shoulders rise dramatically as he takes his next breath. He tears his gaze from mine and stares at my hyperloop capsule, which still lies empty and open on the loading track.

"I don't know," he finally says with a sigh.

"You don't know?"

He shakes his head. "I . . . it just . . . came over me. I couldn't control it. It controlled me. Like it was . . . part of me or something."

"You think it was a stimulated-response system?" I ask, referring to the technology Diotech used to try to make me kill Dr. Maxxer in 2032.

"No," he admits. "It felt deeper than that. I can't explain it. I just knew they were a threat so I reacted."

"It didn't look like they were a threat to you," I say after a moment. "You were a threat to *them*."

Kaelen cringes. "I know. I'm sorry. Will you forgive me?"

"Will you try to figure out what it is? So you can work on controlling it?"

"Yes. Will you forgive me?"

"I'm serious."

"I am, too. Forgive me."

"I will. Eventually."

"No. Now. Forgive me now." He grins. Then he rests his hand on my arm and starts to repeat his plea in our secret code. The same one I just used to distract him from his monstrous trance.

His index, middle, and fourth fingers play the F.

His thumb, index, and middle fingers play the O.

Middle, forth, pinkie = R.

I crack the tiniest of smiles and pull my arm away. "Fine."

"Fine what?"

I cross my arms over my chest. "I forgive you."

"You have to say that, you know. It's in your DNA." I can hear the smirk in his voice.

"To love you? Yes. To think you're not capable of totally glitching up? Not that I'm aware of."

17

HOSPITALITY

Our hotel in downtown Los Angeles is completely empty, just like the hyperloop stations. The streamwork bought up every room. Only a few key employees remain. Enough to get us settled in and prepare our meals. Everyone else has been sent home.

Walking through the well-appointed lobby, I feel as though I'm walking through a ghostly dream. The check-in kiosks have been shut down. The gift shop is dark and closed off behind a syntho-glass barrier. All the tables in the restaurant are set for diners who won't appear.

"Once we reveal you on Mosima's show tomorrow," Crest assures me, "we won't have to take so many precautions."

But after what just occurred on the hyperloop platform, I almost wonder if we didn't take *enough* precautions. And the most unsettling part is that no one seems to be particularly rattled by it except me. Judging by everyone's behavior during the short hovercopter ride here, you would think the whole thing never even happened.

"Why didn't we ride out tomorrow and go straight to the show?" I ask Crest.

"Dane was worried about the effect of the hyperloop. It's been known to disorient people. This way you'll get a nice rest and be completely refreshed and prepared for tomorrow's interview."

It's going to take more than just a night's sleep to prepare me for tomorrow's interview.

"And," Crest adds with a bubbly flourish of her hands, "I hear the view from your room is spectacular. You can practically see all of Los Angeles."

I want to tell her that I don't care about seeing Los Angeles. If anything, I'd like to forget we're even in this city. Los Angeles is where it all started. Where I crash-landed with no memories after escaping with the boy. He found me, swore we were in love, and seduced me into leaving with him again. Sometimes, I like to think about how differently things would have worked out if I hadn't trusted him. If I had let Diotech apprehend me and bring me back right away, instead of leading them on a wild chase through time.

Would Dr. A still look at me with those accusing eyes?

Would the Objective already be complete?

The entire top floor of the hotel is ours. Kaelen and I have our own suites next to each other. Naturally, Dr. A has the Owner's Suite, while Dane and Crest are a few doors away from us. Director Raze has stationed his guards—the ones who weren't injured in the debacle earlier—at various posts down the hallway and throughout the lobby.

Crest sends me to my suite to rest before evening meal. The first thing I do when the door is sealed shut behind me is retrieve the small cube drive from my shoe, where it has been digging into my toes for the past few hours. I turn it over in my palm, studying its sleek metallic surface and wondering if I'll ever know what's inside.

How can I possibly access the drive when I'm watched

constantly? When my DigiLenses and Slate are tracked and my memories are scanned on a weekly basis? How could I ever explain that kind of curiosity to Dr. A? It would be perceived as weakness. It would be perceived as faultiness.

Will I be forced to live forever never knowing what's stored in here?

Crest pings me a few hours later and tells me to join everyone in the Hospitality Suite. I place the drive in the drawer of my nightstand, run to the bathroom, splash some cold water on my face, and gaze at my genetically disfigured reflection in the glass.

Despite the fact I barely recognize the face that stares back at me, despite the fact that she's practically a stranger, there's something achingly familiar about her. Even comforting. Like she's been there the whole time, concealed just below the surface. Hiding behind a layer of flawless golden skin, unnaturally purple eyes, a nose and mouth too perfect to exist outside of a lab. Patiently waiting to make her appearance. Waiting to reveal herself to me.

I'm halfway down the hall when I realize I still haven't changed my clothes. But as soon as I enter the large common room labeled HOSPITALITY SUITE, it becomes evident that no one is interested in what I'm wearing. Particularly not Dr. A, who is currently standing behind his chair, ranting irately about something.

"What do you mean you *can't* find her?" he bellows at Director Raze, ignoring my entrance completely.

I slip into an empty seat at the table, next to Crest, who gives me a warning look and a slight nudge with her elbow.

Just stay quiet, the look says.

Her warning is superfluous. I, of anyone, know how to behave when Dr. A is in one of his moods.

"I mean," Raze replies, struggling to keep his composure, "she's gone completely off-line. Shut down all devices. There's no way to track her unless she turns something on. A Slate. A Lens. Even a glitching oven."

"So you're saying we have *no way* of tracking her?" Dr. A asks impatiently. "She could be raising a goddamn bloody army right now and we wouldn't know."

I sneak a glimpse at Dane, who cringes slightly behind a sip of wine.

"She's not raising an army," Raze assuages. "She doesn't have the reach. Or the influence. Trust me, sir, Jenza Paddok is not the one we need to be worried about. Peder is the one to focus on."

Jenza Paddok.

Should that name be familiar to me?

It isn't.

Dr. A starts to pace behind his chair. He drags his fingers through his silky blond hair, which I notice is fairly disheveled and starting to thin. He hasn't been for a thickening treatment in a while. I wonder when was the last time he slept. "How many did she have before you lost her?"

"Sir, I didn't *lose* her. She disconnected."

Dr. A is clearly not interested in debating semantics. "How many?"

Raze blinks several times, accessing data from his Lenses. "Twenty at the most."

Dr. A scoffs at this. "Child's play."

Dane nods fervently in agreement. "Nothing to concern ourselves with."

"Exactly." Raze jumps back in. "I recommend we continue to focus our resources on Peder. His numbers are growing by the day. He's getting more and more airtime on the Feed. And he'll be all over the Unveiling tomorrow morning."

There's a tense silence as we wait for Dr. A's response. For that long, thick moment, no one even chews.

"Very good," Dr. A finally agrees, lowering himself into his chair and picking up his fork. I feel the room deflate in simultaneous relief.

"Also," Director Raze adds, and my muscles tighten again as I take a hesitant bite from the food on my plate, "I've taken care of the other matter."

Dr. A shares a knowing look with Kaelen. "Very good."

I know that I've missed something in the past few hours and even though my common sense is telling me to tread lightly on this thin sheet of ice Dr. A has frozen around us, I hate being out of the know.

"What other matter?" I ask.

I don't expect to receive an answer, which is why I'm surprised when Dr. A says, "The matter of the paparazzi who found us at the hyperloop station."

My heart starts to pound. "What happened to them?"

"The four who lived to tell won't have anything to tell."

Dr. A's words are like insects crawling up my spine.

The four who lived to tell . . .

That means two of them are dead. The two Kaelen attacked. And the other four have had their memories altered.

Dane catches my eye, offering me a sad smile. "We couldn't have them selling those memories to the tabloids," he explains.

His answer makes me want to scream. Doesn't he get it? It's not the four altered memories that make me want to vomit right now. It's the two people who will never have another memory again. Kaelen *killed* two people. And everyone is sitting around acting like it doesn't matter.

There's an uncomfortable pause and I sense Dr. A studying me. When I look up, his eyebrows are knit together and his head is cocked. "Do you have a problem with how this was handled, Sera?"

I realize that my face has betrayed me. Exposed the horror behind my mask. I will it back into submission. "No. Of course not."

Because how else can I respond? Anything I say that opposes

Dr. A or Director Raze is the same as opposing the Objective. And that will only make things way worse.

I can see Dr. A's tongue stabbing the inside of his cheek. "Hmmm," is the only thing he says. He wipes his mouth with his napkin and sets it down on the table. "Now, I'd like to discuss something very important."

My breath ratchets up a notch. Does he know about the drive? How could he?

I look to Crest for any indication of what this is about. She shakes her head subtly.

"Yes?" I say, but my throat is parched. I take a large gulp of water from the glass in front of me. It burns going down.

"Your first interview is tomorrow morning," Dr. A begins calmly.

Don't remind me.

"It's important that the two of you"—he nods to Kaelen and me in turn—"appear as connected as possible when you're presented to the public. Viewers can see right through romantic façades. They see them every day on the reality shows."

Why would Dr. A ever compare us to a couple on a silly reality show? We are nothing like them.

"So why, may I ask," he continues, "are you refusing to complete the act of ultimate intimacy?"

My cheeks instantly warm. I peer at Dane, then at Director Raze. Both of them are staring awkwardly at their plates. I cast a sidelong look at Kaelen but he gives me an unassuming smile. Does he not find this question inappropriate?

Particularly after the conversation we just had?

"I—I—" I stammer, because Dr. A is staring at me, expecting an answer. "I don't know."

"This act, as I've already explained to you, is what will connect the two of you on a deeper level and bring you closer together."

"I feel close to Kaelen already," I murmur, the words feeling misshapen and swollen on my tongue.

"Not as close as you could be," Dr. A argues. "Kaelen tells me that you continually refuse him into your bed. I'd like to know why this is. It can't be for lack of know-how. I've supplied you with plenty of informative uploads on the subject."

"Dr. Alixter," Crest interjects, "I'm not sure this is an appropriate conversation to have over evening meal."

"This is none of your concern, Crest," Dr. A snaps at her. Crest nods timidly and scoops a pile of food onto her fork. But I notice she never puts it into her mouth.

I clear my throat, buying a little time while I try to come up with an answer that won't set him off again.

Is there such a thing?

My brain squeezes as a memory comes flooding back to me. I fight to keep it at bay. I can tell by the way it twists my stomach that it's not the good kind. It's the other kind. The one that comes with chest pain and nausea and an all-consuming sensation of wretched failure.

"I've just been waiting a long time for this," Lyzender says.

I squint at him. "For what?"

"For you to feel . . ." He looks uncomfortable. Even his face flushes. "W-w-well," he stutters. "For you to feel ready, I guess."

"I'm not ready," I blurt, chasing the memory away before it causes me to lose what little I've consumed of my meal.

"Not ready?" Dr. A repeats with something that sounds like disgust. "How could you not be *ready*? I've built you two to be compatible in every single way. There's no one out there better suited for you than Kaelen."

"I know that—" I try to say but I'm cut off.

"Perhaps there's something you're still holding on to. Or someone?"

The silence in the room slowly starts to suffocate me. I want to run to the window, shove it open, stick my head out, and drink in the warm air.

I will my paralyzed mouth to move. "No," I barely squeak out. "There's no one else."

"Then I don't see a problem."

"Perhaps," Dane says, casting a glance at Crest, "this really is a conversation better suited to a more private setting."

"There's nothing private about their lives," Dr. A argues, his patience dwindling. "They're about to be the most public couple in the world. I didn't create them to live a private life behind closed doors. I created them to be the faces of Diotech. Privacy is not in the equation."

Dane sets a tender hand on Dr. A's arm. He seems to be the only one who can touch him like that. "Yes, I realize. I just meant—"

Dr. A jerks his arm away and rises from the table. "This isn't a discussion. Nor a democracy. I created you two to be hopelessly in love. Now start acting like it."

He stalks toward the door. "Raze," he calls. "How is the network setup coming along?"

Raze straightens before answering the question. "My tech is working on it. The screens in the suites are still connected to the public SkyServer. I'm told it will take another hour or so before our secure internal network is up and running." He gazes around the room. "So be prudent in what you transmit over your Lenses and Slates."

Dr. A doesn't look happy about the news of the delay, but thankfully, he doesn't say anything. He just leaves.

My mind is instantly abuzz.

"The screens in the suites are still connected to the public SkyServer . . ."

Meaning whatever I access on them can't be tracked by Dio-tech. At least not for another hour.

My pulse races as the realization settles in.

Now might be my only chance to find out what's on that drive.

18

RUINS

No one doubts my claim that the hyperloop fatigued me and I'm allowed to retire to my suite without much fuss. Crest reminds me that we'll be leaving for the streamwork at six a.m. sharp.

"Do you want me to walk you to your suite?" Kaelen asks.

I come around to the back of his chair and kiss the top of his head. The coarse hair of his lingering genetic disguise feels foreign against my lips. "No. I can't bear to look at you another second with that face."

Everyone laughs at my joke. I feel disgusted by it.

"I'll be back to my pretty self tomorrow morning," Kaelen replies, playing along.

"Good. I'll admire you then."

Kaelen grins. "I look forward to it."

Once the door of my suite seals behind me, I waste no time retrieving the cube from the drawer, swiping it on, and activating the wall screen. The drive immediately shows up on the list of active devices.

I know my time is limited. The network will be up and running soon and then my window of opportunity will be closed. But I still stare at the drive on the screen for a good two minutes, trying to build up the courage to connect to it.

With the network inactive, whatever I see on that drive can't be traced by Diotech. But there's still the matter of my memories. Our weekly scans are obviously on hold until the end of the tour, but then what?

What will happen when we return to the compound in a month and they find this?

Because they will. They find everything.

I remind myself that it's only a problem if they think I was trying to hide something. If I access the drive, see what's inside, and report it to Dr. A before they have a chance to scan my memories, then I should be safe.

With a deep breath, I initiate the link.

The syncing screen seems to take forever. It's as though time is slowing down the longer the devices try to reach one another. I get a flutter of panic in my chest.

What if the drive has been damaged?

How long was it buried under the hard, unforgiving earth?

Finally, the sync completes and I'm shown an inventory of files stored on the drive.

There is only one.

Everything else has been erased.

And if there was any lingering doubt that the drive was left for me, it's erased as well, as soon as I read the file name.

S + Z = 1609

I cringe as the memory stabs at my heart and my conscience like a vengeful warrior. Like an age-old curse.

"It's beautiful," I say, flipping the necklace over in my palm. I gasp when I see the engraving on the back. I run my fingertip over the text etched into the black heart pendant.

"S + Z = 1609," I whisper, afraid that the clouds might overhear.

"An equation only you can solve," he says.

S + Z = 1609 was our secret code. Along with the symbol of the eternal knot. Back when I used to call him Zen, instead of his full name, Lyzender.

The equation was a plan for our escape. We were going to live in the year 1609. We were going to run away to a time before Diotech. Before science. Before the Objective.

And we did. We made it. He lured me there with all of his romantic words and soulful promises.

Yet it wasn't what it was supposed to be. It was a dangerous time with distrustful people who did not take kindly to my uniqueness.

Dr. A was right about Lyzender all along. His promises were false. His words were contrived. He tempted me into a hell that didn't accept me. It wasn't better in the seventeenth century. It was worse.

Sometimes I wish Dr. A had simply erased him from my mind. That boy and the promises I made to him are my single most powerful source of shame.

I understand why Dr. A didn't, though.

He wanted me to remember. He wanted me to feel this disgrace that doubles me over. He knew it was the only way to keep me from doing it again.

And he's right.

I remind myself that I can use this ghastly sensation to heal. To become stronger. It's just like the training sessions Kaelen and I have back home on the compound. You can't improve unless you face obstacles every day.

Today, this is my obstacle.

With shaky hands, I select the file.

The screen fills with blackness and I see a duration meter appear at the bottom, indicating it's not a memory, but a capture file.

Then suddenly, he's there. Filling my entire wall. His dark, searching eyes lock onto mine, as though he can see me across our eighty-four-year separation.

I instinctively back away from the screen, which is foolish and naïve. Am I really afraid he's going to come through the wall and grab me? I brace myself, grit my teeth, and take a step forward.

I recognize the room he's in. It's the guest bedroom in Cody's town house in Brooklyn. A time stamp appears at the bottom of the frame: September 23, 2032. Approximately seven months after I left with Kaelen and never came back.

He appears older than when I last saw him, his face fatigued and marred by purple shadows. His hair is matted and greasy, as though it hasn't been washed in days. His cheeks and chin, normally smooth and clean, are covered with dark brown stubble.

I remember he used to glow when I looked at him. He used to shine under any light. His deep maple eyes were always gleaming. Now they're dim and faded. Like someone cut the power source.

He looks . . .

My throat goes bone dry as the answer comes to me.

Destroyed.

Like a city that's been bombed beyond recognition. A priceless painting that's been left out in the rain.

"Seraphina," he says, his voice thick with grief.

It's too much. The voice. The lost eyes. The mouth forming a name only he and Rio called me.

"Pause," I practically yell at the screen. He freezes. Safely trapped on my wall. If he can't speak, he can't hurt me. If he can't move, he can't make me feel anything.

But the fact that I feel *anything* means I'm still susceptible.

I'm still failing.

I sprint to the bathroom and activate the cold water. I splash it on my face over and over again until I'm shivering. Until my cheeks are numb.

I return to the living room and resume the file.

"It's been two hundred and twenty-three days since I woke up to find you gone," Lyzender begins. I sit on the foot of the bed and pull my knees up to my chest. It's all I have to protect myself.

"Cody says you left with a Diotech agent to find the cure to save my life. The fact that I'm alive means you succeeded. But the fact that I'm here without you means they succeeded, too. Diotech got to you. Maybe they destroyed your transession gene. Maybe they erased your memories again. I'm not sure. I can only speculate. And trust me, these are the best possible speculations I've had. My mind has come up with far worse. It's amazing the dark places the mind can go if you let it."

As much as I hate to admit it, I know what he's experiencing.

Back when I was still under his spell, trapped in a prison cell in 1609, I thought he had died. My imagination got the best of me. It showed me horrors I never thought I could have created.

"If you're watching this, though," he goes on, "then you found the drive. And that means some part of you still remembers. That's the only thing that gives me hope right now. Knowing that you can never really forget me. Because you never have."

My throat burns as I try—and fail—to swallow.

They are words, Sera. Only words.

He's trying to pull you in again.

He's an enemy of the Objective. His only goal is to destroy Diotech. He doesn't care about you. He doesn't love you.

It's all a ruse to crack your heart open again and make you bleed.

"How many times did they erase me from your memories?" he says. "How many times were you turned into a blank canvas? And yet some piece of you never forgot. If you are watching this, then please try to remember me. Try to remember us. They are not stronger than you. They never have been. Diotech's only goal has been to *conceal* your strength. To fool you into believing you are weaker than them. It's a lie. It's all a lie, Sera. Don't trust them. Don't give up on us. I haven't. Let me not to the marriage of true minds admit impediments, remember?"

I remember. I wish I didn't, but I do.

He's reciting the beginning of our poem. Sonnet 116 by William Shakespeare. He claimed it was my favorite. He claimed it brought us together. Because it was about a constant, unchanging love that withstood the test of time. It was the reason we chose the year 1609, when the poem was first published.

Before I realize what I'm doing, my lips are quietly whispering the words of the next line. "Love is not love which alters when it alteration finds, or bends with the remover to remove . . ."

On the screen, moisture brims in Lyzender's eyes. I want to look away, but I force myself to keep watching.

Fake tears.

Fake emotions.

Fake promises.

"We can still do it," he says, his voice shattering. "Be together. Love's not Time's fool."

I am shaking now. Fighting against the pounding of my own heart.

"Will I find a way back to you, Seraphina?" He leans forward, staring through the drive, through the wall, through time.

Right through to me.

"Yes . . . always *yes.*"

The screen goes dark and the air that's been trapped inside my lungs shudders out. I sit motionless, somewhere between a sob and a scream. The light from the cube drive on the nightstand casts my entire world in a suffocating green glow.

I grab the drive, run to the window, and fumble against the operational panel, swatting it clumsily with clammy fingers. Finally, it slides open and the cool night air hits me in the face. I cock my arm back, ready to throw the drive as far as I can. All the way to the Pacific Ocean. Where this nightmare began.

Do it!

My arm trembles.

Now!

My muscles throb.

Throw him away!

Shaking uncontrollably, I collapse onto the bed. I tuck my knees into my chin, curling my quivering body around the tiny cube.

Maybe if I squeeze tight enough, the green light will extinguish forever.

Maybe if I shut my eyes long enough, I will forget.

19

SILENCED

I don't sleep. I lie in bed for hours, listening to the unfamiliar sounds of this unfamiliar place. A dishwasher running ten floors below. A dog barking in the distance. Someone tapping furiously on their Slate.

At one point, I swear I can even hear the ocean waves crashing on the beach ten miles west of here. Although I know that's unlikely.

When you can hear everything, it's impossible to focus on any one thing. Every little noise is demanding to be heard.

I suppose it's better than the alternative. Being left alone with my thoughts.

Especially given the state my thoughts are in right now.

I turn on my ceiling screen and flip through the streams. The first thing I see is a news bulletin.

The bodies of two paparazzi capturers were found in East LA earlier today.
Police suspect gang members responsible.

I know, without having to click through for more information, that the faces of the capturers will match those of the two people Kaelen killed today at the hyperloop station. So that's how Diotech disposed of the bodies. Dumped them in a bad neighborhood infested with crime, while the memories of the other four were erased and recoded to fill in the blanks.

A far too easy solution for something that shouldn't be that easy to fix.

I flip to the next stream.

Crest's favorite show, *The Rifters*, is on. I try to watch it for a few minutes, hoping it will distract me from the noises that are competing for my attention, but I'm unable to follow the plot. I have a feeling it's the kind of show you can't just start in the middle. I flip streams again and suddenly Pastor Peder is in the room with me. His large, round face projects through the air as though he's hovering over me, talking down at me. Judging me from behind those blue-tinted glasses.

"What exactly are you saying?" an off-screen interviewer asks.

"I'm saying," he replies, looking straight into the cam, straight into me, "Diotech is using these monstrosities they call ExGens as an attempt to control us."

"Diotech's position is that the ExGen Collection is meant to improve our lives," the interviewer argues. "Make us better. Stronger."

Pastor Peder snorts at this and I almost want to check my face for droplets of his snot. "Improve our lives? God created us in his own image. No man—or corporation for that matter—can improve upon that which has already been perfected. These ExGens aren't ideal specimens of humans. They're mockeries of God's will. They're mockeries of us all."

Flustered, I deactivate the screen and grab a pillow, shoving it over my head.

I try to remember Dr. A's assurance to me. That this man is not a threat to us. It would be a lot easier to believe it if he wasn't *everywhere*. If every streamwork in the country wasn't feedcasting his face twenty-four hours a day.

"Those who seek to change the world will make more enemies than friends," Dr. A always says. "If we gave our energy to every person who wanted to stop us, we'd have no energy left to do what we're trying to do."

Through the synthetic down pillow, I hear the sound of music outside, a MagCar taxicab on the street below asking a passenger where he would like to go, Crest's quiet breathing a few rooms away.

I fling the pillow across the room and stand up, padding into the bathroom of the suite. I run a bath, programming my desired settings into the control panel.

Temperature: 108 degrees.

Scent: lavender and honey.

Water tint: aquamarine.

Bubbles: 10 percent saturation.

I slip out of my clothes and into the giant tub. The water feels wondrous. Hot and satiny. I sink in, allowing myself to be drawn further and further into its inviting embrace.

The last thing I hear before my head goes under is a couple having an argument in the building next door.

And then . . . silence.

Glorious, blissful silence.

I could stay here forever. Or until I run out of air. Which would be exactly seventy-two minutes.

Dr. A tested us once.

Being underwater is one of the few places in this world where I can enjoy absolute quiet. It's as though the water is our only weakness. The one thing they didn't account for. I can see through it fine, but my ears are practically useless.

I don't mind one bit.

I close my eyes and bask in the gorgeous nothingness.

When I surface seventy-one minutes later, I hear Dr. A's voice. At first I think he's inside my suite and I jump, the water sloshing around me as I rub my eyes. But I soon realize the sound is not coming from this room, but from down the hall. Most likely the Owner's Suite.

I glance at the clock on the ReflectoGlass: 4:18 a.m.

Apparently I'm not the only one who can't sleep.

"Yes, everything is progressing according to plan," Dr. A is saying. "The first interview of the tour is today. Mosima Chan has the exclusive."

The empty silence that follows indicates he's speaking to someone through an earplant. His voice is terse and edgy. It's certainly not a pleasant conversation. Then again, what conversation at four in the morning is ever pleasant?

"Yes, I realize how delayed we are and I apologize. We've had a few unexpected setbacks, but I've taken care of them."

I start to rise from the tub and reach for a towel but freeze.

Setbacks.

Is he talking about me?

And since when does Dr. A apologize to *anyone?*

"No. There's no need to send someone. You gave me this responsibility and I'm handling it. The girl just took a little bit longer than expected to adjust to the Memory Reassociation procedure, but she's fully functional now. One hundred percent on our side. She won't betray us again."

Memory Reassociation?

What is that? Why have I never heard that term before? I thought my previous uploads included information about all of Diotech's procedures.

I quickly run "Memory Reassociation" through a search on my Lenses but I get no results.

"If you want to help," Dr. A goes on, "may I suggest you do something about Pastor Peder?" He practically spits his name.

"I realize he's popular," he says after a long pause. "That's the point."

He waits. I wait. We both listen. Then Dr. A lets out a sarcastic laugh.

"Rylan Maxxer? I can assure you *she* is not an issue. That problem has been dealt with."

Dealt with?

What does he mean by that?

Is he referring to the fact that the last time I saw her was in the year 2032 and her transession gene had been repressed? Meaning, she can't cause any more trouble in the present because she's trapped in the past?

But there's something about the way he says it—with a chilling finality—that makes me feel like I don't know the full story.

Dr. A sighs as he listens to the other end of the transmission. When he speaks again, I can tell his teeth are tightly clenched. It cuts his words into jagged, tiny pieces. "Yes, of course I understand what's at stake. You don't have to keep reminding me."

He lets out a snarl and a curse that is immediately followed by the sound of something shattering.

The conversation is over.

20

STYLED

The next morning, in my dressing room, an epic debate is waging between Dr. A and the streamwork stylist about whether or not to put cosmetic enhancers on my face. The stylist is in favor. Dr. A is adamantly against it.

"I could give her a very classy look with eye tints," the stylist says. "I have a color palette that would really bring out the purple in her—"

"The whole point is for the world to see how beautiful she is without exterior enhancements," Dr. A argues, and he inevitably wins. Whether it's because he made a valid point or because, like the rest of us, the stylist quickly realized how terrifying Dr. A can be when he's angry, I'm not sure. Either way, it's decided that only my hair needs help.

I'm somewhat grateful there's a professional here so I don't have to do it myself. Or rely on Crest's well-intentioned efforts. Not that Crest would have had time this morning. She's too busy re-making Dr. A's coffee for the fifth time after he swore the last four cups tasted like sawdust.

The stylist is very good at her job. After about an hour, my hair has been washed, dried, waved, and pinned into an exquisite pile of undulating layers atop my head. It looks like every style Crest has ever attempted. Except this one is not lopsided.

When Dr. A comes back to check on our progress, the stylist gestures at my hair with a flourish, seemingly proud of her work. She looks like one of those models on the competition reality shows, when a contestant is trying to win a new hovercleaner.

"Her hair should be down. Not up," Dr. A barks, and then leaves the room again.

The stylist looks like a wilting flower as her arms slowly droop. I turn away and pretend not to notice when her eyes glisten with tears.

Thirty minutes later, Crest breathlessly rushes into the dressing room, carrying a garment bag. She hangs it on the rack and unzips it, revealing a stunning knee-length, A-line dress. The top half is a gorgeous iridescent blue-green that reminds me of Kaelen's eyes and the bottom half is completely covered in nanostitching that has been programmed to reflect. When I glance at the skirt, I see my own mesmerized face mirrored back a thousand times.

"Wow," I say. It really is something.

"You like it?"

I nod. "I do."

Crest's eyes light up at my words, probably because for the first time, they aren't poorly veiled lies.

"Dr. A wanted something that represented the Objective," she explains. "The color is to match Kaelen's eyes, obviously, but the bottom is supposed to symbolize the reflection of what this world can be with the help of Diotech. Everyone who looks at you becomes a part of you. Becomes like you."

My heart swells at her touching description and how much thought she's put into something I thought was just a silly dress.

Crest really does care about the Objective. She takes her part seriously.

I could learn a few things from her.

Once I'm dressed, I slink into the hallway that leads to the soundstage. Kaelen is waiting for me. He's dressed in an immaculate gray suit with purple accents in the hems and collar. A clear reference to my eye color.

Upon seeing me, Kaelen goes deathly still, his eyes slightly unfocused and floating. For a moment, I'm convinced he's staring at something in his Lenses until he blinks hard and smiles at me.

"You are radiant," he says, his voice throaty and thick.

"No. That's the dress."

"No. That's you."

I stand awkwardly, unsure of what to say.

"Thank you." Crest pops her head between us and beams.

I laugh. "It was all Crest. I just stood there while she secured me into it."

"Don't worry," Crest says, winking at Kaelen. "It's not as hard to get off as it is to get on."

I feel my face color. Thankfully, I'm saved from further embarrassment when Dane appears at the end of the hallway. "Are we ready?" he sings in his falsetto voice.

Kaelen reaches out to take my hand. I slide my fingers into his tight, reassuring grasp. For a moment, the image of those same hands pounding against that man's face flickers through my memory but I swiftly push it away. I can't think about that. I can't let myself think about anything else except my obligation right here. Right now.

Crest fiddles with my hair, folding it neatly around one shoulder. Then she gives me a nod.

It's time for us to be unveiled to the world.

21
ENTRANCE

"Well, well, let me have a look at you. Wow, you really are divine. The pair of you. Even more so than they promised. And did they make promises? Did they *ever*! On and on they went about your beauty, your flawless faces. Are you really not wearing any enhancers? Amazing. Skin like polished marble. I could almost convince myself I was looking at a modified projection. This is going to be an interview that the viewers will not soon forget."

The woman in front of me is speaking so rapidly, I find myself struggling to keep up. Her sharp, clipped accent sounds exactly as it does on the Feed.

"Oh, dear me. Where are my manners? I'm Mosima Chan. It's a pleasure to meet you."

She extends her hand and shakes both of ours in turn.

I've always liked watching Mosima on the Feed, but in person, she's positively dazzling. Every facet of her. Down to the way her toes lightly tap the floor when she speaks, as though she's keeping time with the rhythm of her own words.

"It's very nice to meet you, Ms. Chan," Kaelen says. "Sera and I are big fans of your show."

I'm still too overwhelmed to say anything original or creative, so I echo Kaelen's well-articulated sentiments. "Yes. Very big fans."

She places her hand to her heart. "Well, that just melts me to hear you say that. Just melts me to a puddle. Thank you. And please, call me Mosi. That's what my friends call me." She winks. I think it's meant to be directed at both of us, but I notice how her eyes linger a beat longer on Kaelen.

"So," she goes on, clapping her hands together once. "We don't have much time to chat. Gotta save all the good stuff for the viewers, right? So let's get you miked and synced up. Seres, my segment producer, will help you with that. I'm sure they've told you but I'll be interviewing Dr. Alixter, your humble creator, first. Ha! That's amusing to say. *Creator!* And then I'll be inviting both of you on to offer some commentary about your life, your goals, et cetera, et cetera. Sound good?"

She touches a hand to her ear and I assume someone is talking to her through an earplant. "Up, up. Gotta run." She gives each of us a quick squeeze on the arm and then she's gone, zipping toward the stage where she takes a seat in the large red chair I recognize from all of her Feed interviews.

A tall willowy man appears a moment later. His head is shaved and covered in dizzying nanotats. From the looks of it, he's a big fan of animated shows. The kind I thought were produced mainly for children.

"I'm Seres," the man says with a thick accent that I immediately identify as Croatian. "I'm the segment producer."

"*Drago mi je,*" I say with a smile.

He blinks and freezes for a moment. "You speak Croatian?"

"*Govorimo svaki jezik,*" answers Kaelen without missing a beat, informing Seres that we, in fact, speak every language.

Seres is impressed. Even so, he continues to speak to us in English.

"Now, remember. Don't look into the cams, even when they're right in front of you, yes? Mosi will speak to the viewers. You will speak to Mosi. If you've been given any prewritten scripts to memorize, throw them out now. Viewers can tell when you're reciting a line. Natural and organic is better, yes?"

He secures a tiny orange dot to the front of my dress. I watch, intrigued, as the bright color gradually fades and blends into the fabric beneath it.

Nanoflage technology.

"Your mic," Seres explains as he attaches a similar orange dot to Kaelen's shirt. "So the viewers can hear you. And these"—he hands us each a tiny silver disc and mimes positioning it just outside the ear—"so you can hear Mosi and the rest of the production team."

I watch Kaelen secure his into place and I follow suit. Like the mics, the speaker disc adapts to match the color of our skin.

"Larn, in the booth, should be syncing up your Lenses," he goes on. "Tell me when you can see the test capture, yes?"

A second later, a fat brown-and-black-striped furry creature licking its paws pops into the corner of my vision. "I—" I start to say, unsure what I'm looking at.

"It's Mosi's cat," Seres says with a roll of his eyes. "Trust me, not my choice."

"No, if it were your choice, we'd all be watching men take their pants off while we wait for syncs," Mosima calls from her chair, evidently having heard our entire exchange. Seres turns around and sticks his tongue out. She grins broadly in return.

"Three minutes," Seres trills. "Okay, Larn says you're all synced up to our network. If we need to send you any information or cues, they'll come through your Lenses or your speakers, okay?"

"Where do we stand before we walk on?" Kaelen asks.

Seres glances at Mosima. "You didn't tell them about the entrance?"

She lets out a giddy giggle and teeters over to us. "I almost forgot. I asked Dane not to spoil the surprise. I wanted to tell you myself as it was my idea."

I get an inkling I'm not going to like what's coming next.

"We thought it would be fun—and appropriate—for you to have a big entrance. You know, flash and pomp! To really make an impression on the viewers."

Kaelen and I exchange nervous glances.

"And we wanted to come up with something that represents your unique origins."

Definitely not going to like this.

With a capricious flash of sparkly white teeth, she points toward the ceiling. Kaelen and I look up in unison at two giant transparent spheres floating above the main stage.

"How memorable will it be when the two of you arrive into the world—*descending* from the heavens—in *those*?"

Memorable? Maybe.

Ridiculous? Absolutely.

I look to Kaelen, who is nodding politely, but I can tell he's just as put off by the idea as I am.

"When Dane sent me the captures of that fascinating synthetic womb you were grown in, I was struck with an idea." Mosima is still jabbering away even though the clock projected on the window of the control booth above us says we are live in ninety-one seconds. She makes a large sweeping gesture with her hand. "This is your Unveiling. Your birth into the human race. When you emerge from the glass eggs, it will be like you're emerging from the womb!"

"Well—" Kaelen begins, but if he's about to voice his opposition, he's not given the chance.

Mosima lets out a squeak. "Eek! Eighty seconds! Seres will help

119

you into the eggs." She blows kisses to both of us as she scurries back to the stage. "See you soon, my treasures!"

I look to the control booth where Dane, Crest, and Director Raze are watching. Dane catches my eye and gives me an encouraging smile. Did he really approve this?

"Right this way," Seres is saying, and before long, Kaelen and I are following him up a spiral staircase to a platform above the stage. Below us, Mosima is getting comfortable in her red chair while Dr. A sits nearby, looking completely relaxed and at home. As though this is something he does every day.

"After Mosi is finished interviewing Dr. Alixter, we will trigger the eggs to descend. You'll step out—looking graceful, of course— and take a seat on the couch to her right, yes?"

We nod.

The doors of the "eggs" are already open and Seres motions for us to climb in. I peer at Kaelen, who gives me a surrendering shrug in response.

"*¿Qué vas a hacer?*" he says in Spanish.

"*Nada.*" I surrender with a sigh.

I step through the opening and position my feet on the narrow plank that's been built across the bottom. Seres swipes a nearby panel and the eggs seal shut, locking us inside. I gently run my fingertips across the smooth, transparent surface where the door once was. Not even a ridge or seam. It must be synthoglass. Airtight, soundproof, and nearly impenetrable.

Which means we're stuck in here until someone decides to let us out.

A small metal canister is secured to the roof of the ball. I assume it's producing oxygen because the air in here smells fresh.

The clock on the control booth window counts down to twenty seconds.

Twenty seconds?

Is that it?

My stomach flips and I'm suddenly acutely aware of how momentous this really is. Up until now, being kept a secret was such a huge part of my identity. For so long, I was the girl who could never be seen. Who the world couldn't know about. But in less than twenty seconds, that will all be over.

Ever since I returned to the compound and Dr. A told me about the Objective, I knew this day would eventually come. But then, it was just an idea. A futuristic fantasy. Now the future is upon us.

There's no turning back after this, is there? You can't possibly erase a memory from twelve billion minds.

"He's figured out how to work the distributor." Mosima's effervescent voice drifts into my ear. I look down to see a stylist touching up her hair. She must be speaking to him. "So he just sits around and drinks milk all day. I can't figure out how to stop him. That's why he's so fat." It takes me a moment to realize she's still talking about her cat. She closes her eyes so the stylist can paint more powder on her lids.

"Are you ready for this?"

Now I have no idea who she's addressing. It could be Kaelen and me. It could be the technicians in the booth. It could be Dr. A sitting next to her. Maybe it's all of us.

If it were up to me, I would say no. I'm not ready. I'll never be ready for this. I wasn't built for feedcasts and public appearances and changing the world with my mere existence.

But it's never been up to me. And it's too late anyway.

The stage goes dark, and I hear Seres call out, "We're live in 10, 9, 8, 7, 6 . . ."

Hoverlamps and tiny cams start to move beneath me, zigzagging gracefully in the air in a well-rehearsed dance, never missing a step, never colliding. One bulb in particular lowers and twists, pausing just short of Mosima's head.

Seres's menacing countdown continues to echo in my skull. "5, 4, 3 . . ."

Three seconds until my anonymity is gone forever.

Three seconds until Kaelen and I become the most unforgettable faces in the world.

In three seconds nothing will be the same.

There's a hushed, anticipatory silence. I never hear Seres say 2 or 1. Maybe it's implied. Maybe nobody really misses them.

But I feel cheated out of those last two seconds.

22

FALSIFY

Music plays.

It's the familiar song that commences every segment on AFC. An electronic five-note chime with a soft syncopated drum line underneath. A hoverlamp illuminates Mosima's polished face. Through my Lenses, I can see her the way the viewers at home do. The way I'm used to seeing her when I watch the Feed on the compound. I suppose I should be accustomed to the illusion the Lenses project, making it look like she's directly in front of me, talking only to me. But now that I can see the reality offset below, it's unnerving.

Her expression is serious, almost grave as she starts the show. "Welcome to *The Morning Beat* on AFC Streamwork, your number one source for breaking news and real-time world updates. I'm Mosima Chan."

There's a pause. The cams zip around her, repositioning themselves.

"Three weeks ago, AFC reported on some of the most shocking and groundbreaking scientific news ever to be revealed in human history. Diotech Corporation, the largest scientific research and development company in the world, released an official statement claiming that they had synthetically engineered two enhanced human beings in a laboratory. Referring to them as 'ExGens' or 'Next Generation Humans,' Diotech asserts that these two genetically perfected specimens represent the next stage of superhuman evolution, pioneered entirely by science."

My eyes dart to the control booth. Crest catches my eye and gives me a smile.

"Today in the studio," Mosima continues, "I have the distinct pleasure not only of welcoming the president of Diotech Corporation and the man behind this historical scientific breakthrough, but later on in the segment, we will be revealing the ExGens themselves for the first time *ever*, and speaking directly to them. So viewers at home, get your questions ready! I had the privilege of meeting them briefly right before we went live and I can tell you, they are truly remarkable. But first, help me welcome the founder and president of Diotech Corporation, Dr. Jans Alixter."

A hoverlamp glides in front of Dr. A, illuminating his face. The bulb is so bright, I expect him to cower or, at the very least, squint, but he is the embodiment of poise. He smiles at the floating cam that arcs in front of him, and even gives a little wave.

In that moment, I almost don't recognize him.

He's not the short-tempered, grudge-bearing Dr. A who I encounter on a daily basis. This man appears approachable, even charming as he thanks Mosima for inviting him to the interview.

"I'm very excited to talk to you today," Mosima gushes. "And I'm eager to show the viewers exactly what you've created. But first, let's talk a little bit about the history of this project." She blinks twice, accessing something on her Lenses. "My notes tell me that you've dubbed it the Genesis Project. That's rather biblical for a scientific research company."

I cringe waiting for Dr. A's reaction. Mentions of religion always set him off. Everything that man does is an intentional slap in the face of the Church. He even named the company Diotech because it means *God's science*, knowing it would upset all the religious leaders who have ever voiced their opposition to his work.

But his unflappable demeanor never slips, even for a second. In fact, he *laughs*. It sounds completely genuine. I wonder if Dane has been training him as well or if he's simply a natural at this.

"You're right, Ms. Chan. It is fairly biblical. With good reason. When we set out to engineer the first human being ever to be created entirely by science, we wanted to choose a title that would serve to illustrate how connected we still feel to the higher power. We aren't trying to *replace* God with the projects we initiate at Diotech. We're trying to work in conjunction with God. God created Adam and Eve in much the same way that we created Sera and Kaelen."

I can't believe what I'm hearing.

How many times have I listened to Dr. A denounce the Church, claiming that God is a fantasy? A made-up entity to explain things that were once unexplainable? He even told me that science is the "new God." Except smarter and without the jealous nature.

Which means . . .

He's lying.

It's suddenly clear to me. He's lying right to Mosima's face. And to all of the viewers watching.

Does that mean I'm supposed to lie, too?

Dane told us to tell the truth. To speak from our hearts. To show the viewers how real we could be.

Dr. A seems to be doing exactly the opposite.

"Sera and Kaelen," Mosima echoes. "Those are unusual names. Do they have any specific meaning?"

"Of course," Dr. A says. "We don't do anything at Diotech that doesn't have *significant* meaning. It's our mission statement to make the world a better place. And to do that, you have to start with well-intentioned goals. Sera is an alternate spelling of the biblical name Sarah. We wanted to give it a modern twist. Sera was created first. She was our scientific miracle. Life created right before our eyes. It was quite a thing to see."

Another lie.

Sera wasn't even originally a name. It was the sequence of genetic code that led to a successful life-form. Sequence: E/ Recombination: A.

S:E/R:A.

I'm reminded of this every time I walk by that DigiPlaque in the hallway outside my bedroom.

"Kaelen was engineered a year and a half later," Dr. A continues, "using a similar genetic blueprint as Sera but with some important tweaks made to give him his own personality and unique spirit. I named him after my mother. Her name was Gaelen. She died in childbirth."

I never knew the origin of Kaelen's name. I'm not even sure Kaelen did.

And did Dr. A's mother really die giving birth to him?

After the last two lies, how can I be certain anything he's saying is true?

I turn to study Kaelen. The lamps from the stage glow under his handsome face. His mouth is frozen in a slack smile and his aquamarine eyes are sparkling as they stare downward in admiration.

There's simply no other way to describe his expression.

I've seen it on Kaelen's face in the past, nearly every time he looks at Dr. A. But I've never seen it quite so intense before. As though the world could explode outside this studio and Kaelen wouldn't even blink.

"I'm sorry to hear that," Mosima condoles. "It seems natural childbirth is so risky these days. I suppose it's why many parents opt for alternate methods of bringing life into the world. Methods that I know you at Diotech have been pioneering for years."

Dr. A nods, wiping hastily at his eyes.

Is he crying?

"It's been important to me that no child should have to unnecessarily lose his mother the way I did. The artificial wombs that we released into the marketplace have been extremely popular. Far more so than surrogates were in their heyday. Parents can now travel, work, stay out late, eat and drink whatever they want, while the fetus is safely at home, receiving all the necessary nutrients and care it needs to grow into a healthy baby."

Mosima reaches out to touch Dr. A's hand. "I can see this topic is a sensitive one for you."

He nods.

"My reports tell me that Sera and Kaelen were *grown*, for lack of a better word, in wombs not too dissimilar to those currently on the market."

"That's correct," says Dr. A. "Although, because Sera was gestated to full maturity at age sixteen, and Kaelen at age seventeen, the technology of their gestation chamber is significantly more advanced. The artificial wombs available to consumers gestate a newborn baby in the same forty weeks it would take a mother to carry the infant to full term. On the other hand, the more advanced womb used in the Genesis Project is able to birth a fully grown teenage or adult human in only thirty-seven days."

Mosima lets out a low whistle. "Thirty-seven days. That is mighty impressive. Our advance team took some spectacular captures of that womb, which we're going to play for you now. Take a look."

For a moment, I'm actually kind of excited. Are they really going to show Dr. Rio's lab? The one that's been locked up for more than a year? But as the image in my Lenses shifts, I realize they're actually showing the womb where *Kaelen* was grown. Not me.

127

It's housed in a newer, more modern lab in Building 1 that was dedicated to the Genesis Project after Dr. Rio betrayed the Objective.

The cams zoom in on the large spherical capsule positioned atop a steel pedestal in the center of the room. They swirl gracefully around the breathtaking structure to give the audience a 360-degree view of the various tubes and mechanisms that make it work.

I have vague memories of the womb I was created in—mostly from the first few weeks of my life, when they still weren't certain I would survive, and I needed to be monitored twenty-four hours a day in Rio's lab. I can say with certainty that the contraption I'm watching on my Lenses now is definitely an upgraded version from mine, which nearly makes me laugh. Kaelen even got a nicer *womb* than me.

Of course, the chamber itself is empty now. At the time he was grown inside, it was filled with an orange gelatinous substance that served as his embryonic fluid.

I admit, it does remind me of the giant globe I'm currently standing in.

"Truly amazing," Mosima chimes in, bringing the viewers back to the studio. "Now, that womb we just looked at, is it used only for ExGens or could it, perhaps, be used to grow a normal teenage or adult human being?"

"Although we've only used this particular advanced womb to bring our beautiful ExGens into the world," Dr. A replies, "theoretically it could gestate any fully grown human being in thirty-seven days. All you'd need is a piece of DNA and our systems would do the rest."

"Fascinating," says Mosima. "So you previously mentioned that Kaelen and Sera were created from similar genetic blueprints. Does that make them akin to"—she circles her hand as she thinks—"brother and sister?"

Dr. A lets out a hearty chuckle. "Hardly! Their DNA is as unrelated as yours and mine. They are in no way familial. All humans, in fact, share 99.9 percent of the same DNA. What Sera and Kaelen have in common is their perfected genetic sequence and robust enhancements. In essence, they are made from the same mold, but contain very different materials. At their core, however, they are quite connected. Which is probably why they fell in love so quickly."

Mosima reacts as though this is the first time she's heard this piece of the story. Even though I know it's not. "In love, you say?"

Dr. A's expression turns whimsical. I didn't know he was even capable of whimsy. "Yes. Very much so. In fact, we created Kaelen and Sera to be partners. In life and in love. They are what I like to refer to as 'Print Mates.' "

"Like soul mates?"

"Exactly. A scientific soul mate, if you will. Literally made for each other."

Mosima puts a hand to her heart. "That's lovely. I can tell you are a romantic at heart, Dr. Alixter."

He lets out a sigh. "Guilty."

"So." Mosima turns serious again. "Is it safe to say that you are the brains behind this project?"

Dr. A pauses to reflect.

I feel myself leaning forward in anticipation of his answer. Will he mention Rio? The man he destroyed? Who is now absentmindedly snipping hedges on the compound, completely unaware of his own lost brilliance?

Will he give Rio any of the recognition he deserves?

"It's impossible for me to take all the credit," Dr. A says, rubbing his chin. "Especially when so many talented scientists at Diotech headquarters contributed to the success of this project. But if we're speaking exclusively about who did the actual scientific 'grunt work,' so to speak, of bringing these beautiful souls into the world, then yes, I suppose that would be me."

Something hot starts to bubble and burst in my chest.

Pop, pop, pop, pop, pop.

I can feel Kaelen eyeing me from the adjacent sphere but I don't turn. This time, it's me who stares straight ahead. It's not fascination that holds my gaze. It's not admiration. It's not worship.

It's an emotion I only recognize once it's fully coursing through me, boiling my blood and souring my tongue.

Disgust.

Suddenly I feel as though I can't breathe. The curved walls of this egg are closing in on me. I glide my hands against the surface, searching for a lever, a button, a latch. Anything!

I can't do this.

I *can't* do this.

I push against the glass, checking the integrity of the construction. But I already know it's synthoglass and that means I'll never be able to break through.

And even if you could, a voice in my head demands, *where would you go?*

They'd find you.

I brush a fingertip across the genetic implant—the tracking device—on the inside of my left wrist. The voice is right. The satellites would locate me in seconds.

But I'm not trying to run away. I'm not trying to escape again.

I'm trying to get *home.* Back to the compound where I belong. Back within its safe walls and the anonymity of its isolation.

Are you okay?

A ping flashes across my right Lens. It's from Kaelen.

I glance over at his sphere to see he's still staring at me, concern etched into his face. He must be able to sense my panic. I want to reach out to him, to fall into him, let him wrap me up in those strong arms. He would make everything better. If he were next to me now. If I could touch him.

I'm about to send a response when the interview beneath us suddenly comes back into focus.

Mosima is speaking. "Well, you must have seen the droves and droves of protesters outside of the studio this morning when you flew in?"

Dr. A sighs. "I did, indeed."

"I've never seen such a strong opposition in all my life. Is it safe to say you have a few enemies out there?"

Dr. A smiles wryly. "Yes. It saddens me greatly. But what important figure in history who sought to do things differently wasn't met with resistance? It took Christopher Columbus seven years to find a country willing to financially back his new route to India. Everyone thought he was crazy. Martin Luther King Jr. was killed trying to change the way we think. Would I love for everyone to be on my side? Certainly. Will I stop moving forward just because they aren't? Of course not."

"Well put, Doctor," Mosima approves. "I think the question on everyone's mind, however, is . . . *why*? Why create these two superhuman ExGens? Are you saying that we normal humans aren't enough?"

"Not at all," Dr. A is quick to reply. "I'm simply of the opinion that if we *can* become better, why don't we?"

"Care to elaborate?"

Dr. A crosses his legs and leans back in his chair. He's ready for this question. It's the one he's been preparing for from the very beginning.

"Look around you, Ms. Chan," he says in a relaxed but formal tone. "The world is at war. *We*, as human beings, are at war. With disease, with climate changes, with natural disasters. Last year the POK virus wiped out two million people across the globe. Two months ago, Hurricane 981 wreaked havoc on the east coast. Mother Nature is trying to destroy us. We have to evolve. And fast. We don't have time for natural evolution to take its course and make us stronger and more resilient. We won't last that long! The next step in human evolution is through *science*. We have to fight back. And the only way to do that is to make *ourselves* stronger and more resilient. To become more like Sera and Kaelen, who you will soon meet and marvel at for yourselves. I created them to show humanity what our true potential is. To show us that we don't have to lose these battles. We can adapt. We *can* fight back. And more important, we can *win*."

Dr. A has managed to affect every single person in this studio and, I'd venture to guess, in the world as well. Mosima sits back in her chair, staring openmouthed at him. Activity in the control booth has died down. The technicians appear to have been lulled into a semitrance. Even Crest and Dane—who have heard this before, who work to achieve this every day—are visibly moved by Dr. A's conviction.

And me.

I feel every muscle in my body unclenching. The bitterness in my mouth dissolving. The heat in my blood gradually simmering and cooling.

Dr. A's passionate words have reminded me of why I'm here. Why we're *all* here.

The Objective.

I don't think he's ever described it so eloquently before. So persuasively.

This is what it all comes down to. Saving the human race from extinction. If it takes a few small lies to get us there, who am I to complain?

Who am I to judge Dr. A for a little necessary manipulation? If it saves us in the end, it will be worth it.

This glass ball isn't a prison. It's a display case.

And we are the key to everything.

The Objective is the only answer.

Anyone who opposes it, who stands in its way—Dr. Rio, Lyzender, Pastor Peder, all those protesters outside—should not be trusted.

So when I hear Mosima say, "Well, after that inspiring speech, I think it's time to bring out our special guests," I am no longer outraged.

I am determined to be the powerful face of the next generation that Dr. A created me to be.

When I feel the plank beneath my feet begin to rumble as the sphere prepares to lower—to deliver me to the world—I am no longer hesitant.

I am ready.

I am fearless.

23

REBIRTH

The studio goes dark again as we start our descent from the sky. The fanfare begins the moment we clear the rafters. Multicolored lights dance, artificial smoke wafts into the air, music blares. It is a spectacle like I've never seen on Mosima's show before.

And Kaelen and I are smack in the middle of it.

I hold still, trying to maintain my composure. Out of the corner of my eye, I watch Kaelen for cues. He looks stoic in his open-legged stance, arms to the sides. I emulate his posture, reminding myself that this is second nature. Don't think, just react instinctively. Everything I've ever needed to survive the next thirty minutes has already been uploaded into my brain, wired into my skin, programmed into my blood.

When the spheres are only a few inches from the ground, the doors unseal and we step onto the stage. Kaelen's hand finds mine almost instantly. Mosima rises to make grand sweeping gestures toward us. "Look at them!" she's shouting over the thrumming beats. "Just look at them!"

As instructed, we take our seats on a love seat as the music dies down and the lights return to a simple, daylight white.

"Closer together," Seres's voice booms in my ear, causing me to jump.

Kaelen must have gotten the same order because we simultaneously move toward each other until I'm practically in his lap. He drapes one arm around my shoulder and I place my hand on his leg.

I check my Lenses to see what we look like to the audience but apparently they've deactivated that view. Maybe it's too unsettling to see your own capture playing back while you're sitting here.

But whatever we're doing must be working because Mosima looks exuberant.

"Aren't they divine, everyone?" She's speaking into one of the countless DigiCams that are buzzing around our heads like a swarm of bees. I have to fight not to swat them away.

She turns to Dr. A, who is seated to her left. "You weren't exaggerating, Dr. Alixter. These two are something special."

Dr. A beams. "Aren't they?"

"Unbelievable. Truly unbelievable." She focuses back on us. "So tell me. Is this terribly overwhelming for you two? I'm told that you'd never left the Diotech headquarters before yesterday."

Dane's words race through my mind. A warning that was repeated over and over in the days leading up to this moment.

Whatever you do, don't mention your failed escape.

"It's certainly different," Kaelen says.

"What's been the craziest part of your journey into the outside world so far?"

"The hyperloop," I say, my voice cool with just a tinge of playfulness. "That was pretty warped."

I steal a glance at the control booth and catch sight of Dane nodding. I knew he'd appreciate my use of modern slang. And apparently Mosima does as well. She seems positively tickled by my response as she says, "I agree. I've never liked traveling that way. I just gobble down a Relaxer and blitz out. But you probably don't even get motion sick, do you?"

"Not that I'm aware of," Kaelen says.

"We don't get sick," I add confidently.

My tone, my eyes, my posture. It's exactly as we rehearsed countless times with Dane and I'm actually surprised by how easy the poise comes to me now. Even if it feels like I'm wearing clothing that's three sizes too small.

"That's right," Mosima chimes. "That's what my notes tell me. Fascinating. Simply fascinating. So you've never experienced even so much as a common cold?"

"No," replies Kaelen.

"Well, then that means you've never experienced the bliss of a nighttime cold Releaser!" She cackles at her own joke, as does Dr. A.

"Sera and Kaelen have been created with immunity to all known diseases," Dr. A puts in. "A luxury we hope to be able to offer the general public very shortly."

"Won't that be nice? And I'm told a simple cut on your finger heals in less than ten minutes, is that correct?"

"That's correct," Kaelen says.

Mosima looks into the cam hovering in front of her. "Ten minutes. Can you imagine? Not very fun for you cutters out there, is it?" She seems to find great humor in this and her high-pitched snort of a laugh grates on my eardrums.

"So," she goes on, her face serious again, "immunity to disease, obviously extremely good looks—which we can see. I'm also told that you have superhuman strength and speed."

"That's right," Dr. A answers for us. "Do you want to play the capture we took during their training session last week?"

Surprised, I blink and turn to Kaelen. I didn't know they had captured our training session last week. Did he?

Mosima nods like it's the best idea she's heard all year. "Yes. Let's do that. Larn, can you patch that in?"

My Lenses flicker and a view of our most recent challenge course comes into focus. I watch as Kaelen and I, dressed in red training suits, take our positions at the starting line and he counts us off in Russian.

"*Odin, dva, tri.*"

It's always Russian in the training dome. I've never asked him why, but I think the feel of it on his tongue puts him in a running mood for some reason.

I watch us both sprint into the course, tackling each element with speed and precision. The footage contains a digital overlay of the virtual obstacles so the audience can see them the way Kaelen and I saw them through our Lenses during the challenge.

In a span of three minutes, we outrun a high-speed train, leap five-hundred-foot chasms between the roofs of towering skyscrapers, swerve around MagCars on the expressway, and then at the end of the course, we have to lift a small hovercopter from the ground to rescue a dying child pinned underneath. I watch myself wince against the reverse pull of the electromagnets that were used to simulate the weight of the vehicle. My knees wobble and shake as I lift the virtual object from the ground, crouch under it, and, with the strength of my legs and back, hold it up so the child can be rescued.

I remember this specific course vividly. After all, it was only last week. But it's strange to be watching it from the outside. I don't think I've ever actually seen myself in action before. I really am *fast*.

Of course, not as fast as Kaelen. He beats me to the finish line by twenty-two seconds. His superior DNA has always given him an advantage in the training dome.

"Impressive," Mosima commends, and then with a laugh she adds, "I wish I looked that good in a bodysuit."

There's a pause that I assume is meant to allow her joke to resonate with the viewers. Then she turns to us. "And was that Russian I heard you speaking in that capture? What other languages do you speak?"

"All of them," Kaelen responds.

"All of them?"

"We speak every language."

Mosima peers back at the floating cam in front of her. Her eyes open so wide I'm afraid they might pop out of their sockets. "Stupendous!" she trills. "What a talent to have! And at such a young age! You're both only eighteen, is that right?"

We nod.

"Kaelen, you were created at the age of seventeen, but Sera, you were sixteen when you were born, so you've been around a bit longer."

"Yes, I'm definitely older and wiser," I say with a smirk.

Kaelen tickles my waist, which causes Mosima to giggle even harder than me.

"Isn't he breathtaking, ladies?"

Kaelen grins, revealing two rows of perfect teeth.

"Simply ah-dorable." She regains her composure. "So, how does it feel to have all those skills?"

"I can't really say," I reply. "We don't know any different."

"Touché!" Mosima replies with another chuckle. I can tell by her reactions that Kaelen and I are doing precisely what we're supposed to do. Precisely what we've been created to do. We're charming her. We're charming everyone.

But then why do I feel so horribly out of place up here?

If this is what I was made for, shouldn't I be enjoying it? The way Kaelen genuinely seems to be?

"Dr. Alixter," Mosima coos, "wherever do they get their dazzling personalities? Are those engineered in a lab as well?"

Dr. A gives her a coy smile. "Now, now, Mosima, we can't reveal *all* our secrets, can we?"

"Does your predicament bother you in the slightest?" she asks us. "Having been born on a research compound with no chance of ever having a normal life?"

I hear the question but my mind is still trapped in the previous one.

Where *do* we get our personalities?

Kaelen and I are so different. He's ambitious and charismatic and optimistic. And, as it turns out, might possibly have a disturbing violent streak. While I'm . . . I don't even know what I am anymore. I've been too many different people to keep track. The dutiful prisoner. The escaped convict. The amnesiac supermodel. The truth-seeking skeptic. The loyal lover. The heroic savior.

And now, the defective traitor trying to redeem herself.

Deep within all of those personas, is there something that might tell me who I really am?

Is there a common denominator I can cling to?

"No," Kaelen answers Mosima's question, drawing me back to the interview. "We don't mind what we are. We are fortunate to have been given such gifts. Our lives are enriching and fulfilling. We have everything we could ever want."

"Including love," Mosima adds with a wink to the viewers. "Dr. A was just telling me before you came on that you two were genetically engineered to be perfect matches for each other."

"That's right," Kaelen answers, tightening his arm around my shoulder. "I'm head-over-heels in love with her."

Mosima practically swoons right out of her chair.

"And you feel the same way?" she asks me. "At least I hope you do. Otherwise, we're in for a very awkward interview."

I laugh, knowing it's the appropriate thing to do. "Yes. He is the perfect person for me."

Mosima sighs into the cam. "Doesn't that just melt you? Let's take some questions from the viewers. Larn, do you have a few good ones lined up for us?" Mosima pauses to watch something on her Lenses. "User Jennz122 from Portland, Maine, has posted a question on the comment bar. She asks, 'If it doesn't work out between you two, Kaelen, would you ever consider going on a reality show to find a wife?' "

Kaelen and Dr. A laugh in unison. I don't find anything particularly humorous about the question. "Well," Kaelen says jovially, "fortunately I won't have to worry about that. Sera and I are bonded for life."

"Yes, they are! Thanks for your question, Jennz122. Who's next?" Another pause. "Oh, this is a good one. We have a question from user SZ1609."

The breath traps in my lungs and for a second the world loses color. Loses shape.

It's a coincidence. It has to be.

There are only so many combinations of numbers and letters out there.

I peer at Dr. A and Kaelen to gauge their reaction. Neither one of them seems to have caught the significance.

Not that I would expect them to.

$S + Z = 1609$ was our secret code. Lyzender's and mine. Even if Dr. Alixter saw it on a memory scan, I doubt he would recognize it here. It's too out of context.

But not for me. Despite my efforts, I can never seem to shove the dark-haired boy out of context. He's always right there, lingering behind my subconscious, like shoes peeking out from under a curtain.

"This question is for Sera," Mosima goes on. "Our viewer wants to know, 'If you've never left Diotech headquarters, how can you know for certain that Kaelen is the perfect person for you? What if there's someone else out there who could possibly be a better match?'"

My blood turns to ice.

It's him. It has to be him.

But *how*? How is that possible? He's supposed to be trapped in the past. He's not supposed to be *here*.

I know Seres told me not to look directly into the cams, but I can't help myself. My head slowly turns—as though acting entirely on its own—and I stare straight into the object hovering in front of my face.

A shiver passes through me. It's almost as though I can *feel* him staring back. As though his liquid-chocolate eyes are reflected in the lens of this tiny cam.

"The viewer asks a very good question," Mosima goes on, oblivious to my reaction. "How can you possibly be sure you are right for each other when your exposure to the rest of the world has been so limited?"

There's no way I can answer. I can't even move my lips, let alone form coherent sounds.

Thankfully, Dr. A swoops in to rescue me, stealing the audience away with his unrivaled composure and articulate speech. "Let me ask you this, Ms. Chan," he begins. "How many times have you been in love?"

She looks taken aback and her face colors slightly. "Well, that's a rather personal question, Dr. Alixter."

He tilts his head, leaning forward in his chair. "Fine. I'll put it another way. How many times has the average person been in love?"

She considers. "Two, maybe three times."

"And how many times has the average person had their heart broken?"

"Countless, unfortunately. Or maybe that's just me." She turns toward her viewers and cackles.

"What if you could love without the risk of ever getting hurt?" Dr. A goes on. "What if you could love with a one hundred percent certainty of being loved in return? With no jealousy. No insecurity. No doubt. Sera and Kaelen's love was perfected by science. They will never hurt each other. They are incapable of doing it. Just as you are incapable of flying." He leans back in his seat. "I don't know about all of you at home, but I'd take that over meeting someone randomly on the SkyServer any day."

Mosima wobbles her head from side to side. "You do make an excellent point, Dr. Alixter. I can tell from the influx of comments we're getting right now, it seems there are many viewers who agree with you. And some who don't. But let's move on, shall we?" She focuses back on us. "So, you lucky lovebirds. You are physically flawless, built like superheroes, and have brains that rival today's computers . . . and you've found your soul mate by the age of eighteen!"

"Print Mate," Dr. A corrects her.

"Of course. Print Mate. Gotta get my Diotech lingo down." She guffaws. "You are clearly the envy of everyone on this planet right now. Can we get a little kiss from you two?"

The request startles me but I don't have time to process it. Kaelen is already turning his mouth to meet mine. His eyes are already closing. Suddenly all I can think about is Lyzender. Could he really be out there? Watching us on the Feed right now?

"What are you waiting for?" Seres barks in my ear. "Kiss him already!"

He's right.

What am I waiting for?

Even if Lyzender is out there—which I'm still convinced is impossible—he shouldn't matter to me. He doesn't matter to me.

All that matters is here in front of me. Leaning in to kiss me right now.

I take a deep breath and close my eyes. I can feel his lips before

142

they touch me. Like they have their own energy. Their own atmosphere. When our mouths meet, I'm suddenly transported to another world. Where Kaelen and I are alone and there aren't billions of people watching this intimate moment between us.

Where SZ1609 is just an unfortunate coincidence of letters and numbers.

Everything in our past is erased. Our flaws are unremembered.

But the sound of Mosima's "awww" breaks through my mental barrier and I feel Kaelen smiling against me. His hand grazes the side of my face before he pulls away.

"Our comment bar is exploding right now!" Mosima tells us. "That was so special. I'm pretty sure you two just warmed every heart in America. Mine included. Can we play that back, Larn?"

My Lenses flash and I can now see what the world has just seen. Kaelen and I coming together the way we've been engineered to do.

They've slowed the capture way down. It takes forever for his lips to reach me. But when they do, I feel the kiss all over again. I feel it in my toes. In my stomach. In my carefully styled strands of hair.

I've never actually seen myself kissing Kaelen before. Now it's easy to see the effect it has on me. The way my eyes willingly sink closed, as though they don't care whether or not they ever open again. The way my mouth reaches for his, forever hungry and forever satiated at the same time.

All of this plays out in front of me like a silent song. A perfect symphony.

"It's easy to see from this playback that Dr. A is right," Mosima observes. "You two are positively meant for each other."

"Yes," I say softly, knowing the whole world is listening. "Yes, we are."

24
INVITATION

The pop of the champagne echoes through the entire Hospitality Suite as Dane fights to catch the overflowing liquid in tall, narrow glasses.

Champagne flutes. I access the correct terminology.

He offers a half-full glass to me and I take a tentative sip. The fizzy drink tickles my tongue and throat as it goes down. But overall, I enjoy the taste. Even Kaelen takes a few sips. I never see him drink alcohol.

Dane raises his glass in our direction. "You two were spectacular today. The audience *loved* you. AFC reported it was one of their most-watched segments of all time."

I immediately notice the discrepancy in his statement. Most-*watched* segment. Not highest-rated or most-positive viewer reaction. I have yet to be able to view the playback on my Slate, but I have a feeling if I'm ever brave enough to watch it, I'll find more than a fair share of negative comments in the side bar. Particularly if the group of protesters who waited for us outside the studio is any indication of how much the audience "loved" us.

The mass of bodies seemed to have quadrupled in size since we arrived. Thankfully, we didn't actually have to maneuver through them. We took off from the hovercopter landing pad on the roof of the building and were able to fly over them. But I did notice the pilot subtly dodging a few unidentified projectiles that were launched in our direction.

Kaelen told me not to look but I couldn't help it. I stared down at them from the window of the hovercopter, feeling the deep-seated hatred they cast up at me from so far below.

How can you feel such strong emotion for someone you've never met?

"They don't hate you," Crest reassured me once we arrived back at the hotel. "They hate what you represent. What Diotech represents. It's just like Dr. Alixter said during the interview: you can't change the world without making enemies."

As I gazed down at their irate faces and the loathsome messages that flashed on their handheld screens, I willed myself to be stronger. I prayed for the resilience and thick skin that Dr. A promised the world I have.

That they could soon have, too.

But the sights below me and the emotions they stirred up hit too close to home.

I was suddenly back in 1609, strapped to a wooden stake as the ruthless flames of misunderstanding and fear clawed at my legs, burned through my clothes, and scorched my skin black.

They hated me then. They hate me now.

This was supposed to be the place where I belonged. This was supposed to be the time period where I would finally be accepted for who I am. Where I didn't have to hide. Now, all I want is to bury my head under the blankets and do just that.

Hide.

"To the Objective!" Crest chimes in, and everyone raises their glasses, clinking them softly against one another. I follow suit. Kaelen catches my eye as he holds his flute up to meet mine.

"You were wonderful today." The lilting Italian runs off his tongue, a melodic song in my ears.

I tap my glass against his and take a sip. "You have to say that," I tease, keeping with his chosen language. "It's in your DNA."

He smirks and I lean in to kiss him. The champagne tastes better on his lips than it does from my flute. When I pull back, Kaelen is grinning at me. I take another drink, draining the glass.

I like the way the bubbles warm me. Loosen me. They have a rare ability to heighten some senses while dulling others. I notice the more I drink, the easier it is to forget things I don't want to remember. Block questions I don't want to answer. Like:

Who is SZ1609?

I suddenly realize why so many people drink alcohol. It's a self-administered memory modification. It numbs the parts of yourself you don't like. The parts you wish were different. For a brief moment, it turns you into the person you want to be. And the person everyone else already thinks you are.

But I have a feeling it won't last.

I have a feeling, with my ExGen blood, I will be cheated out of several hours of forgetful bliss.

Kaelen grabs me by the hand and starts to pull me toward the hallway. "C'mon," he whispers.

My feet feel sluggish and heavy as I follow him. "Where are we going?" I try to replicate his whisper but I just end up giggling instead.

He doesn't answer. He doesn't have to. As soon as we arrive at the door to his suite, I know. "Will you come inside?" he asks, bending forward to brush his lips against the curve of my neck, sending tiny shivers down my arms.

"Are you asking me because you *have* to? Because it's coded into your—?"

Kaelen stops my question by pressing his finger to my lips. "I'm asking you because I *want* to."

Without turning around, he swipes the panel on the wall. The door unseals and he backs inside, keeping his burning gaze on me the whole time. His hand tugs on mine. His eyes beg for me to follow him.

His smile makes it impossible to say no.

25

UNWELCOME

Kaelen's suite looks identical to mine, except reversed. The bedroom is where my living room is, the bathroom door is on the opposite wall. But everything is different once we're both inside it. And I have a feeling everything will forever be different once we leave it.

Kaelen takes both my hands in his and kisses me gently on the nose. Then on the cheek. Then on the mouth. My lips part and I inhale him. Inhale the promise of being with him. Of joining back together with him. Like the way we started. Two people created from the same beginning.

His hands slide down and find the hem of my dress. I lift my arms over my head to help him remove it, but he surprises me by ripping apart the fabric instead. I giggle as the tattered dress slips to my feet. "Crest will not be happy with you."

"I don't care about Crest right now."

"I thought you liked that dress," I tease with a mischievous smile. The champagne is making me bold. Improving my ability to make jokes about things I only understand because of a series of uploads.

"I like it better now." He casts his eyes down the length of my body. He does little to hide his fascination with my bare skin and the sparse undergarments Crest made me wear.

"Fair enough." I reach up and easily resign his shirt to the same fate as my dress. The frayed pieces fall from his lean, muscular torso, revealing beautifully sculpted shoulders, defined chest muscles, and skin softer than anything I've ever felt. I run an exploratory palm across his collarbone.

And then he's devouring me. His lips kneading against my neck. My shoulder. His tongue tracing lines in the grooves between bone and muscle. We stumble toward the bed, the downy fabric of his comforter absorbing our fall. Kaelen is on top of me, his weight bearing down on me. Two bodies creating fire against each other. His mouth reaches for mine. When our lips collide, a surge of electricity passes through me, lighting up every skin cell and every nerve.

"Do you know what comes next?" I whisper, suddenly feeling foolish and naïve. Seeing two strangers in an upload is one thing. Working out the logistics yourself is another.

"I know what comes next."

Suddenly his hand is on the inside of my thigh. I gasp in surprise. In delight. I'm starting to think Kaelen's uploads were slightly more thorough than mine. My body responds to his touch immediately.

Made for each other.

His lips reach for mine again as his hand starts to move. My breath shudders. I close my eyes.

And I see his face.

Not Kaelen's.

His.

Lyzender's.

"I've just been waiting a long time for this," he says, gazing tenderly down upon me.

"For what?"

"For you to feel . . . well . . . for you to feel ready, I guess."

I shut my eyes tight and try to push it away but the imagery is too strong. Or the champagne is too weak. It's a battle and the memory is winning. The guilt is standing by, ready to consume me and splinter me apart from the inside.

"Something that will bring us closer together. As close together as we can be . . . it's not really something I can explain. I mean, I could . . . but I think I'd rather just show you. It would be more meaningful that way."

I want to cry out. I want to scream for him to go away. Get out of my mind. Get out of my thoughts. You're not welcome here anymore.

But there's something about his intense eyes that I can't chase away. No matter how hard I try. No matter how much I want to.

The sickness starts to bloom inside of me. The unrelenting shame that always accompanies his memory spreads like a deadly virus. It will consume me. It will double me over in wretched agony.

"Stop!" I shout. Kaelen jerks up, regarding me with concern.

"What's wrong?" he asks. "Did I hurt you?"

I shake my head. I want to tell him that it wasn't *him* I was shouting at. It was Lyzender. It was the image of his face bubbling to the surface whenever it pleases. Regardless of where I am, who I'm with, what I'm doing.

I just want to be left alone!

I push Kaelen off me. "I'm sorry," I say, my voice trembling beyond recognition. "I can't do this."

I launch out of bed and am halfway across the suite in a nano-second. I'm fast but Kaelen is faster. He always has been.

He's in front of me before I can blink. His strong hands gripping my arms. His eyes full of questions. "What's going on? Is this because of what happened on the platform yesterday?"

The tears are coming. They well up in spite of myself. Just another part of me that I have no control over. I shut my eyes, trying to trap the tears inside but they leak out anyway, tracing jagged, insolent paths down my cheek.

"Yes," I begin, and then change my mind. "No. Not entirely. I . . . I can't do this." The words are so cracked.

"It's okay." Kaelen pulls me to him, wraps his arms around me. "We don't have to. We can just be here. Together."

I can't do that either. Not when Lyzender's face is forcefully monopolizing my thoughts. Not when he's out there, sending me messages, burying memories in the ground, asking me questions on the live Feed.

I shove Kaelen away. I admit it's too hard. Too rough. Not that it would hurt him. At least not on the outside. But it's enough to keep him from following me. And that's all that matters right now.

"I'm sorry," I say again, refusing to look at him for fear his expression will destroy me.

I pull on what's left of my ruined dress, holding the top up with one hand so it doesn't plummet to the ground again. I charge the door, open it with a swipe of my finger, and rush through.

As I walk down the hall, swatting tears away, Dr. A's words from the interview today haunt my mind.

"They will never hurt each other. They are incapable of doing it. Just as you are incapable of flying."

I'm beginning to wonder how many other things Dr. A has been wrong about.

26

CONVICTION

The guard stationed outside Kaelen's door pays me no attention as I stagger down the hallway, drunk with emotion and guilt and whatever's left of the champagne.

I don't go to my room. It's too close. I would be able to hear Kaelen breathing through the adjoining door. A heartbeat and a knock away.

We're not allowed to leave the floor. Raze has given his guards specific instructions to contain us. That leaves only one place I can go.

When I burst through the door of the Hospitality Suite, I'm surprised to see it's not empty. I'd assumed everyone would have gone back to their rooms by now. Particularly given the early hyperloop we have to catch to San Francisco in the morning.

Dr. A stands in the center of the room. Dane is dangerously close to him. They are speaking in harsh whispers. Dane has his hands on the sides of Dr. A's face, as though he's literally holding him up. Keeping him from toppling over. But Dr. A isn't looking at him. His gaze is focused just to the left of him. Eyes distant, lips clenched shut, while Dane pleads for his attention.

My entrance isn't graceful. I accidentally knock into a table with my hip, sending the empty flutes that haven't been cleared away crashing to the floor. The collision nearly makes me lose hold of my dress. I pin my elbows tightly against my ribs to keep the shredded fabric around me.

They turn in unison and Dane's hands instantly fall to his sides.

"Sera," Dr. A says, his voice strained. Like he's trying to sound happier to see me than he is.

"I'm sorry," I say for the third time in the past five minutes. "I'll go."

"Don't be silly," Dr. A says. "Dane was just leaving."

I don't miss the pointed look Dr. A gives Dane right then and the wounded expression he gets in return. But I also know better than to comment on it.

"Weren't you?" Dr. A prompts.

Dane grits his teeth. "I was." He walks briskly from the room, not looking back once. He doesn't say good night. To either of us. Which is very unlike Dane.

Dr. A lowers himself onto the sofa and gives the wall screen the command to unpause. "Sit down," Dr. A says, patting the space next to him.

Actually, the last thing I want right now is Dr. A's company, but I sit anyway. Because that's what I do. I obey.

I pray he won't ask me where I've been, why I'm not with Kaelen, and why my dress is nearly ripped in half. Fortunately, he seems too weary and preoccupied with whatever just happened to put the pieces together. In fact, his eyes barely even leave the screen as I sink into the couch.

I turn my gaze to the wall, surprised to see Pastor Peder on the Feed. He's wearing the same wide-brimmed hat and blue-tinted glasses, giving another impassioned, long-winded speech to an audience of thousands. Today, I recognize the familiar monuments of the nation's capital behind him.

"These abominations," Peder is saying to the crowd, "these *ExGens*," he spits the word, "are not the work of God. They are the work of a much darker, more sinister force. They're soulless monsters that Dr. Jans Alixter is trying to pass off as human beings."

The throngs of people break into cheers of concurrence.

Why is Dr. A watching this? Why is he subjecting himself to this torture?

Out of the corner of my eye, I see him reach for a glass on the table next to him. It's not champagne, but something stronger. I can smell its noxious odor as he takes a long, sturdy gulp. Like he's trying to swallow the strength to keep watching.

"Have you ever noticed," Peder goes on, "that *Diotech* and *devil* both start with the letter D?"

The crowd loves this. The hovering cams pan the rows and rows of people packed into the outdoor venue. Their faces are distorted mirror images of one another, sharing the same ugly hate that fuels them.

"Look at them," Dr. A murmurs. The charming, charismatic leader from today's interview is gone. The man who sits next to me is balancing precariously close to the edge of defeat. One strong gust of wind and he'd be gone. "So blindly faithful. So . . . *brainwashed*."

The languid, almost garbled quality of his voice makes me think he's not really talking to me, but rather to himself.

"This is what happens when you believe in things you can't prove. It makes you crazy." He points his glass to the screen, as though he's toasting Peder's success. "If he asked them to throw themselves in front of a speeding MagCar they would do it. If he asked them to light themselves on fire, they would do it. Without even questioning."

Fire.

The word sends a shiver of fear through me. It bounces around my brain, trying to find a familiar place to land—a synapse to attach itself to—before finally giving up and fading into the background noise of my mind.

I don't say a word. Something tells me he's forgotten I'm even here. Until he says, "You know, Sera, we've come so far with technology. We've done so much." He stops, closes his eyes. "So much. Yet we're so stalled when it comes to our views about the world."

His words slur, each one bleeding into the next. That's when I realize he's intoxicated. The idea astounds me. I've only ever seen an inebriated person on the Feed. Never in real life. And never someone like Dr. A.

"I could have sworn by the time I became an adult, this religious crap would have finally blown over. How many times do we have to prove to them that they're wrong? How many scientific breakthroughs must we have before these idiots finally understand the truth? There is no God. *We* are God."

He's still staring at the screen but he's not listening to Peder's sermon anymore. I steal a glance at him and notice how bloodshot his eyes are. How saggy his skin looks. They must have put enhancers on him for the interview today. Enhancers that are now wearing off.

"Faith is a powerful thing, Sera," he says, growing quieter, more introspective. "A foolishly powerful thing. It keeps people stupid."

"Dr. Alixter wants to debate science," Peder bellows from the screen. "Fine. Let's debate science! Did you know there is scientific proof of the existence of a soul?"

The mob falls quiet, waiting for his next words with intense eagerness.

"That's right," Peder goes on. "It has been proven that when a human body dies, it loses an infinitesimal amount of mass. What could we possibly attribute this to? A freak physiological accident? Or the departure of a heavenly spirit? A soul returning to its maker?"

Screams from the audience. People are shouting, "Yes! God lives!"

"I bet," Peder says, staring right into the cam, right into my eyes, "that if you cracked open those two ExGens, if you peeled away their glossy exteriors and squeezed out their last breaths, you'd find *nothing* inside."

The applause escalates to a deafening level. I'm grateful when Dr. A finally pauses the playback, running a shaky hand across his damp forehead.

As I stare at the eerie frozen image of Pastor Peder on the wall—the brim of his hat casting a shadow over his sharp features, his eyes visibly ablaze behind his glasses—I can't help but wonder if he's right. Is that what's been missing my entire life? A soul? Some kind of invisible essence that differentiates the Normates from the ExGens? Is that the widening hole that seems to follow me wherever I go?

Dr. A sets his empty glass down with a *clank* and stands up. He stretches his arms above his head. "I better get to sleep. We have an early day tomorrow."

"Why does Peder hate us so much?" I blurt out. I realize it's the first time I've ever used the word *us* in Dr. A's presence.

"Because he's afraid of us," he says.

That wasn't the answer I was anticipating. I find it hard to comprehend—or accept—such a simplistic explanation. "Then why do *you* hate *him* so much?" I ask, expecting to challenge him. Expecting to stump him.

Dr. A just looks at me, as though he's studying data on a Slate. He takes my chin in his hand, rotating it left, then right. "You know," he says pensively, "sometimes when I look at you, all I see is her."

I frown. "Who?"

But he doesn't answer that question either. He releases me and turns for the hallway, letting out a long, stale sigh as he goes. "Good night, Sera."

27

BREAKAGE

I lie on my bed and stare at the ceiling of my hotel suite. Right now it's programmed for night, made to look like there is nothing between me and the star-cluttered sky. Even though I know there is so much more than nothing.

A historical upload once told me that ancient people believed superior beings lived up there. In something called "the heavens." They were referred to as "gods" and they were revered. Respected above all other people. Because they weren't people. They were something more.

More powerful.

More knowledgeable.

More resilient.

Dr. A says there are some Normates who still believe in this archaic way of thinking. Who still think that somebody watches over us. He says these people are the enemies of science. The enemies of the Objective.

"Science has answered all of the questions that were posed at the time the gods were invented," Dr. A once told me. "Those mythical beings are obsolete in our time. Fairy tales. Anyone who says differently is only fooling themselves."

When I ran away with Lyzender we traveled to a time when mythical gods were still revered as the keepers of the secrets.

This was evident six months after we arrived and my special abilities landed me on trial for witchcraft. I would have burned on that stake had it not been for Kaelen. Had it not been for Diotech. They rescued me. Then Dr. A shared the truth with me, invited me into his secrets. Fixed me.

Now when I look up at the sky, I see sky.

I see oxygen molecules and vaporous gases and the helium beams of the sun. I don't see fantasies or poetry or dreams of far-off places.

That's the way it should be.

Yet something inside me still stirs for more. More information. More insight. More answers that can't be found in an upload. My brain craves it like dry, cracked skin craves moisture.

"Activate Feed," I tell the ceiling, and the image instantly shifts. A live broadcast of a professional MagBall game is streaming. But I'm not interested in sports right now.

"Search function."

The MagBall game is reduced to a small square that zips off to the corner of the ceiling and a search box appears in the center. I give it my parameters.

"Dr. Jans Alixter."

I've searched his name so many times. I've scoured through hours of archived footage of his life, trying to unlock the secrets of the mysterious man who controls my destiny. Decides my fate. I don't quite know what I'm looking for now. I don't know what I expect to find that I haven't already devoured during my countless searches in the past year. But something still motivates me to scan the results that fill the screen.

I filter the list by format, opting to view all the Feed footage first. There's not much available before March 28, 2091, the date Diotech was created. Dr. A was clearly a very private person before he cofounded what would become one of the most powerful corporations in history. It's almost as though his life began when his company began.

I locate archived Feed footage of a press conference dated May 5, 2110, and command it to play. I've seen this before, during one of my many searches. It's the first public announcement of Diotech's synthetic meat product. Dr. A is at the podium, speaking eloquently to the cam, while Rio is standing in a corner, fidgeting with what I recognize as an earlier model of the DigiSlate.

Dr. A finishes his short speech and turns the attention over to his colleague. I watch in fascination as the man who created me, who helped me escape, shakily steps up to the podium and reads a prewritten speech from his Slate about the science behind the synthetic food. His voice is trembling. His back is hunched slightly forward. His eyes never leave the screen. It's obvious he's extremely nervous and uncomfortable at that podium.

I suddenly realize that's exactly what I would look like in Feed interviews if it weren't for the countless uploads and genetic programming I've received to make me articulate and charming.

My eyes flick to Dr. A, now standing off to the side. He's trying really hard to hide the annoyance he feels about his partner's stage fright.

Dr. Rio finishes speaking and hurriedly steps away. Dr. A resumes his position at the podium to answer questions from the reporters.

I'm about to return to my search results because I've already seen this footage, when something on the far edge of the screen catches my eye. I'm not sure why I didn't notice it before. Probably because I was too focused on Dr. A's Q&A to pay attention to what was happening offstage.

The visual is slightly cut off due to the edge of the cam's frame.

But I can just make out Rio—who has literally run away from the podium—bending down low to pick something up. A moment later, I see he's lifted a small child—a little girl—into his arms. His previous anxiety instantly vanishes. He's smiling now, kissing the girl's cheek.

I command the screen to pan left and zoom in tight. I can see most of Rio's body but still only half of the child's face. She looks to be about four years old. With dark honey-colored hair, golden skin, and as Rio bounces her slightly in his arms, causing her to smile, I can see a small pink birthmark just under the right side of her jawline. I zoom in farther and see that it vaguely resembles the shape of a maple leaf.

Familiarity tugs at my subconscious.

I recognize the girl. I've seen her before. In a memory. In Rio's memory. It was a little over a year ago, when I returned to the compound with Kaelen in search of the Repressor for Lyzender. Rio was in a vegetative state in the Medical Sector, before they replaced his brain with a computer. His memories were scrambled and chaotic, but I was able to see one.

Or, perhaps, he was able to show me one. The only one that mattered.

It was of her.

She had the same sweet, heart-shaped face, the same clear and curious mahogany-brown eyes. The same miraculously uplifting effect on the man who's holding her in this footage.

A man who is now—for all intents and purposes—gone.

But what about her? Where is she? Why have I never met her or heard a single utterance about her before?

My mind flashes to the day we left the compound. To Rio's stony, warped face as he stood motionless under that creepy cottonwood tree.

Sariana.

That's what he called me.

My thoughts racing, I return to my search page and speak new terms. "Sariana Ri . . ."

But my voice trails off when I see a result from my last search farther down the screen. It's a link to archived footage labeled DIOTECH VS. JENZA PADDOK.

Jenza Paddok. Weren't Dr. A and Director Raze discussing someone by that name the other night at evening meal?

I select it and the ceiling begins to play a capture from what looks to be the outside of a courthouse. A small crowd has gathered, and a tall, slender woman with dark skin and a long face descends the steps of the large stone building.

Feed reporters surround the woman as hovercams buzz around her head.

"Ms. Paddok," one of the reporters asks, "what is your response to the unexpected dismissal of this lawsuit against Diotech Corporation?"

I access my brain for a legal definition of *dismissal*. One comes back immediately from an upload I received months ago about the U.S. legal system: a judge's ruling that all or a portion of the lawsuit is terminated or thrown out, at which point no further evidence or testimony may be provided.

A well-dressed woman, presumably her lawyer, blocks the reporter from getting closer. "This setback is unfortunate but Ms. Paddok is not finished seeking justice from Diotech for the crimes they have brought against humanity. We will find another way to fight this battle."

A second reporter tries to ask a follow-up question but Paddok blocks him with a raise of her hand. It's then that I notice the small mark on her palm. It's not swirling or animated like a nanotat. It looks to be a *real* tattoo. The kind they used to ink directly into your skin before the less invasive nano version was invented.

I rewind the footage and pause on the image of her hand thrust toward the cam. I command the screen to zoom in on the tattoo, studying the curious image.

It's a red crescent moon.

But as the footage expands across my ceiling, getting closer and closer to the peculiar symbol, it's not the red moon that snags my attention. It's the blurry face peering out from behind the woman's outstretched hand.

Someone buried deep within the crowd of spectators and news crews.

A crop of thick, dark hair. A pair of liquid-chocolate eyes. Lips that would feel all too familiar against my own.

"Zoom out," I yell frantically at the screen.

It obeys. And suddenly there he is. Barely visible amid the sea of onlookers. His usual easy smile is gone. Replaced by a somber look of determination.

"Transfer to Lenses!"

I sit up and watch the same frozen capture fill up my peripheral vision. My eyes dart downward, searching for the metadata. This capture is from two years ago. Almost to the day.

"No," I say aloud to the empty room.

It can't be him.

It's not possible. It's not possible. It's not possible.

But now suddenly all I can think about is his face on that drive. That heartbreaking capture he buried for me to find.

"Yes . . . always yes."

In a whisper, his name is out of my lips before I can stop it. Before I can hold back the tidal wave of emotion that comes crashing down with it. "Zen."

28

RECALL

I reverse the footage and replay it countless times. He's only there for a moment. When Paddok raises her hand to block the hovercams. Then her arm is back at her side and his face is concealed again. The cams follow her to an awaiting MagCar and he's never seen again.

Common sense.

That's what Dr. A would tell me right now. Half of being a good scientist is knowing when to use common sense. And common sense tells me it can't possibly be him.

Lyzender Luman is in the year 2032. In Brooklyn, New York. I left him there with no transession gene and no way to get back here. Which means now, eighty-five years later, he is most likely dead. Or incredibly old.

It has to be someone who looks like him.

Remarkably like him.

But my mind immediately flashes back to our Feed interview today. To the viewer who asked the question. Who called himself SZ1609.

I'd finally managed to convince myself it wasn't him. That it was just a strange, unnerving coincidence.

But now . . .

I don't know.

I pause the footage again and zoom into his dark, endless eyes.

I used to stare into those eyes for hours.

I used to watch him sleep.

I used to count the minutes until he woke.

That was back when I was weak and susceptible to temptation. When I was broken. Now what do I feel?

I don't let myself answer. Because it's a moot question. It's not him. It can't possibly be.

Lyzender Luman is gone. That's not his face. Those aren't his eyes. That's not his mouth.

His mouth . . .

"You need to come with me." The urgency in his voice cuts me so deep, I can't look at him. I cast my gaze to the ground.

"If I go with you," I say, fear nearly choking the words, "will you kiss me again?"

Suddenly, he is next to me. He places his warm, soft palm against my cheek. I close my eyes, memorizing the feel of his skin on my skin.

"Every day."

The sickness starts to well up inside of me. The writhing desperation to escape my own body.

Hastily, I blink the Feed capture from my Lenses, watching his frozen face disappear from my vision.

But even after it dissolves, those eyes seem to linger. To cling like the stars that dance on the backs of your eyelids when you're falling asleep.

I blink again hard, willing them to leave. I can still see the blacks of his irises. The delicate curve of his long lashes.

I run to the bathroom, activate the sink, and splash water into my eyes, watching my reflection blur and ripple before it settles back to normal again.

His face is still there. His lips are still reaching for mine.

I tear the Lenses from my eyes and toss them into the basin, running the water on full power. I watch the small, helpless domes fight to cling to the sides of the sink. But the riptide is too strong and finally they succumb to their fate, swirling away. Vanishing down the drain.

I stare at the emptying sink for a long time. Much longer than I'm sure Dr. A would approve of.

I'm already practicing the story I will tell Director Raze tomorrow morning when I ask him for a new pair of Lenses. I will say they accidentally popped out when I was washing my face. I will say I fought hard to catch them before they were washed away.

And I will pray that my dangerous lie will never be caught.

The Lenses were clearly defective. And defective things should be replaced.

29

SUMMONS

The next day, we board a hyperloop for San Francisco. After that it's Portland and Seattle. We do a Feed interview in each city, followed by a public appearance in a grand amphitheater or arena. Just as Killy promised, the hyperloop rides do get easier. My stomach adjusts, my brain learns how to blitz out.

The protests are getting worse. It seems that in every city we stop, the angry crowds waiting for us are larger and more fearsome than the last. Our hotels are always vacant, entirely bought out by Diotech or a local sponsor. Director Raze brings in extra security—hired freelancers who help him secure the perimeters and guarantee our safety.

Yet I never feel safe.

I wonder if anyone else does.

Conversely, our fans and supporters have grown in vast numbers, too. Every public appearance is sold out. Every local feedcast has millions of live viewers. When we exit the hyperloop stations, alongside the dissenters, there are also admirers. They call out our names, take our capture, hold up signs proclaiming their adoration.

Sometimes it's hard to remember that there are actually more people in this country who love us than hate us. Dane says the protesters are such an infinitesimal percentage of the total population. "Not even a blip on the radar in the grand scheme of things."

Maybe it's because hate tends to resonate so much louder than love. And the ones who abhor us somehow always find a way to push themselves to the front. To make their infinitesimal percentage heard.

After Seattle, we travel east, stopping in Salt Lake City and Denver before making our way south to Albuquerque, El Paso, Dallas, New Orleans, Nashville, Birmingham, and Atlanta.

Kaelen and I have yet to talk about the incident in his hotel room in Los Angeles. Thus far, we've both managed to avoid the topic completely. It hasn't affected our performance onstage, though. I still love him and I still have no trouble feedcasting it to the world. But he hasn't asked me to come to his room again, even though Dane booked us adjoining suites at every single hotel, and I haven't invited him to mine either.

By day, we are inseparable. We hold hands, we kiss, we speak to each other in romantic Italian. By night, we are alone. I lie in bed and think about him in the next room. I listen for his breathing and try to match mine to his. It's a way to stay connected to him even when we're apart.

I know I could ask him to sleep with me. Just lie next to me and hold me until the night is chased away. But I'm afraid to. I don't know why. Afraid of the memories it will trigger? Memories of another boy who held me through another darkness? Or afraid of the emotions that always seem to come with those memories?

Either way, that night in Los Angeles drove a wedge between Kaelen and me. A wedge that I'm not sure how to remove without the possibility of driving it deeper.

Fortunately, the tour is going so well the rest of our group doesn't seem to notice. Not even Dr. A. The Diotech stock continues to soar to new heights. The ExGen Collection ad runs constantly on the Feed. Our faces are on the cover of every DigiMag and DigiJournal in the country. And Dane says preorders for the genetic modifications have already started pouring in by the millions. According to him, it will be the most successful product launch in Diotech history.

When we get back to the hotel in Atlanta, I murmur a good night to everyone and go straight to my room. Physically, I feel fine—as always—but emotionally, I'm drained. Each day, I grow more and more tired of the act I'm expected to perform. The show Kaelen and I put on for the countless people who come to see us. At least, it's a show for me. For Kaelen, it still appears to come naturally. Like he was born to be onstage. Born to be in front of an audience. His smiles for the cams seem so effortless. His interactions with the screaming fans feel so genuine.

I, on the other hand, have to fake it. Although my body language and delivery are always impeccable (according to Dane), I never feel at ease in front of all those people, all those cams. Again, I wonder how Kaelen and I can be so different, when we're supposedly cut from the same scientific cloth.

I've gotten into the habit of retreating to my room the moment we return to the hotel and not resurfacing until the next morning. The thought of being on display after I finish being on display is too much to fathom.

But tonight I'm barely in my room for five minutes when Dane knocks on the door.

"Jans sent me to fetch you," he says, and I swear I see a flash of apology in his eyes. Dane is the only one who calls Dr. A by his first name. Really, the only one who's allowed to.

"Fetch me? For what?"

He looks like he's considering answering the question but decides not to. "He told me to bring you to room 702."

I nod and reluctantly rise from the bed where I collapsed the minute I closed myself inside the room. There's no use stalling or trying to negotiate for more time. Dane and I both know that when Dr. A summons you, you go.

I slide my feet into my shoes and follow him into the hallway.

Room 702 is only a few doors down. Dane moves to swipe his finger against the panel but stops and turns to face me.

"Sera," he begins cautiously. "What you saw the other night—between me and Dr. Alixter."

I shake my head. "It was none of my business. I'm sorry I intruded."

Dane lifts his hand in the air, as if to silence me. "No. I want to explain. Dr. Alixter and I . . . we have a . . . well, he's a complicated man," he finally finishes after much stumbling.

I nod, waiting for him to continue.

His eyes dart toward me, then to the ground. "He grew up in a family who didn't accept him. His parents and brother were very religious people. They believed that science was the enemy. When he told them that he wanted to be a scientist, they essentially disowned him. He ran away and hasn't spoken to them since."

I find myself wondering why he's telling me this. "Is that why he hates religion so much?"

Dane bites his lower lip. "For the most part, yes."

When it doesn't seem as though he's going to elaborate, I ask, "What does this have to do with the other night?"

He blinks, as if he's just remembering why he started this conversation. "Oh. I guess what I wanted to say is . . . seeing Pastor Peder on the Feed, it always puts him in a sour mood. Because it hits him a little too close to home, you know? You shouldn't take it personally. He loves you. You and Kaelen. You are like the children he never had."

Well, Kaelen is, at least.

Once again, I remain quiet, thinking he'll add more. But he doesn't.

"How do you know all of this?" I ask.

Dane smiles. It's a reserved smile that barely scratches the surface. "I suppose when you work with someone for a long time, you pick up a few things."

"How long *have* you worked for Diotech?"

He chuckles and rubs his chin. "Wow, I don't even know. I was hired to manage the announcement of the synthetic meat line. And that was . . ." He pauses to think.

"May 5, 2110," I say, remembering the archived footage of the announcement that I watched the other night.

He smiles. "You're right. So that would make it—flux—more than seven years already."

I think back to that footage. How captivating and composed Dr. A was. How miserable and awkward Rio was. That is, until he lifted the little girl into his arms.

Suddenly, I'm struck with a thought. I know it's dangerous to ask questions about Rio, but maybe if I frame it right. If it seems to have come up organically . . .

"You said Dr. A had a difficult childhood?"

"That's right."

"Is that why he never had children of his own?"

Dane clears his throat uncomfortably. "Probably."

"What about Rio? Did he have any kids?"

"One," Dane says, a sadness unexpectedly clouding his eyes. "A daughter. Sariana."

A shiver passes through me at the sound of that name again.

Sariana.

It feels like so much more than just a name. It feels like the whole sky.

I swallow. "What happened to her?"

"She died about three years ago. It was horrible. Rio was devastated. She was only eight."

"How?" I manage to squeeze out.

171

Dane sighs, blinking out of his gloom. "Broken neck. She fell out of a tree in the Agricultural Sector."

My blood turns to ice. I don't have to ask. As soon as the words are out of his mouth, I know which tree it is.

The cottonwood. The one that I can't bear to walk past. The one that screams at me when I turn around. Just the thought of those gnarled branches and that warped bark makes me shudder.

"And they couldn't save her?" I ask, my voice trembling.

He shakes his head. "By the time they got to her it was too late."

I want to know more. So much more. But I have to tread carefully. Too many questions about the daughter of an enemy might raise suspicions.

"Anyway," Dane says, effectively ending the conversation, "best not to keep him waiting."

Dane turns and swipes his finger against the door panel of room 702. It slides open and all harrowing remnants of our previous conversation instantly vanish when I see what's waiting inside.

Or rather *who* is waiting inside.

I have to work hard to hold back the gasp that threatens to escape.

"Hi, Sera," the man says in a friendly voice.

But it's not his cordialness that confuses me. He's always been kind to me. In fact, he's probably one of the nicest people on the compound. I just never expected to see him in our hotel. A thousand miles *away* from the compound.

"Sevan." I barely manage to squeeze his name through my constricting throat. "What are you doing here?"

I don't know why I even bother to ask. There's only one reason Sevan Sidler, Diotech's chief Memory Coder, would be here. But his answer still sends a tremor of dread through me.

Sevan smiles innocuously. "Dr. A asked me to scan your memories."

30

ABNORMAL

Dr. A has been ordering random memory scans for both Kaelen and me for the past year. He says it's his way of making sure we stay true to the Objective and, in my case, making sure my devious tendencies don't resurface. The scans never bothered me before. They were supposed to be superfluous.

I never had anything to hide before.

Now, as Dane mutters a goodbye and Sevan leads me into his suite, I think about all of the things I've hidden in the past few days. All of the things that will undoubtedly show up on this scan.

The cube drive that was buried in the dirt and that I've been stupid enough to carry with me on every stop of this tour. Lyzender's distraught and heartbroken message vowing to find me. Seeing his face in the Feed footage. My inability to push that face from my mind.

These are the kinds of things that should be reported. The kinds of things that threaten the Objective. Yet I deliberately kept them to myself. I *chose* to disobey.

My legs tremble as I make my way farther inside room 702.

Sevan has built a temporary memory lab in the dining room of the suite. It's nowhere near as menacing as the real thing. Still, staring at those instruments—the computer terminal with the special coding keyboard on the desk, the injector lying next to it, the chair with the synthosteel clamps—I feel a cold sweat trickle down the back of my neck.

I also wonder *why* Dr. A ordered this scan in the middle of the tour. Has he had it planned from the beginning or does he suspect something? Did Kaelen get scanned, too? Or is it just me?

Maybe Kaelen told Dr. A about my warped behavior that night in Los Angeles.

My breathing grows shallow.

Should I refuse?

Should I ask to talk to Dr. A first?

Maybe if I run to him now and confess everything, he'll understand. He'll forgive me.

I chastise myself for being so foolish and naïve. Of course he won't understand. Of course he won't forgive me. I knowingly kept secrets from him. I knowingly deceived him. That's unforgivable in his eyes.

"How are you?" Sevan asks, seemingly oblivious to the terror ripping me apart. "How's the tour been going?"

Small talk.

He's making small talk like he always does. He has no idea what he's about to find. What he's going to have to report.

"Fine," I manage to utter as I try to keep my lips from trembling.

He waits for me to say more and then releases a short laugh when I don't. "Well, that's not what I've heard."

"What did you hear?" I ask, panic flaring up.

He gives me a strange look. "I've heard that it's been far better than *fine*. Dane has transmitted nothing but glowing reports back to the compound. Apparently the world loves you two."

I relax somewhat but the relief is short-lived.

"Shall we get started?" Sevan motions to the chair. With a deep surrendering sigh, I lower myself into it and place my arms on the armrests to activate the restraints. The thick synthosteel instantly clamps around my wrists, holding me in place.

Since I'm never conscious during any of the scans, I don't know if the clamps are there as a precautionary measure, or if people actually do struggle when their memories are being evaluated.

"Connecting to your vitals now," Sevan says.

I've always liked Sevan. Despite the nature of his job—invading people's minds—he's nice to me. He tells me what he's doing as he's doing it. After all this time, I don't need each step of the process explained to me. I know his computer is linking to the signal transmitted from the nanosensors that live in my bloodstream, sending data and information to his system about my physical condition.

But it's reassuring to hear him say it anyway.

I lean back and wait for him to inject me with the serum that will send me into a dreamless sleep and steal hours from my life. It will only seem like a few seconds to me. I will wake up in this chair feeling groggy and disoriented. And there's always a chance that some of my memories will be gone when I do.

Like the night before we left the compound. When I woke up in Sevan's lab with hours missing from my day. I knew I had seen something. Something I wasn't supposed to see. And now I'll never know what it was.

The same thing could very well happen tonight.

It's impossible for every single memory in our brains to be reviewed by a human being, so the scans are programmed to look for abnormalities. Thoughts and memories that vary from the everyday routine of our lives. They're usually accompanied by nanosensor reports of elevated body temperatures, augmented heartbeats, strained breathing.

All the things that will surely expose me for the deviant I still am.

"Okay, looks like we're ready." Sevan glances one last time at his screen and then picks up the injector. He offers me a smile before placing it against my neck. Even though I know he doesn't mean it to be, it's the most menacing gesture I've ever seen. "See you in a few hours."

I feel the pressure of the injector against my skin and a moment later everything grows heavy as my brain shuts down and the familiar wave of darkness consumes my consciousness.

By now I am used to the sensation of being taken. Of falling into shadows.

But today, I am terrified. Not of the black curtain itself. But of what I will find waiting for me when it's finally lifted.

31

PARADOX

When I come to, light is already breaking outside the window. It must be early morning. I was out for the entire night—more than eight hours. Much longer than my usual scans. That can't be a good sign.

I peer drowsily around the room. Sevan is at his monitor, furiously typing code into the keyboard. A faint beeping alerts him to my consciousness and he turns and smiles.

"Welcome back."

I attempt to blink the bleariness away but it doesn't want to let go.

I do what I always do when I wake up from a scan. I try to focus on the last thing I remember before losing consciousness. It comes to me easily today. I remember the fear.

My eyes dart back to Sevan, who has resumed typing, his eyes focused, his mouth slightly ajar. It's strange. He doesn't look like he's just witnessed a major infraction. The cuffs around my wrists release and I flex my fingers.

I'm afraid to move. To stand up. Terrified that the worst

has not yet arrived, and I want to be sitting down when it does. But after a moment, Sevan lifts his gaze from his screen and regards me with an inquisitive expression. "You're free to go," he reminds me. As if I haven't done this numerous times in the past year.

I try to speak but only air comes out.

"Do you feel all right?" He frowns at his screen. "Your stress levels are a bit high, but it's probably just anxiety from the tour. Nothing to be alarmed about."

"I'm okay," I finally manage to say.

He flashes me a goofy smile. "Good." Then, when I still don't move, he asks, "Was there something else?"

"The scan," I begin warily. "It went . . . smoothly?"

He spins back to his coding keyboard. "Yup. All clear. See you next time."

All clear?

That can't be right. There was nothing about the last few days that would warrant an all-clear status.

Is there something wrong with the equipment? Was it damaged during travel? Did Sevan not read the output correctly?

The memory of the cube drive should have jumped out at him like a fish in the desert. As well as the boy's face in the Feed footage. There's no way those recall patterns looked anything like my normal day-to-day routine.

Perhaps he's lying. Perhaps the infraction is so big, he's been ordered not to discuss it with me. Which would mean any minute now I'll receive a ping from Dr. A asking to see me. Or worse, one of Director Raze's lackeys will be waiting outside the door to personally "escort" me to Dr. A's suite.

I rise unsteadily from the chair. "Thank you, Sevan."

He looks up long enough to give me a wave. It's an unusually slow movement. Like he's tracing the sun's arc with his fingertips. On the palm of his hand I notice he has a nanotat. I find that odd because I don't remember ever seeing it before. Also, because Sevan doesn't seem like the kind of person to get one. Nanotats are normally imprinted by artistic types. Sevan always struck me as more rational and scientific.

The design is fitting for him, though. It's a scrolling line of code. It must be Revisual+, the language of memories, because I can't read it. I've never received an upload for a computer language before. To me, it just looks like an indecipherable sequence of gibberish.

"Goodbye," I say, mimicking his strange, slow wave. Maybe it's some kind of Coder salute.

He repeats the gesture and I'm debating whether I should as well when I notice the nanotat on his hand change. It's only for a flicker of an instant. Not long enough for any Normate eye to catch, but I can see the shift. If Kaelen were here, he would as well.

For a sliver of a second, the palm of his hand is no longer decorated with streaming lines of code, but rather an unadorned image.

A red crescent moon.

When I blink, though, it's gone. Replaced by the same repeating progression of numbers and symbols. Mesmerized, I take a step forward, watching his palm. I wait for it to change again, but it never does. He soon lowers it to his lap.

"I like your nanotat," I say, feeling unexpectedly brave. "Is it new?"

He flips his palm up and runs his fingertips over the animated text. "It is. I thought I'd give it a try. See what all the hype is about."

"What does it mean?" I meet his eye, probing him for truth with my gaze. "The code?"

"It's stupid actually. A Coder's paradox. It's the memory of a Coder programming his own memory. Basically a circular reference. It goes around and around forever. Like looking into a mirror within a mirror."

"An infinite loop."

"Exactly." He flashes me an unassuming smile and I swear I see the reflection of a thousand secrets dancing in his eyes. "Well, I guess I'll see you later."

I nod and slip out of the room. Once in the hallway, I press my back against the wall and suck in large gulps of air, willing my heart to stop galloping in my chest before its frantic activity shows up on someone's Slate.

I don't know what just happened back there. I don't know why my perfidious memories didn't set off warning alarms from here all the way back to the compound.

But I do know, whatever it is, Sevan is in on it.

32

RUPTURED

When our hovercopter arrives at the local Feed station in Miami the next morning, Director Raze receives orders to touch down on the grass in front of the station, as opposed to the roof where we usually land.

"Not a chance," Raze says into his earplant, glaring out the window at the throngs of people below us. "Patch me through to the streamwork manager."

Kaelen and I sit in the row of seats behind him, our hands tightly clasped together, staring out opposite windows. I turn to watch Raze as he waits for a connection.

"This is Director Raze, head of Diotech Security. There is no way we are landing in the middle of that mayhem."

He pauses, listening. A moment later, he bangs his fist against the window.

"What's going on?" Crest asks. She's seated in the last row of the hover, behind Kaelen and me.

"Their roof pad is under construction. They say it's impossible to land up there."

I gaze down at the swarm of bodies and my throat tightens.

"Agent Thatch." Raze initiates contact with his second-in-command, who's riding in the hover behind us with Dane and Dr. A. "We're being forced to land out front. Contact the private security detail. Tell them we want a protected path cleared from the front lawn to the entrance. Synthoglass barricades. No one can get through. Is that understood?" Raze pushes back against his headrest and sighs. "What a glitching mess."

We're forced to circle for thirty minutes while the sea below is parted by a group of uniformed guards and large plates of synthoglass are set up to create a secure pathway for us.

As we wait, Crest fiddles with my hair, pulling out pins from my swept-back bangs and reinserting them. I don't think my hair actually *needs* work, it's just her way of expending nervous energy. None of us are excited about having to wade through that chaos down there.

After she secures the last pin and leans back in her seat, I feel a light tapping on the inside of my hand. I look down to see Kaelen's fingertips moving in rapid succession, typing out our secret code against my palm.

CAN WE TALK?

So this is it. We're finally going to address what happened back in Los Angeles. Right here, hovering five hundred feet above a swarming Miami Feed station.

I take a breath and drum out a response.

YES.

He turns to me and speaks in hushed Hindi. I almost want to laugh at how unnecessary his whispers are. It's not like anyone in this hover can understand Hindi.

"I'm sorry. I shouldn't have pushed you."

"*Nahīṁ*," I say, accessing the dense, melodic language. "I handled it horribly."

Kaelen shakes his head, appearing frustrated. He runs his fingers through his glossy hair. "I sometimes forget that I'm competing with someone else."

This takes me by surprise. "What? No. You aren't competing with anyone."

"I'm competing with your past."

We both know who he's referring to. We don't have to say his name. Even though it bounces through my brain like an echo in eternity.

Lyzender.

Lyzender.

Lyzender.

"My past is gone," I assure him. "It's literally in the past."

"Then why are you so scared to be with me?"

I bite my lip. "I'm not scared."

"What is it then?"

I want to scream that I don't know. That I can't put it into words. That I've tried to explain it to myself but it refuses to make sense.

I'm grateful when Raze interrupts us, barking orders about what will happen when we get to the ground. I feel my stomach drop as the hover begins to make its descent.

"Can we finish this later?" I whisper in English.

Kaelen nods but won't meet my eyes.

We land in the center of the cleared pathway and my heart squeezes as I take the first step down the hover's staircase. The crowds are barricaded behind the high walls of soundproof glass but their voices rise over the top, infiltrating my space. Some are screaming for our attention, wanting us to face them so they can grab a good capture. Some are screaming for us to go back to where we came from, or worse, to hell, where we belong.

Uniformed guards are lined up along the blockade to protect the seams between the glass panels. Kaelen takes my hand as we start the terrifying journey through the parted crowd. Director Raze walks alongside Kaelen, Crest, and me, while Agent Thatch escorts Dr. A and Dane, who have just stepped out of their hover.

We're nearly to the door of the station when I hear the cracking sound. My gaze flicks toward the noise and I watch in horror as an industrial MagTractor backs up, revs its engine, and comes crashing through a gap between two of the synthoglass panels.

Kaelen pushes me aside, out of harm's way, and Director Raze does the same to him. A man—a farmer based on the way he's dressed—jumps out of the tractor. He hurls insults at us as he stalks in my direction. I stand, sick and paralyzed with fear.

Everything that comes next appears to be happening in slow motion. I can see the drastic shift in Kaelen's face. I can almost hear it. The *snap*. The creature breaking free from its shackles.

In a split second, the man is on his back, cowering while Kaelen sits astride him, striking his face with his closed fists. His hands move so fast, they blur through the air. The only sight I fully register is the splatter of blood that sprays with every punch.

The rage hollows out his eyes. In that moment, he looks exactly as Pastor Peder described us: like a soulless monster.

It takes five security guards to pull Kaelen off the man. The first two who try are thrown back immediately, tumbling through the air and crashing with a sickening *crunch* against the synthoglass on either side of us.

When they finally manage to untangle him from the man's pulverized face, Kaelen is covered in the farmer's blood.

We're ushered toward the building. Kaelen is breathing hard. Not from the effort of the fight, but from the storm raging inside him. He's still thrashing and growling as he's hurried inside the Feed station by Director Raze and his men.

I stop just short of the door, long enough to take in the pandemonium that has erupted in our wake. The guards are having a difficult time keeping everyone back. People are pushing to get closer, to steal a peek.

Last time they erased memories to hide the truth about Kaelen. They won't be able to do that this time.

There are too many people. Too many Slates. Too many witnesses.

Through the mesh of the bodies, I manage to catch a glimpse of the man who attacked us—who never even got close enough to breathe in my direction before Kaelen intercepted him. His face is completely disfigured. His eyes are swollen shut. His nose sits blood-spattered and crooked above his busted lips. The skin of his cheek is peeled back, barely hanging on.

My heart stops when I realize he's not moving.

Something screeches and scrapes inside my ears. A panic so loud it blocks out all other sounds.

I step slowly away from the growing unrest. My feet stumbling over each other. I hit a hard surface. When I turn around, I see it's the door to the station. It's been closed on me. In all this commotion, they don't even realize I'm still outside.

Suddenly, warm breath tickles the nape of my neck. A large hand wraps around my stomach, yanking me back hard. I scream but no one can hear it above the turmoil.

My reflexes are slow, dampened by the spiral of shock I'm spinning in. By the time I even think to fight back, the sizzle of a Modifier stings my skin and I wilt into the arms of a stranger.

PART 3

THE UNRAVELING

33

CLEANSED

In the darkness of my mind, I remember my birth. Emerging from the thick, gelatinous fluid of the womb. Opening my eyes to the world.

The face I saw before me was Rio's.

Not the empty shell of a person who now roams the compound. A strong, vibrant man with bright eyes and a smile that made me feel like I was home. Even before I understood the concept of home.

He slapped me on the back and told me to breathe.

I remember the oxygen. That first sip of air. It was sweet honey to my lungs.

A MedBot came to clean me. It cleared the fluid from my nose. It washed the residue from my skin. It combed the tangles from my long, damp hair.

Then there were tests. So many tests. Injectors pressed against my skin. Blood drawn from my veins. "Perfect," was the word I kept hearing. "Absolutely perfect."

I was so very tired. Somehow Rio knew. He put me in a bed and told me to sleep.

I drifted off to the sound of him sobbing quietly.

"You're here," he kept saying, over and over again. "You're finally here."

I awake to voices.

Frenetic movement all around me.

Two pairs of eyes floating above, like stars in a black sky.

The darkness comes and goes. I'm injected with something that makes my limbs feel sluggish and then my eyes grow too heavy to open again.

I can't move. I can't speak.

Even if I could, the only name I would call out would be Kaelen's. What will happen to him now? Now that the world has seen what he can do? I used to think I was the flawed one. I was the one who ran away. But I'm starting to wonder if we're both inherently defective.

"Make it fast," a woman says. "It won't take long for them to notice she's gone."

I hear the sound of strained breathing. A man. His voice is vaguely familiar but I'm too disoriented to place it. "He killed him. He wasn't supposed to kill him. I didn't think he would—"

The woman barks a response, harsh and impatient. "Graw was prepared to die for the cause. He knew the risks."

Are they talking about the farmer? The one who Kaelen beat senseless?

Is he really dead?

My mind flashes back to those two helpless paparazzi on the hyperloop platform and my stomach starts to cave in on itself. I want to vomit but even my gag reflexes are paralyzed.

The air moves around me. The flurry of hands working.

I feel a pinch in my leg, just above my knee. My skin catches fire. It burns like an inferno inside my veins. But I can't cry out. My mouth is frozen. My tongue is so numb, it may as well have been cut out.

Something beeps near my head. It starts out loud and cacophonous. Like a chorus of tiny chirping insects. But as the unbearable pain travels through me, spreading like wild flames, the song starts to die down. One by one, the beeping insects are killed off.

"Did you get them?" the woman asks.

"Just a few more," the man says. Another injection of searing liquid lava erupts through me and my brain shrieks. I'm reminded of being burned alive at the stake. The pain was so intense, it eventually knocked me out, stole my consciousness. My body was merciful enough to shut down.

I can only pray that it does the same now.

The final insect beeps its last dying breath.

"Done," the man says.

"Good. Now that."

Another pinch near my left wrist. I recognize this anguish. The way it twists my bones and claws at my muscles. Rearranging cells. Reprogramming my blood. It's the same excruciation I remember from the genetic disguises we were forced to bear when we first left the compound.

This time, it's not focused on my face. It's focused on my wrist. Where my implant is. My tracking device. The permanent piece of me that connects me to my home. To Kaelen.

The pain keeps exploding in my lower arm. Like tiny detonations one after another. I want to scream for them to stop, but my voice is gone. Everything is gone except for this blinding cloud of torment that has settled around me.

One at a time, my eyelids are pried open. I hope to catch sight of whoever is doing this to me, match the dimly familiar voice with a face, but all I see is a giant hand descending. Its fat fingers rip the Lenses from my eyeballs. Then my lids snap closed again.

"Destroy them," the woman orders.

"On it."

I hear a rustle of movement. "We're running out of time. Are we clear yet?"

Someone grabs hold of my wrist, lifts it off the hard surface I'm lying on. "I think we're clear."

"You can't *think*," the woman scolds. "You have to *know*. If Alixter tracks her back to the camp, we're all dead."

There's a long, uneasy silence. A wordless war being waged somewhere above my head.

The man swallows. I can almost hear the lump in his throat scratching its way down. "We're clear," he finally says, uncertainty rattling his words.

"Take us up!" A shriek of an order. But it's obeyed. I feel a low rumbling beneath me, the stomach-dropping sensation of a hovercopter rising from the ground.

Once again, I try to cry out for Kaelen. Once again, I'm denied a voice.

"This plan of his better work," the woman mumbles under her breath as we soar higher and higher into the sky. "Otherwise, this will all be for nothing."

34

STRANGERS

I wake up in an arctic tundra. A freeze that clings to my bones. That saturates my blood, turning it to a river of floating ice.

I shiver violently, the contractions tensing my sore, listless muscles. The chill surprises me. I've never felt anything like it before. My body is designed to stabilize in extreme temperatures. Keep me warm when it's too cold and cool me down when it's too hot.

But this is something else.

My eyes flutter open. I blink and try to make sense of my surroundings. I'm outside. No, I'm inside.

No . . .

I'm outside, but shielded by cloth walls. Some kind of makeshift house?

The answer lumbers into my brain a moment later, far too slowly. Like my mind is struggling to access everyday definitions. Words and meanings that should come instantly, but don't.

Tent.

It's a tent. I'm lying on a rickety metal bed with no blankets. Nothing to shield me from this insufferable cold.

It's almost impossible to move, as though my limbs are literally frozen solid. Wiggling my fingers is a chore. Pivoting my head takes all my strength. But finally, I'm able to cast my gaze to my left arm, which is outstretched, draped across the edge of the bed. I follow it down, past my elbow, until I see my face-up palm.

My wrist.

Something is wrong with my wrist. It's completely smooth. Not a scar, not a freckle, not a thin black line.

My genetic implant is gone.

I sit up abruptly, seizing my wrist with my other hand. The sudden movement makes everything spin and warp. Like I'm seeing the room through one of those humorous distortion apps you can run on a ReflectoGlass.

What is happening to me?

I run my fingertip across the skin where my implant used to be.

I fight to access my most recent memories. I remember the farmer who charged the barriers with his tractor. I remember Kaelen attacking him. I hung back to assess the damage and that's when it happened.

I was taken.

By who?

What did they do to me? Where did they bring me? Wherever it is, I have to get out of here. I have to find a way to contact Director Raze.

It takes so much effort to pull myself to my feet. And when I do, the room does another full rotation, pulsing like a human heart. I grab on to something to steady myself. It's a pole in the center, presumably holding up this archaic structure.

The whole tent trembles under my weight.

I wait for another teeth-chattering shiver to pass through me before continuing toward a sliver of light coming from a small gap in the fabric wall of the tent.

"I wouldn't go out there," a voice says from somewhere

behind me. I jump and spin. My vision blurs, distorting the dark silhouette of a person sitting in the corner. Who has apparently been there the entire time.

How did I not hear him breathing?

My vision readjusts a moment later and a face finally comes into focus.

His face.

The boy who ruined my life. Who haunts my dreams and fuels my guilty conscience. The boy I can't forget, no matter how hard I try.

His name echoes deep in my brain, shuddering through me like a sob.

Lyzender.

He sits in a chair, his legs propped up on a small folding table. The soles of his shoes are coated in dark red dust. I squint to make out the object in his hand.

A book.

A real book made out of board and paper. Like the kind Dr. Rio used to collect.

I know that seeing him here in front of me—in this time— should make me lose my balance again. Should make it hard for me stand, speak, breathe. I should doubt his existence. Doubt my sanity. Argue with reason.

But I don't do any of those things.

Because in truth, it makes perfect sense. All the pieces fit. His promise to find me. The question asked during our live Feed interview. His blurry face in the footage from Jenza Paddok's court case.

I tried to convince myself none of it was real. A cruel trick of the imagination. But somehow, I could never quite succeed. No matter what I told myself, no matter what Dr. A assured me, one way or another, Lyzender's return seemed inevitable. Like I've been subconsciously waiting for it.

What *doesn't* make sense—what I find myself observing anxiously—is the unusual severity of his features. The hard line of his jaw. The dimness in his eyes.

"The tent is guarded," he goes on, glancing back at his open book, as though he couldn't care less about my presence. "They don't trust you."

He's not the boy from my memories. The boy who won me over with smoothly delivered lies and flowery promises. He looks older and there's a darkness about him. A sun that's forgotten how to shine.

Not that it matters to me in the slightest.

All that matters is that I find a way out of here.

"I'm the only reason you aren't in iron chains right now," he tells me, flipping the page.

"Where am I?" I ask.

"In a tent."

I'm racked by another chill. "Where? Antarctica?"

He raises a single eyebrow as he watches me shake. His face twitches ever so slightly—a flash of something, but it's gone before I can identify it. "Not exactly."

"Look," I say sharply, trying to ignore the bolt of electricity that passes through me when I look at him. "I don't know why you're working with a nutcase like Pastor Peder, but—"

"I'm not."

I'm startled by his admission.

He's not working with Pastor Peder?

Who else would want to kidnap me?

"Well, regardless, Diotech will find me here. They have methods to track me wherever I am. And when they do, they will punish you. In ways you don't even want to know."

"I'm quite familiar with Diotech's methods of punishment," he says casually, flipping another page. "As are most of the people here. But in regard to them locating you, I wouldn't count on that."

I rub my fingertip against my bare wrist, where my genetic implant used to be. Lyzender notices. "If only I'd been able to do that earlier, huh? This story would have turned out very differently."

I stop rubbing.

He closes the book and places it on the table. "Anyway," he goes on, stretching his arms above his head, "it's all gone. The implant, your Lenses, your Slate, even your nanosensors." He pins me with a gaze that I can feel deep in my gut. "Trust me, no one is going to find you here."

So that's what they were doing in the hover. That's what the fire blazing through me was. They were destroying my sensors—the microscopic robots programmed to transmit information about my vitals back to the Diotech network. It's how Dr. A knew I had snuck back onto the compound with Kaelen one year ago. When I was searching for the genetic Repressor to save Lyzender's life.

It's how I was counting on them finding me now.

But if he's telling the truth and they're really gone, it's hopeless.

"Who did this to me?" I demand.

He doesn't answer. He leans back in the chair, balancing on its rear legs.

"Lyzender," I growl.

"Oh, so you *do* remember me?"

"Of course I remember you."

He nods, as though he was expecting me to say that. "Sevan said you would."

Sevan.

I was right. He is involved in whatever this is. But where is he now? Is he *here*? Was he the voice I heard on the hovercopter? Was he the person who grabbed me in the crowd?

I try to boil all my questions down to one. "What is his part in all of this?"

Once again, I'm refused an answer. The only response I get is, "He warned me about what they did to you this time."

"What *they* did to me?" I snarl. "*They* fixed me! They made sure I wouldn't fall for your lies again. They *saved* me. From *you*."

"From *me*?" He slaps a hand to his chest so hard the sound makes me jump.

"Yes."

He tips his head back and lets out a deep, mocking laugh. There isn't an ounce of joy in it. "Wow. I'm flattered. Truly flattered. That I'm high enough on Alixter's flux list to be considered such a dangerous *threat*." He rubs his chin pensively. "Although that really doesn't say much about *them*, does it? That a harmless guy like myself could be so intimidating to a corporation as powerful as Diotech?"

His rant has left me speechless. I've never heard such venom come from his mouth before. The boy from my memories was sweet and gentle and mellow. He told stories to the children on the seventeenth-century farm where we lived. He won over the horse that hated me. He spoke to me with such tenderness.

Now something ugly and poisonous lives within him. It infects his voice, twists his laugh, tightens my chest.

"So that's it, huh?" He's glaring at me now, but it's not the same pair of eyes that stared back at me through the wall screen of our Los Angeles hotel. Those eyes were weary and distraught but there was no observable hate.

Not like now. Not like this.

"I'm out and he's in? Just like that?"

He doesn't actually say Kaelen's name but I can only assume it's who he's referring to. If it really was him who asked that question during the Feed interview, then he's seen us together. He watched that kiss.

"All because Dr. *Alixter*"—I despise the way he says his name, as though it's a made-up word—"convinced you I was the enemy?"

198

"You *are* the enemy," I whisper.

Because it's how Dr. A would want me to respond.

Because it's how Kaelen would respond.

Because it's the truth.

He launches to his feet, sending the chair clattering back. "Why?" he roars, color rushing to his face. "Because I loved you? Because I would have done *anything* for you?"

I catch his blatant use of the past tense. But it doesn't affect me. I don't love him anymore. Why should I care if he still loves me?

Especially when it wasn't even real.

What Lyzender and I had was an illusion.

"Because," I correct him, "you are working with your mother, Dr. Maxxer, to destroy Diotech."

He lets out another one of those unnerving derisive laughs. It sounds like a knife is chafing the inside of his throat. "Is that what he told you? Your precious Dr. *Alixter?*"

I nod but stay silent. Lyzender's erratic state is starting to frighten me. Not that I couldn't fight him and win. That's not what I'm afraid of.

I'm afraid I might have to.

"Well, at least Alixter got half of it right," he says. "I *am* trying to destroy Diotech. And I'm not the only one. But my mother is dead."

Dead?

The word sinks into my stomach and begins to rot.

"You mean," I begin tentatively, "because she eventually died? Of old age?"

I never assumed Dr. Maxxer would still be alive today. The last time I saw her was in the year 2032 after her transession gene had been repressed. She had to be at least fifty then. Which means today, in 2117, if she were alive she would be over 130. Normates have been known to live to 120. But 130? That's a stretch.

"No," Lyzender replies darkly, "because Dr. Alixter sent someone to kill her. On July 14, 2032."

"The day after I left her," I say aloud.

"Cody and I saw it on the news. A mysterious submarine bombing in the Kara sea, off the coast of Russia. Cody recognized the location immediately. He said you went there to find my mother."

"Rylan Maxxer? I can assure you she is not an issue. That problem has been dealt with."

Dr. A swore she was too crazy to be a threat. That her rants about a secret organization called the Providence were only signs of her delusion.

If that's true though, then why kill her?

"H-h-how?" I stutter. "How did he get to her? He outlawed transession a year ago. The gene hasn't been reproduced since."

"Maybe he sent someone before he outlawed the gene. Maybe even your boyfriend. Or . . ." Lyzender screws his mouth to the side, feigning deep, profound contemplation. "Maybe he lied to you." His mouth drops open, aghast. "But no! That's impossible. Dr. Alixter would never *ever* lie to anyone."

I shake my head in bewilderment. That scathing tone. That bitter sarcasm. Who is this person? Where did he come from?

Has he really changed that much in a single year?

"Diotech is trying to help people," I tell him boldly.

"Diotech is trying to *control* people."

No! a voice screams in my head. *Don't listen to him. He's trying to lure you back in. He's trying to deceive you again.*

"That's a lie," I assert, keeping my voice stern.

"Like all the other lies I told you?" He smirks, the sarcasm still thick in his tone.

"Yes."

He takes a step toward me. I instinctively take a step back. "So when I told you I loved you?"

I feel my legs starting to wobble. "Lie."

He takes another step. I retreat again. The tent wall is at my back now. I can't move any farther.

200

"And when I told you I'd always protect you?"

He's too close. His scent has reached me. It's masked by a layer of sweat and dirt, but my nose can still identify it. My mind can still pair it to memories.

Memories that should keep me from him.

Not draw me in.

"Lie," I say again.

Another step and he's upon me. His nose is inches from mine. The air that leaves his mouth is the same air I breathe in. "And when I told you I'd never stop looking for you?"

My throat is dry. I try to wet it but there's nothing to swallow.

Somehow, I am no longer cold. And I hate him for that.

I will my body to shiver again.

"Lie," I finally manage to squeeze out. But even I can hear the waver in my own voice.

He smiles. It's not playful. It's not spiteful. It's something else.

"Yet here we both are," he says.

His eyes travel to my lips. He watches them tremble. I press them tightly together.

"Don't," I warn him, hoping it will make me seem strong. Resolved. No longer the girl who was so easily tempted by those lips.

His mouth lingers close. His nose brushes against the tip of mine.

"Don't what?" he asks, presuming innocence.

I can hear my heart thundering in my chest.

Can he hear it, too?

After everything we've been through together, does he just know it's racing?

"Are you afraid I'm going to kiss you?" he asks. "Is that what you think?"

I draw all the oxygen in the world into my lungs and hold it.

I will push him away. I will muster all the pitiful strength I have left and use it to put as much distance between us as this tiny tent will allow.

"I want to talk to the person in charge," I assert, then I close my eyes. It's easier that way. Not to have to look at him.

I feel a rush of cold come back to me, like an arctic wind has swept in. When I open my eyes, he is already halfway out of the tent. "C'mon," he mumbles, "I'll take you."

35

HEROISM

I follow Lyzender out of the tent and into a world unlike anything I've ever seen. The site is so daunting and awe-inspiring that I involuntarily stop walking. It's nothing like the Diotech compound with its sleek metallic edges and synthetic walls and Versa-Screens that will show you anything you want. It's nothing like the cities we visited on the tour with their skyscraping towers and bustling MagCar expressways.

This is not a city at all.

It's a camp.

In the middle of the desert. A desert that looks not too dissimilar from the landscape that surrounds the compound.

A dozen or so people flutter through the maze of tents and fold-up tables. Some stop to stare at me like I'm an alien visiting from another planet. Most are too busy to notice me.

I once received an upload about the ancient cultures of our world. Savages, the upload called them. Long before technology and science and modern amenities, there were people who lived like this. In tents. With no climatization. No power. No sturdy walls to keep intruders out.

I can feel how hot the air is. I can see it in the damp clothing of the passersby, the sheen of sweat on their foreheads and necks. But inside, my body is still frozen. How can I possibly be this cold in the middle of the desert?

So many questions filter through my mind at once.

What is this place?

Who are these people?

Before I can take another step into their strange, primitive village, the barrel of a shotgun is thrust against my right temple. Out of the corner of my eye, I can just make out the weapon's owner: a tall man with green eyes and a tired, pinched face.

"Where do you think you're going?" he barks at me.

"Jase," Lyzender says, pushing the gun from my head. "It's fine. She's with me. I'm taking her to the war tent."

"Why isn't she cuffed?"

Lyzender chuckles. "She's not going anywhere."

I almost laugh at his ignorance. At his blind trust. Dr. A was right. Faith does make people stupid. If Lyzender thinks I have any loyalty to him—that I won't run from this place the moment I find the right window—then he's put his faith in the wrong person.

Jase looks unconvinced. Smart man.

"I'll take her there and escort her right back." Lyzender's patience is dwindling. "She won't leave my sight."

Has he completely lost his mind? Does he not remember how fast I can run? How strong I am? What makes him think he could stop me if I wanted to leave? The only reason I'm still standing here is because I choose to be.

The man stands firm, shaking his head. "No can do. Boss's orders. The girl is to remain in this tent."

"I don't take orders from your boss," Lyzender sneers.

"And I don't take orders from *you*."

I glance around the camp, searching for guard towers or borders, but for some reason I can't seem to see past the next row of tents. When I try to focus on the horizon, my vision swims and smudges. Like I'm looking through a dirty window.

I blink hard. What is wrong with my eyes?

I can hear Kaelen's voice in my head, telling me what to do.

Don't wait.

Run, Sera. Get help. Count your steps, remember landmarks, and lead us back there.

He's right. I don't know who is in charge of this camp, but I can't wait around to find out. I have to get back to the compound. This is my chance to be a hero in Dr. A's eyes. To prove my redemption once and for all.

After this, he'll never be able to doubt my devotion to the Objective again. He'll never be able to look at me like I'm a traitor. He'll see me as he sees Kaelen. A confidante. A friend. A daughter.

Lyzender is still arguing with Jase. Would this man shoot me if I ran? Would he even be able to hit me?

It depends on how good his aim is. How fast his reflexes are.

Not that I wouldn't heal if he does turn out to be a good shot.

I gauge my best route, quickly determining it's behind me, around the back of this tent, which appears to be positioned at the far edge of the camp. I blink again in frustration but something still seems to be malfunctioning with my vision.

I tell myself it doesn't matter. Once I get back to the compound, the scientists will be able to fix whatever's wrong with me.

I need to devise a distraction first. Something to divert Lyzender and Jase's attention and give me a head start. Just in case that hover they transported me on is still lurking around the camp somewhere. It shouldn't make a difference, though. With my speed, by the time they're able to get to it and start the engine, I'll be a mirage on the rippling desert horizon.

But a head start never hurt anyone.

I eye the small rickety table beside me, next to a chair I'm assuming Jase was occupying before our exit. On the table sits a jug of water, a plate of what appears to be browned meat, and an ancient communication device that my sluggish brain is telling me is called a walkie-talkie.

I take a deep breath, steeling myself for the challenge.

I hold Kaelen's bright blue-green eyes in my mind. This is what he'd want me to do. I'm sure of it.

His voice is back in my head, counting in Russian the way he always does when we start a challenge course in the training dome.

The training dome.

The compound.

Home.

I'll be home soon.

Odin, dva, tri!

I kick out one foot, knocking the table over with a splash and a *clatter*. As expected, Lyzender and Jase both startle and look to my left. I duck right, around the back of the tent, and take off.

Into the desert.

Into the unknown.

Toward redemption.

36

LEADER

I only make it a few steps before my lungs start to burn. I cough up hot, angry air. My legs tremble beneath me and I can tell from the passing scenery that I'm not moving very fast. I will my body to speed up. To run like only Kaelen and I can.

But it refuses to cooperate.

I'm still shivering but now I'm sweating as well. Sweating from the effort. From the heat. From the frustration.

What is happening to me?

I stop to catch my breath—something I've only ever seen people do on the Feed shows. My chest feels as though it's on fire. Fighting for oxygen. I rest my hands on my knees, panting wildly. I turn and look back to see if anyone is following me. I think I see silhouettes in the distance but my vision only blurs again. Everything melts together until I'm squinting at nothing but a smudged canvas of colors.

Keep going! I hear Kaelen's voice in my head. *Keep running!*

He's right. I don't know what's happening to my body, but I can't stop.

I turn my back to the camp and will my legs to move again. They reluctantly oblige. My lungs scream with every step. My thundering heart protests in my chest.

My feet slow, dragging heavily beneath me, until I'm barely shuffling through the desert dirt.

And then I collapse.

Hitting the ground hard.

Feeling the collision everywhere.

When I wake up, I'm dizzy and my head is throbbing. I'm back inside a tent. A different one. It's much larger and with better appointments. From the bed I'm lying on, I can see a large table in the center, littered with various maps and documents printed on real paper.

If I didn't know any better, I would think I had transessed two hundred years into the past. But my transession gene is gone. Dr. A made sure of that.

My whole body aches when I attempt to sit up, and I quickly find that my hands are bound to the bed frame with a pair of heavy handcuffs that feel like they're made from real metal, not the lightweight synthetics.

I blink the room into focus and see Lyzender standing by the entrance. He ducks his head out the flap and calls, "She's awake."

A moment later a woman strolls in. She's tall and slender with skin slightly darker than mine and thick, black hair that's been braided down her back. She's dressed in a simple pair of green pants and a soiled gray T-shirt. The sleeves have been torn off, exposing muscular arms and bronzed shoulders. Her skin is covered in markings. Not nanotats, but old-fashioned ink tattoos. The kind that are etched into your skin forever.

Even without spotting the small red crescent moon on the inside of her right palm, I recognize this woman from the Feed footage I watched in my hotel room.

Jenza Paddok.

The woman Director Raze promised me wasn't a threat.

I wonder what he'd say if he knew she'd successfully kidnapped me from right under his nose.

She's less polished than the woman I saw on my wall screen. A layer of grime and sweat almost baked into her skin. I can't help thinking that she would be pretty if it weren't for the animosity weighing down her features.

"Hello, Seraphina." I place her voice right away. She was with me in the hovercopter when they injected my veins with liquid fire.

"It's just Sera," I mumble.

She shares a quick glance with Lyzender before grabbing a chair from the table and straddling it. "As you wish, Sera."

"I don't think any of this is what I wish," I snarl.

Paddok turns to Lyzender. "Will you give us a moment alone?"

Lyzender stiffens, his eyes darting between us.

"I'll be quick," she assures him.

Reluctantly, he exits the tent, but I'm certain he hasn't gone far. My body heaves with a barrage of nasty coughs. It reminds me of the horrific sound Lyzender made when the transession gene was slowly killing him.

"Yeah, about that." Paddok offers me a cloth handkerchief but I refuse it and wipe the spittle from my mouth with my shoulder. "We had to take precautions to avoid"—she pauses and smiles— "well, what just happened."

Precautions?

"What did you do to me?"

"Don't worry. It's only temporary. A little concoction devised by a member of my team to dull your enhancements. An inhibitor of sorts. Essentially, it's keeping you sick and blocking your body's natural ability to heal itself." She lets out a soft laugh. "Welcome to the real world. It's flux, isn't it?"

"You turned me into a Normate?" I say it with such disgust I surprise even myself.

209

Paddok barks out an empty laugh. "Is that what Alixter calls us? It certainly has a nice ring to it."

There it is. Just for a flicker of a moment, I see behind her façade. I see her loathing for the man who created me.

"Anyway, you should be grateful that's *all* we did to you. Jase wanted to kill you and Feedcast it live."

I fight back a shudder. If Kaelen had to watch me die on a wall screen, he'd lose himself.

"He can be a bit dramatic," Paddok adds. "I, on the other hand, feel that you could be much more useful in other ways. Namely, getting us onto the Diotech compound."

"Well, you're wrong. It's a fortress. Even I don't know how to get in."

She smiles. "We'll see about that. I imagine Alixter will be pretty anxious to get his precious science experiment back."

"So that's your big plan?" I mock. "To use me to gain access to the compound? Then what? A few shotguns aren't going to stand up against Raze's security force."

She chooses not to respond to this. Instead, she says, "So, Lyzender tells me that you two used to be something of an item. Is that true?"

I turn my gaze to the ceiling. If she won't answer my question, there's no reason for me to answer hers.

"It's why he persuaded me not to lock you up." She nods toward my restraints. "I hope you'll forgive my change of heart."

When I don't speak, she goes on. "He also seems to think that given enough time here with us, you might actually come around. Join our side."

"I'll never join your side," I spit, breaking my vow of silence.

She sighs. "That's exactly what I told him. But he has this crazy notion that somewhere deep inside of you, there's a *real* person. With morals and a conscience and all that fancy stuff."

If she's hoping to get a reaction from me, she's going to be disappointed.

"I warned him though," she continues, "that you're a product of Diotech. That evil and corruption run in your blood. Quite literally. He refuses to believe me. He still thinks there's something redeemable about you."

Without my permission, my eyes drift to the entrance of the tent.

"I have to say," Paddok goes on, "I admire his faith. Even if I don't agree with it. I guess we all need to believe in something, right? It gives us a reason to get up in the morning. Something to fight for."

When I don't say anything, she stands and returns the chair to the table. Then she sticks her head out the flap and beckons Lyzender back inside. "Return her to the medical tent, will you? Our strategy meeting starts in an hour."

37

OFF-LINE

The last time my hands were bound was in the year 1609, when the townspeople of London believed I was a witch and arrested me. I had shown my special abilities in public. I had moved faster than their eyes could keep up with.

I had done it to save Lyzender.

And it landed me in prison. On trial for my life, and eventually, on a stake being burned alive.

That should have been my first clue right there. That should have alerted me to the fact that being with him is not safe. That it is not my true purpose.

But it didn't.

I was too far over the edge to recognize the dangers of loving him.

I won't make that mistake twice.

He doesn't hold on to my shackles as he guides me through the camp. He must know I'm not going to try to run away again. Not when the truth has been revealed to me and this debilitating poison is coursing through my blood, keeping me weak.

The bottom line is, I need another plan.

"So," I say to him, jogging slightly to walk by his side. The minimal effort leaves me winded. "Are you going to tell me how you got here?"

He flashes me a sideways look. "Whatever do you mean?" There's a playfulness mixed in with his acidic tone.

"Last time I saw you was in the year 2032. You were dying in a bed in Cody's town house."

He lets out a biting laugh. "I bet that pleased you, huh?"

"What? Of course not." The words are out of my mouth before I can stop them. Before I can analyze where they're coming from.

But it's evident to me now that they're coming from the past. From the girl who stood by his bedside weeping over his frail body, wondering if she would ever see him alive again.

Not the girl I am now.

He kicks a rock with the tip of his shoe. "Right." His sarcasm hangs in the air, swirling into the dust that's being roused by our footsteps.

I open my mouth to protest but to be honest, I don't know how to handle this brooding, rancorous boy I've never met before. The hopeless romantic spouting devotion and poetry? I had prepared myself for that. I had spent the last year building up a tolerance to it.

But this?

I just don't know what to say.

So I settle for the truth.

"I certainly didn't feel that way then," I admit softly.

He stops and faces me. "And now?"

I try to turn away but he grabs my chin and forces me to look at him. "No," he asserts, "you don't get to do that. You don't get to avoid me. Not anymore."

I tremble at his touch. It warms my glacial skin. For a moment, the shivers stop and I feel my blood heat again. Then his hand falls away and the cold front returns.

"And now what?" he asks. "You'd step over my dead body and keep on walking?"

I shake my head. Hoping it's enough. Knowing that it's not.

"What?" he demands.

"I . . ."

He bends to meet my downcast eyes. "You?"

"I . . . don't want you dead."

He tips his head back and laughs. "You don't want me dead? Really? How sweet. That's touching."

I shut my eyes tight, berating myself.

What kind of an answer is that?

It's a truthful one, sure. But it's not a complete one. I don't want to see him die. I don't want to see *anyone* die. I just don't want him here. With me. Touching me with those hands. Challenging me with those eyes.

I want him in the past where he belongs.

He keeps walking. I assume I'm expected to follow him so I do. The day is almost over. The sun is starting to set. As we pass through the camp, people stop what they're doing to watch us. To watch *me.*

I'm the anomaly. The one who doesn't fit in. The high-value prisoner whose face has been on every streamwork. On the cover of every DigiMag.

No one speaks to me. I wonder if they've been ordered not to.

I silently count them as we walk by. Twenty-two that I can see.

The conversation between Dr. A and Director Raze filters back through my mind.

"Child's play," was Dr. A's reaction to the size of Jenza's nonexistent army.

I wonder what he'd think of her now that she's managed to take me prisoner.

214

We've reached the tent on the far side of the camp. The one I woke up in. I now see the small white cross on the front, labeling it as a medical facility. Although the word *facility* is a stretch. The only things inside are a bed, a table, and a few outdated medical supplies that I somehow failed to notice when I was here before. I have a vague recollection of these supplies from my short stay in the hospital in the year 2013. My brain stretches to access the correct names for each instrument: stethoscope, blood pressure cuff, thermometer. Devices that have become obsolete since the invention of nanosensors.

I recall my nurse, Kiyana, fitting the stethoscope into her ears, pressing the cold plate against my chest. Waiting. Listening.

The memory of her causes me to ache a little. She was the first person to treat me like a human being. Not a miracle. Not a freak.

It suddenly hits me that these are all manual tools. Nothing that requires power or a SkyServer sync.

"She's gone completely off-line. Shut down all devices. There's no way to track her unless she turns something on."

She's staying off Diotech's radar.

A strategy I remember all too well.

I sit down on the bed and Lyzender comes over to fasten one end of my cuffs to the metal bed frame. Now if I want to go anywhere, I'll have to take this whole rusty contraption with me.

Once he's finished, he moves away quickly. As though being that close to me is dangerous.

I'm unsure what I'm supposed to do now. Wait? For what? For them to use me as bait?

Lyzender stands awkwardly in the center of the tent, equally unsure what comes next. Our eyes meet for a tense moment before he turns away and heads outside.

It's exactly what I want. I want him to go.

I used to pray for real silence. I used to savor any piece of it I could find.

But this is a new kind of silence. The kind that comes from being imperfect. And suddenly the thought of being left alone in it terrifies me.

"Cody," he says softly.

It takes me a moment to realize he's speaking to me. He hasn't left. He's standing in front of the flap, looking back at me.

"What?"

"Cody is the reason I'm here. He figured out how to reverse engineer the transession gene from the blood he took when I was sick. Before the gene was deactivated by your boyfriend." The disdain he places on the word *boyfriend* is palpable, but it's not the part I'm focused on.

"Cody rebuilt the gene?" I'm still having a hard time believing it.

"It took him three years."

Three years.

The number bounces around in my brain like a floating Mag-Ball caught between two goalposts.

It's only been one year for me, but for Lyzender, it's been three. Which means he's now twenty-one years old.

He waited that long to come back here? Just so he could stop the Objective? Just so he could see Diotech destroyed?

Why?

As soon as I ask myself the question, I realize I don't know the answer. It's the first time I've ever wondered about Lyzender's motives.

Dr. A told me that Lyzender's mother, Dr. Maxxer, wanted to destroy Diotech because she was angry. Because Dr. A exiled her from the compound.

Does Lyzender share those same motivations?

Is he trying to avenge her death?

But he never liked his mother. He always spoke about her with such contempt. Was that all an act, too?

216

It suddenly seems so incredulous that he would hold someone else's grudge for that long.

Is it possible he came back for another reason?

"What did you do during those three years while Cody worked on the gene?"

"I waited." He looks down at his dirt-caked shoes. "For you."

"For me to do what?" I ask, even though I already know what he's going to say.

"For you to come back. For you to send me a sign that you were okay. When you didn't, I knew they had gotten to you again."

Somewhere inside of me I'm screaming.

Don't listen. Don't believe. Don't fall.

He scoffs, "But those are all just lies, right? I never *really* loved you."

"Right," I whisper. Whether or not he heard me is irrelevant.

I heard.

The conviction is logged in my memories.

He doesn't speak again for a long time. It feels like every possible combination of words flits through my mind at once. None of them are the right one.

"Well," he says after a while, clearing his throat. "Good night."

The flap swishes closed behind him, and just as I suspected, the silence is deafening.

38
PARTS

Night settles in. One by one, I watch lanterns illuminate, casting misshapen shadows on the cloth walls. Every once in a while, a figure will tromp past but no one bothers to enter. I count how long it takes for them to disappear and the silence to return.

The inhibitor in my blood keeps me chilled in the evening desert heat. I find a blanket under the bed and struggle with my free hand to spread it over me. It's thin and made from a scratchy material. It does nothing to stop the shivering.

After almost an hour, a girl ducks through the flap. She's pretty and petite with dark skin and silky black curls that frame her slender face. She looks to be about my age and I wonder how someone so young could be involved in something like this.

She stands by the door with her back to me. I hear the striking of a match and then the lantern on the table is illuminated. The warm light is a welcome addition to this dreary place.

I used to be able to see in the dark. Now that my abilities have been blocked, I understand what it means to be afraid of it.

She sets a plate of food down on the floor near my bed, just barely within reach. I squint at the murky brown lumps but fail to identify them.

"Thank you," I say, my teeth chattering.

She turns to me and I see a face devoid of sympathy. "Paddok told me to do it."

The message is clear. She's not doing this for me and therefore she won't accept my gratitude.

She pauses, glancing up and down my covered body. I can't help but notice the repulsion that distorts her features. Then she leaves. And I'm alone again.

I count three minutes of absolute stillness after her footsteps fade.

It's enough for me to deduce that no one else is coming this way. Stretching my bound arm as far as it will go, I hook the bottom of the plate with the toe of my shoe and drag it toward me. One sniff informs me that it's meat. And not the synthetic kind. The scent of cooked flesh rolls my stomach and I push it away again, even though I'm pretty much famished. I haven't eaten since the meal at the hotel before we left for the Feed station.

It feels like a century ago when it was really only this morning.

I wonder what Kaelen is doing right now. I wonder how long it took them to notice I was gone. They must be going out of their minds trying to locate my signals. Running their satellite search for my genetic implant.

Did they return to the compound? Did they cancel the remainder of the tour? I can't imagine they'd proceed without me. How would they possibly explain that to the public? No doubt whatever story Dane concocted to cover what really happened earlier today is all over the Feed right now.

If only I could figure out how to get a message to them.

Just as the thought enters my mind, I'm struck with an idea.

Lyzender knows about Kaelen. He was the one who asked that

question during the first live interview. Which means there has to be a device somewhere around here—a screen, a Slate, something!—that can connect to the SkyServer. Maybe it's simply been turned off. Or maybe its signal has been scrambled to make it untraceable.

I yank my cuffed hand, cringing at how loudly the metal bangs against the bed frame. I try to squeeze my hand out, but the hole is too narrow. I'd surely take off several layers of skin in the process. And in my current condition, who knows how long that would take to heal.

I lean forward and examine the cuff itself. The keyhole is small and round. I saw Lyzender put the key in his pocket after securing me, but perhaps there's something else I could cram in there to try to trigger the locking mechanism. Something very straight and narrow.

Something like . . .

I reach up and feel my hair. Although the half-swirl that Crest attempted is now a giant mess, there are still some nanopins intact.

I pull one of them from my head and insert it into the lock, maneuvering it around until the end catches on something. I give it a firm tug and the cuff slides open.

"Thank you, Crest," I whisper as I reinsert the pin into my hair, just in case I might need it later.

The camp is empty when I slip outside of the tent. I assume everyone is at the strategy meeting Paddok mentioned but since I have no idea where it's being held, I'm going to have to tread as quietly as I can.

Balancing on my toes, I weave through the tents, stopping behind each one to listen for voices before proceeding inside. I find it difficult to maneuver in the dark. I trip over many unseen things and barely manage to stop myself from falling.

Is this what it's like for everyone else?

Being blinded by the darkness? Left vulnerable by the night?

I riffle through boxes and bags and search under beds, but I find nothing capable of transmitting a signal.

Most of the tents are arranged for sleeping, except for one particularly large one that clearly serves as some kind of food pantry. The stench of death instantly fills my nostrils, making me queasy. On a large table in the middle lies an assortment of dead animals in varying stages of preparation. Several skinned rabbits, an unidentified creature that's been hacked to pieces, and a fully intact deer with eyes frozen open in terror.

I hold back the bile rising in my throat and duck outside.

I'm able to check four more tents before I hear the soft din of voices. I follow the sound as it guides me to an outdoor dining area of sorts. Wooden tables and benches are set up around a dying fire. Every seat is taken. I count twenty-five people in all, including Paddok, who stands in the center. I scan the small crowd but it's too dark to make out any of their faces.

They seem to be in the midst of some kind of debate. They talk over one another, fighting to be heard. Paddok eventually quiets the dispute with a raise of her hand.

"There will be no more discussion about the girl." Her voice is firm and decisive. Her eyes flick in my direction and I duck behind a tent before she can spot me, straining to hear what's being said.

"We will use her to gain access to the compound and plant the device in the underground server bunker as originally planned."

I feel my breath catch. No one is supposed to know about the server bunker. It's where *all* of Diotech's data is stored. Project files, memory downloads, personnel records, system backups. Everything. Dr. A didn't trust any outside data security firms to protect the data, so he built an impenetrable bunker somewhere underneath the compound and told no one about it. Except the man tasked with keeping it a secret.

The only reason I'm even aware of its existence is because I once overheard Dr. A and Director Raze talking about it in the late hours of the night.

Every other Diotech employee believes the data is housed in a server room in the Intelligence Command Center, but it's just a front. A room with a bunch of processing servers and pods of dummy data. Fool's gold. The true heart of Diotech is buried deep within the earth.

And somehow someone here knows about it.

I try to assure myself that it doesn't matter. Even if they know about the bunker, they'll never be able to get this mysterious "device" Paddok is talking about past Director Raze. Every vehicle that enters the compound is thoroughly scanned. There's a force field protecting the airspace that no unauthorized hovers can pass through. Not to mention the agents in the ICC always override control of any visiting crafts as a safety protocol.

Sneaking *anything* into that compound is virtually impossible.

"So far everything has progressed smoothly," Paddok is saying. "Thanks to Sevan, the girl is no longer traceable by any of Diotech's technology."

I was right. It was Sevan in that hovercopter filling my veins with lava. I bet it was him outside the Feed station as well. Who Modified me and carried my body away. He might know about the bunker from scanning my memories, but he wouldn't know *where* it was located.

"There is still much to be done before we can launch this attack," Paddok goes on. "We all have our roles and we certainly all have our motives."

A round of hushed murmurs permeates the group.

"The most important thing to remember, however, is that we work together. If we want to pull this off, there is no room for error or discord. We must cooperate as a single unit. That is the only way we will successfully bring this company to justice."

I struggle to make sense of what I'm hearing, but my thoughts are wispy and chaotic and I can't seem to hold on to any of them long enough. My heart is racing so fast, I swear it must be feed-casting my location to the entire camp.

"Diotech issued an official statement today," Paddok continues. "As suspected, they aren't mentioning anything to the public about the kidnapping. Here's the playback from the Feed earlier today."

My hopes lift as I hear a shuffling of some sort and then the unmistakably cheerful voice of Dane. I peer my head around the tent to see Paddok hoisting up a rectangular screen for the rest of the group to see.

A Slate!

I knew they had to have one here. Which confirms my original thought. The signal must be masked or scrambled.

I squint at the tiny screen and listen to Dane's speech from a Diotech-monogrammed press podium. "We are saddened to have to delay the remaining stops of our ExGen publicity tour due to a sudden illness that has befallen Dr. Jans Alixter, the president of Diotech Corporation. I assure you he is being treated with the best possible care and we expect a speedy and complete recuperation, at which time we will resume the tour and continue to the designated cities on our itinerary."

So that's how they're covering for my absence. Making up an imaginary illness for Dr. A. Obviously they couldn't claim that I'm sick.

"Dr. Alixter wanted me to express his apologies for this delay and pass along this personal message to you." Dane clears his throat and blinks twice, accessing something on his Lenses. " 'I look forward to the day when our ExGen product line will finally be available to the public and neither I nor anyone else will be burdened by the inconvenience of illness.' " Dane flashes a hurried smile. "Any questions?"

The cams pan to the audience as hundreds of hands go up at once.

"Can you comment on the attack earlier today? Has this in any way impacted the schedule of the tour?"

Dane shifts his weight from foot to foot. "The attack was unfortunate. For reasons we cannot even fathom, this madman, who goes by the name of Graw Levens, felt the need to try to inflict harm on our ExGens."

I hear someone at the camp snort. "*You people* are the madmen."

"Fortunately," Dane goes on, "we had Kaelen's reflexes and strength to protect us from the wrath of this clearly troubled soul. But no, the episode today and the timing of our tour delay were purely coincidental."

Paddok lowers the screen, clearly not interested in hearing the next question, and I slip back behind the shield of the tent.

I have to get to that Slate.

"As expected," Paddok says to the group, "they are lying to cover up what really happened. But they'll be using all their resources to get to the bottom of it. So we have to stay on task and move forward as quickly as possible. How is the device coming?"

"The device is almost finished," someone replies. A male voice. "Lyzender is going to retrieve the final part we need tomorrow. It will take me a day or two to install it and make it compatible with the other components, but we should be ready to go in a few days."

"Thank you, Klo," Paddok says. "You've been an invaluable asset to this team."

Klo?

Klo Raze?

As in Director Raze's son?

Once again, I steal a peek around the edge of the tent and stifle a gasp as I make out the blue tips of his hair, confirming that this *is*, in fact, the boy from the compound. The one who watched me so curiously from the Rec Field the day before we left for the tour.

Pieces are falling into place faster than I can process them. If Klo has access to any of his father's security clearances, there's no end to what he can accomplish.

I retrace the last twelve hours in my mind. The transmission to Director Raze in the hovercopter, alerting us that we couldn't land on the roof. The makeshift barriers that were erected on the ground. Graw Levens smashing through the gaps in the syntho-glass on his MagTractor. Paddok said something about how he died for the cause.

There was no construction on the roof.

It was all a setup. The transmission. The farmer. The tractor.

A necessary distraction.

They knew it would cause a big enough commotion to divert attention so they could deactivate me with a Modifier and carry me away without anyone noticing. They just weren't counting on Kaelen's violent streak.

They weren't counting on anyone dying in the process.

Klo helped facilitate the whole thing. He knew where we were going to be. He would have had access to the tour schedule, to Raze's earplant, to everything. I expect he's the one who has been masking the Slate signal. So they can turn it on without the risk of being tracked down by Diotech.

And worst of all, he's probably the one who told Paddok about the bunker.

How is it possible that a traitor has been living within the compound walls, in the same *apartment* as the head of security, and no one knew?

Dr. A evidently has more enemies than he realizes.

My mind is yanked back to the meeting as Paddok asks Klo another question. "And you're certain they won't be able to detect the device once it's complete?"

"No way. The origins of the pieces are too diverse. They'll never register on a Diotech satellite scan. My father built these systems. They're programmed to pick up frequencies from devices created in the last fifty years. Lyzender hasn't brought us anything from the past century. We'll be able to pass it right under their noses. They won't even know what hit them until it's too late."

"Very good," Paddok commends. "Okay, people. Excellent work so far. Only a few more days to go and this nightmare will be over. Are there any other discussion points before we wrap up for tonight?"

I know I should move. I should get back to the tent before this meeting is adjourned and someone finds me here, but the shock of everything I've overheard has rendered my legs useless.

"Lyzender hasn't brought us anything from the past century."

I don't know how I didn't put it together before. I suppose I was too busy dealing with his presence here to fully analyze his involvement in the plan.

The shotguns. The walkie-talkies. The manual medical instruments. The books.

Old, outdated equipment that hasn't been in supply for over fifty years. And all of it is small enough to be carried by hand.

Lyzender has been using his reengineered transession gene to transport supplies from the past. And tomorrow he's retrieving the final piece to some undetectable explosive device.

He didn't come back for me.

Dr. A was right all along. Lyzender is here for one reason and one reason only: to destroy Diotech.

And it's up to me to stop him.

39

PRETENSES

Somehow I manage to slip back into the medical tent, into my cuffs, and under the scratchy blanket before anyone seems to notice that I'm gone. When I hear the first sets of footsteps outside, I pretend to be asleep. I don't want to talk to anyone right now. I have too much to think about.

This crazy group of people—these terrorists—are going to use me to destroy Diotech.

It wasn't Pastor Peder that Dr. A needed to be worried about. It was this tiny, seemingly insignificant army hidden in the desert. It was his own people. People he trusted. People Raze trusted.

As I lie in the dark and listen to the camp grow still, I make a decision. I make my own pledge for revenge.

They betrayed us and now I will betray them. I will find a way to warn the compound about their plan. I will make sure they never succeed. But before I can do that, I have many holes to fill. There's still so much I don't know.

Primarily, their plan for getting past Raze's security and getting this device onto the compound.

Paddok said they're going to use me to gain access, but how? Even if I'm sent in there alone, Diotech will still conduct their usual scans of any vehicle I'm traveling in. This device Lyzender is helping to build may not register on Diotech satellites but it'll certainly be detected during an internal inspection.

I need more information.

Several more pairs of feet pass by the outside of the tent before I hear someone stop. The tall, thin silhouette of a man appears on the fabric wall. He seems to be debating whether or not to enter.

I hold my breath and wait. Hoping it's him and praying it's not at the same time.

A moment later, the flap pulls away and Lyzender appears. His features catch the light of the lantern on the table. He doesn't smile when our eyes meet. The change in him still disorients me. He always used to smile when he saw me. No matter what was happening, no matter what danger was lurking just outside our reach, he would always take the time to smile. To promise me that everything would be all right.

Now, those kinds of assurances seem to be very far down on his list of priorities.

"Did you enjoy your late-night stroll through the camp?" he asks, one eyebrow arching.

So much for going unnoticed.

His gaze slides to my chained hand, still secured to the bed frame. "How did you get out of the cuffs?"

I feign innocence. "I don't know what you're referring to. I've been here the whole time."

His expression tells me this game is not worth my time.

"Did you pick the lock?" He glances around the small space. "With what?"

"Maybe I transessed out of them?" I keep my voice light,

almost playful. "Maybe I traveled to the past and stole the key? Oh wait, I forgot—stealing things from the past is *your* job."

I watch his jaw tighten. "Paddok sent me here to find out what you overheard. I guess that answers her question. Not that it matters. The plan is moving forward regardless of what you know. In your condition, I doubt you'll be able to do much to stop it anyway."

"What makes you think I *want* to stop it? Maybe I want to help."

He cackles. "Somehow I doubt that."

"You don't know what I want."

"I know *exactly* what you want."

I mirror his eyebrow arch. "Then tell me."

He stalks purposefully toward the bed. I have to fight the instinct to push myself back against the frame. When he reaches me, he places one hand on either side of my covered legs and bends down so that we're eye to eye. So that I can't look anywhere else but at him.

"You want to get back to your glossy ExGen boyfriend. You want to prance around in sparkly dresses and be the good little spokesmodel you were built to be. You want to prove to your precious Dr. Alixter that you're not the traitor he thinks you are. But what you don't know—what maybe someday you'll actually realize if you wake the glitch up—is that you'll never succeed. Because you'll never be able to prove something that's not true. I know you better than you know yourself, Seraphina. But that's easy when all you do is lie to yourself."

For a tense moment, the only sound is the rattling my cuff is making against the bed frame as I try to keep my hands from shaking. Lyzender's breath is hot on my mouth. His fierce stare is almost frightening.

"What about you?" I manage to fire back.

He stands up with a chuckle and crosses his arms over his chest. "What about me?"

"What are you getting in exchange for being Paddok's transession errand boy?"

He doesn't understand the question.

"What did she offer you in return for confiscating goods from the past?" I rephrase.

"What makes you think she had to offer me anything? Our agendas are perfectly aligned."

"Destroying Diotech?" I confirm.

He nods. "Right you are."

But there's something insincere in his voice that sets off an alarm in my brain.

"You look disappointed," he remarks. "Were you hoping I'd say I'm doing it in exchange for you?"

"For me?"

"I help her out, I get you in the end."

"I'm not a commodity you can trade," I argue.

He tilts his head, pondering. "That's not technically true. You certainly are a commodity to Diotech."

Irritation boils in my chest. "Well, that's not what I was hoping you'd say, anyway."

He finds amusement in my reaction. "Good. Because I'm not doing this for you. For once in my whole glitching life, I'm not doing something for you."

"Good."

"Good," he says again.

Silence falls upon the tent. Neither of us dares to speak or move.

I start to shiver. I despise my own weakness right now. I despise how vulnerable it makes me feel. I command my teeth to stop chattering. My skin to stop prickling with tiny, unsightly bumps.

It's no use.

Lyzender lets out an exasperated sigh, as though this whole

exchange is terribly inconvenient for him. He stalks out of the tent without another word.

I roll onto my side and face the wall, resting my cheek uncomfortably on my bound arm.

Surprisingly, Lyzender returns less than a minute later. I turn to see he's carrying a blanket. This one looks much thicker and warmer. He tosses it haphazardly over me, as though he couldn't care less where it lands.

We both know he could leave right now. He could walk out and not look back. And for a moment, that appears to be exactly what he's going to do.

But after another loud sigh, he approaches the bed and takes the time to tuck the edges of the blanket under my trembling body, capturing the wondrous heat inside.

A memory begins to form in my mind. One that I'm sure will bring its fair share of grief and remorse. Like they all do. I try everything I can think of to keep the memory at bay—counting, multiplying, dividing—but it crashes through my mental barriers.

Lyzender wrapping me in a blanket.
Lyzender catching me in his arms as I fall.
Lyzender carrying me to a makeshift bed on the floor.

It was the year 2013. In an empty kindergarten classroom. The mysterious boy had just told me his version of the truth about who I was. Of course, it was mostly fabrication. Embellished to make me feel anger toward the scientists and corporation that gave me life.

But the sensation is what I remember most clearly now. The way it felt to be so close to him. Wrapped in his steady compassion.

For a spark of a moment, I feel traces of that same compassion as he reaches over me to secure the final corner of the blanket under my shoulder. As his hand lingers a second too long on my arm. His gaze a second too long on my face.

Then, like a gust of cold air, the moment is over.

The compassion is gone.

Because he's gone.

40

NOURISHED

I sleep horribly. I don't know if it's a side effect of whatever toxin they've pumped into my veins, the fact that this is the farthest I've been away from Kaelen in over a year, or the memory of my conversation with Lyzender replaying over and over in my mind, but the next eight hours are racked with nightmares and restless tossing and damp sweat that freezes to my skin like a layer of winter frost.

I'm grateful when I open my eyes and see that daylight has finally broken outside my tent. I count the minutes until the footsteps start—twenty-two—and until someone enters my tent—another seventeen.

It's the same girl who came to bring my evening meal and light my lantern the night before. She's holding another plate of food. Without uttering a word to me, she sets it down next to the untouched plate from yesterday and turns to leave.

I wince when I look down to see more cooked animal flesh. I'm almost hungry enough to give it a try but then I think about the poor deer lying dead on that table and my appetite vanishes.

"Is there anything to eat besides meat?" I ask, stopping her at the flap.

"Unless you want to use your superpowers to magically sprout vegetables out of your ears, then no."

I can't help wondering if everyone here is as disgusted by my presence as this girl is. How can they hate me so much when they don't even know me? Is it because of where I come from? Because I was created by Diotech? What reasons do they have for despising a company that has cured countless diseases? Prevented a disastrous energy crisis? Improved the standard of living all over the world?

Why would they want to destroy an entity that's trying to help people?

"What's your name?" I ask the girl, hoping to draw some information out of her. Start a dialogue. Maybe if I can understand their motives better, I'll have an easier time stopping them.

"Why? So you can report me to Dr. Alixter and have my face mutilated or my brain turned to mush?"

I blink in shock. "What? No. He wouldn't do that."

Even as I say it, I see a flash of Rio's dull, unblinking eyes from that early morning in the Agricultural Sector. When he called me Sariana. His daughter's name.

We have to punish our enemies. Otherwise, how will we stop more people from betraying us?

The girl laughs. It's a hard, abrasive sound that chafes the air. "You clearly don't know him as well as I do."

"I . . ." I fumble to form a sentence. "I thought since you seem to come in here often, I should know your name."

She gives me a harsh stare that chills me even more than I already am. "I'm not here by choice. Trust me, it's not my lifelong dream to bring you deer meat."

My stomach rolls. So it is the deer on my plate.

"But you're *here* by choice, aren't you? In this camp? With these people?"

She doesn't respond. Although she looks like she wants to.

"Or is Paddok holding you against your will?" I push, seeing that I'm having an effect on her.

"Paddok is doing what needs to be done. It's about time someone did."

I nod like I see her point. "No one can deny her passion. It's certainly inspiring. I'm just wondering where it comes from."

"Where what comes from?" she snaps.

"All that energy. That drive. I mean, what could Diotech possibly have done to her to warrant such an excessive reaction?"

The instant it's out of my mouth, I know it was the wrong thing to say.

"You don't have a glitching clue what you're talking about!" she roars. "So I suggest you keep your pretty mouth shut."

"Whoa, whoa, what's going on in here?" The flap swings open and into the tent walks the tall and gangly Sevan Sidler.

Under normal circumstances, I would be happy to see him. He's always gone out of his way to be nice to me. He's always felt trustworthy. Now I know the truth about him. How he betrayed us. How he kidnapped me. Injected my veins with a fiery poison.

His eyes dart uneasily to the girl.

"Xaria," he says to her, "your mother is looking for you."

She gives me one more venomous glare before turning to leave. As she goes, she scuffs the ground with the toe of her shoe. It catches the side of the plate she just set down, spilling the meat into the dirt.

Sevan bends to scoop it up. "Don't mind her. She's been grouchy since you got here." He dusts off the meat and returns it to the plate, offering it to me. I shake my head.

"You have to eat something."

"I can't eat that."

"Believe me, it's much better than the synthetic flux they serve on the compound."

"The synthetic flux was never alive."

"Can't argue with that." He peers over his shoulder at the tent door, then slips his hand into the pocket of his pants, drawing out two small capsules. "Here," he says. "You didn't get these from me."

Warily, I take the pills. "What are they?"

"NutriCaps. All the nutrients and hydration your body needs. Plus, they curb the hunger cravings. They're manufactured by Diotech. That's why they're not very popular around here. But if you don't eat, you'll die."

I guess that would be one way to foil their plan.

I stare down at the two clear capsules in my hand. After what Sevan did to me yesterday, can I even trust these are what he says?

"Don't worry," he says, reading my hesitation. "I'm not trying to poison you."

"Yeah, because you already did."

He chuckles. "Touché. And sorry about that, but it had to be done." He nods toward the pills. "They'll help with the cold, too."

I toss the capsules into my mouth and swallow. I feel the hollowness in my stomach start to disperse almost instantly. "Thanks."

"Don't mention it. I've got a whole supply in my tent. I wasn't sure how my body would handle real meat." He picks up a chunk of dusty venison from my plate, rips off a piece, and chews. "Turns out it's pretty good."

"Who was that girl?"

Sevan glances behind him. "Who? Xaria? She's the daughter of a former Diotech employee. Her mother, Dr. Solara, used to run the memory labs. She was actually my boss, but she was terminated after a bunch of files were stolen under her watch."

"What files?"

He takes another bite, chomping furiously. "Your files."

This surprises me. "Someone stole my memory f—?"

But the answer hits me before I even finish the question.

"Lyzender," I murmur.

He returned to the compound after we escaped and I woke up in the year 2013 without any memories. He stole them for me and transported them on the cube drive so he could show me the truth about my past.

Or rather his distorted, glitched-up version of the truth.

"Is that why she hates me?" I ask. "Because her mother was terminated after he stole memory files for me?"

Sevan teeters his head from side to side. "Among other things, yes."

"What other things?"

He pops the last of the meat into his mouth and wipes his greasy hands on his pants. "Let's go for a walk."

"Where?"

"I thought I'd show you around the camp."

I shiver at the thought of leaving this bed and the warmth of my new thick blanket. "No, thank you."

"C'mon," he urges. "It'll be fun. Well, maybe not like fun fun but it'll be good for you to get out of this tent, stretch your legs, breathe some fresh air. I'll introduce you to some interesting people."

The thought of possibly gathering more intelligence about Paddok's plan of attack is what eventually convinces me to mutter my agreement.

I clank my cuff against the bed frame, reminding him that I'm not exactly free to roam around.

Sevan snaps to attention. "Oh, right." He pulls a key from his pocket but doesn't completely release me. He unlocks the cuff from the bed and swiftly fastens it to his own wrist.

237

"Now you can't go anywhere without taking me with you," he jokes.

I glare at him.

"Look, it's not for me," he explains, nodding toward the outside. "It's for them."

He gives my wrist a tug. I brace for the cold and peel the blankets from my body with my free hand. He helps me out of the bed, offering his shoulder for me to lean on as we shuffle toward the door.

"It's warped, isn't it?" he asks.

"What?"

"Being a Normate."

"Are all of you this helpless?"

He laughs. "Not all of us."

"This is what Dr. A is trying to prevent, you know? This kind of weakness."

Sevan pulls back the tent flap and guides me through it. "Dr. Alixter is trying to prevent a lot of things, Sera, but human weakness isn't one of them."

41

INCENTIVES

"How long have you been a part of this?" I ask Sevan as we hobble into the center of the camp. I lean on his arm way too much but he doesn't seem to mind. So far, he's kinder than anyone else has been to me since I got here. We've only been outside for a few minutes and already I've gotten half a dozen repulsed glares.

"For a while now."

"Dr. A never knew?"

"The only people who knew are here right now."

I think back to the last time I saw Sevan. At our hotel in Atlanta. "You destroyed my memory files, didn't you? After that last scan? That's why I was out so long."

He cocks an eyebrow. "We were so close to extracting you. If Dr. Alixter got wind that anything was amiss, we wouldn't have been able to go through with the plan."

"Why?" I ask, doing little to hide my disapproval. "Why would you deceive him like that?"

Sevan smiles. "You and I are acquainted with two very different versions of Jans Alixter."

I scowl. "And what version are *you* acquainted with?"

He doesn't answer. Instead, he points to the man who shoved the shotgun barrel in my face yesterday. He's sitting at one of the wooden tables in the dining area, chomping ferociously on a chunk of deer meat. When he sees me, he eyes his shotgun leaning against the edge of the table. "That's Jase Plummer. He's from New Orleans. Three years ago, his baby daughter died during childbirth. Not even a minute old."

I recoil. "That's horrible. Why didn't they use an artificial womb?"

"They did. Diotech-manufactured. Their doctor convinced them it was the safest option. Little did they know, the womb they ordered was part of a faulty batch that shouldn't have been released into the marketplace. Diotech failed to test it properly. About three thousand babies died that month. Jase's wife killed herself shortly after. By pumping her veins full of Cv9."

Cv9. A heavy sedation drug. Ten times stronger than a Relaxer. Also manufactured by Diotech.

"You can't be sure that Diotech was responsible for the faulty wombs," I argue. "A lot of other factors could have contributed."

Sevan snickers darkly. "You sound just like the Diotech lawyers. Dr. Alixter was able to pin the blame on one of their distributors, claiming that the wombs were damaged in transit."

He points in the opposite direction, toward a man working on the engine of a hovercopter, presumably the same one that was used to transport me here. "That's Davish Swick. Former owner of Swick Worldwide, the transit company that used to handle the bulk of Diotech's distribution. The company was obliterated after Diotech claimed they were responsible for the death of three thousand babies. The case went to trial. Diotech won. No surprises there. Some might argue it was because Swick really *was* responsible for the faulty wombs. Others—like, say, a Memory Coder who was in charge of altering the memories of the technicians who tested the wombs—would probably argue differently."

Davish Swick watches me with distrustful eyes as we pass.

Next, Sevan points to a short raven-haired woman carrying a wicker basket full of clothes. "Leylia Wong. She was a scientist on the verge of a miraculous breakthrough that would have allowed us to use our waste as fuel. It would have solved the energy crisis and the pollution crisis, but her lab was suddenly shut down. Without warning. Her funds were cut. When she tried to move her research to her own garage, she found all of her files had mysteriously vanished from the SkyServer. Maybe it's just a coincidence that Diotech was about to announce the four-trillion-dollar implementation of the nationwide MagLines, a project that would have been rendered completely irrelevant if Leylia's research had seen the light of day." He shrugs. "Or maybe not."

He gestures toward a stout, unkempt man exiting the food tent where I stumbled upon the dead animals last night. "And that's Nem Rouser. His family owned a small cattle ranch in Montana for almost two hundred years. Until Diotech released a new line of synthetic meats and all the cattle ranches were shut down."

I shake my head. "Now you're stretching the truth to try to make a point. Diotech *had* to create the synthetic meat because the cows were dying from Bovine Liver Disease. I learned about it in an upload *you* gave me."

Sevan shrugs. "Chicken or the egg, I suppose."

I frown. "What does that mean?"

"It means, it's just a little suspicious that Diotech had the synthetic meats ready to launch into the marketplace *right* as the BLD crisis hit."

"Are you claiming Diotech purposely spread liver disease to the cows?"

He raises his eyebrows, mocking me. "Wouldn't that be scandalous?" Then he points toward a bulky, muscular man walking in the direction of Paddok's tent. Although *walking* is a nice way to put it. It's more like a rickety hobble. His shoulders are hunched forward and one of his feet drags heavily and lifelessly behind the other.

"You probably never met Olin Vas during your time on the compound."

"Okay, okay." I stop him, not wanting to listen to another devastating story. "I get it. You all have a reason to hate Diotech. It still doesn't mean—"

But the breath is knocked out of me when Olin, having heard his name, turns to look at us. I have to stifle the scream that bubbles up in my throat at the sight of his face. It's the most ghastly thing I've ever seen. The left side is completely deformed. Like someone stretched out the skin and rearranged his features. His eye droops past the tip of his nose. His left ear is completely gone, and his hair on that side only grows in small tufts, leaving behind giant bald spots that are patched in ugly red sores.

Not unexpectedly, he gives me a scowl and pushes his way into Paddok's tent. I'm grateful for his disappearance. I'm not sure how much longer I'd be able to look at him.

"That is how Diotech treats its ex-employees," Sevan says. If I didn't know any better I would think he was actually *enjoying* my reaction to all this.

"He worked for Diotech?" I ask in disbelief.

"Agent Vas used to be on Director Raze's security force. Until he was framed for one of the director's mistakes."

Director Raze makes mistakes?

Well, underestimating Jenza Paddok was certainly one of them.

"What was it? The mistake?" I ask.

"You," he says casually.

"Me?"

"The first time you and Lyzender attempted to escape."

A hint of acid stings the back of my throat.

I know about this. It was one of the erased memories that was restored after my return to the compound last year.

Lyzender convinced me to run away with him. He showed me captures of snow-capped mountains and exciting foreign cities. He made me absurd promises about being together forever. And like the fool that I was, I believed him. I went blindly.

That was before Lyzender discovered the existence of the transession gene. We attempted to escape by boarding a delivery van exiting the northwest gate. We were tracked down a few miles outside of the compound after they did a satellite scan on my implant.

I always wondered how we were able to slip out under Raze's careful watch.

Was it because he was being careless?

Did he really blame his mistake on that poor man?

"His punishment was genetic mutilation," Sevan explains. "Not one of the products Diotech advertises to the public."

I think about the genetic disguises Kaelen and I were given when we left for the tour. But that was different. A few small tweaks, a few *temporary* imperfections. That man's face is ruined forever.

My voice is shaking. "You mean, they . . ."

"Sent a scrambling signal to his DNA? Yes. The same way they were able to program your DNA with the genetic implant that held your tracking code. His DNA has been programmed to make him look like that. It's quite a painful process. Having your face rearranged while you're still awake."

I reach down and touch the smooth, flawless skin of my wrist, where the black line used to be. "You changed mine. Why can't you fix him?"

"It's too extreme," says a voice behind me. I spin to see

Paddok standing there. She's still dressed in her green pants and gray sleeveless shirt, but her skin appears to have been recently cleaned, which makes me wonder if there's a water source nearby. "Trust me, we've tried. We don't have the technology, and it would simply be too painful."

I remember the unbearable agony that twisted my bones and clawed at the inside of my arm when they removed my implant. And that was only a little black line.

"Diotech doesn't just discharge you," Sevan tells me. "They mutilate you. They destroy you. So you never forget."

"What is she doing out here?" Paddok asks.

"I thought it would be good for her to see the camp. Learn why we're here."

"You're wasting your time," she tells Sevan, her distrustful eyes lingering on me when she says it. "She's gone. Alixter's brainwashing is far too deep."

I want to argue but I'm suddenly at a loss for words. Besides, what can I say in response to that?

That I'm not brainwashed?

That Dr. A is not the monster she thinks he is?

That all of these people are making it up? Fabricating stories about loss and heartache and pain just to have a valid reason to take down Diotech?

Paddok flashes me a tight-lipped smile before disappearing into her tent.

I think back to the capture I saw of Paddok emerging from the courthouse. The one where Lyzender was hiding in the crowd. The digital docket announced that her case had been dismissed.

What was the case?

Why was she fighting them?

I'm about to ask Sevan this very question when something catches the corner of my eye. Or rather someone.

He's tall and slender, standing with his back to me, talking to the man Sevan identified as Davish Swick. It's not his body that catches my attention, however, it's his hair. Blond and unruly, a mess of tangled curls. He turns his head ever so slightly to the side and I'm able to see the profile of his narrow face. His achingly familiar face.

I feel a squeeze in my chest. My mind is playing tricks on me. That's the only logical explanation.

Because it's the year 2117. If he were still alive, he would be one hundred and seventeen years old. But this boy—this young man—can't be older than twenty-five. And yet it's him. I know it's him. His nose, his cheekbones, his hair are identical to the boy I once knew. The boy who used to blush when I looked at him.

As I call out his name, my thin, frail voice nearly vanishes into the air. "Cody?"

He turns. And that's when my legs finally give out from under me.

42

HERITAGE

The impact of my sudden fall knocks Sevan off balance and, with his wrist still handcuffed to my own, he nearly tumbles down next to me. He manages to catch himself just before hitting the ground and bends to help me up.

I'm rambling now, barely making any sense. Words are spilling chaotically from my mouth. "How is he here? He can't be here! Did he give himself the gene? Why would he do that? Is he looking for me? Did he come with Lyzender?"

But that's impossible.

The Cody who reverse engineered the transession gene for Lyzender was thirty-two. This man is way younger than that.

Did Lyzender transesse back in time to give a younger Cody the gene?

As these thoughts tumble around in my head, the man stares at me completely dumbfounded. As if he doesn't even recognize me.

"Why is he looking at me like that? Doesn't he remember me?" I stab an accusing finger into Sevan's chest. "Did you recode his memories?"

"Sera," Sevan says sternly, placing his palms on my cheeks and forcing me to look at him. "It's not him. It's not Cody."

"Yes it is!" I scream. "It's him! It's Cody Carlson. My foster brother. He's just older. Or younger. Or I don't know but it's him!" I try to turn my head to look at the man again, but Sevan holds me in place.

"Listen to what I'm telling you, Sera. It's *not* him."

I rip his hands from my face and stomp over to the man, dragging Sevan with me. My emotions are all tangled up. I can't tell if I'm angry or happy or fearful or some noxious mix of the three.

"Cody!" I bellow. "What are you doing here?"

The man backs away, seemingly afraid of me.

Why would Cody be afraid of me? Did Paddok get to him, too? Has he been manipulated into distrusting me like everyone else in this place?

"Sera!" Sevan calls behind me, still attached to my wrist. I try to block him out. "That's Niko. He works for Paddok."

Niko?

I stare at the man with the curly blond hair, trying to meet his eyes, but he drops his gaze to the ground. It's then I start to see the small differences. A squarer chin. Higher cheekbones. A more pronounced brow.

"Who are you?" I ask, my tone transitioning from forceful to inquisitive.

"I'm Niko." He repeats the unfamiliar name. "Niko Carlson."

A shiver runs down my arms.

Carlson.

When I speak again, my voice is shaky. "Why do you look like him?"

The man finally finds the courage to meet my gaze and I stare into his blue eyes.

The exact same blue eyes.

"Because he's my great-grandfather."

247

43

TAINTED

I sip the water slowly, just as Sevan instructed. The lukewarm liquid feels slimy as it navigates down my throat. It doesn't taste like the water we drink on the compound. It's thicker, meaning it's organic, not synthesized to improve taste and purity.

It has a metallic flavor that makes me think about the billions of little microbes swimming around in every drop, waiting to infect my weakened system.

We're seated at one of the wooden picnic tables in the dining area of the camp. People are fluttering around us doing whatever it is they do here. Sevan sits next to me, his cuffed wrist lying on the table beside mine. He says nothing. I say nothing in return.

I'm still trying to process what happened.

Cody's great-grandson is here. Working to take down Diotech. The very company that created me. That also created a gene that sent me into the past. To the year 2013, where I first met a gangly, awkward thirteen-year-old boy named Cody Carlson.

It's too much to be a coincidence.

There's a bigger story here. Unfortunately, Niko walked away before I could say anything else. Then Sevan led me here and handed me a cup of disgusting, bacteria-laden organic water.

I take another sip.

I haven't thought much about Cody since I returned to the compound. I haven't had any reason to. He belongs in that other part of my life. The part that brings me nothing but shame.

But lately it's become more and more difficult to forget it.

This camp is crawling with reminders.

"Better?" Sevan asks, gesturing to my cup.

I nod.

"Maybe I should take you back to your tent. I think you've seen enough for one day."

He starts to stand but I don't move. "What about you?"

"Sorry?"

"You never told me why you hate Diotech."

Sevan slowly lowers back down. "I'm not sure you're ready for that story yet."

I pin him with a glare. "Just because you've seen my memories doesn't make you an expert on my mind."

He chuckles. "Very well."

He doesn't speak right away, though. He stares into the distance, as though something out there has momentarily snagged his attention.

"When I first started working at Diotech, I was a shy, lonely programmer. An outcast with no friends and no family to speak of. All I wanted was to fit in somewhere. I worked hard. I got promoted quickly. When I was finally assigned to the memory labs as a Coder, I thought, this is it. I've made it. It was a prestigious position within the company. The memory labs have an elite status on the compound. After Dr. Solara, Xaria's mother, was terminated and they placed me in charge, I thought I was living the dream, you know?"

249

I don't know. Is there a common dream that all people share? Why have I never dreamed this dream?

But I nod anyway and he continues. "Then I learned about you and Kaelen. I knew higher clearance levels would mean access to some disturbing information. I knew there would be times I would have to shut off my conscience and pretend things didn't bother me. I just didn't expect . . ." His voice cracks slightly and he trails off, looking uncomfortable. "For glitch's sake. Human beings? Manufactured? Brainwashed?"

"I'm not brainwashed." I wish everyone would stop using that word to describe me.

"That's exactly what someone who's been brainwashed would say."

"But—"

"Who do you think received the order to administer the alterations on you? Who do you think went into your brain and twisted every single memory by hand?"

Twisted?

"What are you talking about?" I demand, feeling irritated by my own confusion. "Dr. A let me keep my memories. He even restored the ones they'd taken before."

"Yes," Sevan admits. "He let you keep them, but they still had to be versions he approved of."

"Versions?"

He sighs and rubs his eyebrow. "Dr. Alixter quickly figured out that simply erasing things from your mind wasn't working. It wasn't keeping you from him."

He doesn't have to say who him is. We both know.

"So he decided to try something else. It was a new procedure. It hadn't been fully tested yet, but Dr. Alixter insisted we implement it on you. It's called Memory Reassociation."

His words set off alarm bells in my brain.

"The girl just took a little bit longer than expected to adjust to the Memory Reassociation procedure."

I overheard Dr. A saying this to someone on the other end of a transmission the morning of the Unveiling.

"What does it do?" I ask, my mouth suddenly bone dry.

"The idea behind it is that your brain can be programmed to associate a certain memory with any emotion we choose. It twists your recollection of events. It warps your past into anything they want it to be. Do you want someone to feel nostalgic about an abusive parent? Done. Do you want someone to feel betrayed when they remember a happy childhood? Done. We associate the desired emotion, your brain distorts the memory to make it fit. It's that simple. Do you want someone to feel guilty about a love that changed her life forever?" His voice gets very quiet. Like he's run out of fuel. He locks onto my eyes. "Done."

The shivering intensifies. "That's a lie." I can barely manage to keep my teeth from chattering.

"You're programmed to think that, Sera. Your brain wants it all to make sense. Even if it's illogical. Think about it. Why else would Lyzender be here?"

"For the same reason you're all here!" I try to shout but it comes out strained. "To destroy Diotech."

Sevan shakes his head. "Not him."

"Yes, him. He told me so himself."

"Now that was a lie."

My head is pounding. The thoughts are jumbled, shoving against one another. Like a drunken brawl in my brain. I press my palm against my temple, begging it to stop.

Just stop.

"Dr. Alixter wanted you to feel allegiance to Diotech. To what they're trying to do. But to accomplish that, he also had to make you feel betrayal when you remembered your past. It was all spelled out on the order. I coded the emotions in myself. Everything you feel—about Dr. A, about Diotech, about Lyzender—it's manufactured. I would know, I put it there. And I couldn't live with myself afterward. That's why I'm here."

"I don't believe you," I whisper.

"You're not supposed to. I'm a good Coder."

Somewhere inside of me, I find the strength to scream, but it's a waning force that's only good for one word. So I choose it wisely. "No!"

I stand up and try to walk away, but I'm yanked back, still cuffed to Sevan. I pull hard, imagining that my abilities are back and I can rip his arm clean out of the socket, but I don't even seem to be making a dent in his skin. "Release me," I beg quietly.

Surprisingly, he does. Without argument or hesitation. He pulls the key from his pocket and unlocks his end. The vacant cuff dangles from my wrist.

He must know I won't try to run.

He must know I barely even have the strength to make it across the camp to my tent.

Everyone here is a liar. Lyzender, Paddok, Sevan. They'll say whatever it takes to break me. To make me believe I'm on the wrong side.

I'm on the side of humanity. The side of doing good for the world. That's the right side.

I start limping back to my tent.

"Remember the fire," Sevan calls from the table.

My footsteps slow to a stop.

Fire? What fire? The one that burned me at the stake in 1609?

But instantly I know that's not what he's referring to. His words. They spark something. An image stirs in my brain. An imprisoned memory struggling to break free. An unforgotten nightmare.

And suddenly I see it. I remember it.

A blindfolded woman standing in the desert. Flames roaring inside a glass cage. She walks mindlessly into the inferno.

She doesn't even scream.

But I do.

At least I try. Kaelen's hand muffles the sound. Kaelen's words attempt to soothe me. Kaelen's arms carry me away.

Across the compound. Under the glinting metallic archway. Through the doors of the memory labs.

I slowly turn around. Sevan has stood up from the bench. He stares at me expectantly. As if he knows what's happening in my brain right now.

"The memory you erased," I say numbly. "The night before we left."

"I gave it back," he confirms. "During your last scan. It just needed to be triggered."

My throat is dry. Scorched from the recollection of the flames. "Why?"

"So you could see the truth for yourself."

"What truth? What did I witness that night?"

"The *real* Objective," he replies calmly.

"Burning people?"

He takes a step toward me. "*Controlling people.*"

I shake my head.

He takes another step. "Every product in the ExGen Collection contains an untraceable piece of nanotechnology."

I shut my eyes tight. It's crazy. It's delusional. It's exactly what Dr. Maxxer claimed, and *she* was crazy. She was delusional.

Another step. "A stimulated-response system. Just like the one they used on you in 2032. It will embed itself in the consumer's brain and lie dormant until the day Diotech decides to switch it on."

I cover my ears with my hands. "Stop! That fire never happened!

You coded that memory to mess with my mind. You are the brain-washer! Diotech is trying to *help* people!"

"Think about it, Sera." Sevan's tone sharpens. "Diotech has nothing to gain from making people stronger. The *world* has nothing to gain from making people stronger. A controlled population is a weak population is a safe population."

I won't stand here and listen to this. I won't let myself be manipulated by these lies.

I turn again and walk away, determined to huddle under my blankets until I drift to sleep.

But just as I reach the tent I catch sight of the dark-skinned girl. The one who brought me my food earlier. Who Sevan called Xaria.

She's standing on her tiptoes, her lips curled into a coy smile as she whispers into someone's ear. Then she wraps her arms around his neck and pulls him toward her, steering his mouth to hers.

It's then that I'm able to see Lyzender's face. As it rotates toward me to welcome her kiss.

44

ANSWERS

He sees me as soon as his lips touch hers. His mouth falls open and his eyes widen. For a moment, he stands completely still, unsure what to do. When she realizes he's not kissing her back, she pulls away, murmuring something inaudible against his chin.

Then she looks my way and her gaze slices into me.

I duck into the tent and collapse on the bed, facing the cloth wall. The air comes out of my lungs rough and ragged. I try to take deep breaths but it only results in a coughing fit.

I tell myself it has nothing to do with what I just witnessed. My shortness of breath is one hundred percent attributable to my walk through the camp. And to the disturbing lies that Sevan tried to force on me.

Why should I care what Lyzender does?

Who Lyzender kisses?

I shouldn't. I don't. He can kiss every girl within a fifty-mile radius if he wants. It doesn't affect me at all. Actually, that's not true. It's *better* for me. Better that his attention is focused elsewhere.

Better that he's not trying to manipulate me anymore. He's clearly found another, more agreeable subject.

One less thing for me to have to worry about.

I need to concentrate on my mission to warn the compound about the imminent attack.

There is nothing else.

I hear the tent flap swish a moment later. I don't have to roll over to know who's standing there. I recognize his breathing. His silence. The way the air in the room bends toward him.

"Seraphina—" he starts to say.

"It's Sera."

"Seraphina," he repeats with even more persistence. "We need to talk. What you just saw out there—"

"Has nothing to do with me."

"Has everything to do with you." His voice is thick and pleading. I can hear his feet shuffling around the interior of the tent. It's what he does when he's trying to find words.

I remember.

How I wish I didn't.

"You don't have to explain anything to me," I tell him.

"No!" he shouts, causing me to jump. I've only ever heard him shout once before. It was at Rio. Before he discovered that Rio was trying to help us.

"No," he says again. This time more quietly. More controlled. But still packed with intensity. "You don't understand what I've been through. Those three years trapped in time without you. I finally understood what all those religions mean when they talk about hell. They were the most agonizing years of my life. I lost myself. Cody almost lost his family trying to help me. Then he had a breakthrough, and I thought the agony was over. I thought as soon as I could get back here, all those long, hellish years would be behind me." He pauses. I still don't turn around to look at him. "Then I saw you on the Feed."

A chill racks my body. A chill that has nothing to do with the poison in my blood.

"You asked that question, didn't you? SZ1609?"

"Yes," he whispers.

I don't know why this answer crushes me. It only confirms what I already knew. Maybe because now it's a fact. Not just a theory. Maybe because I suddenly see that interview in a new way. Through his eyes.

The hand-holding.

The flirtations.

That kiss.

I remember how it reached my toes. How it looked on the slow-motion playback. Like two people hopelessly in love.

Like two people who have never been in love with anyone else.

For a single moment—as long as it takes for me to count to three—I allow myself to feel the grief that washes over me. I allow myself to ponder the heartbreak that Lyzender claims he felt when he watched that. I allow it to consume me.

1, 2, 3.

Then it's over. I bottle it up. Push it down. I remind myself that he doesn't really love me. He never did.

It was an act.

Just like this is.

"It twists your recollection of events. It warps your past into anything they want it to be."

NO!

I curl myself into a ball and shake. I want it all to stop. The noise. The chatter in my mind. The voices telling me what they want me to believe.

I can't believe everything. I have to choose. And I choose the Objective.

I choose Kaelen.

"I saw you with him," Lyzender goes on after a heavy silence.

"I saw the way you looked at him. The way you kissed him. It destroyed me all over again. I descended into darkness. Xaria was there. She's been trying to pull me out."

"Good," I mumble into my kneecaps. "Now we both have someone." The tears are coming. I can't stop them. They will have to fall. But as long as I stay curled up here, as long as I refuse to face him, he will never have to know.

I silently will him to leave. Walk away. Let me crumble to pieces alone.

"Yes," he agrees. "Now we both have someone."

I hear his footsteps retreating. I hear the flap being pulled back. And then I hear nothing.

The first tear treks a path down my nose, falling onto the lumpy pillow. The sob rises up inside of me, threatening to convulse my entire body. Threatening to bring this tent to the ground.

"Can I ask you one thing?"

It's him. He hasn't left.

I don't speak, in fear of revealing everything. My brokenness. My fear. My treacherous relief that he's still here.

"When you saw us just now," he says softly. The edge to his voice is completely gone. Vanished without a trace. "When you saw her kiss me, did it make you feel *anything*?"

The truthful answer is right on the tip of my tongue. Ready to implode.

It made me feel everything.

But that's not an answer I can give.

That's not an answer that makes things easier. That simplifies life. That improves situations.

That's an answer that erases progress. That turns back time. That destroys.

I manage to hold back a shudder. It feels like holding back the tides.

"No," I say.

I count the seconds until he leaves again. It's all I can do not to scream.

This time he makes his departure clear. Hard footfalls on the ground. A violent clattering outside. Hushed voices speaking calming words.

I'm grateful for the commotion. It stifles the sound of me shattering.

45

STAGED

That afternoon, I'm roused from a deep sleep and led into the dining area of the camp. Everyone is already assembled for what looks like another meeting. They watch me as I'm paraded in—Sevan, Paddok, Klo Raze, Davish Swick, Olin Vas with his disfigured face, Nem Rouser who cooks the meat, even Niko Carlson, Cody's great-grandson. Twenty-five faces. Twenty-five distrusting stares. All directed at me.

I cough a little but try to stand up straighter. I'm not sure what's happening or why I've been brought here to be gawked at, but I'm not about to let these people threaten me with their hatred.

I am an ExGen—at least I was before they filled my veins with liquid weakness. I am the face of the future. I will not believe their lies, or be intimidated by their vengeance, or be trapped by their manipulations.

I will fight. I will keep fighting until Diotech has destroyed them. Or they kill me. Whichever comes first.

Lyzender suddenly appears in front of me, his face distraught, his eyes pleading. "Please just do exactly as she says," he tells me urgently.

Before I can ask him what he's talking about, Jase nudges me forward with the barrel of his shotgun and sits me down at one of the wooden tables. I'm positioned so that the entire camp is facing me. They're all clustered in a tight group behind Paddok and Klo. I suddenly feel like I'm onstage again. Back in the spotlight. Except this time, I don't know what's expected of me.

"Do you want me to dance?" I ask, trying for sarcasm, but my voice is too frail—too sickly—to be taken seriously.

Ignoring my joke, Paddok steps forward. "Here's how this is going to work," she addresses me sharply. I've never seen her look so anxious.

What the glitch is going on?

Paddok shoves a piece of paper into my hand. On it, she's scribbled something in messy handwriting. "This is what you will say. This is all you will say. If they ask you questions, you will ignore them. If they try to get more information out of you, you will ignore them." She nods to Jase who stands just off to the side, his gun aimed at my head. "If you fail to comply with any of these guidelines, your precious Print Mate will be forced to watch your brains splatter all over his wall screen. Is that clear?"

Print Mate?

Kaelen!

Is he here?

My gaze darts around the camp, but I see no sign of him. Then, out of the corner of my eye, I notice Klo pulling something from his pocket. My head whips back as he unrolls the familiar item and my entire body starts to hum.

The Slate!

A connection to the world.

To Diotech.

My arms tremble, wanting to reach for it. If only I had my full strength I could tackle him to the ground and confiscate it. Then again, if I had my full strength, I suppose I wouldn't need the Slate in the first place.

I watch anxiously as the flexible screen blinks to life, emitting a soft glow across his face. A few taps before he brandishes it toward me.

I inhale sharply when I see the familiar dining room of the Owner's Estate framed between his hands. Sitting at the long polished-marble table, staring at me as though they're looking out of a glass prison, are Director Raze, Dr. A, and my beloved Kaelen.

My heart pounds wildly in my chest. I briefly glance down at the piece of paper in my hands, skimming the barely legible handwriting. I catch key words like kidnappers, ransom, bank account.

That's when Paddok's warning finally makes sense.

That's when another piece of their plan clicks into place.

I'm here to negotiate the terms of my release.

46

SUBTEXT

There is no doubt in my mind what I must do. This might be my only chance to get a message to Director Raze. To warn him about what's coming.

"I said," Paddok growls, jolting me out of my thoughts, "is that clear?"

"Yes," I say, eyeing Jase's gun a few feet away.

It's perfectly clear. I disobey, Kaelen watches me die.

Paddok is smart. She knows the threat of death alone is not enough to make me comply. But if Kaelen has to witness my murder, it will destroy him.

Glancing back at the Slate, I now realize that although I can see Dr. A, Kaelen, and Director Raze, they still can't see me. Or hear me. This side of the connection hasn't yet been activated.

"If you try to give up our location, Jase will shoot you," Paddok goes on.

"I don't know our location," I remind her.

"If you try to warn them about anything you've overheard, Jase will shoot you. If you try to—"

"I understand," I tell her, my temper starting to flare. "Read the script and say nothing else."

Her jaw flexes. "Good."

I glance again at my script. They're asking Diotech for a two-billion-dollar ransom to be transferred to a bank account. After that I'll be returned to them safe and sound.

So that's their plan. They're trying to make this look like a basic kidnapping. I admit it's pretty clever. Kaelen and I are two of the most famous people on the planet right now. It's not hard to believe that someone would want to trade us for a bunch of money.

And then what? How are they planning to get that device into the underground bunker? There are still too many details I don't know.

"Are we ready?" Paddok asks Klo.

Klo nods. "Ready to transmit on your order, boss lady."

I look out into the sea of faces huddled behind Klo and Paddok. Judging by the fact that the entire camp has gathered to witness this, it's a key moment. The rest of their plan hinges on what's about to happen.

The only person on this side of the Slate with me is Jase, standing just outside of the cam's frame.

I catch sight of Lyzender and can tell from the uneasy way he glances between me and Jase that he doesn't approve of the use of the firearm. He gnaws at one of his fingernails until Xaria comes up from behind him and wraps her arms around his waist. I'm sure she means it to be a calming gesture but it only seems to make Lyzender more nervous.

I look away, directing my gaze right at the Slate. Dr. A, Raze, and Kaelen are still sitting at the table, waiting for the transmission to go live. Kaelen drums his fingers apprehensively on the tabletop.

"Remember," Paddok warns. "No deviations from the script."

"I remember," I mutter.

She gives the sign to Klo. His fingertip swipes across the screen, activating the cam. Kaelen, Raze, and Dr. A all sit up a little straighter at the sound of the small ding that announces the connection.

"Sera!" Kaelen calls out. I've never heard such fear in his voice. Such angst. I feel like the mass of the moon has been dropped into my lap. "Are you all right? Did they hurt you?"

I keep my right hand resting on my leg. With the other, I raise the trembling script and begin to read. I fight to keep my words steady and even.

" 'My kidnappers are sending this transmission as a show of good faith and innocuous intentions. And to prove to you that I'm still alive and not injured.' "

"Tell us where you are!" Kaelen screams at the cam. Dr. A puts a hand on his shoulder, attempting to relax him.

My eyes dart nervously to Jase, who gives his gun a little bump.

"She can't," Raze tells Kaelen. "She's being threatened. I can see it in her eyes."

Dr. A turns his head and mouths something I can't interpret, most likely a curse.

I swallow and keep reading. " 'If you would like for me to return alive, a two-billion-dollar ransom must be transferred to the following bank account number in the next forty-eight hours.' "

I pause, positioning my right hand in the center of my thigh and spreading my fingers. I try to make direct eye contact with Kaelen through the screen, urging him to pay close attention.

My gaze darts to Paddok. She gestures for me to continue.

As I slowly begin to read the account number on the page, I lift the fingers of my right hand ever so slightly, hovering them just above my leg.

"7," I announce slowly.

Subtly, I press my thumb, middle finger, and pinkie into my pants. Like I'm playing a chord on a piano.

"9." I reveal the next number with delicate precision as my fingers rise back up, and my middle, ring, and pinkie fingers tap out another letter.

I watch Paddok for any sign of suspicion, but she's not focused on my hand. She's focused on my lips. Making sure nothing spills out that's not written on this piece of paper.

I promised her I would read the script and say nothing else. And I'm keeping that promise. I'm not *saying* anything else.

"4." I announce the next number of the account. My thumb plays the imaginary keyboard on my leg.

"1."

All five fingers come down. The sign for the letter P. I've now spelled out the first word in my message.

I watch Kaelen's face for a reaction. So far, I've yet to see one. Does he understand what I'm doing? Is he even looking at my hand? Or is he just smart enough to hide it?

With the final numbers of the bank account, I'm able to spell out two more words.

"0."

Tap.

"2."

Tap.

"2."

Tap.

"3."

Tap.

"8."

Tap.

Director Raze is entering the account numbers into his Slate. Dr. A is seething quietly in his chair. And Kaelen remains as emotionless as a statue.

Paddok nods toward the script, urging me to finish up.

There're only a few more lines to read and I still have two more

266

words to silently convey. Up until now, I've been very slow and delicate with my finger movement, afraid that anything more might tip off one of the twenty-five people watching me. I have to pick up the pace if I want to communicate the final piece.

" 'Once the money is transferred to the account,' " I say deliberately while I press down my thumb and forefinger, followed by my index finger, " 'I will be returned to the compound by way of hovercopter.' "

Index, middle, ring, and pinkie.

" 'You may take control of my hover as soon as it's within Diotech airspace.' "

Thumb, index, and pinkie.

Only one more line to go. The movement of my fingers is fast but barely visible. Hardly a twitch.

" 'Any failure to comply with their terms . . .' "

Thumb.

All five fingers.

Thumb.

" 'And I will be killed . . .' "

Thumb, index, middle, ring.

" 'On live Feed.' "

I watch Kaelen leap up from his chair, lunging toward me. He slams his fist hard against the wall screen, causing my view to rattle. "You glitching bastard! I will kill you! I will desecrate you. If you hurt her, I swear, I will hunt you down and rip your heart out of your chest."

Raze is out of his seat, attempting to restrain Kaelen, but he's beyond restraint now. He's snapped. The rage has been triggered. There will be no controlling him for a long time. It's exactly the reaction that landed me here.

It's not that I blame him for this predicament, but right now I need him to help us get out of it. I need him to calm down and look at me. *Notice* what I'm trying to tell him.

Paddok pokes Klo in the arm, indicating the end of the script.

I jab my fingers against my leg, rushing to spell out the last three letters in the message just as Klo cuts the transmission.

"Clear," he calls.

Chatter recommences among the group as I breathe out a shuddering sigh. My entire body is shaking with fear and relief and, for the first time in two days, the tiniest glimmer of hope.

I did it. I sent a warning to Diotech. It was all there. Played out by my trembling fingers.

TRAP.

BOMB.

BUNKER.

JENZA PADDOK.

It wasn't elegant. It wasn't thorough but it was as clear a message as I was able to convey.

Whether or not Kaelen received it is another story.

47

INSULTS

As the hours tick by, the members of Paddok's team grow more and more antsy. They gave Dr. A two days to transfer the money but no one seems entirely certain he's going to do it. Except for Paddok. I hear her murmuring to people outside my tent, reassuring them of my value. "He'll never allow her to die on live Feed. Never."

I'm fairly convinced Paddok is bluffing. I don't think she'll actually go through with a public assassination. I'd like to think I have enough supporters here to prevent that from happening. Lyzender would never allow me to be killed, would he? Even if his feelings for me were a sham, would he really want to see me die?

And what about Sevan? Doesn't he care about me on some level? Was his kindness all an act, too?

And finally there's Klo. I don't know much about him but he doesn't seem to despise me the way the others do. He wouldn't vote for me to be put to death, would he?

As for the rest of the people here, I'm sure they'd pop

champagne and throw a party on my grave. To them, I'm just an extension of the Diotech beast. Another sector of the compound. Chop it off and you have that much less beast to kill.

In the end, two billion dollars to Diotech is nothing. A raindrop in a canyon. But if Kaelen was able to successfully translate my code, they'll know that the ransom demand was just a ruse. A veiled scheme to get an undetectable device onto the compound.

How they plan to do that, I still don't know.

What I do know is that if the message *was* conveyed, that ransom may not be paid. And I may very well die.

If it wasn't, Dr. A will transfer the money, I'll be returned home, and everyone at Diotech could perish.

Only time will tell at this point.

And that makes time my worst enemy and my only friend.

———————

That night, I'm invited by Paddok to join the group for evening meal. Apparently my good behavior during the transmission has earned me the right to sit with everyone else instead of being holed up in my tent alone.

I can immediately tell from the glares as I walk back to the dining area that Paddok did not poll the rest of the camp before extending the invitation. I try not to cringe at the smell of cooked meat that lingers from the fire pit in the center as I stand in line, waiting for Nem Rouser to dump a filet of unidentified dark red meat on my plate.

I scan the tables set up around the fire pit for a place to sit. Lyzender and Xaria are nestled together at the nearest one. He looks rigid and uncomfortable as he eats, while she giggles and whispers things in his ear. When she catches me staring at them, she leans in and kisses his cheek.

I roll my eyes and move to the table farthest away from them.

As of right now, Klo Raze is the only one sitting there. I set my plate down and slide onto the bench across from him.

He looks up, grins a dimpled boyish grin, and returns to devouring his meat.

I'm going to have to ask Sevan for some more of those nutrition capsules after the meal is over.

"Vegetarian?" Klo nods at my untouched food. He tears a strip from the rib in his hands and chews with his mouth open.

"I prefer the synthetic variety," I say quietly.

"That stuff'll kill you."

I shoot him a dubious look.

"It's true," he vows, holding up red-stained fingers like he's swearing an oath. "Nature didn't intend for us to eat fake flux. Our bodies don't know what to do with it."

"The synthetic meat is designed to be healthier for your body," I argue. "Easier to digest. Enhanced with nutrients."

He chokes out a laugh. "You're a walking Diotech commercial, aren't you?"

I fall silent. I suppose that did make me sound pretty brainwashed.

He pulls another strip of flesh from the bone. "You see, when you mess with nature enough, there comes a point when it stops being good and starts being destructive."

"Is that why you're here?" I ask.

He sucks the rib bone clean and drops the bloody appendage onto my plate, even though there's plenty of room on his own. I take that as a sign he's not going to answer my question.

"It was you, wasn't it?" I ask. "Who told them where the server bunker was?"

He performs an awkward seated bow. "Snitch extraordinaire. At your service."

"Your father trusted you with that information."

His playfulness slips away. "My father never trusted me with

271

anything. I learned a long time ago that if you want information, you have to find it yourself."

"And the transmission about the rooftop landing pad being under construction? You sent that."

He beams, revealing shreds of meat stuck between his teeth. "You're welcome."

"That wasn't a thank-you."

"You're welcome," he repeats, picking up his next rib and devouring it the way he did the first.

"That farmer is dead because of what you did."

I expect my comment to sting. To elicit some kind of reaction from this boy. But it doesn't. He sucks on the end of his bone. "No. That farmer is dead because of what you *didn't* do."

I recoil. "Excuse me?"

"You were the only one with the strength to stop Kaelen. Yet you did nothing. You just stood there."

"Actually," I begin, growing flustered, "I don't have the strength to stop Kaelen. He's always been stronger than me."

"But you didn't even try. Do you enjoy watching your boyfriend kick the living flux out of people?"

"No."

"Then?"

"I . . ." I stop when I realize that I don't know the rest of the sentence.

"You were scared," he answers for me.

I laugh. "No, I wasn't."

"Sure you were."

"You don't know me." I pick at the smallest piece of meat on my plate, wondering if it tastes as foul as it smells.

"I know enough," he says, flicking a strand of blue hair from his face. "I saw you around that compound. I watched you for months. You were such a good little girl. So afraid of upsetting anyone, you wouldn't even risk having a single thought of your own."

"That's completely untrue," I argue, even though the words feel lumpy and awkward on my tongue. I hide my discomfort by popping the morsel into my mouth and attempting to chew.

"It *is* true. I saw the footage from the attack outside the Feed station. When Kaelen lost it. You looked like a . . . like a . . ."—Klo nods toward the meat on my plate—"well, probably a lot like this deer looked right before it was shot."

The soggy flesh in my mouth suddenly tastes like blood and I spit it out.

The boy laughs. "You don't even have the guts to eat a glitchin' piece of meat."

I flounder for something to say in response, but all that comes out is, "I'm not a coward."

He cleans the last rib bone and tosses it down, sucking the juice off his fingers. "Look around you. The truth is right here in front of you. Carved into the faces of all these people. You're so terrified that your precious Dr. A might be wrong—that your entire existence might be a big fat lie—that you refuse to see it. *That* is the very definition of a coward."

He stands and picks up his empty plate, delivering it to the bin of dirty dishes. For a moment I think he's going to come back, call me more names, accuse me of more things, but he does something even worse. He walks away.

His hasty departure surprises me at first, but my shock quickly slips into anger.

Who does he think he is? He can't just sit there and accuse me of being a coward and then leave without giving me the opportunity to defend myself.

I leap from the bench. My voice is hoarse and raspy as I call out, "Hey!"

When he spins around, that annoyingly smug grin is still plastered to his face.

"What did I ever do to you?" I shout, causing a few people to stare. "I've never even met you!" I turn to address the rest of the onlookers. "Any of you! And you hate me. You treat me like a criminal. Because of where I come from. Because of who made me. And I'm the coward!? I can't help being born in a lab any more than you can help being born outside of one. I've been nice. I've sat in that tent for hours pretending that what you're planning to do to the only home I've ever known doesn't devastate me. Well, you know what? I'm done being polite. You can all go to hell."

I stomp in the direction of my tent. But I'm slow and frail and Klo catches up with me easily, grabbing me by the arm and pulling me to a stop.

"What?" I growl.

He's going to insult me again. I can see it in his eyes. This argument is not over for him.

"Look," he says, his tone surprisingly mild. And quiet. As though he doesn't want anyone else to hear. "I know you're not on our side and that's fine. I don't give a flux. But you at least need to be on *his* side."

I toss my hands up, exasperated. "Who?"

But we both know who. Which is probably why he doesn't say his name.

"We practically grew up together on that compound. We used to be best friends. Then he left to be with you and I never saw him again. Until he showed up here, heartbroken and dangerously hopeful.

"His whole glitchin' life has been about you. About saving you. He was one of the smartest kids I knew. He could have been great. But he gave it all up for you. Don't make his sacrifice be for nothing."

I swallow and look to the ground. The image of Xaria's lips on his plays over and over again in my mind like one of Crest's looping nanotats. "He didn't love me," I murmur to the dirt. "I was just a means to an end."

Klo's grasp slips from my arm and I feel the blood rushing back to my fingers.

Anger flashes on his face but it's quickly replaced by a sad, withering smile. "That's the most cowardly thing you've said yet."

48

LEGACY

I wait for the camp to fall asleep. I wait for the sounds of footsteps to disappear completely. Then I grab my lantern and tiptoe into the night. No one has bothered to lock me up again. I've proven to be a good little hostage. Sticking to the script, not trying to run away anymore, making conversation with my captors. Apart from my outburst at evening meal today, I think I've been fairly cooperative, given the circumstances.

Of course, they don't know about the hidden message in my transmission.

There's a chance Kaelen doesn't even know about it.

I steal quietly through the slumbering camp. I know which tent is his because I saw him retreat into it earlier, after the excitement of the hostage negotiation was over.

I slip inside.

He wakes when my light floods the small space, and sits up in his bed with a start. From the widening of his eyes, I think he might believe I'm here to kill him. But the truth is, I just want answers.

Not that I could kill anyone in my current state.

I don't wait for an invitation to sit down. I know I'll never get one. I sit on the edge of his bed and set my lantern on the nearby table. I have to reach over him to do it, my arm brushing against his. The faint beam of light reveals a tint of red on his face.

I fight back a smile.

Cody used to blush around me, too.

Maybe it's genetic.

"Hi, Niko," I say.

"What are you doing here?" Despite his fear, he manages to infuse an impressive amount of annoyance into his tone. As if the only thing he's concerned about right now is being woken up in the middle of the night.

I stare at him, unable to keep the amazement from my face. He looks *so* much like Cody. They share the same faded blue eyes, the same round face, the same curly blond hair. I imagine this is what Cody would have looked like in his twenties.

"Did you know him?" I ask. "Your . . . great-grandfather."

It feels so strange to think of Cody as a great-grandfather. It was hard enough to think of him as a father.

"A little," he says guardedly, refusing to take his eyes off me. "He died when I was eight."

Died.

The word feels like a slap. Even though I know it shouldn't. I never expected Cody to be alive today, but hearing it aloud is something altogether different.

"Has anyone ever told you how much you look like him?"

He nods. "My grandfather Reese used to tell me we looked alike. He showed me a few captures of when he was younger. I guess I could see the resemblance."

Reese.

The memory instantly floods my mind. The little boy with red hair who came barreling down the stairs of Cody's town house.

Who taught me how to play his favorite virtual simulation game. Who called my once thirteen-year-old foster brother "Daddy."

Unexpectedly, black guilt and red rage flare in my throat. I feel them gnawing at me, strangling me.

Cody was an enemy to the Objective, I remind myself.

Even if he didn't fully understand what he was doing, he still helped me evade Diotech countless times. And now his great-grandson has pledged himself to the other side. The side that wants to see the compound obliterated and Diotech destroyed.

"Are you okay?" Niko asks.

"Yes. Why?"

"Your face," he says, "it got all, I don't know, screwy."

"Screwy?"

"Like you smelled something bad."

"Why are you here?"

My abrupt question takes him by surprise. "Excuse me?"

"Why are you fighting against Diotech?"

A long silence passes between us as Niko seemingly considers whether to respond. I'm sure he's been warned more than once not to trust me. Not to divulge any information that might compromise their plan.

"I was born to fight Diotech," he finally says.

"What?"

He appears to relax a bit—now that I've proven I'm not here to suffocate him with a pillow. "I guess you could say it was my legacy." He laughs weakly.

I shake my head. "I don't understand."

"I didn't for a while, either," he admits. "The only thing I really remember about my great-grandfather was how old he was. And how *crazy* he seemed."

Crazy? That's not an adjective I would have used to describe Cody. "Did he get warped in his old age?"

I've heard of it happening to people. Especially those born before the latest advancements in neurotechnology. Or those refusing to trust them.

"I certainly thought so," Niko replies. "As did the rest of the family. He would go on and on, ranting like a lunatic about some evil corporation that wouldn't exist for another few decades. A corporation that would build human beings in science labs and manipulate people's brains and try to control the world. We all thought he'd lost his mind. I mean, that's what you think when someone claims to know the future, right?"

A shiver runs through me.

"Anyway," Niko continues, "I didn't like him very much. As a kid, he scared the flux out of me. Every time I saw him, he would force me to listen to his raving stories about this diabolical company and how one day I'd be the one who could stop them. I was the generation that would *have* to stop them."

"Diotech," I whisper, almost inaudibly.

I remember when Cody watched my memories from the cube drive. It was in the guest room of his town house when we were trying to save Lyzender's life. He saw everything that had happened to me since I woke up in the wreckage of the plane crash.

For me, it was just another act of betrayal—sharing confidential information with an outsider—but for him, it was apparently the start of something else.

"I thought he was just old and delirious," Niko says. "Like maybe he was confusing real life with some random sci-fi movie he'd seen as a kid. Then one day, an ad came on the Feed for the artificial womb. I saw the company logo, and every hair on my body stood on end. That's when I realized he wasn't crazy. He was . . ."—his voice grows soft and reflective—". . . something else."

He stares into the flickering light of my lantern. "Of course," he continues forlornly, "by the time I realized how right he was, it was too late. He was gone. But I knew what I had to do. It's almost as though he'd been preparing me for it. I had to stop them. So I found Paddok and the others and I told her I wanted in. Later I met Lyzender and found out about you, the transession gene, and the time he spent with my great-grandfather before he came back here. Everything made more sense at that point."

My breathing has become shallow. I can't bring myself to speak.

There's a war waging in my head. The person who once cared for Cody, who once loved him like a real brother, is clashing against the person who is supposed to condemn him. Cody and I are not on the same side. We never were. If it wasn't clear before, it is now. He raised this man to be my enemy.

He may not have known it at the time—it may not even have been a conscious choice—but he was a traitor. Just like Rio. Just like Lyzender. Just like me.

Yet there's an unfamiliar emotion welling up inside me, fighting for my attention. An emotion I can't identify. It warms me where I should be cold. It softens me where I should be unyielding.

I stand up a little too quickly. The room does a full spin. I hold on to the bed frame to steady myself.

"Are you sure you're all right?" Niko asks, and I nod. There's a tenderness in his voice that wasn't there before. He must hear it, too, because his next words are sharp with impatience. "Is that it? Is that why you came here?"

I don't reply. I grab my lantern and start toward the door.

But I can't leave. Not without asking the one question that's been plaguing me since I first laid eyes on Niko. Possibly even longer.

The loyal soldier in me insists the answer doesn't matter. But the traitor in me has to know.

Some battles are won. Some are lost.

I slowly turn around, swallow the rough lump in my throat, and ask, "Do you know how he died?"

Niko raises an eyebrow and peers inquisitively at me. "He was old. A hundred and two. He died in his sleep. His heart just . . . you know, stopped."

A ripple of grief passes through me. I don't fight it off. I don't erect walls to keep it at bay. But I don't let myself cry either. I bow my head and hastily blink away the tears that sting my eyes. "Thank you," I murmur.

"He was a great scientist," Niko says softly. "From what I've heard, he won a bunch of awards for his work."

I lift my head and look at him. In the dim light, he appears to be studying me, measuring my reaction. For some unfathomable reason, I think he's trying to console me.

I slink back into the night and disappear behind the flap of my tent. By the time I lie down on my own rickety metal bed, my eyes are wet with unwelcome tears.

I shouldn't mourn the death of an enemy.

I shouldn't cry over a silly boy who once had a silly crush.

And I certainly shouldn't let the words of a stranger console me. But I do.

49

UNCLEAN

Early the next morning, Klo receives an alert that the money has been transferred into the specified account. A smattering of cheers and applause wakes me from my restless sleep and Paddok herself enters my tent to bring me the news. I think it's the first time I've ever seen her smile.

It's decided that I will be delivered to the compound at seven the next morning.

As Paddok's team buzzes around the camp getting ready for the big event, I lie on my bed and let the implications sink in.

I failed.

Failed to escape.

Failed to warn them.

Failed, failed, failed.

Once again, I let Dr. A down. And now Diotech will suffer the consequences.

I drift in and out of a dreamless, guilt-plagued sleep for the rest of the day. When the sun is low in the sky, Lyzender comes to wake me. He tosses a questionably clean towel on the bed.

"Time to get cleaned up," he says, the now-familiar sharpness coating his words like liquid glass. "Paddok doesn't want you going home looking like"—he pauses, gives me a once-over—"like you are now."

I haven't seen my reflection in over two days. Appearances haven't exactly been high on my priority list lately. Not that they ever are. I want to ask why I should bother making myself presentable when I'll be covered in the dust and ashes of my home in less than twenty-four hours.

I keep this inquiry to myself.

I grab the towel and Lyzender guides me outside. We walk for about a half mile from the perimeter of the camp until we come to a small meadow. I halt and stare in wonderment at the thousands upon thousands of tiny white flowers covering the ground like a sprinkling of fresh snow.

Dandelions.

The weed that marks the first day Lyzender and I met. The weed that he plucked for me and brought me in a vacuum-sealed tube.

The weed that Diotech eradicated, along with so many others. Or so I thought.

Looking out on this sea of white cotton, I realize that Diotech has no power here. That Dr. A's reach has a limit.

In this wild meadow, miles from civilization, miles from the innovative science of the compound labs, some things are safe from extermination.

Some things still survive.

Lyzender has stopped, too. I can feel his eyes on me, watching my reaction. Is that why he brought me here? To try to stir up some buried emotion? To poke at the wounds of my betrayal?

Well, it won't work.

I keep my expression neutral. Indifferent. "Where exactly are we going?"

He starts walking again. "It's just over this ridge."

A few minutes later we arrive at a small lake cut into the desert floor. Like the towel over my shoulder, its cleanliness is debatable.

"Be quick about it," he says shortly.

He takes a seat on a boulder near the shore and leans back on his hands. Like he's waiting for his favorite show to start on the Feed.

I scoff. "Well, at least turn around. I'm not taking my clothes off in front of you."

He smirks. "We lived together for over six months in a seventeenth-century farmhouse with no running water. I've seen you naked plenty of times."

"It's different now."

"Yeah," he mutters. "You weren't in love with someone else then."

He turns around.

I pull off my filthy clothes and wade into the cool water. Clean or not, it's still refreshing. Even though I shiver under the surface, I like the sensation of the lake on my body, washing away the dirt on my skin and hopefully on my soul. If I even have one of those.

The people around here don't seem to think so.

I watch Lyzender's back as he sits patiently on the rock, staring into the horizon. "Will you tell me more about tomorrow?" I ask, cupping a handful of water in my palm and letting it sift through my fingertips.

Silence, and then he says, "I can't."

"There are people on that compound who I care about, you know?"

His shoulders stiffen. "I know." His tone is glacial.

"Not just him," I correct. "Other people. Innocent people. People you must have known when you lived there."

"Paddok is not interested in taking innocent lives. She's only interested in protecting the rest of the world from Diotech."

"So you're saying you won't kill anyone."

Another long, dreadful pause. "I'm not saying that."

I bite my lip and brace myself for another onslaught of tremors. "What happened to Jenza Paddok?"

My question takes him by surprise. "What do you mean?"

"Sevan took me on a tour of the camp. He said you all have your reasons for wanting to destroy Diotech. What is hers?"

He hesitates. "I don't know. She never told me."

"You're lying," I accuse.

"That again? Why do I always have to be lying?"

"Because you were there. At that courthouse. The day her case was thrown out. I saw you in a Feed archive. You transessed there to check up on her, didn't you? You wanted to make sure her claims against Diotech were legitimate before you joined her team. Before you trusted her with your secret."

He picks up a rock and throws it hard into the dirt. "Yes. Fine. I was there, okay? I sat in the back row of the courthouse and watched Diotech get away with murder."

My chest tightens. "Murder?" I try to sound skeptical. But I'm not sure how convincing I am.

"Her son," Lyzender says. "They killed her ten-year-old son."

I hop up and down in the water to keep warm. "How?"

Lyzender sighs. "Nerve gas. A new fast-spreading variety Diotech was working on for the government."

I know from my many uploads on the subject that modern wars are mostly fought with these kinds of silent weapons. Deadly vapors that can be released by undetectable drones. But I've never heard of a nerve agent killing an American child. Their uses are limited to foreign-war fronts and battle zones.

"Before the latest batch could be sold to the government, it had to be fully tested," Lyzender goes on. "On both adults *and* children. So a drone carrying the gas was delivered to the playground of an elementary school. Fifty-two students were killed."

I exhale a breath that has turned stale and moldy in my lungs. I've seen what nerve gas can do. The convulsions. The salivation. The complete loss of all bodily function. Imagining fifty-two children going through that is too much to bear.

I swiftly push the thought from my mind.

"Paddok tried to file a class action lawsuit against Diotech. It was thrown out for lack of evidence." He chucks another rock at the ground. "But you and I both know the real reason it was dismissed."

My brow furrows.

"The Providence," he says.

The water around me suddenly turns to ice and I'm frozen in place.

He knows? About the Providence? Did his mother, Dr. Maxxer, share her crazy conspiracy theories with him?

"Trestin told me," he answers my unspoken question, referring to one of the men who was working for Dr. Maxxer.

"You knew Trestin?"

"He came to visit me when I was staying with Cody. After they murdered my mother. He was sick, dying. The transession gene was killing him, like it nearly killed me. He wanted to tell me why my mother left me. What she died fighting for."

A small part of me is desperate to ask him if he believes it. If he's crazy enough to think that Diotech is being controlled and protected by a secret organization of the most powerful people on the planet. But the rational part of me insists it doesn't matter. It's a preposterous explanation that's founded on the ramblings of a madwoman.

"Lyzender—" I begin quietly, but he interrupts me before I can finish.

"Why do you call me that?"

"Because it's your name."

"That's never been my name. Not to you, anyway."

I know what he's referring to. I know what he *wants* me to call him. I can remember the day I named him. It was one of the memories that was originally taken from me and later returned. I bravely recall it now, even though I know it will bring me nothing but harrowing grief.

"Zen." The three letters drift from my lips like an exhale.

He looks at me, eyebrows knit together.

"It's a word," I try to explain. "I read it in one of the texts you brought me. It means—"

"At peace," he answers.

"Like you . . . Lyzender."

As expected, the torment begins. The stabbing guilt, the despairing anguish, the fervent desire to crush my head between my hands until it bursts. Until it stops.

". . . your brain can be programmed to associate a certain memory with any emotion we choose."

Stop!

My emotions aren't fake. They're not coded into me like a glitching Slate. They're mine and they're real.

Real because Lyzender was a mistake. Every part of my past—a mistake.

"You're so different." He huffs out the words like they weigh a thousand pounds apiece. And then, a moment later, more quietly, "So different."

"Why?" I demand, furiously splashing the water with my hand. "Because I don't fall all over you whenever you walk into a room anymore? Because I'm strong enough to resist you now?"

Abruptly, he spins around. My body is submerged in water, but still I attempt to cover myself with my hands.

"Hey!" I protest.

But he keeps looking. Not at the parts I'm trying to hide, but at the parts I didn't know I had to. My face. My eyes. *Me.*

"You used to have this fire about you. This fierceness. Even when they erased everything—when they made you a blank page—it was still there. The girl I met in that cottage never would have sided with them. Never would have loved who they told her to love. Kissed who they told her to kiss. *She* was the strong one. Not you. It's like"—he closes his eyes, searching—"it's like they extinguished your fire. The thing that made you Seraphina is gone. Now you're just Sera. I prefer the blank page."

"I don't love him because they told me to." Right now, it's the only accusation I can dispute. "I love him because he's him."

Lyzender sighs as his head lolls forward, like he's fallen asleep. Like he's given up.

"Because he's like you," he whispers.

I wade closer to him, uncertain I heard him correctly. "What?"

"I knew eventually there'd come a day when I wouldn't be good enough for you. When my *ordinary* was overshadowed by your *extraordinary*. The day I saw him on the Feed for the first time, some part of me knew that it was over. That I'd never be able to compete with that kind of perfection. You found your match. Even if Diotech had to manufacture it for you. In a way, I guess that makes sense."

He turns back around and I float in silence. The tiny ripples my body makes as I maneuver in the water are the only sound for miles.

I don't know how to respond to what he's just said and from his closed-off posture, I'm not sure he even wants me to try.

The sun is starting to set. It will be dark soon, and I imagine Paddok will want us back before then. So I emerge from the water and wrap the towel around me. Shivering, I slide my feet into my shoes and bundle my clothes under my arm. Without saying anything, I stand next to Lyzender and cast a sidelong glance at him.

He extends his hand toward me. I look down to see a dandelion lying in his open palm, its fragile white fibers still intact.

I stare at it, unsure what to do. I'm afraid of what it will mean if I take it. But I'm more afraid of what it will mean if I don't.

I gently pinch the stem between my fingers, flinching slightly when my skin touches his.

He nods too many times for it to look natural. Then we start back to camp.

With the heavy shadows that follow us, the ten-minute walk feels like an hour. The air is so thick around us, it's like walking through mud. The ground seems to sprout fingers that grip my ankles, making it nearly impossible to take another step.

When we finally reach my tent, he doesn't make any move to accompany me inside. Not that I expected him to. Not that there's any reason for him to.

Still, it disappoints me.

And I hate myself for it.

Lyzender has already started to walk away.

"He's not perfect," I say to his back. He stops but doesn't turn around. "He has a temper. I don't know where it comes from, but he can't control it. He becomes irrational. Fueled by anger and rage. You can't calm him down. It's like something takes over him. Something living and breathing inside of him."

I watch Lyzender's shoulders rise and fall with his steady breath.

What do I hope he'll say to me now?

I don't know.

I don't even know why I told him what I did.

At the very least, I pray that he'll face me again. So that I can see if my words have changed him. Swept away some of the weariness from his features. Erased some of the burden from his eyes.

But like so many of my prayers lately, this one also goes unanswered.

And I watch Lyzender walk away.

50
ILLOGICAL

By morning light, the camp is abuzz with activity once again. Everyone is preparing for the big day. The day I help a group of rebels destroy my home.

I lie on my bed, holding the stem of the dandelion Lyzender gave me. I'm not sure how it survived the night. I take it as a good omen. Maybe it means I'll somehow survive this day.

Dr. A doesn't believe in omens. He doesn't believe in signs.

I can picture him now, snatching the dandelion away, crushing the soft fibers between his fingers.

"Omens are for people who lack a solid understanding of science," he would say. "Who lack logic."

I want to yell back at him that logic can't help me now. In my mind, I've played out every possible *logical* outcome of this day and none of them are good. All of them mean disaster and the death of people I love.

The glitch with logic. I need something else now. I need something that defies common sense.

I need a miracle.

A shuffle of footsteps outside my tent alerts me to a visitor. I set the dandelion carefully back down on the table. Sevan enters a moment later, his expression grim. Despite all the lies he's told me, he's not like Paddok and the others. I can see it in his somber eyes. He's not celebrating this day. He's mourning it like me.

He must have people on that compound he cares about. He must not want to see them all perish. So why is he letting this happen? Why isn't he trying to stop it?

He steps toward me and opens his palm, revealing a nutrition capsule. "Take this," he urges. "You'll need your strength."

That's the understatement of the century.

I don't hesitate. I place the tiny pill on my tongue and swallow.

"And take this, too."

He reaches into his pocket and pulls out a small silver cube drive.

My cube drive. The one Lyzender buried in the earth for me.

I sit up. "How did you—?" I begin to ask.

But Sevan is already rushing to explain. "It was in your pocket when we took you. I was directed to search you and throw away anything that might emit a signal, but I kept this. I turned it off so it couldn't be traced but Klo said it was probably too small to register anyway." He holds it out to me. "I thought you might want it back."

I stare at the cube drive. It looks even smaller in Sevan's large palm. I think about the memories that were once stored on it. Memories taken from my own mind. Then I look up at Sevan and his dark, weary eyes, and I think about how tiny this drive is compared to the server bunker. How many memories are trapped down there? Memories stolen by Diotech and altered by Sevan's hands.

I take the drive and slip it into my pocket.

He flashes me a gentle smile. "I'll be out here when you're ready." Then he leaves.

I pick up the dandelion from the table and hold it in front of my lips. I'm supposed to make a wish. That's what people used to do with dandelions. But I don't know what to wish for anymore. Everything my heart wants feels like a betrayal to someone.

So I just suck in a breath and blow.

The feathery seeds scatter throughout the tent before settling like dust at my feet.

I stand and, careful not to step on them, slowly walk outside, into the fresh morning air. Sevan offers his arm and leads me through the camp, to where a hovercopter is waiting to take me home.

51

REQUESTS

The device is smaller than I imagined. It's encased in a sturdy metal box that Klo carries delicately on to the hovercopter.

Fifteen people are accompanying me to the compound: Paddok, Klo, Jase, Lyzender, Davish, Nem, and nine others I've never formally met. I'm relieved when I find out that Niko isn't one of them. A relief I probably shouldn't feel, but do all the same.

Every single one of my chaperones carries a firearm stolen from the past.

I point to Lyzender, who is packing a bag with supplies. "Why is he going?" I whisper to Sevan.

"He insisted. I'm assuming it was part of his arrangement with Paddok."

Something about the way Sevan says the word makes me instantly suspicious. "What kind of *arrangement*?"

He shrugs. "I don't know. Some sort of deal was struck when he joined up. That's all I've been told. I'm not surprised, though. Why would he jeopardize his life hopping through time without getting something in return?"

"Jeopardize his life?"

"I thought you knew," he says in surprise. "The transession gene? It kills you. And quite painfully from what I've heard. It's why it was banned. No Normate system can withstand the strain."

"But I thought . . ." My voice fades.

It suddenly occurs to me that I didn't think this through. Of course, I know what the transession gene can do. I'm the one who nursed Lyzender when he was sick. I'm the one who risked everything to save his life. When he told me Cody had reengineered the gene, I guess I just assumed he had also figured out a way to make it safe. I never even considered the possibility that Lyzender might get sick again. Why would he purposefully choose to go through that a second time? He could die. He will die if he doesn't get another dose of the Repressor from Diotech.

"All I know is," Sevan goes on, oblivious to the internal battle waging in my mind, "it must have been one hell of a request."

Sevan is staring pointedly at me. I meet his gaze. "What?"

"*What?*" he repeats, almost laughing. "Are you really that warped that you can't figure it out?"

"You said you didn't know!"

"I can take a wild guess and bet two billion dollars that I'm right."

"You think it's me," I say, kicking the dirt. "You think he's doing this for me."

"Can you think of anything else?"

I turn my attention back to Lyzender. Xaria is now dramatically throwing her arms around his neck and crying into his shoulder.

Sevan follows my gaze. "Think again."

Lyzender disentangles himself from her, casting a hasty glance at me. His expression is dark and unreadable. He kisses her cheek, murmurs something I can't hear, and jogs up the stairs of the hover.

I think back to the conversation Lyzender and I had in the tent. I accused him of striking a deal with Paddok. I asked him what he was getting in return for his help. He swore there was no deal. That he was only doing this because their goals aligned.

Was he lying to me then?

My head starts to throb at the thought. I can't keep track of everyone's deception. I can't figure out who is telling the truth and who is telling me what they want me to hear.

Or are they the exact same thing?

"You don't know anything," I say to Sevan, pushing past him toward the hovercopter.

I hesitate at the base of the stairs. Jase is ready to nudge me with his shotgun. I grab the handrail and hoist myself up the first step. But I'm yanked back down by a hand on my wrist. I spin around to find Xaria glaring at me like the world is ending and it's my fault. I think she's going to scream at me again, like she did in the tent, but her face softens and when she speaks, her voice breaks a little.

"Whatever he's thinking of doing, don't let him do it."

I forcefully pry my wrist from her grasp. It takes way too much effort for my liking. "I don't have the slightest idea what he's thinking of doing, nor do I care."

I start to turn back but this time it's her desperate plea that stops me.

"Then let him go," she says.

"What?"

"If you don't love him, let him go. Let him be with someone who cares about him."

"I'm not stopping him from doing anything," I shoot back, irritation sharpening my words.

"But you are." Her eyes are welling with tears now. It makes her look so much younger. Like a broken doll. "You are and you don't even realize it. Do you know how hard I worked to make him forget about you, to help him move on from the girl who smashed his heart into a thousand pieces?"

I press my lips together, saying nothing. This girl has treated me horribly ever since I arrived. Why should I have any sympathy for her now?

"And it was working!" she cries. "I was finally getting through to him. Then you showed up and he fell apart again. Like someone set off a bomb inside of him."

I find her word choice ironic given what's about to happen.

I bark out a laugh. "You act like it was my *choice* to be here. Trust me, there are so many places I'd rather be."

"He's hanging on to something," she says, and for the first time I see the pain in her eyes. It's magnified by the tears. "He's still foolish enough to think he can fix you, but now it's time for someone to fix him. I can do that. But first, you need to let him go. *Please.*"

"Don't worry," I tell her. "I did that a long time ago."

I continue up the stairs and disappear inside the hover. It's larger than the ones we rode in during the tour. The SWICK TRANSPORTATION logo on the side indicates it was originally intended for transporting cargo. Not people. The sixteen seats look like they were added as an afterthought. I take the only empty one. It's next to Lyzender. He's twisted his body so that he can see out the window, his head resting dejectedly against the glass.

"We're clear for departure," Paddok says into her walkie.

Klo engages the autopilot system. Like he did with the Slate, I imagine he's already scrambled the craft's signals.

"What was that about?" Lyzender asks me without looking up.

I realize from his vantage point he must have seen me talking to Xaria.

"She thinks she can fix you," I mumble, pressing back into the seat and closing my eyes as a painful chill shudders through me. The hovercopter lifts into the air, dropping my stomach.

Lyzender keeps his forehead glued to the window. "She's wrong."

He says it so quietly, I wonder if he even intended for me to hear.

52

SURPRISES

Twenty minutes after we've left the camp, the center of the hover floor splits open, revealing an auxiliary smaller craft attached to the belly. A series of blinking lights and screens flash from below. Klo jumps in and starts running system checks.

"What is that?" I ask Lyzender, who is out of his seat, leaning over the gap in the floor.

"It's your hoverpod."

My hoverpod?

Meaning, I'm riding in that? By myself?

"We're good to go," Klo announces, climbing back out. He gives me a grin. "You won't plummet to the earth in a fiery crash. I checked."

"Thanks," I mutter, although maybe that would be the best scenario at this point.

Paddok jerks her chin in my direction, ordering me to get in. There's no point in arguing now. This is happening. Fighting is out of the question in my condition.

I move toward the pod but Lyzender grabs my arm. "Wait."

Paddok rolls her eyes. "We don't have time for this. Klo's scrambling loop will only last another thirty minutes."

"I know!" Lyzender snaps, irritated. "Just give me a glitching minute, will you?"

He pulls me to the far back corner of the craft. The interior of the hover is small enough that everyone can hear what he's saying, but the extra inch of privacy does seem to make a difference. If only to make me more uncomfortable. I fidget with my empty hands.

Is this a goodbye speech? If it is, I need to put a stop to it. I'm not sure I can get through it.

"Sevan told you why all these people hate Diotech." He rushes through the words, racing to get them out before Paddok rips me away. "You remember all the stories he told you?"

I nod, but don't look up.

How could I forget that horrific tour of the camp? Vas's disfigured face. Davish's heavy heart. The resentment that Nem carries around like a weight strapped to his back.

"But you haven't heard the story about why I hate Diotech."

"I know," I mumble.

Suddenly his hand is on my chin, lifting my face to him. "No," he growls. "You don't."

You would think I'd have gotten used to his hostility by now. This new hardened Lyzender. But it still makes some lost, abandoned part of me ache. Like a deeply buried scar that never healed. That still throbs when it rains.

"You think you know, but you're wrong. You only know whatever warped, twisted version they convinced you was real."

He lets go of my chin but I don't turn away.

"What did they make you believe?" he asks. "That I stole you? That I forced you to leave against your will?"

I open my mouth to argue that it's not just a belief. It's the truth. But the only thing that comes out is a shiver.

"Seraphina."

"Sera," I whisper.

"Seraphina," he repeats insistently. "I hate them for what they did to you. For what they continue to do to you. Even now. They lie to you. They manipulate you. They brainwash you. I didn't steal you. *They* stole you. They stole your whole life. Then they stole you from *me*."

I want to close my eyes to him. Close my ears to him. Shut it all off.

"Okay," Paddok says impatiently, stepping between us and taking me by the arm. "That's enough soap opera for today. When are you going to get it through your head, Lyzender. She's one of them. Through and through. You're wasting your breath."

I'm guided toward the hatch. I step down the five-rung ladder and lower myself into the seat in the center of the pod. The space is small and cramped, only big enough for one passenger. It's clear from the bare-bones command center in front of me that this is an autopiloted device. No human interference is allowed or intended.

"You okay down there?"

I look up to see Klo hunched over the opening, his hands on his knees. He sweeps his dark blue hair out of his eyes.

"Fine," I mumble.

"Remember," Paddok is saying to Klo somewhere above me, "everything by the book until we're clear. Don't hack her in. They need to grant the pod access. They need to think we're following their commands to the letter. No movement on our part until the gas is released."

Gas?

The air inside this tiny contraption starts to suffocate me.

What gas?

What is she talking about? Is this the missing piece I've been trying to figure out? Is this how they plan to get past Director Raze? With some kind of poisonous gas?

Then I remember what Lyzender told me at the lake. About Paddok's son.

"Before the latest batch could be sold to the government, it had to be fully tested. On both adults and children. So a drone carrying the gas was delivered to the playground of an elementary school. Fifty-two students were killed."

Fear kicks my pulse into overdrive. I can hear the blood pounding in my ears. She's going to kill them all. She's going to murder them the same way she thinks they murdered her son!

"Got it, boss lady." Klo nods. Then he looks back at me, his finger on the button to close the top. "How long can you hold your breath?" He laughs. "Just kidding."

The lid to the pod starts to seal. I hear a scrambling above me. "Flux. Wait!" Lyzender says, his face suddenly appearing in the closing gap. Something about his wide, unblinking eyes sends a wave of anxiety through my gut. Is he not as certain about this plan as Paddok seems to be?

"Seraphina," he says. "I'll see you soon." It sounds like a promise. One that he's making more to himself than to me.

Lyzender's mouth opens as he begins to say something else, but the pod seals shut, silencing his words. Concealing his face.

I stare helplessly at the darkened ceiling.

And then I let out a scream that ruptures the sky.

PART 4

THE UNDOING

53

DETACHED

There once was a time when human beings traveled the world in giant metal birds. With steel wings and tails. They flew thirty thousand feet above the ground. They tore through the air, etching white scribbles into the sky.

Then came the Great Oil Collapse and everything changed.

Cars fueled by gas became museum relics.

Airplanes were grounded forever.

Wheels became obsolete.

The human race was saved by magnets and vacuums. Hover-copters, MagCars, and hyperloops.

Of course, Diotech was at the forefront.

They were working on it far before the oil vanished. It was almost as if they knew exactly when the last drop would dry up. Timed to the very second.

When I received the upload on the history of transportation, I never questioned Diotech's participation as the pioneers of the industry. The headlines hailing Diotech's supremacy in the race to a new energy source streamed into my brain and implanted in my mind. But I never wondered beyond what those headlines claimed.

The command screen of my tiny pod blinks with a foreboding message:

Detachment initiated

The pod rumbles as it comes loose. I feel a sense of weightlessness for a second and then the engines kick in and I'm thrust back into my seat.

I think about Sevan's tour of the camp. The people he introduced me to. The rebels willing to do anything to exact revenge on the world's largest, most powerful corporation.

". . . his baby daughter died during childbirth. Not even a minute old."

"Dr. Alixter was able to pin the blame on one of their distributors . . ."

". . . it's just a little suspicious that Diotech had the synthetic meats ready to launch into the marketplace right as the BLD crisis hit."

So many stories. So many broken hearts. Shattered lives.

Too many to be a coincidence?

Too many to be a lie?

Pressure builds between my temples. My brain starts to throb.

The pod banks left and I peer out the tiny windows at the earth below. I can just see the tip of Paddok's hovercopter as I sail away from it.

For some reason, I can't bring myself to watch it disappear.

A few minutes later, the sleek buildings of the compound come into view. That's when I really start to panic.

I have to stop this. I have to at least try. I can't just sit here. They have no idea what's about to happen to them.

Think, Sera.

What would Kaelen do?

What would Director Raze do?

I look at the command screen. Perhaps I can warn them from here. Send a message through the system. I tap the glass but nothing happens.

"Communication mode!" I yell at it.

The display doesn't change. The progress along the pod's preset course still glows ominously back at me.

Arrival in 2:42

2:41

2:40

"Redirect course," I try.

No response.

"Flux!" I swear.

Klo must have locked me out.

I'm completely powerless. I don't have what it takes to be a hero. I don't know why I ever thought I did. In less than three minutes this pod will land in the center of the compound and release some awful gas that will . . .

I don't even want to think about what it might do.

Suddenly a new idea forms.

The gas.

It has to be somewhere on board. How else will they release it? There has to be a capsule or a container. If I can locate the contraption that is meant to disperse it, maybe I can disable it. Or at the very least delay it until I have time to warn them.

I leap to my feet and rotate slowly in the small space, feeling the walls for doors or levers. Anything that might serve as storage. But it occurs to me that the container could very well be on the *outside* of the pod. Strapped to the roof or the belly, ready to diffuse its poison the second it lands.

A beeping sound grabs my attention. The command screen. It's changing.

A communication is being sent. The pod is requesting access to enter the compound's force field.

"No!" I dive toward the controls, hitting every button I can. Screaming into the unresponsive interface.

"Director Raze! Dr. A! Can you hear me! It's Sera! Don't grant access. It's a trap! Destroy the pod! Can anyone hear me? DESTROY THE POD!"

Tears of frustration—of helplessness—are streaming down my face.

The screen flashes again. For a moment, I feel a dangerous hope rising in my chest.

Did someone hear me?

Are they responding?

System override by Diotech Corporation

The standard protocol has been initiated. Diotech is taking control of the pod.

Activating internal detection devices

A bright crimson light flares across my vision and I watch my infrared silhouette appear on the screen in deep reds and glowing oranges. My still capture appears next to it. An openmouthed, panicked expression distorts my features.

Scanning for prohibited materials

YES!

I shudder a sigh of relief.

They're inspecting the pod. They're checking for hazardous items. Weapons. Biogerms. Mysterious canisters full of deadly gas.

They have to find it. And once they do, the pod won't be granted entrance. Raze will never allow it to land.

I feel my spirits lifting.

It's not over. This morning won't end in catastrophe.

But then I see what flashes on the screen next and my hope shatters into tiny irreparable pieces.

Access granted
Initiate landing procedure

54

CHAMBER

How could the scans not find it? Where could they possibly have hidden this gas that Diotech wouldn't be able to detect it?

Did Klo rig the scanning devices before we boarded the hovercopter?

That doesn't seem likely. Paddok was adamant about playing by the rules. No hacks. They wanted Diotech to trust my pod. To let me land without hesitation.

My chest tightens as the ground below me grows nearer. The sight of the familiar buildings and manicured pathways should bring me comfort. All I've wanted for weeks was to come home.

I press my forehead to the glass and search for signs of life. So far, I've yet to see a single person walk by.

Maybe they *did* get my message after all. Maybe they've evacuated the compound. Transported everyone to safety.

Then a flicker of movement catches my eye and I see the first agent appear, dressed in his usual black uniform, brandishing a mutation laser in one hand.

It won't do him much good once he's breathing in toxins.

Several more agents emerge from the Intelligence Command Center. I want to shout for them to go back inside. Get as far away from this pod as possible. But they just keep coming. Dozens of agents armed with Modifiers and mutation lasers and other useless weapons.

A higher-ranking agent shouts orders to the others and they align in a formation around the pod.

I land softly in the center of the ICC courtyard. Barely even a jostle. Desperately, I paw at the hatch above me, trying to get out. With an exhale and a groan, the door unseals and the pod releases me.

I scramble up the ladder and burst into the daylight, waving my arms frantically over my head. "Get away!" I shout at them. "Run! Now!"

All the guards look to their commander, who I now recognize as Thatch, one of Raze's senior agents. He gives me a puzzled look.

"It's a trap!" I scream. "There's—"

I double over as something explodes inside of me, stealing my breath. My stomach contracts like I'm going to vomit. I open my mouth and heave, but nothing comes out except dry air that stings my throat.

It takes me a moment too long to realize that something is amiss. That it's not air escaping my lips, but a thick, orange mist. It slithers sinuously into the air. By the time I think to close my mouth, it's too late. The gas is already spreading, dispersing.

It moves faster than I can comprehend.

Like a soldier on a mission.

The first agent starts to convulse. His body shaking violently. An earthquake going off inside his brain. His eyes roll back into his head as saliva drips from his mouth, running down his chin. I immediately notice its distinctive orange tint.

It's in me.

I'm the chamber. I'm the dispenser.

I think back to the nutrition capsule Sevan gave me before I boarded the hover.

It wasn't filled with nutrition.

They must have triggered it somehow. Did Klo do it remotely? Or was it the open air of the compound itself?

The writhing guard starts to fall. His closest neighbor runs to catch him. He fights to hold his comrade still but it's not long before he succumbs, too, thrust back by his own fit of vicious seizures. A pool of liquid blooms in the front of his pants.

The first agent collapses. Hitting the ground hard. The uncontrollable thrashing continues. More orange bile is expelled from his mouth and now his nose as well. Hideous welts start to boil up on his skin, covering his face.

Not even a minute passes. It all happens in a matter of seconds.

One by one they're seized by this merciless poison that I've brought upon them. They don't even have time to cry out. The gas traps the noise inside them.

Their convulsions are their screams.

Still perched on the top rung of the ladder, I take in the scene around me in horror. I am completely powerless. Completely useless.

Is this what happened to the children? Is this how Paddok's son died?

Tears rain down my cheeks as I wait for the gas to take me, too.

Please take me.

I suck in deep lungfuls of air, hoping to speed the process along. I brace myself against the open hatch, waiting for the seizures to commence.

Nothing happens.

No matter how much toxic air I breathe, I seem to be immune to the gas. Immune to this horrible fate.

I look past the circle of fallen agents, toward the rest of the compound. A pair of lab assistants in white coats are walking from the Administration Sector to the Medical Sector. They stop when they see the spectacle.

"No!" I try to call out to them, but no sound emerges. Only sobs.

A moment later, they are writhing on the ground as well.

Innocent people. Just doing their jobs.

How long will it take to spread to the rest of the compound? How long will it take to reach the Owner's Estate? Is that where Kaelen is right now? I pray he's as far away from here as possible.

I pray he's on the moon.

I hastily wipe my cheeks with the back of my hand and scramble out of the pod. I drop to the ground and start to run in the direction of the Residential Sector. Maybe I can warn them. Maybe I can get them out before it's too late.

But the first people I pass are infected by the gas instantly. The poison overtakes them. Controls them. Until they can't stand up.

I'm only spreading it faster by moving around.

I turn and dash back to the pod, just in time to see the hover-copter coming in for a smooth, uninhibited landing. I skid to a stop.

The door unseals. Paddok disembarks first.

She glances casually around her, surveying the carnage like a prospector surveying land. Her satisfied expression makes me sick. Heat spreads through my body. My hands tighten into balls.

"Nice work," she commends. I don't know if she's talking to me or Klo or even to herself, but it doesn't matter.

I charge toward her and send my clenched fist sailing into her smug face.

55

BELOW

Klo and Lyzender pin my flailing arms to my sides and yank me back, while Jase jumps out of the hover and wields his shotgun at me. I could care less about his stupid weapon. Let him shoot me.

Thankfully, I was able to get one decent punch in before they restrained me, and I can already see the effects of it on Paddok's left eye. The skin is pink and broken just below her eyebrow, blood trickling down. She dabs it gingerly with her fingertip. I'm expecting her to lash out at me in return, but she doesn't. I almost wish she would. I could use a fight right now.

"You killed them!" I scream at her, wrestling against my captors. Given my limited capabilities, I only manage to elbow Klo in the ribs.

He groans. "Lyzender, control your woman."

"Just be grateful she doesn't have her full strength," Lyzender says with a chuckle. "Or we'd all be dead."

I'm still shouting, "You killed innocent people! You are a murderer!"

"They're not dead," Paddok mumbles, wiping her bloody fingertip on her shirt.

I stop thrashing and stare incredulously at her. "What?"

"I said, they're not dead. Flux, Sera. I'm not Jans Alixter. It's a disabling nerve gas but it's been modified so the effects are temporary. You can thank Leylia Wong for that. It'll wear off in a few hours."

"Temporary?" I confirm.

"If it was deadly it would have been green. The green stuff is what killed my son."

I shake off Lyzender and Klo.

"Although I should have killed them," Paddok grumbles. "God knows they wouldn't have shown us the same mercy."

"Why doesn't it affect us?" I ask.

"We've been injected with a blocker," Klo explains.

"Enough chitchat. Get the device," Paddok orders, holding a palm to her swelling eye. Jase and Nem stand guard with their weapons as Lyzender carefully removes the metal box.

"Klo." Paddok points at him. "Wait here with the hover. Keep refreshing the scramble loops if necessary. The rest of you are with me in the bunker." She stops to shoot me a vicious glare. "And you. Try to keep your fist away from my face, okay?"

I nod. A small part of me feels like I should offer her an apology. But then I remember what's inside the box cradled in Lyzender's hands and all inklings of remorse die.

Klo climbs back into the hover, and Lyzender starts walking toward the Medical Sector. The rest of the group follows him. I don't want to be anywhere near Paddok so I keep pace with Lyzender in the front. We pass several more unconscious bodies—all with the same orange-tinted bile oozing from their lips and hideous boils covering their skin. The gas spread quickly, but I notice it's no longer dispersing from my mouth. I hope this means it will eventually stop affecting people. That the worst is over.

But I know the worst is yet to come.

I glance down at the metal box in Lyzender's hands. It's only about ten inches wide and four inches high. I still can't believe it's enough to destroy an entire compound.

We walk under the archways of the Medical Sector and up to the main entrance of Building 2. Lyzender pauses to hand the device to Jase and pulls a small container out of his bag. When he pops open the lid, I see that it's lined with several nanostrips in the shape of fingerprints. He selects one, slips it on his finger, and runs it across the door panel.

Access is granted.

We proceed down a long corridor past several smaller labs until we reach a flat gray wall. But I quickly realize it's not, in fact, a wall when Lyzender locates the square panel and swipes his fingertip across it.

A VersaScreen.

Designed to look like a wall.

"Director Raze's print," he says proudly, peeling off the nanostrip and returning it to the case. "Courtesy of Klo."

The screen splits open and the fifteen of us cram into an awaiting lift. Lyzender removes a flat, rectangular device from the same case and holds it in front of his mouth. When he speaks, his voice is distorted, making it lower and more gravelly.

"Bunker floor."

He sounds *exactly* like Director Raze.

The lift descends. It feels like light-years before we reach the bottom.

We're released into another long corridor. This one is bare and dimly lit. There are no windows and no doors. The only exit is the way we came in.

"I don't understand," I whisper to Lyzender as we gradually make our way to the end of the hallway. "Why don't you just transesse into the bunker with the device?"

He laughs. "Do you remember what happens when you transesse? What it feels like?"

I think back to the swirling nausea that overtook me every time I jumped across space and time. "It feels like your insides have been ripped apart and put back together."

"Well, imagine doing that with a device that could destroy a small village."

"Oh."

He nods toward the end of the hallway, at the massive silver wall that awaits. "Synthosteel," Lyzender whispers to me.

I know what it is. It's manufactured here. The most impenetrable substance ever created. Known to withstand nuclear blasts.

"When the device detonates within these walls," he explains, "no one will even hear it. But anything inside doesn't stand a chance."

The group stops in front of the wall. Lyzender reaches out and strokes the steel, as though he's admiring its strength.

"The server bunker," he says quietly to himself. Then there's a long, heavy silence as Lyzender simply stares at the dense steel, his palm resting against its unyielding surface.

If I didn't know any better I would think he was praying.

"I had nothing there. Except a mother who cared more about her latest research project than her own family. And a father who left because of it."

Those were Lyzender's words to me that early morning we sat outside the Pattinsons' farm house in the year 1609 and watched the last rays of sunlight burst into the sky. His hatred for Diotech runs so deep, it's become a part of him. Like an extra limb or appendage. He's carried it around with him for so many years, he's permanently hunched under the weight of its hostility.

Now he's come to accomplish the one objective that has

fueled him and defined him for longer than he can remember. The one goal he probably never imagined he would ever achieve.

He turns to me, his gaze pleading, as though he's begging for forgiveness. "Every piece of data ever created or collected by Diotech is behind this door. Every memory they've confiscated, every life they've ruined, every heart they've broken."

Suddenly, I understand. And relief washes over me.

It's only the data they want. Not the hundreds of lives. Or the buildings. Or the money. Just the information. The intellectual gold.

The rest is just a pile of synthetics.

Moisture is pooling in Lyzender's desperate eyes. He wants me to tell him it's okay. He wants my permission to obliterate it all.

But I can't give him that and he knows it.

It's not mine to give.

And even if it was, I think he knows what my answer would be.

He wipes his eyes and taps the panel on the wall. A digital keypad appears. He inputs a ten-digit sequence. Paddok sucks in a breath behind me as the screen announces:

First Security Measure Bypassed

A retina scan appears next. Lyzender removes another nanostrip from his case, this one fashioned into a Lens. He slips it into his eye and aligns his face with the screen while a green light flickers across the bridge of his nose.

Second Security Measure Bypassed

Finally, the screen displays a small square, big enough for the tip of an index finger. Lyzender produces the first nanostrip he used and hands it to Paddok. "Would you care to do the honors?"

She looks surprised by the offering but carefully takes the strip and presses it to her finger, jumping slightly as the molecules fuse to her skin.

But she doesn't reach for the screen. At least not right away. She closes her eyes for a moment and bows her head.

"This is for you, sweet Manen," she whispers, almost inaudibly. "I'm sorry."

Månen.

Norwegian for moon.

We step aside as Paddok extends her hand—the red crescent moon on her palm flashing in and out of view—and holds her disguised fingertip up to the screen.

This is it.

It's all over.

In a few minutes, Diotech will be nothing but a memory.

It seems to take forever for the system to verify. I start to count the seconds.

1, 2, 3, 4 . . .

I never reach 5.

Because the large slab of steel in front of us glides open, revealing the eerily dark chamber of the server bunker. Inside, a single pinpoint of red light blinks on and off. By the time any of us recognizes to whom the weapon belongs, the molecules in the air around me are already quivering. Then I watch in horror as Paddok's body flies halfway down the length of the corridor.

56

RIPPED

Gunshots echo inside my skull. The sound of bodies collapsing. Thunking against the ground.

Paddok's people are firing.

But on who?

That's when I see them. Emerging from the darkness of the bunker like ghosts. Dozens of them. Dressed in black, wielding long-range mutation lasers.

Diotech agents.

I feel another ripple of air inches away from my nose and Davish sinks to the floor next to me.

They were here all along. Waiting in the dark.

An ambush. A *trap*.

Kaelen got my message.

Relief wells up in my chest, flooding my eyes with tears. The lights go out. I can't see anything. There's more desperate gunfire, but they are firing into the dark. They don't know if they will hit anything. Or anyone.

"Hold fire!" Jase calls out. They can't risk shooting their own people.

I hear the soft whizz of the lasers. Direct shots. The agents must have night vision installed on their Lenses.

Someone tugs on my hand and suddenly I am running. Running through the blackness. I nearly trip over something. My whirling mind tells me it's a body.

Paddok perhaps?

Is she dead?

Or just stunned?

How high did they set those lasers? Were they as considerate as Paddok was? Choosing to temporarily debilitate? Or did they opt for a more permanent solution?

The hand around mine tugs harder, willing me to run faster. My legs beg me to stop. My lungs burn. I cough and stumble and collapse to my knees. But I'm scooped into the air before I even hit the ground.

The ride is jostling. My head bangs against my chest. It's like the world is coming apart beneath me.

I can feel us ascending. We're in the lift. Riding it back up.

Then more running.

The daylight blinds me as we reach the outside. I blink and shield my eyes with my hands. It's then I look up and see Lyzender's face above me. His skin glistens with sweat. His mouth is pulled tight from the effort of carrying me.

He sets me down on my feet and I sway slightly before leaning against a cold surface for support. I hear a scraping sound and turn to see Lyzender fidgeting with a metal grate built into the wall of the building.

I glance around. We are alone.

Where is everyone else? Did we leave them down there to perish?

Lyzender manages to pop off the grate and then he's hoisting me up, shoving me into the narrow hole.

"Go!" he yells in a hoarse whisper. "Get in!"

I scurry forward on my knees and Lyzender climbs in behind me. He fumbles with the grate, securing it back onto the opening, sealing us inside.

"Keep going!" he commands.

I crawl on my hands and knees. Lyzender is right behind me, urging me along, telling me to turn left and then right and then left again. I want to stop. I want to curl up into a ball and wait for them to find me. But Lyzender doesn't let me. He keeps screaming for me to move forward.

To go deeper into this maze of tiny hallways.

I had no idea this even existed inside the compound.

It seems like we're crawling forever. The light in here is murky at best and the haze that has settled around my vision doesn't help. The metal surface chafes against my palms. My arms give out multiple times and I stumble, nearly knocking my chin on the hard surface beneath me. Finally, Lyzender gives me the order to stop.

I collapse, gasping for air. I tuck my knees into my chest and bury my head between them.

I start to cry.

Lyzender is suddenly in front of me. So close. So dangerously close. I can feel his own labored breath against my face.

"Seraphina," he says, placing a hand on each of my knees and shaking me gently. "It's going to be okay."

His words are useless, though. Empty syllables with no meaning.

"Why am I here?" I scream at him, feeling my face flush with bitter heat.

He looks taken aback, fumbling to answer. "I saved you."

"What about them?!" I yell.

But I don't even know who *them* is. Dr. A? Kaelen? Paddok? Klo? Who am I crying for? Who am I grieving?

I start to tremble. "Diotech is good. They're good. They're good."

I will keep saying it. I will say it until I can't speak anymore. Until they're the only words I can hear.

Lyzender grabs me by the shoulders and shakes me. "Sera. Listen to me!"

I rock back and forth, repeating my mantra. "Diotech is good. The Objective is good. They're good."

"Sera!" He shakes me harder. "Let go! Let them go! You are stronger than this. You are stronger than them. I know you are. Why do you think they keep erasing your memories? Why do you think they need to tangle them up with false emotion? They are *afraid* of you, Sera. Afraid of what you can do. You are more powerful than they want you to realize. But you have to believe it. You have to know that you can beat them. I can help you. Let me in, damn it!"

His urgency shocks me into a stunned silence. I stare into his weary, fervent eyes and lose myself for a moment.

"Diotech is good," I hear myself whisper again. But it's not me. It's a voice coming from far away. From years ago. From another dimension.

He falls back in exhaustion, resting his head against the opposite wall of the air duct. He closes his eyes.

As I continue to rock back and forth, his face starts to shift. His angry façade is falling away. Lyzender Luman is coming back. The boy I met when I was locked in a restricted sector of a compound. The boy I let lure me away from the only life I'd known. The boy who vowed to save me over and over again.

"Diotech is good," I murmur. "Diotech is good."

He winces at my words. Like every syllable is a dagger in his chest.

"They erased me from your memory so many times," he whispers. "And yet you always remembered me. You never forgot."

More and more of his emotional disguise is stripped away. Until it's only him left. The way I always knew him. The way I loved him with so much of myself.

"Remember me now," he pleads.

Yes . . . always yes.

"Diotech is good. Diotech is good."

Lyzender's eyes fly open again. A renewed determination in his gaze.

"Diotech is—"

In a flutter of a heartbeat, he's there. His hands on my face. His mouth on my mouth. He kisses me hard, stealing the words from my lips. Stealing the sensation from my fingers. My head knocks back against the steel duct, but I feel no pain. I only feel him. On me. In me. Around me.

Consuming every part of me.

I wrap my arms around his neck and draw him closer to me. I open my mouth to him. He wastes no time filling the empty space. Filling the empty time.

Time we could have been doing this.

His hands move from my cheeks to my hair. Twisting, tangling, grasping.

The words keep echoing in my mind.

Diotech is good. The Objective is good.

I silently beg for them to stop. They can't be true while this is happening. They can't exist while this feels so amazing. Those two worlds can't survive in the same universe.

A million images flood my mind at once.

Dr. A's disapproving eyes.

Kaelen's soft lips.

Mosima Chan's openmouthed laugh.

Rio lifting his daughter into his arms.

Paddok's body blasting into the air.

One by one I try to block them. Chase them away with the heat of Lyzender's lips on mine. But the images return like angry insects. Wanting to feed on my flesh.

With a single violent thrust, I push Lyzender back. I'm surprised by how hard he hits the wall behind him. Either my strength is returning or I've found a new source.

I touch my fingertips to my mouth. My lips still tingle. They no longer feel like my own.

I am not myself. I am a stranger trapped in my skin. Or maybe the skin is the stranger and I'm the real person.

My vision starts to swim.

I collapse forward. Lyzender is there to catch me. His arms encircle me. His chest breaks my fall. His breath on my neck warms my cold, cold heart.

"Shhh," he coos into my ear. "It's okay. It's going to be okay. I'm right here."

I sob silently against him, wanting to pound his chest and pull him closer to me in the same breath.

"I did this," I murmur. "I did this."

"No you didn't."

"I did. I warned Dr. A about your plan. I sent Kaelen a message during the transmission. I used a secret code that we invented. That's why they were there, ready for you."

Lyzender doesn't say anything for a long time. But he doesn't let me go, either. He keeps stroking my hair. He keeps holding me. I don't even feel his embrace loosen.

How can he not hate me? How can he not shove me away and call me a traitor?

Because that's what I am. I betray everyone.

Apparently it's just what I do.

"I wish I could have met you under different circumstances," he says wistfully. "Far away from this terrible place." I feel his lips press urgently against the top of my head. "I wish I could have fallen in love with you in a different world."

I lift my head to meet his eyes, but instead I meet his lips. My mouth finds its way back to his. Entirely on its own. My lungs breathe him in, like he's the only oxygen they'll ever need. My arms encircle him, like they've never held anyone else.

What is happening to me?

Where did I go?

Where did I come from?

I feel like I'm being torn in half. Split right down the middle. A ragged, bloody seam the only evidence that I was once whole.

I pull myself away from his warm, inviting lips. "I'm not the girl you met in that cottage," I murmur. "Not anymore."

"You'll always be the girl I met in that cottage," he says. "They can't change that. They can't break that."

The sobs come again, violent and reckless. Tormenting me as the weight of a century crushes down on my heart.

They already did, I want so desperately to tell him. *I'm already broken.*

But I'm not given the chance. Because somewhere in the distance, the loudest, most deafening thunder is ripping the air apart.

An explosion big enough to tear the world in two.

57

TEMPEST

My knees bang against the metal underneath me as I fight to find my way back through the tunnels of air ducts. Lyzender is somewhere behind me, calling my name, calling me back.

I don't turn around.

Something unfamiliar fuels me now. Something not in my blood. Not hardwired into my genes. A squeezing panic that threatens to suffocate me if I don't move faster.

As I round one of the sharp corners that wasn't designed for human traffic, the sharp edge slices across my arm. I bite my lip as the pain spirals my vision and the blood starts to flow. But I can't stop to tend to the wound.

I keep crawling. Willing myself forward. The memory of that horrific, teeth-rattling blast is enough to make the throbbing in my arm feel like background noise.

"Flux! Sera!" There's terror in Lyzender's voice. He's reached the first puddle of blood.

I find a grate that leads to the outside. I pivot around so I can kick it out with my feet. It gives way easily and I scoot to the edge of the drop and let myself fall. I land in a crouch on the ground.

"Sera!" He's behind me now, pushing himself out of the opening.

"What did you say about the explosion?" I scream at him.

He blinks. "What?"

"You said it wouldn't make a sound. You swore we wouldn't hear it. Because it would be contained by the bunker."

Comprehension weighs on his face.

That blast was deafening. Earthshaking.

Which means it didn't detonate in the bunker.

Which means it wasn't contained.

"Seraphina," he tries.

I don't wait for him to finish. I take off at a run, scanning the Medical Sector with my limited vision as I go. Everything looks intact. There doesn't seem to be damage to any of the buildings. Even the pathways are perfectly manicured. Not a flower petal out of place.

I know we entered the bunker through the Medical Sector. Lyzender guided us right under that familiar rectangular archway. The VersaScreen that concealed the lift was in Building 2.

I remember!

But I also remember that long, white corridor that seemed to stretch on for miles.

"Which way was it heading?" I whisper. I close my eyes and try to picture the way we were facing when we stepped off the lift. I spin in a slow circle, trying to align myself in the right direction.

When I open my eyes, I feel my knees give out. The world collapses around me.

I'm looking right at the Residential Sector.

Lyzender's winded voice is behind me. "Sera, wait! It's not safe!"

I take the shortcut through Buildings 3 and 7, sprinting as fast as my weak legs will carry me. I'm still frustrated by my inadequate speed. When is this glitching inhibitor going to wear off?

By the time I reach the school, I can hear the screaming. Anguished cries from people in pain. People in mourning.

When I turn the corner and burst onto the Rec Field, I see the smoke. Rising up from a giant chasm carved into the ground. It's three times the size of the field I'm standing on. A jagged, gaping hole where the residential apartment buildings once stood.

Where Diotech employees and their families slept and ate and shared stories about their day.

Gone.

Gone.

Gone.

My legs go numb. The only organ I can feel is my pounding heart.

The only thought in my brain is that it's my fault.

It's all my fault.

If I hadn't warned them—if I hadn't sent Kaelen the message—none of this would have happened. The plan would have gone off without a hitch. The device would have been triggered inside the airtight bunker. The explosion would have been contained.

All that would have been lost was some stupid useless data!

But instead, it ripped a hole in the earth, leaving behind nothing but rubble and ash.

And bodies.

Bodies everywhere. More than I can count. More than I woke up with in the ocean after Freedom Airlines flight 121 plummeted from the sky.

I feel a similar chasm opening up inside of me. Threatening to consume me whole. Swallow me into the darkness.

And wouldn't I love to let it?

Wouldn't I love to just disappear right now?

Fall into this giant crack in my heart and never resurface.

I nearly trip over a large piece of rubble. It looks like a chunk of ceiling. Angrily, I bend down and push it. It takes all my strength to move it even an inch, but somehow I manage to roll it over.

I immediately wish I hadn't. More bodies await me underneath. I stagger away, my vision tunneling. My knees buckling.

A sharp wail slices through the air, snapping me back into myself. I turn around to see Crest, my darling friend. I want to kiss the sky and thank the heavens that she's not dead.

She's alive. Alive and running.

Not to me, though. To a contorted body splayed on the ground. When she reaches it, she drops to her knees. I hurry toward her, stopping short when I see the face of the man she's huddled over. He's handsome. With a chiseled jawline and high cheekbones. His eyes are closed, revealing long vibrant green lashes.

"*Those lashes,*" I can hear her say. "*They can turn a good girl bad in three seconds flat.*"

This must be Jin. The lab assistant she always talked about. The one she called her Dark Matter.

He's so still. So very still. The only movement is a single nanotat on his left arm. A swirling, high-speed journey through dark sky and blinding white stars.

I feel a hand on my shoulder and I jump.

"Sera?"

It's Lyzender. But I don't turn to look at him. Instead, I look up. Into a morning sun that shouldn't be shining. That shouldn't be so eager to get up and brighten the day with its luminance.

My body is heaving in dry sobs.

He steps in front of me, his expression grave. "Sera. We need to get out of here. We need to get back to the hover."

I shake my head. "No."

"Seraphina."

"NO!" I scream, shoving him hard. "I did this to him! I killed him! I'm not leaving!"

I turn back to Crest. She's pushing Jin's hair from his forehead and brushing the dust and ash from his cheeks, revealing cuts in his skin. Blemishes in his pale white skin. With her thumb, she rubs at a gash above his eyebrow, trying to erase it. But her hands aren't magic. She only manages to smear the blood across his forehead. And now he looks worse.

This makes her cry even harder.

"I'm sorry," I whisper to her. "It's my fault. All my fault."

She doesn't seem to hear me over the deafening noise of her own pain.

Suddenly, behind me, there's a deep, angry roar. The sound of trapped wolves and vengeful murderers. When I turn around, I expect to see someone charging toward me, a weapon drawn and poised to slay, but instead I see someone running away from me. Running like the world is chasing him.

It's Lyzender.

Finally giving up on me. Finally accepting the fact that I'm a lost cause, just like Paddok said. That I will never be me. I will always be them. Diotech—good or bad, helpful or evil, protective or destructive—runs in my veins. Their science is my body. Their inspiration is my life.

I was made here.

And here is where I must stay.

A voice calls my name from across the chasm. A voice full of desperation and heartbreak. I look up and see the face I was made to love. The face that lifts me from nightmares, quiets fears, and makes earth-splitting chasms feel like mere cracks in the ground.

His dark blond hair shines brilliantly in the sun, finally giving reason to the yellow orb's presence on this dark morning. His eyes sparkle as they meet mine across the great divide. There is no smile on his face. I'm not sure how anyone could smile in this devastation.

But there is relief.

The same relief that's coursing through me right now, giving me the will to move. To run to him.

"Kaelen!" I cry as my feet falter uneasily on this rubble-laden path. I don't look down. I refuse to see what I'm stepping through. I know it's more than rubble. I know it's people, too. People I once knew. People I might have said hello to in the mornings. Faces I would surely recognize.

Right now I have to stay focused on the one thing that's keeping me from collapsing in on myself: Kaelen is alive. He didn't perish in this disaster.

My foot catches on something and suddenly I'm plummeting downward. Into the horrors that lie beneath me. I thrust my hands out to break my fall and something sharp slices through my right palm.

"Sera!" Kaelen calls. Even though I know he's moving toward me, it sounds as though he's getting farther away.

Blood gushes from my hand. I lift it up to see what cut me and my gaze falls on a pair of red-handled trimming shears.

No.

Please, no.

I'm crying again before I even look down. Before I even see his face.

I lost him once before. Logic tells me it should be easier the second time around. Like I've had practice or something.

But logic is nowhere to be found in this chaos of smoke and death.

There is only sorrow. There is only pain. The kind that blinds you and makes you feel like you're drowning on land.

I pull Rio's head into my lap and stroke his face. It's marred with scratches where the demolished building came crashing down on him. He was probably outside trimming the hedges.

So many hedges.

I can feel blood from a gash in the back of his head trickling between my knees.

I open my mouth, open my throat, open my soul, and let out a wail.

The gruesome sound terrifies me. I have trouble believing that it actually came from me. It was animalistic. No, more like someone ripping something animalistic apart. I've never heard such a noise escape me before.

A quiet groan startles me and I look down to see a tremble of movement on his face.

"Rio!"

"Sera." I can hear the injury in his voice. The fading strength. Death waits nearby, ready to take him from me, but somehow he's still here.

He coughs, a spittle of blood trickling from his mouth. I wipe it away with my hand.

His eyes fight to open. I feel a clench in my chest as I wonder which eyes will be staring back at me. The Rio I remember? Or the eerie barren version they replaced him with?

I resolve to stay with him no matter which one I see.

"Seraphina?" he says again, and I wilt in relief.

Seraphina.

Rio was the one who gave me that name. The real Dr. Rio. The man who created me. Who brought me to life and treated me like a daughter.

When his eyes drag open, I see him again.

I grab his hand and squeeze it. "I'm here."

Another cough as he struggles to speak. "Do you know why I helped you escape?"

I bite my lip and shake my head. I only know the reasons Dr. A told me. And who knows if those are true anymore.

"Because you're free," he tells me. "You were always free."

"Rio, I—"

"I never told you who you really are. I should have told you."

"I'm an ExGen," I say numbly. But the title no longer holds the same pride it once did.

He tries to shake his head, but the movement only makes him cough up more blood. He winces against the pain.

"Stay still," I urge him. "Please."

He tries to speak again but the words are too quiet. I lean down and press my ear to his lips. "Find out who you really are," he says.

I feel a delicate shudder of breath against my cheek. There's a finality about it. A release of suffering. He's gone. No longer suspended between life and death. Between sanity and madness.

I didn't think there were any tears left inside me. I thought I had cried them all. But somehow, from somewhere, a single drop of rain leaks onto his cheek.

Like a miracle.

Like the beginning of a storm.

58

CROSSING

"Stay right where you are, lover boy."

I feel the sharp steel against my neck before I see the man holding it. I look up. Kaelen has crashed to a halt only an arm's reach away. He glares somewhere above my head, at the knife's owner. Then his gaze finds me and I watch the fear take shape in his eyes.

"Up you go," the man says to me, easing me to a stand by the elbow. The blade stays firmly pressed against my throat. "Very good."

Kaelen is frozen. Everything is still except the twitch of his fingers. He can't decide whether to follow the man's orders or charge and take his chances.

"Thought you could get away with it, didn't you?" The stern voice is breathy and warm at my ear. He smells of smoke and desert dust and deer meat.

"Jase." I finally place him. I assumed he was dead.

"You thought you could tip off your little Diotech friends and not pay for it, huh?"

"I didn't—" I start to argue, but the blade crushes my wind-pipe, rendering me silent.

"Shut the glitch up," he roars. "How'd you do it? How'd you warn them?"

I flash a look at Kaelen but don't answer. The truth will only aggravate him more.

"You got out," I squeak.

It's not a question. It's a statement of hope. If he got out of the bunker before it blew, maybe others did, too. Maybe they're not all gone.

He laughs maniacally. "What? Are you disappointed? That you weren't able to kill us all? I escaped the same way you and that coward Lyzender got out. I ran. But not before detonating the de-vice on those glitching baby killers."

"You . . . " I'm unable to finish the thought.

"I had no choice," he growls, pressing the knife harder against my skin. I feel it prick the surface. A dribble of warm liquid trails down my neck. "They are all dead. Paddok, Davish, Nem, all of them. Because of you. Now Manen's death will never be avenged. Or my daughter's. Or any of them."

Kaelen takes an uneasy step toward us. "Jase, is it?"

Jase whirls me toward him. "Don't move. I'll slit her throat. I swear."

"She'll heal," Kaelen challenges.

Jase lets out a dark laugh. "Not with the inhibitor running through her system."

Kaelen tilts his head, not fully understanding.

"That's right. We weakened her. Took away her superpowers. So she couldn't beat the flux out of us."

Kaelen looks to me. Is it true? his eyes ask. I respond with the subtlest of nods. Comprehension passes over him like a shadow. He gets it now.

If Jase cuts, I die.

334

"Look," Kaelen tries. "Dr. Alixter will pay you whatever you want. Just let her go."

"The glitch with Dr. *Alixter*," Jase spits. "Where is he anyway? Hiding in his mansion? Too much of a coward to come out here and fight his own battles? Instead he sends his warped army to do his dirty work. Well, joke's on him. Because they're dead, too. None of them could have survived that blast."

All those agents in the bunker.

Gone. Killed in the wake of my stupidity. I thought I was helping. I thought I was *saving* lives, not annihilating them.

"What do you want?" Kaelen asks diplomatically. But I can see his composure slipping. His temper flaring. If that monster comes out now, we might both die.

"I want her to apologize. For all of their deaths. For existing. And then I want *you* to watch her die."

"Do it," I tell Jase, leaning into his blade. "Cut me. Slice me to pieces. You're right, I deserve it. I'm not meant to be here. I never should have been created."

"Sera, no!" Kaelen cries, trying once again to inch forward. But one flicker of movement from Jase's knife causes him to retreat.

"It's okay," I tell Kaelen. "This is how it has to happen. You don't know how many people have died because of me. How many lives have shattered just because I exist. I've done enough damage. I don't need to live to do any more."

He shakes his head quietly, moisture pooling in his eyes. His shoulders start to shake.

I've never seen Kaelen cry. I didn't know he was capable of it.

The sight sends another deep splinter through my already shattered heart.

A commotion behind us snags my attention. Without releasing the knife, Jase turns us both until we're facing the giant chasm. I hear Lyzender's voice bark, "Move! Come on! Let's go." Then I see two people shuffling toward us. One hidden behind the other.

I gasp when I finally make out the man in front.

A bound and battered Dr. A. His face is covered with gray ash. A purple bruise is forming above his left eye.

He stumbles toward us and I can see Lyzender trudging behind him, shoving a gun barrel into his back.

"I found him clutching some dead guy's body," Lyzender says.

Dane, I think with dread.

Lyzender lurches to a halt when he sees the situation in front of him: Jase's arm around my neck, the edge of his knife piercing my skin.

"Jase!" he yells, momentarily losing focus on Dr. A. "What are you doing?"

Dr. A uses the distraction to run. He doesn't get very far, though. Lyzender yanks him back and points the gun at his temple. "You stay," he commands.

"I'm doing what should have been done from the beginning," Jase replies. "She warned the bastards and led us right into an ambush."

"Jase, don't do this. She's not your enemy. Diotech is your enemy."

"She *is* Diotech!" Jase bellows. "You're the only one too stupid to see that."

"I'm afraid he's right." Dr. A speaks for the first time. It's not in his usual charming, cocky voice. He sounds defeated. He sounds broken. "She is very much a part of this corporation. Just like God, I created my children in my own image."

"For glitch's sake, shoot him already!" Jase screams at Lyzender. "That's what you wanted, isn't it? Why you're here. Paddok promised you'd get to kill him when the time came. So do it."

Paddok promised . . .

Is that it? That's what Lyzender got in return for helping her? A chance to kill Dr. A?

This whole time, it had nothing to do with me, but everything to do with revenge. He's not here to rescue me. He's here to murder the founder of Diotech.

Lyzender's gaze flashes to me and I glare back at him.

"Wow, Lyzender. I'm flattered, really," Dr. A says. He tries for sarcasm but it comes out tired and too heavy. "You've spent so much time and energy thinking of me and I haven't given a second thought about you."

"That's flux." Lyzender slaps the gun hard against Dr. A's temple. Dr. A sinks to his knees. "You've spent years of your life trying to make me disappear. You've erased me, you've warped me, you've banished me into the past, you've even tried to replace me." He juts his chin toward Kaelen. "But I keep coming back, and you despise me for it. Just as much as I despise you. Because no matter how many little experiments you whip up, no matter how hard you try to produce love in a glitching test tube, nothing compares to the real thing. Admit it, you hate me because I can give her the one thing that you can't manufacture in a lab. You hate me because you can't duplicate me."

In the distance, I hear sirens. Lyzender must hear them, too, because he looks to the sky. Emergency hovers are inbound.

"Your time is up, little girl," Jase growls at me, angling his knife so the blade is perfectly poised against my vein.

I glance from Lyzender to Kaelen. The two people I have loved with everything I have. As different as wrong and right. Land and sea. Mountain and sky.

At this very moment, however, they are identical. Twins in their fury. Companions in their hatred of the man threatening to slice open my throat.

But I'm surprised to see that neither one of them is looking at me. Or at Jase. They are looking at each other.

Kaelen gives Lyzender the subtlest of nods. I don't know what is exchanged in that minuscule movement but whatever it is, Lyzender understands.

Kaelen leaps backward, fast enough to make the air spin. Jase startles, turning his head away from mine in an attempt to follow Kaelen's blur.

This movement is all Lyzender needs. He releases Alixter, shoving him to the ground. He takes aim at Jase's exposed head and fires.

59

EQUALITY

Dr. A crawls hastily away, pulling himself to his feet and darting in the direction of the Intelligence Command Center. Lyzender aims the gun at his vanishing form but he's knocked off balance when Kaelen charges him, slamming into him from the side. The gun plummets to the ground but neither one goes after it. Instead, they lunge for each other.

I watch in horror as the two people who each hold half of my fractured heart punch wildly and sloppily in the air, each hoping to land a strike. I'm surprised by how inept they are. Especially when I've seen both of them fight so elegantly before.

There's something about this ruined place and the emotional stakes of what they're fighting for. It slows Kaelen down and trips Lyzender up.

Kaelen swings fast and hard but Lyzender miraculously manages to duck the blow and charges headfirst into Kaelen's stomach. Growling and snarling, he knocks Kaelen onto his back. But Kaelen is on his feet again in a blur, rushing toward his opponent. This time they both go down. Lyzender twists his body so he can wrap his legs around Kaelen's neck. He squeezes, but it's no match for Kaelen's superior strength. He breaks from the hold in a flash and positions himself atop Lyzender, pinning him down with a knee to the chest.

He manages to deliver two firm blows to Lyzender's jaw before Lyzender wriggles away, jumping to his feet and landing a kick squarely between Kaelen's shoulder blades.

Kaelen groans but doesn't fall. He whirls around, striking Lyzender's knees until they're both on the ground again and Kaelen is once again taking his aggression out on Lyzender's defenseless, Normate face.

"Stop it!" I scream. Because it's not fair. It will never be fair. No matter how quick Lyzender is. No matter how much he *wants* to win, he's no match for Kaelen's unparalleled power. The capability programmed right into his DNA.

Nature can put up a good fight. It can scrap like the scrappiest of fallen warriors. It can kick and bite and punch, but science will always be one step ahead. In technique. In force. In adaptability.

Because it can move faster. Evolve faster.

"Stop!" I cry again. But no one is listening to me. They're still grappling on the ground, jockeying for control. Lyzender is tiring. He's throwing everything he has at Kaelen and it's not enough.

So he fights with words. Because it's all he has left.

"She will never love you the way she loved me!" he yells in between Kaelen's blows. "You are a poor replacement. A stand-in. A *fake*."

I hear a frightening growl come from the entanglement of bodies and my stomach contracts.

I know that sound.

It's the same sound Kaelen made when he attacked that farmer outside the Feed station and the paparazzi on the hyperloop platform. The same sound that escaped him when he protected me in the subway back in 2032.

It's the other Kaelen. The terrifying version of him that I can't control.

I don't know where that monster lives. He seems to come out only when he's threatened, challenged, or, in this case, insulted.

I saw what became of that farmer in Miami. I remember the way he looked when they finally tore Kaelen away from him. His eyes had rolled back in his head. His mouth was slightly agape. He looked broken. And not just because his skull had certainly been cracked. But something else in him had been cracked, too. Some part of his humanity.

I fling myself toward the boys still wrestling on the ground. I know my strength is no match for Kaelen's. Not even when I'm at my full capacity. But he won't hurt me. He won't risk it.

"Stop! You'll kill him!" I manage to wedge myself between them, lying protectively over Lyzender who now has only his bruised and bloody hands to protect himself from Kaelen's wrath.

Kaelen is so lost in himself, so lost in this fiend that pilots him, he doesn't even notice that I'm there. His fist strikes down hard. I turn my head. It lands squarely on my ear.

I scream. The pain rockets through me, vibrating my brain. The whole world seems to hum and flicker. Like a broken screen that's trying to hold on to a signal.

When I look up, Kaelen's face reflects the horror that I know he feels.

"Sera," he breathes. It's all he can say. He's too shocked for words. Even though my head is throbbing and my ear is ringing like it's the only sound I'll ever hear for the rest of my life, I know I've accomplished what I set out to accomplish.

I've ruptured his crazed, monstrous state.

I've pushed him back over the edge. Back to the sweet, caring, protective Kaelen I love.

He thrusts himself backward, landing on his butt, and holds his head in his hands, rocking slightly.

"Kaelen." I reach toward him. "It's okay."

"Like hell it is!" Lyzender struggles to sit up, but he's weak and battered. "He could have killed you. He could have killed us both! He's a glitching maniac."

I place a hand on Lyzender's chest. "Please. Just go." I glance at the sky and we're both reminded of the incoming hovers full of people who will be none too happy to find him here. Especially after Dr. A explains the part Lyzender had in today's devastation. "Get out of here. Find Klo. Take the hovercopter back to the camp."

"Seraphina," he argues. His fury has not subsided. Not one bit. "I will not leave you here with that monster."

"I'll be fine. I promise. Now GO." I give him a shove. He winces against it and it pains me to watch. But it will pain me even more to see him captured by whoever Dr. A has called in to deal with him. Dr. A won't be kind. It's not in his nature.

"No," Lyzender resolves. "Not without you. Not again. We belong together, Sera."

"I belong here."

He starts to shake his head.

"Zen," I say forcefully. My voice is breaking. I catch his chin in my hand and hold it. I won't look away until he understands. "You have to leave. If you don't, Dr. A will kill you, or worse."

"Then come with me." The pleading in his tone—the aching, the desperation, the history—it's almost too much. I feel myself crumbling.

I close my eyes. "I can't."

"Why not? Sera, you can't stay here either. You will never be free if you do—"

"BECAUSE I CAN'T LOVE YOU!"

The words echo deep within the chasm that was formed in the earth today. And the one that's been forming in my heart since the day I was brought into this world. I fear neither one can be completely refilled. The new dirt that they'll pile in, the new foundation that they'll lay will only serve to hide the raw, pulsing wound that will forever remain underneath.

The injury on Zen's face is unmistakable. It cracks me wide open. It steals everything I have left.

But if it saves his life, then I have no other choice.

"I can't love you the way you want me to," I whisper. I pray he can't hear the uncertainty in my voice. If he does, he'll never leave. "It's like Paddok said. I'm too far gone. I'm too broken. I can't go with you when I'm meant to be here. This is where I was made. This is where I must stay." I shut my eyes tight, gritting my teeth. "Please, just go."

I wish I could have fallen in love with you in a different world.

I start counting. It's all I can do to keep the tears at bay.

When I reach 41, I hear him rise to his feet. When I reach 50, I hear his quiet, uncertain footsteps. But they don't recede. They come closer. I keep my eyes firmly closed.

57: his breath on my face as he bends down to me.

60: his hand on mine, prying my fists open with his fingers.

68: something cold and hard placed in my open palm, my fingers closing around it.

"I will wait for you." His whispered words are cracked and wounded.

83: the sound of hovercopters descending, sirens blaring, his lips brushing against my forehead.

89: his warmth disappears.

95: the sound of running, running, running . . .

100: gone.

60

MOURNING

The world is quiet now. Finally quiet. The bulldozers and cranes outside the window that cleaned up the mess I made have stopped for the night. The sounds of parents calling for lost children and children crying for lost parents have subsided.

The compound—or what's left of it—has gone to sleep.

Tomorrow will be another day. Tomorrow Diotech will be rebuilt. But the shame imprinted on me will never go away.

I listen to Kaelen's deep, easy breaths beside me. I was supposed to fall asleep in his arms. After he pulled me to him, kissed me deeply, and whispered Latin in my ears. But it was he who succumbed to the night first.

I am still awake.

He tried to apologize. He started so many times. But I never let him finish. I promised him we didn't need apologies. We were beyond that.

"We beat each other up all the time." I attempted a joke. "It's what we do. We can't hurt each other, remember?"

He touched my bruised cheek with the back of his hand. Ever so gently. The remorse clouded his eyes. "I hurt you here."

I take his hand and place it on my chest. "But it doesn't hurt here."

As I lie in bed, I can already feel the skin healing. The pain being chased away as my genes grow stronger. As the inhibitor works its way out of my system. Tomorrow I will be whole again. I will be strong.

I will be me.

If only I knew who that was.

One hundred and twenty-one people are dead. And the counters are still counting.

Tonight we gathered around the dining room table and ate our evening meal like nothing had happened. But it was an act no one could really keep up. Kaelen and I picked at our food while Dr. A stared vacantly at the empty seat where Dane used to sit.

Director Raze joined us toward the end of the meal after he'd sent the police away, insisting he could handle things from here. We listened numbly as he chewed on his synthetic steak and drank his wine and recounted the whole painful saga from his side. How Kaelen translated my message. How he set up the trap for Paddok. How we lost so many good people but ultimately won the war.

The bunker was not destroyed.

Diotech's precious data is safe.

The company will live on.

Meanwhile, my head has been a cacophony of what-ifs.

What if I'd never sent that message to Kaelen?

What if I'd never stopped to watch the commotion at the Miami Feed station?

What if I'd never fallen for the boy?

I don't have answers to any of them.

"You did the right thing," Kaelen tried to assure me after

Dr. A excused himself and Director Raze returned to the ICC. "If you hadn't warned me, they would have destroyed it all. Diotech will recover because of you."

I nodded numbly.

Diotech may recover. But I fear I never will.

When I'm certain Kaelen is asleep, I untangle myself from him and slip into the bathroom, sealing the door behind me. Motion sensors activate the Feed on the ReflectoGlass when I walk in and I see the familiar images of the ExGen Collection ad playing.

"Be stronger. Be faster. Be smarter. Be more," the deep, commanding voice says.

"Deactivate Feed," I nearly scream at the glass.

The ad vanishes just as the Diotech logo appears.

I turn on the water in the tub. No scents. No enhancements. Just clean, clear, scalding water.

I strip off my pajamas and sink under the surface.

The hot water stings my bruised face but I brace against it. The whoosh in my ears brings me a fleeting peace. I close my eyes and let myself float.

The water can't wash away what I've done.

Can't wash away the look in Zen's eyes when I told him I couldn't love him.

Can't mend my brokenness.

But it can bring me blissful silence. Even if just for a moment.

And then the moment is over. I think of Crest sobbing over Jin's body. I think of Rio. I think of Raze's agents and Paddok and even Jase. All the people who won't see tomorrow.

They each lived for something different—rebellion, change, science, revenge—and yet they all died for the same thing in the end.

The grief weighs upon me so heavily, I feel it pinning me to the bottom of the tub. I feel it soaking into me like a wet cloth that will never dry. I will carry it around with me wherever I go. Sodden, dripping limbs that will slow me down no matter how fast my legs can carry me.

At least the water can wash away my tears.

61

HOPEFUL

When I rise from the tub, it is almost morning. My fingers and toes are wrinkled from the saturation of the water. I step into the Demoisturizer and lean against the wall for support as the dampness is sucked from my skin.

I dress and sit in front of the ReflectoGlass. In the same chair I always sit in when Crest attempts to do my hair and tells me about her Dark Matter. She returned to the estate after evening meal but immediately locked herself in her room and hasn't come out since.

I pull open the vanity drawer and find what I've hidden there.

A tiny vial filled with a sparkling clear liquid. It's what Zen placed in my hand before he left. Before the hovercopter took him away from this place forever.

It didn't take me long to realize what it was.

A dose of the transession gene. Cody engineered two. One for Zen and one for me. One last hope of escape.

I stuffed it down my shirt as soon as I made the connection.

Kaelen was too drowned in his misery over accidentally punching me to notice.

"*I will wait for you.*"

That's what Zen said as he gave me the vial.

And I now know it's a promise he will keep.

I doubted his devotion to me. I doubted every time he ever told me he loved me. That's something I will have to live with for the rest of my life.

I don't doubt it now.

There's no way I could.

He had his chance to kill Dr. A. He had his chance at revenge, but he threw it away to save my life.

There is no arguing with that.

There is no hidden meaning or agenda in his actions.

There is only truth.

A truth that was there all along but that I refused to see. I was programmed *not* to see it.

There's only one doubt left in my mind now.

But it's not about Zen. It's not about Kaelen. It's not even about Diotech.

It's about me.

I need to know who I am. I am not a Normate. But I am not purely an ExGen either. I am something in between. Something intangible. But hopefully not unknowable.

And it's that hope that steers my hand toward the injector Crest keeps in my bedside drawer. It's that last strand of dying faith that secures the vial in my hand to the injector's reservoir and pilots the pressurized tip to my vein.

62

TRESPASS

The Genesis Project began in the year 2101. Dr. A likes to recount the chronicles of its success like it's a children's bedtime story.

Sequence: A / Recombination: A – Failed

Sequence: B / Recombination: F – Failed

Sequence: D / Recombination: R – Failed

One hundred and four disappointments until finally they stumbled upon the one that worked.

Sequence: E / Recombination: A

S:E/R:A was a success.

That was almost three years ago, in the early summer of 2114. June 27 to be exact. The date has been etched into my mind thanks to the DigiPlaque that hangs in the hallway outside my bedroom, cycling through the dates of the failed attempts until finally landing on the only date that mattered from then on.

My "birth" day.

Before Kaelen was brought into existence. Before a boy named Lyzender stumbled upon me locked away in a prison cell in the now-forsaken Restricted Sector. Before my escape and my return.

What was so special about S:E/R:A?

Why did it succeed where the rest failed?

If I can answer that question, I think I can answer all the others that have plagued me since I woke up in that womb.

"Find out who you really are."

Dr. Rio gave me the first clue before he died. The real Dr. Rio. Not the artificial one who occupied his body for the past year. He gave me an invitation to search for the truth about myself. To trespass into his secrets.

I don't have to go far to find what I'm looking for. I don't have to intrude into the past or peer into the future. The answers have been here the whole time. Less than a mile away. It's only now I've had the courage and the will to seek them out.

I close my eyes and focus on my destination.

On the other side of the compound, in the middle of the Medical Sector, there's a door that's been locked for almost three years.

And I finally have a way inside.

63

WOUNDS

It's been a long time since I've transessed. I almost forgot about the toll it takes on your body. The unsettling twist of the stomach and joints, the upheaval of molecules and cells. I feel the air shift around me, indicating my relocation. When I open my eyes I haven't moved in time but am now inside Dr. Rio's former laboratory and office. It's been securely closed off and locked up ever since it was discovered that the cofounder of Diotech Corporation was the one who helped me escape. Since then, all access to this place has been restricted.

I always expected a new scientist to one day move in here and make it his own, but Dr. A never allowed it. It's almost as though he wanted to preserve it. Or maybe this room—where they worked side by side as partners, where they created a new life together—was simply too difficult for Dr. A to look at anymore. Maybe that's why he moved the Genesis Project to its current home in Building 1, where he brought in new and improved equipment to create his new and improved ExGen.

The nostalgia of this space hits me like a boulder. From the glossy blue-and-white countertops to the sloped ceilings to the synthetic fish tank embedded in one of the walls. Dr. Rio always used to joke that synthetic fish were the only pets he could remember to feed.

The empty, spherical womb sits untouched in the center of the lab like an abandoned planet.

That giant globe brought me to life. Inside those domed synthoglass walls, a sixteen-year-old girl was grown and birthed into the world.

I brush my fingertips gently across its surface, imagining what it must have been like to be trapped inside, breathing fluid, looking out on the world that I would soon awkwardly inhabit. That would eventually reject me.

If I crawled back inside now and ran the process in reverse, could it erase the past three years? Would it shrink me down to nothing more than a speck of dust?

As I glance around the deserted lab, it becomes apparent just how long it's been since anyone has set foot in here. The hydroponic flowers that used to frame his wall screens have died. The room is still scattered with empty plates and coffee mugs. Dr. Rio was known for refusing to grant access to anyone when he was in the middle of a project—not even a cleaning bot. And the white DigiBoard where he used to brainstorm his ideas is still covered in his indecipherable scribbles and virtual pins.

I spot his desk in the corner of the large room. I tread lightly across the floor, suddenly grateful that Paddok's people removed my implant and my nanosensors. With Director Raze still trying to pick up the pieces from the attack and restore order to a disorderly place, reinstating my tracking protocols hasn't been top priority.

I guess they don't consider me a flight risk anymore. After all, I was the one who warned them about the attack.

I guess I've finally proven my trustworthiness.

Just as I've lost all trust in them.

I tap the screen on Rio's desk, activating it after its very long slumber. It blinks to life, somewhat slowly, like it's remembering how to function again. A password prompt appears and I input the only word I can think of:

Seraphina

It works.

I access the file manager and stare in wonderment at the rows and rows of data pods, each holding countless files. The list goes on forever. I don't even know where to start.

I barely know what I'm looking for.

I opt for the search function instead, entering the first name I was ever given:

S:E/R:A

The results are generated instantly but it's another daunting catalog that would take me years to sort through, not to mention the fact that I probably wouldn't understand most of what I'm reading anyway. I silently curse myself for never requesting an upload on advanced genetics.

My eyes quickly skim the file names. My vision seems to be improving by the second as the final effects of the inhibitor wear off.

I stop when I reach a pod labeled JOURNALS.

I open it and find thousands of motion capture files, arranged by date. I locate one imprinted with APRIL 23, 2114—the day of the last failed sequence, S:D/R:Z.

The next combination will be a success. But not for another three months.

I lower myself into the chair and activate playback.

Rio's weary, larger-than-life face projects onto the wall screen above me. He looks younger than I remember him, but his features are weighed down by fatigue and constant failure.

He speaks directly into the cam, directly into my awaiting gaze.

"April 23, 2114. S:D/R:Z has failed." He stops, wipes his eyes, and sighs. "As you can see, the embryo reached full maturity inside the artificial womb, but like its predecessors, it did not survive the birthing process."

The perspective switches. A new cam has been activated. I'm now staring at the giant womb. Its portal has been opened, the fluid drained, and just to the left of the massive orb sits a hovering gurney with a dead, naked girl laid out upon it.

She doesn't look like me. She has lighter skin and darker hair. Her face is rounder.

Before I can study her further, Rio is back on the screen.

"S:D/R:Z is the thirteenth embryo we've been able to gestate to full maturity. As with the previous embryos, the gestation was completed in thirty-seven days, two hours, forty-two minutes, and sixteen seconds. Zero of those thirteen have survived past birth."

Thirteenth embryo?

There are thirteen more dead bodies like that?

"For reasons we have yet to identify," Rio goes on, his eyes misting slightly as he talks, "the specimens simply do not want to survive outside of the womb. It's almost as though they were not meant for this world."

His words echo hauntingly through my brain.

"Not meant for this world."

He sounds eerily like Pastor Peder. Did Rio have doubts about this project before it was a success? Was he starting to question the creation of life in a lab? I wonder if he ever voiced those concerns to Dr. A. If he was smart—and if he knew his cofounder as well as I assume he did—he would have kept those hesitations to himself.

There's a long silence, during which Rio stares pensively into the cam. Then, without warning, he snaps back to attention and continues talking. "Tomorrow, we will begin work on Sequence: E / Recombination: A. In an attempt to eliminate the issues we experienced with Sequence: D / Recombination: Z, we will be making the following adjustments to the genetic code." He squints at his screen, just to the left of the cam. "Adjustment one—"

Rio is interrupted by a faint *beep*, followed by the soft whimper of a little girl's voice.

"Daddy?"

His body becomes hyperalert. With a swipe of a finger against his desk, three VersaScreens descend from the ceiling behind him and to the sides of him, morphing his enormous lab into a quaint little office and blocking the open womb—and the dead girl—from view with a digital projection of a tropical beach.

In his haste to conceal everything, he forgets to turn off the cam.

Another swipe unseals the main door to the office and a young girl comes barging into the room, face flushed, tears streaming down her face, and blood trickling from her left knee.

This is Sariana.

The same little girl I saw in the archived Feed footage of the synthetic meat announcement. And the same girl I saw in Dr. Rio's memory when I returned to the compound last year with Kaelen.

For some reason, every time I see her, I find myself drawn to her in an unusual, almost familial way. Like I've dreamed about her my whole life. Like I see her silhouette out of the corner of my eye every time I turn around.

And now, I'm struck by how strangely we almost look alike. I didn't notice it the past two times I saw her. She was younger then. But now that her face is less like a baby's and more like a young child's, the resemblance stands out.

Our hair is almost the same shade of honey brown, our skin

almost the same caramel color. And our noses and cheekbones have a similar shape and slope. Her eyes aren't purple like mine, but they're such a deep reddish-brown they could almost look purple in a certain light. While my skin is completely smooth and unblemished, hers is covered in tiny freckles, and she has that pink birthmark under her chin—the one shaped like a leaf.

Staring at her on the screen, I'm suddenly reminded of the genetic disguise I wore at the beginning of the tour. It dulled some of the gloss and silkiness of my enhanced ExGen features, replacing them with something more Normate.

Something that looked a lot like her.

"Sari, what happened?" he coos, and I instantly notice the shift in his voice. He's still exhausted, still weighted by failure, but this little girl—with her knobby knees, uncombed hair, and radiant brown eyes—will never know. She brightens him up like a tiny sun.

She points to the small gash on her knee. "I fell out of a tree in the Aggie Sector." The memory of the wound makes her start to blubber.

Rio scoops the girl into his lap and examines her wound. "Hmmm. Let's see. Oh my, that does look bad. Did it hurt?"

She sniffles and nods.

He leans in closer, his face turning playfully serious. "That looks really bad. My professional opinion? I'm afraid you're not going to make it. You don't have much longer. Maybe a few minutes. Tops. I hope you have all your affairs in order."

This makes her giggle.

"This is *not* a laughing matter," he goes on. "I just told you you're going to die in a matter of minutes and you're *laughing?*"

She giggles harder. "No, Daddy."

"No, what?"

"I'm not going to die," she reasons. "It's just a scrape."

"Hey, hey," he argues, mocking offense. "Who's the doctor here? Who's the one with the fancy lab?" He motions to the space

357

around him. "Are you really going to argue with my professional assessment?"

She nods vehemently. She's loving this.

He rubs his chin. "I see. A differing of opinion. Interesting. And what are your qualifications, Doctor Sari?"

She shrugs. "I'm eight."

"Eight," he says, feigning great fascination, his eyes widening. "Well, why didn't you say so in the first place?" He sets her down on her wobbly, slender legs and proceeds to bow down in front of her. "I yield to your unrivaled genius."

When Rio stands up again, they're both smiling. I feel my own lips involuntarily curl. This is what kept him going through one hundred and four failures.

"So," Dr. Rio says to the girl in the capture as he places a nano-patch over her cut. She hisses through her teeth as it fuses to her skin. "What did we learn today about climbing the trees in the Aggie Sector?"

Petulantly, she stomps her foot. "But they have the best trees for climbing."

He challenges her with a look. "Mrs. Gleist says you haven't been turning your assignments in on time."

She sticks out her lower lip but doesn't answer.

"Sariana," he prompts.

"It's boring. She's boring. School is boring. I don't wanna go anymore."

He chuckles. "If you don't go to school, how will you possibly grow up to be a brilliant scientist like me?"

"I'm already smarter than you," she points out.

He considers. "That's true, but you need to be a zillion times smarter than me." He gives her a pat on the back, nudging her toward the door she came in. "Now, I have to go back to work. No more tree climbing, please. Okay?"

Her shoulders slump as she walks dejectedly toward the door. "Okay."

"Go finish your assignments for tomorrow."

Her head hangs dramatically low. "Okay."

The door seals shut behind her and Rio focuses back on the cam in front of him. It's only now he realizes it's been capturing this whole time. "Oh, flux."

He jabs at his desk and the screen above me goes black apart from one line of text.

End of file

"Diotech personnel search," I bark at the computer.

Anyone living within the Diotech compound has to have a record in the personnel system. It catalogs countless pods of data about every employee, spouse, and child, including name, age, birthday, physical characteristics, security clearance, diet, salary (for employees), grades (for children), daily health vitals, even sleep patterns to measure stress levels.

I think about the horrific story Dane told me on the tour and tears mist my eyes. But I want to know more. I want to know why this little girl is so achingly familiar. Why looking at her makes my skin tingle.

A search box appears and I carefully pronounce her name. "Sariana Rio."

Immediately, something starts to happen.

But it doesn't originate from the screen. It comes from somewhere inside of me. A secret buried long ago. A truth concealed by time and technology.

My brain feels like it's being carved open. A gnarled, clawed hand reaching deep within, pulling the memory out, like lava being scooped out of a bubbling volcano.

I press my palms to my temples, shut my eyes, and bite my lips against the scream.

Somewhere in the blinding white pain, the recognition of what's happening to me surfaces.

Time Delayed Recall.

A memory that's been sitting dormant and encrypted inside my mind, just waiting for the correct trigger to activate it.

I've experienced the anguish of TDRs before. Dr. Maxxer used them to bury a map in my mind that would lead me to her. But I've never felt anything quite like this.

This is an ache like no other. This memory fights back. It holds on. Bracing against the pull of the claws. Like it doesn't want to be unwrapped. It doesn't want to be triggered.

Finally, I can't fight it off any longer. The scream erupts from my lips, sliding across the sleek synthotile floors of the lab. Echoing off the walls.

Meanwhile, the battle continues. My brain versus the technology implanted inside of it. One wants to show me what it's been programmed to show me, the other wants to protect me from it.

I have no say in who wins. I have no say in how long they will struggle against each other. All I can do is clench my fists, squeeze my skull harder, and pray that it will be over soon.

Please, one of you just surrender.

But neither one is willing to admit defeat. On and on they fight. My body is their battleground. My whimpers are their casualties. My misery is the fuel that drives them.

Until eventually, after what feels like centuries, a victor emerges.

Its identity is no surprise to anyone, least of all me. As always, technology wins, bashing in my poor, defenseless brain like the obstinate warrior that it is. With one final blast of sharp, jagged agony, the war is over.

The memory comes sprinting into focus, eager and desperate, like a released prisoner afraid of being captured again.

I crumple back against the chair and let it come. Let the victor bask in its hard-earned glory. But as the images start to infiltrate my mind, bombarding my senses, I realize it's not one of my memories that's been locked behind a mental fortress all this time.

This fragmented piece of the past belongs to the man who put it there.

64

APPEALS

He sits in his office. The sun shines high in the sky outside his window. He stares at it with remorseful eyes, apologizing for not being able to give in to its temptation.

"PLEASE come play with me," the little girl says again, her precious face reappearing on his screen after he's already dismissed it twice. "We can play your favorite game," she negotiates.

He activates the cam and smiles back at her. "Not today, Sariana. I'm sorry. I have to work."

Her lips fall into a pout. "You always have to work."

He sighs. She's right. He does. But it won't be forever. As soon as this project is a success, he can relax. He can take time off. He can watch his daughter grow up.

"Why don't you go play with Ren or Phillina?" he suggests to the girl's projection.

This is clearly not a viable option. "Ren is doing schoolwork and Phillina just wants to play virtual games."

"You should be doing schoolwork, too," he reminds her. It's always been a struggle with Sariana. She's loved the outdoors since she was a baby. She used to cry when she was taken inside.

Maybe because inside is where her mother died.

"Did you finish your math assignment?" he asks when she turns away from the cam and lets her cheek do the protesting.

"No," she admits begrudgingly.

"Well," he prompts, "maybe you should."

"Math is stupid," she argues. "I can find anything I want to know on the Slate."

"What happens if you don't have a Slate and you want to do complex calculations in your head?"

Her scowl deepens. "Why would I want to do that?"

His patience is dwindling. The coffee he downed just a second ago is already wearing off. "Sari," he says with a huff, "I can't have this same argument again. Do your assignment and then ping me when you're done."

She does nothing to hide her frustration as she cuts the connection and the small frame where her face once appeared fades to black.

He turns and looks out the window again. The sun continues to call to him with a warm smile. The cloudless sky sings his name.

Agitatedly, he swipes his finger against the desk to activate the glass's projection program. The bright, colorful window mutes to a dark gray wall.

He will not be enjoying the day today.

He will be here.

He will be with S:E/R:A. The beginnings of a new life.

Hopefully.

The last one hundred and four attempts have failed, but he feels good about this one. For the first time in a long time, he feels optimistic.

He spends the next thirty minutes inputting the last of the modifications into the sequencer. The digital rendering of the girl's face on his screen doesn't change. But somewhere deep within her DNA she is being improved. She is being given another chance at life.

Hopefully.

He gazes into her luminous eyes, which are still no more than a collection of supreme definition pixels. "This time I'll get it right," he promises her, even though he knows it's a promise he can't keep. "This time, I'll finally get to meet you."

He turns and looks at the massive, effervescent globe behind him. The sparkling orange liquid is rippling with anticipation, ready to receive the materials from the sequencer. Ready to cocoon the precious, fragile cells deep within its core and harvest them into a living, breathing, surviving sixteen-year-old girl.

Hopefully.

His fingertip hovers over the surface of his desk, shaking as it readies itself to send the final command.

If this works, she will be the most perfect human being in existence.

If this works, she will be beautiful. She will be infamous. She will be a scientific miracle.

If this works.

His finger starts to tremble. The doubt starts to seep in.

Can he really handle another failure? Can his heart, his resolve, his career really survive another broken, lifeless corpse on his table?

He pushes the thought from his mind. He wills himself to stay positive. To stay optimistic.

To stay hopeful.

S:E/R:A will be the one. The one that survives. He doesn't know how, but he feels it in his bones.

Maybe it'll be the modifications he's made to the DNA sequence that finally do the trick.

Maybe it'll be a miracle.

He takes a deep breath and prepares to send the initiation command. But just before his finger brushes against the cool surface of the desk, another ping appears on his wall screen.

Without even bothering to look at the metadata, he angrily accepts the incoming request. The reprimand already bursting from his mouth. "Sari! This is not a debate! I'm—"

He's halted by the sight in front of him. It's not the face of his daughter that greets him on the other side of the connection. It's his business partner.

"Alixter," he says with relief. "Sorry, I thought you were my daughter. You'll be happy to know I'm just about to implant the next sequence in the gestation chamber. I've made some significant tweaks to—"

Once again, Rio is cut off.

And it is not words that immobilize his tongue, but rather an image. An expression. A burdensome silence.

"Alixter?" he asks warily. "What is it?"

The blond man on his screen anxiously wets his dry lips.

"Havin," he says, addressing him by his first name, something he rarely does. Rio is already out of his chair. "What? What's wrong?"

His business partner hesitates. As if time is irrelevant. As if he knows it won't change anything. "You need to come to the Health Center right away."

65

REARRANGED

He bypasses the hovercart, opting to run on foot. It's a little less than a quarter of a mile, on the other side of the Medical Sector. The cart would be decidedly quicker, but there's something about the running, the sweat, the heavy breathing, that makes him feel as though he's getting there faster.

As if effort somehow equals efficiency.

He always thought this compound was designed poorly. It should have been set up in adjacent rings, spiraling outward with the most important buildings huddled close together in the center. As opposed to these alienated, squared-off sectors.

He also never understood why the Health Center was housed in the Medical Sector as opposed to the Residential Sector where it could be closer to the people who actually use it. Not that many people get sick on the compound. Illness is a rarity here.

But the layout of this place was never up to him. That was his partner's domain. They had agreed early on to split the division of labor by specialty. As Dr. Rio was clearly the more gifted scientist, he would oversee the research projects and experimentation, while Dr. Alixter, who was innately more charismatic and articulate, would handle operations and public relations.

He bursts through the doors of the Health Center a few minutes later, drenched and panting. He skids to a stop when he sees the crowd of people gathered around the gurney parked in the lobby.

The body it's supporting is covered in a pristine white sheet. The shape is too small to be a scientist. Too narrow and slender to be an adult.

Why are they just standing there? he thinks, pushing through the small swarm.

Why aren't they doing anything?

Upon seeing his face, the people surrounding the gurney disperse. Breaking apart for him. Clearing a path to the worst sight his eyes will ever be forced to take in.

It's not her, he thinks as he peels back the sheet and takes in the child's freckled face, light brown hair, and thick eyelashes. She's too small. Too fragile. Too . . .

Still.

Then his brain gets a precious moment to catch up. His brilliant mind slowly processes the data. The details. The facts.

And then he's screaming. "What the glitch is the matter with you? Why are you all standing there? Get me a resuscitation pack NOW!" He leans close to her breathless lips. "Sari," he pleads. "Can you hear me? Sari?"

He winces as his cheek brushes against hers and he feels the coldness of her skin.

When he stands up, no one has moved.

"Flux!" he shouts. "Get out of my way! I'll get it myself."

Dr. Alixter is the one who catches him as he shoves his way through the crowd. Dr. Alixter is the one who holds him as he thrashes. "She's gone," he says, his voice gentler than Dr. Rio has ever heard it. Gentler than anyone has. "There's nothing we can do."

But Rio won't hear that. Can't hear that. He breaks free. "Like hell there isn't."

He sprints down the hall, returning a moment later with a small, unmarked box. He rips off the sheet, exposing all of the girl's frail body. That's when he sees what they've already seen. That's when he knows what they already know.

The unnatural angle of her neck. The slight protrusion of bone.

"She fell," the familiar voice narrates from a safe distance behind him. "From a tree. It happened instantly. She felt no pain. I'm sorry, Havin."

The world starts to turn an angry shade of red. The temperature of the planet rises until he swears he lives on a furious, bitter sun. The same sun that invited him to play only moments ago.

Someone pulls him away, trying to shield his eyes.

Someone else mumbles illogical ramblings into his ear. Nonsense about how life is a mystery, and we can't always understand the deeper meaning.

He breaks from the feeble grasp and suddenly he's running again.

Lies, he thinks as more sweat pours down his face.

All lies.

He won't stand for them. Not when rational things can be done. Things that make sense. Problems don't get solved by tricking yourself into thinking they don't exist. By believing in manipulative malarkey.

Problems get solved by logic and reason and hard work.

And he knows, better than anyone, that science can fix everything.

66

CONVERTED

His fingers fly over the surface of his desk. He moves so fast, his brain can barely keep up. It's his anger at the universe that powers him now.

I will show you who's in control, he wants to shout at the sky.

You can't make these kinds of decisions for me!

With a swoop of his hand, S:E/R:A is pushed from the screen. Her DNA will receive no more real estate in his mind—or his processor—today.

He pulls the single strand of hair from his pocket. The one he took from his daughter's head as he bent down close and whispered to her. The one they didn't see him steal.

He inserts it in the sequencer and the code of her life appears on the screen. All three billion lines of it. He wastes no time or thought or consideration. His finger doesn't hover or tremble or hesitate.

This is what needs to be done.

He encodes the age. Eight years, three months, eleven days, and twelve hours.

She won't have to miss a second.

His finger slams down on the initiation button. The sequencer rumbles to life. Building, coding, resurrecting. In a few short hours, the stems will be complete. In less than a day, the cells will be implanted. Tomorrow her body will begin to grow.

And in thirty-seven days, she will be here again.

In thirty-seven days, he will leave this place with her in his arms and never look back.

He watches the sequencer work. He can almost see her crimson-brown eyes and honey hair reflected in the endless patterns of genes. He can almost hear her laughter echo in the biopolymers. Smell the sweet scent of her skin in the nucleotides.

But no matter how hard he focuses on the maze of genetic code streaming like rain before him, no matter how many times he orders himself not to think about it, the image of her motionless body—her deoxygenated lips, her slender, fractured neck—penetrates his mind every time he blinks.

He is haunted by her vulnerability.

He is plagued by how quickly her fragile life was stolen from her. From him.

As he stares at the endless rush of data on his screen, he can no longer see her. Hear her. Smell her.

All he can see are her weaknesses.

Rippable skin and crushable bones. Collapsible lungs and a stoppable heart. Feeble, slow muscles. Fallible health. A mind too quickly fatigued.

A body too easily broken.

And he knows it's not enough. It will never be enough. Not until she's protected from this cruel and unforgiving world.

Swiftly, he aborts the procedure, which has barely reached the 2 percent mark. The overworked sequencer whines to a stop. He reopens the uninitiated code for S:E/R:A, the girl who will show that same cruel and unforgiving world what indestructibility looks like.

He's never believed in the existence of a soul. It requires too much faith and offers not enough proof. But as he carefully extracts portions of his daughter's DNA—the very pieces that make her her—and inserts them into the awaiting sequence, he prays that he's been wrong all along.

He prays for that miracle.

67

HER

Time is a funny thing.

I've traveled within it so many times. I've disappeared into the past, I've returned to the future. I've lingered in so many precious present moments.

To most people, I imagine time is like a highway, stretched out before you and behind you. You can only see so far ahead, you can only remember where you've been. Someday you may reach those faraway signposts in the distance, but you'll never return to those ever-shrinking landmarks of the past.

To me, however, time is happening all at once. It's not linear. It's everywhere I look.

Somewhere out there, right now, a seventeen-year-old boy is climbing a concrete wall that was meant to keep him out. A girl with no memories is waking up in a vast ocean, surrounded by the wreckage of a plane that was never meant to crash. A thirteen-year-old boy with curly blond hair is lying in his bed, reading *Popular Science*, dreaming of amnesiac supermodels. A seventeenth-century farmer and his wife are welcoming a young couple into their home. A silver-haired physicist is injecting herself with a gene that will allow her to travel through time.

And right now, somewhere in the middle of the Nevada desert, hidden deep within a top-secret research compound, a brilliant scientist is watching the most perfect human being emerge from an artificial womb and take her very first breath of air.

That girl is me.

And also her.

Sariana, the eight-year-old daughter of Dr. Havin Rio, was taken from this earth too early.

And she was returned to this earth thirty-seven days later.

She was the missing piece. The reason so many dead ExGens were pulled from that chamber was because they were lacking the one thing Dr. Rio could never manufacture in his lab.

Humanity.

Sariana is the reason I am here. Her death is the reason I live and breathe now. Without ever knowing it, I stole life from her. I claimed it as my own. I pranced around the compound and the past and the nation, pretending it was me. But it was never me.

The body may belong to Diotech.

But I belong to her.

I always will.

Rio wanted me to know. He wanted me to find the answer if I ever knew to ask the question. I wonder how long that memory has been buried inside me. I have a feeling it's been there from the very beginning.

———

I know exactly what needs to be done.

I work quickly, accessing the memory servers from Rio's screens. I'm now extremely grateful that the server bunker wasn't destroyed.

That the heart of Diotech is still intact. Because that's how you take down a beast. You aim for the heart.

I find the memory files I need and upload them onto a public pod on the SkyServer. Then I dig the cube drive out of my pocket. The same one that Zen buried for me in the Restricted Sector. It's saved me more than once. Now I hope it can save me one last time. I place it on Rio's desk, swipe it on, and initiate the connection.

I erase everything that's stored on it. There's only one memory that will help me now.

The memory of what I'm about to do.

My hands don't shake or tremble as I work. My mind isn't full of doubt or reservation. My breath remains steady and rhythmic. My heart certain. For the first time in a long time, I know I am doing the right thing.

When I leave Rio's lab two hours later, the clock on his screen has already started ticking. Counting down the seconds until a new beginning.

"I wish I could have fallen in love with you in a different world."

In the end, this will be my legacy.

In the end, this is how I will be remembered.

68

SOMEWHERE

The sun is just beginning to appear over the horizon when I transesse into the boy's tent. I sit on the edge of his creaky, metal bed and stare at his beautiful face. The one I've fallen in love with so many times I've lost count.

Or maybe it was *her* who fell in love with him.

Maybe it was *her* heart guiding me all along.

He's no longer a boy. He's a man now. Time stole his childhood from him. Then it turned around and stole his love, too.

He doesn't wake when the weight of my body presses down on the thin mattress. Or when I brush his dark hair from his sleeping eyes.

It's not until I bend down and touch my lips to his that he stirs.

At first he returns my kiss, his body stepping in to respond while his mind is still waking up. His arms wrap around my neck. His hands compel me closer.

But then panic overtakes him. He pushes me away and sits up, blinking against the vanishing darkness to make out my features. To confirm it's really me.

"You can't be here," he whispers hoarsely. "They know you sabotaged the attack. They'll kill you if they find you here."

"I'm not staying," I tell him. I reach out to touch his lips. They're so warm. Just as I remember. "I can't stay."

My fingers find his. I tangle them together in no particular order. A clutter of thumbs and pinkies. I hold on tight. Then I close my eyes and transport us far, far away. To another place. Another time.

A time where Diotech doesn't exist.

Where the stars aren't crossed.

Where wood is wood. Glass is glass. And people fall in love with people. Not synthetic hybrids.

We land on a soft bed of leaves. The change in the air is the first thing I notice. There's a chill. A sweet humidity that the desert can never provide. Zen fights against the wooziness that accompanies such a long journey and glances around, recognizing our destination immediately. The tall trees, the supple moss, the smell of embers burning on a stove somewhere in the distance.

"Our woods," he says in astonishment.

"Our time," I answer.

I smile and lace my fingers through his. This time lining them up properly. His thumb, my thumb, his index finger, my index finger. His heartbeat, my heartbeat.

Nearly five hundred years before Diotech was built, Zen and I lived in a tiny farmhouse not far from this very spot. We worked the land and fed chickens and darned socks. And every night, we retreated to these woods to be alone. Zen taught me how to fight. How to overcome the instincts programmed into my DNA. Just in case they ever found us here.

In these woods, I defeated an imaginary Diotech.

In these woods, we lived out a promise we made to each other.

But it wasn't long before the world surrounding these woods closed in on us and stole that promise away.

I take a deep breath. There is so much to say and yet there is so much I would rather leave unsaid. Saved for another time. Another world. Another me.

But I know there are things that can't be set aside. Apologies that can't wait. Truths that must be stated.

"I don't blame you for hating me," I tell him.

"Sera—"

"I don't blame you for your anger," I go on. "Toward me, toward Diotech, toward the world. I'm sorry for what they did to you. For what they did to us. I'm sorry for letting them do it so many times. For not being stronger. I want so badly to be the person you think I am. But—"

My voice begins to crumble. Zen places a hand on my cheek, quieting me.

"I never hated you. I tried. God knows I tried so many times. Three years is a long time to hold on to something that slips farther away every day. Hating you would have been the easier thing to do. Would have been such a beautiful release. But I could never do it."

"Until you saw me with Kaelen?"

He shakes his head. "Even then."

"Until I betrayed you and Paddok's entire team?"

"Seraphina." He says the name so delicately. Like it might shatter between his lips. "When are you going to understand? When are you going to get it? Diotech is the monster here. Not you. Every time you hurt me was when they were controlling you. Every time you loved me, was when you managed to break free."

"No!" I push his hand away from my cheek. "I can't keep blaming them for my mistakes. I have to take responsibility for the things I've done. For the things I've made you feel. For the agony I've put you through." I stop. Because I'm crying now. Because the words are caught in my throat. Somehow, I still manage to choke them out. "I have to let you go."

The tears are falling down my face like fat drops of rain. Zen leans forward and carefully kisses each one of them, absorbing them into his lips until my skin is dry.

"You can't let go of someone who won't stop holding on," he whispers into my ear.

I melt into him. He wraps his arms around me and draws me to him. His heart pounds against my cheek. So strong. So steady. So unwavering.

"What I said yesterday," I murmur into his chest. "When I told you I couldn't love you . . ."

"I know you didn't mean it."

I close my eyes and draw strength from the parts of me I never knew existed until just a few hours ago. "I did," I whisper. "I meant it. I can't love you. The girl you fell in love with—the girl you climbed walls for, and traveled through time for, and nearly died for—she's not me. She's a ghost living inside me. Who never deserved to die. She fell in love with you, too. But it's not me. It's never been me. I am just an empty vessel with bones that can't break and lungs that don't tire and eyes that see in the dark."

Zen pulls away from me so that he can look into my eyes. Her eyes.

He doesn't know what I know. What I've seen in Rio's memories. Yet somehow he understands.

"Sera," he says intensely. "I fell in love with you. I climbed that wall over and over again for you. I came back for you. Whoever you think you are, or think you're not, it's all the same to me. It's always been you."

His words sink deep into me. Like boulders settling to the bottom of a lake. At first they don't fit. They feel out of place. They feel like strangers. But slowly, the water begins to welcome them. The moss grows up around them, embracing them, rooting them to the ground. Making them feel like maybe they've never been anywhere else.

Maybe they've never *not* been true.

Sariana may be the life that breathes inside me, but I've kept her alive these past few years. I've allowed her to run faster than she's ever run, travel farther than she's ever gone, fall in love deeper than she'll ever know.

Maybe that's worth something.

Zen slips his hand into my hair and guides my mouth to his. The kiss is unlike any of the thousand kisses that live in our past. It isn't angry or desperate. It doesn't scream goodbye or murmur hello. It isn't searching for something missing or recovering something lost.

Science brought us together. Science kept us apart. And this is the kiss that unchains us both.

Somewhere out there, right now, two business partners are preparing to build a corporation that will one day dominate the world. A Jamaican nurse in a hospital is tending to a plane-crash survivor with no memories. A fire is burning the skin of a convicted witch. A pastor is telling stories about monsters. A child is falling from a tree.

And on the soft, mossy floor of a forest in the English countryside, a girl who has finally discovered the truth is kissing a boy who has known it from the very beginning.

And that brings them closer together than they've ever been.

69

NOW

I lie beneath the canopy of trees and listen to the forest breathing. The sun will be rising soon. Zen is fast asleep by my side, his arm draped over me, just as we used to sleep when we lived here. When this forest was our backyard and that sunrise was our morning ritual. At one time it seemed like we could live forever here. Peaceful, undisturbed, far away from the horrors that brought us together.

Then new horrors found us. The people we hoped would help shield us, exposed us. The gene that ran through Zen's blood turned on him. Our serenity became a nightmare in the blink of an eye.

I'd like to think that maybe we could have done things differently. Maybe if my abilities hadn't been revealed, maybe if I'd been able to find a cure for Zen's illness and bring it back to him here, maybe if I had never met Kaelen, never learned about the Providence from Dr. Maxxer, never watched so many innocent people die, then we would have been able to stay. Our fantasy of spending the rest of our lives together buried in the past might have lasted.

I know that's only wishful thinking. I know that five hundred years in the future, there are problems that won't simply go away. There's a corporation wreaking havoc on people's lives, and there are souls that died because I couldn't stop it from happening.

There is one battle I still have to fight. There is a monster I still have to destroy. And I have to do it in the present. In the time where I belong. I can't keep running away and disappearing into the past. The past is not where this war will be won.

I know Zen will hate what I'm about to do. I know he would never approve of me doing it alone. But alone is the only option.

Carefully, I remove his arm from my body and sit up. I pull the injector from my pocket and secure the first vial I brought into its reservoir.

He doesn't flinch even when the pressure of the tip pinches his skin.

I wait for the drug to enter his system. For his sleep to become deep and dreamless. The Releaser works better on him than it ever did on me.

When I'm sure that he won't wake, I wrap my hand around his and I take us back. Back to reality. Back to the present.

The bed in Zen's tent creaks as our weight materializes upon it. I close my eyes and count to ten while the dizziness and nausea subside. Then I remove the second vial. The one I stole from the Medical Sector before I came here.

"I'm sorry," I tell him as I attach the vial to the injector and position the tip against his vein again. "We can't travel the universe forever. Sooner or later, we have to come home."

I release the serum that will repress his transession gene, save his life once again, and turn time back into a highway.

Like it is for everyone else.

I bend down and brush my lips against his, stealing one last kiss. From my pocket, I withdraw the small silver cube drive. There was a time when Zen buried it deep within the earth with a message for me to find. With a promise to return to me. Now it's my turn to leave something for him.

I place the cube in his palm and close his warm fingers around it. Slowly and carefully, I trace the symbol of our eternal knot across his hand and the tops of his knuckles. Once, twice, again.

Two hearts, forever intersected. In a loop that never ends.

"Fall in love with me in a different world," I whisper.

And then I vanish.

I can't stay. I was never meant to stay.

70

LEGEND

Once upon a time, there was a brilliant scientist named Dr. Rylan Maxxer. She discovered that human beings could travel through time and space with a single tweak to their DNA. A transession gene.

But she was convinced that the people who hired her to develop this gene would use it for the wrong purposes. So she injected herself with her creation and disappeared into the past. That's when she stumbled upon a secret organization called the Providence: a collection of the most powerful people on the planet. A secret society that has been around for centuries. Their number one priority has always been to maintain control over the human race and keep the power in their own hands.

At one point, not so long ago, when they felt that control might be slipping, they invested in a small biotechnology company called Diotech. Although Diotech launched many important experiments, the Providence really only cared about one.

The Genesis Project.

The creation of two superior life-forms that would serve as

promotional tools for a new line of genetic modifications to be released into the marketplace. Little does the public know, the enhancements will do more than just enhance. They will control. The injections will be laced with undetectable stimulated-response systems that can be activated whenever the Providence wants. Humankind manipulated at the touch of a button.

This is the story Dr. Maxxer told me when I was brought to her submarine in the year 2032.

This is the story she devoted her life to.

And for the past year I've believed it was exactly that—a story. The rantings of a lunatic.

What do I believe now? I'm not sure. I know that Diotech is not what it seems. I know that Dr. Alixter has lied to me, manipulated me, and used me in a game bigger than what I can see.

When I think back to everything that's happened over the last few weeks, crucial moments stand out more prominently than the rest.

Dr. Alixter's mysterious conversation in the early morning.

Dr. Maxxer's death in the year 2032.

Countless reports of people who suffered at the hands of a corporation that has somehow always managed to be vindicated from the consequences of their mistakes.

Seemingly protected by an invisible, all-powerful entity.

If I list the evidence I have, the truth is almost obvious.

The Providence is real.

They are out there. They are watching. They are maneuvering us like pieces on a chessboard.

But I still don't know for certain. I still have never seen them with my own eyes. Never heard their voices with my own ears. All I've witnessed is the destruction others claim was left behind by their hands.

If this organization is as secretive, as unknowable, and as

powerful as Dr. Maxxer says it is, then I may never have the ultimate proof that it exists.

It's something I have to choose to *believe*.

Or not.

Dr. Maxxer died trying to track down the Providence. Trying to destroy them. But how do you destroy an enemy you can't see? How do you defeat a monster that has the ability to hide in plain sight?

The answer is you don't. You can't.

The only thing you can hope to do is take away its power. Take away its fuel. Figure out what it feeds on and obliterate it.

Then maybe it will die in the very place it's been hiding.

––––––––

When I open my eyes, I see my own face. It's staring back at me from a large ReflectoGlass. At first, I don't recognize it. The eyes are too old. The mouth is too stern. The posture is too upright.

But there's really no mistaking that it's me.

Behind me is a rackful of dresses and pantsuits. A wall of dazzling custom-cut and nanostitched fabrics. In front of me, on a long tabletop, is a collection of beauty enhancers. Creamy skin ointments, nanoconcealers, and vivid eye tints.

I am inside a dressing room.

It belongs to the woman who is sitting in the nearby chair, reading a Slate.

She startles when she sees me. As I expected. I'm not sure she'll ever understand how I magically appeared in front of her without ever touching the door.

"Sera," she says, recognizing me immediately. "What are you doing here?"

I step toward her, keeping my shoulders back and my confidence high. "I want to go back on the Feed. Today. Right now."

She laughs like this is all a big prank that someone put me up to. "Okay. Do you have more to say about Diotech?"

I don't join in on her laughter even though every single one of my uploads on social etiquette tells me it's the appropriate thing to do. "Yes, Mosima." I pronounce her name with purpose. With conviction. "I have a *lot* more to say about Diotech."

71

LIGHT

"We're live in 10, 9, 8, 7, 6 . . ." Seres's accented voice slips into my ear as the hovercams whiz above my head. Right now they're all pointed at Mosima, who has promised to introduce me. Soon, they will be turned to me. They will be feedcasting my face to the nation. They will be transmitting my story.

My *true* story.

Not the one Diotech made up to fool the nation. Not the one Dane softened and polished to help improve my likability. I don't give a flux who likes me anymore. And I have a feeling *no one* will like me after they hear what I have to say.

"5, 4, 3 . . ."

Just like during my previous appearance on the segment, the last two seconds are omitted, but the lamps and cams don't appear to need them. And neither does Mosima. The light directly in front of her flicks on and illuminates her warm, shining face to the world.

"Welcome to *The Morning Beat* on AFC Streamwork, your number one source for breaking news and real-time world updates. I'm Mosima Chan."

She pauses as the cams navigate around her, finding her from another angle. I wait in the darkness with my heart in my throat.

"We have a special guest this morning. An *unexpected* special guest. You've seen her before. Right here on this stage actually. And you've been seeing her for the past few weeks all over the media. She's here with a special message for our viewers. Please help me welcome back Diotech's own ExGen Sera!"

The hoverlamp that's been waiting patiently before me activates and suddenly I'm in the spotlight. In that very moment I'm struck by how lonely it feels to be here on this stage. Not just because Kaelen and Dr. A aren't with me.

This is a different kind of loneliness.

The kind that runs deep in your veins. That echoes against your bones when you're trying to sleep at night.

The kind you were born with. And will die with.

Even though Seres, once again, warned me not to, I look straight into the hovercam that settles in front of me as Mosima launches into the interview.

"I'm glad to see that you're okay, Sera. I read that Diotech headquarters had a little bit of an accident the other day. Something about a faulty foundation causing a building to collapse."

I continue to look straight into the cam, into the eyes of the viewers, as I utter the first of many disheartening truths. "That was a lie."

Mosima is completely caught off guard. She coughs slightly. "Excuse me?"

"There was no foundation problem. Diotech was attacked. Many people died. Including several that I loved."

Out of the corner of my vision, I can see Mosima deliberating on how to proceed. A digital press release was obviously sent out about the collapsed building, and this is a far cry from what was in it.

I'm sure Mosima Chan is used to breaking-news stories, but this won't be like anything she's ever broken before.

She's about to get the exclusive of her life.

"Are you saying Diotech lied in their press release about the building?"

Gaze forward. Don't blink. Don't waver.

"Yes. And that's not all they've lied about."

Another long, pensive pause as Mosima gathers herself and her thoughts. I expect her to ask something thoughtful and profound but all she says is, "Please, go on."

"The compound was attacked by a group of people led by a woman named Jenza Paddok. This same group of people was also responsible for the unexpected halt in the publicity tour last week. The tour was not cut short, as it was reported, because Dr. Alixter was sick. It was cut short because I was kidnapped."

"Kidnapped?" Mosima repeats in disbelief.

"Yes. By Jenza Paddok. Jenza, like every single member of her team, was wronged by Diotech. Jenza's son, Manen, along with fifty-one other children, was killed because a drone released a canister of deadly nerve gas in a school playground."

"You're referring to the incident at Hillview Elementary School a few years back," Mosima confirms. "I was told the drone collided with a bird, causing it to crash-land in the school playground."

"That's what everyone was told. It was another lie. Diotech had developed a new variation of the nerve gas. But before they could sell it to the military, it had to be tested on a myriad of life-forms— plants, dogs, lizards, adults, children. That drone was *sent* to that school on purpose."

Mosima leans back in her chair. I can't help but notice the skepticism painted on her face. "These are some pretty weighty accusations, Sera. Do you have any proof?"

"Yes. I have the memory files of the Diotech employee who programmed the drone. This particular memory was erased from his mind so he could never reveal the truth and never testify against them. I also have the archived memory files of every high-ranking employee and scientist who ever worked at Diotech."

I hear a quiet gasp and it takes me a moment to realize it didn't come from Mosima. It came from someone in the control booth. Maybe everyone.

"Well," Mosima says, sounding slightly winded, "I'm sure we'd all love to get a look at those files. Perhaps Seres can—"

"I'm not finished."

Mosima blinks wide-eyed at my brazenness but allows me to continue.

"Jenza Paddok and the majority of her team were killed during the attack on the compound, along with several Diotech employees. Jenza is only one of the thousands of people whose lives have been destroyed by this corporation. Mine included." I lean forward and pin my gaze on the small floating object that hovers so effortlessly before me. I try to imagine the faces of everyone I've ever met and everyone I've ever lost, condensed into that tiny blinking red eye. "But it is my hope, that with your help, she will be the last."

72

UNBLINDED

"In June of 2114 I was created by Diotech Corporation. I was manufactured in a lab to prove the supremacy of science and to show all of you how much better you could be with the help of the genetic modifications that Diotech is scheduled to release over the course of the next year." I glance at Mosima, then back at the cam. "But you already know all of that. What you don't know is why they're doing it."

I hear a commotion through the speaker Seres placed next to my ear. I peer up at the control booth. Someone—a man in a suit I've never seen before—has burst into the room. Mosima's eyes are darting nervously between him and me.

I focus back on my audience. I wonder how many viewers are watching right now. Five billion? Seven billion? All of them?

"Diotech doesn't want to make you prettier, or stronger, or faster, or more impervious to disease. Diotech wants to control you. You see, inside every genetic enhancement of the ExGen Collection, there will be an untraceable piece of nanotechnology. When triggered, this technology can manipulate your actions and your thoughts. It has the ability to control everything you do and say."

The man in the suit is shouting at the technicians now. "I have twenty-five angry Diotech lawyers on my Lenses threatening to sue our asses into the ground if we don't shut her down right now!"

"No." It's Seres's voice that answers him. But he's not in the booth. He's down here on the stage floor with us. "This is your producer speaking," he yells at the technicians. "I order you to keep this transmission hot."

I steal a glance at Seres, the bald Eastern European man with the countless swirling nanotats competing for attention on his head. He's no longer watching the stage. His eyes are cast upward, to the booth above. He's fighting back. He's probably risking his job to keep me live.

But it will only be a matter of time before Diotech wins again and my face disappears from people's screens. I have to get through this as calmly and quickly as possible.

My stomach is gurgling, threatening to dispel its contents over this polished stage floor. I take a deep breath and will myself to keep talking. "I know you're probably outraged to hear what I'm telling you. But the truth is, I don't blame Diotech for what they've done to me. And what they're trying to do to you. I blame you." I pause, letting my accusation sink in. "Yes, all of you out there watching. When you trust something so blindly that you don't even question its motives, you give up your power to it.

"Diotech is the most successful corporation in the world. It reigns over everything else. But only because you put your faith in it. You purchase its products and buy into its claims and want so badly to have the things it promises you.

"When Kaelen and I came on this stage two weeks ago and showed you how beautiful you could be, how fast you could run, how sharp your mind could become, you didn't doubt it. You asked how you could get it and how long you'd have to wait.

Diotech knew what you wanted and you proved it right. You chose to make it a god. But gods can only survive if you believe in them."

"If you don't cut this transmission RIGHT THIS GLITCHING SECOND," the man in the suit bellows in my ear, "I will fire every single one of you!"

Out of the corner of my eye, I see Seres bounding up the stairs. A moment later he appears through the synthoglass of the booth. An argument commences but I try to block it out as I battle to keep going.

I'm starting to feel woozy. Disoriented. A hundred sights and sounds swirl through my mind at once.

The dying light in Rio's eyes as I held him in the wreckage of the compound.

The rage in Pastor Peder's face as he called me a soulless monster.

The sorrow in Paddok's voice as she whispered a prayer to her departed son in front of the bunker door.

I can feel Mosima next to me. Watching me. Stunned into silence. But still wanting more. I struggle to find my next words. To put order to the chaos that's reigning in my head. To transform muddled emotions into syllables.

When I speak again, my voice has softened. Almost to the point of breaking.

"A very brave woman once told me, 'We all need to believe in something. It gives us a reason to get up in the morning. Something to fight for.' I never believed in much. I always thought it would make me weaker. I was told science had the answer to all my questions, and therefore, I didn't need to ask any. I was given thoughts to think and truths to memorize. I was brainwashed by Diotech, too."

Up in the booth, both Seres and the man in the suit are

screaming into opposite ears of the poor technician whose shaking hands are poised precariously over the control panel.

I close my eyes for a brief moment. Somewhere out there, Kaelen is watching. And Dr. A and Director Raze and maybe even Zen. As I pull the last ounce of strength from the depths of myself, I try to forget everyone else. I speak only to them.

"Belief doesn't have to make us weaker, though. It can make us stronger. But there has to be a middle ground. At some point, we have to think for ourselves. At some point, we have to believe in what we already know and ignore the rest. Faith is only evil if it's used to control you. But it doesn't have to. It can enlighten you, too."

"For the glitching love of Christ!" I hear the booming voice in my ear. I glance up just in time to see the man in the suit launch his body toward the control panel, knocking the technician out of his chair. Seres lunges after him, trying to pull him away. But it's too late. The man's hand must reach its designated target because just then every light in the studio dies and I am returned to the darkness.

73

RESEMBLANCES

I am breathing underwater. I am drifting in space. I am not part of the world that surrounds me. I am in my own realm of existence. Separate from the anarchy that erupts around me. Distanced from the screaming, the franticness, the calls of guards. I observe them like a goldfish observes life from a tank. Their footsteps stomp below me, disturbing the water, quivering my view. But I just float. And watch. And wait.

Wait for the results of my actions to take effect.

Wait for Seres to find the link to the public SkyServer pod that I transmitted to his Lenses. The pod that contains all the incriminating memories I stole from the Diotech servers before I left.

Wait for the world to change.

No matter what happens now, my words have set me free.

Unbound.

Even as Diotech guards storm the studio, shoving the chaos aside, breaking limbs to get to me.

Unshackled.

Even as they press the prongs of the Modifier to my temple.
Unchained.
Even as they take me away.

I come to in a metal room. There are no doors and no windows.
I imagine myself twenty floors below the ground, below even the
server bunker that Paddok failed to destroy. But really, I've probably just been stuffed into one of the cells in the Administration
Sector that they use to hold volunteers who come to the compound
to test out new products.

I attempt to transesse from one end of the small square room
to the other, less out of a will to escape and more out of basic
curiosity. As predicted, I go nowhere. My gene has been repressed
again.

Just as it should be.

No one should have the ability to move through space and time.
No one should be able to dodge the consequences of their actions
by vanishing into thin air. Everyone should have to face life as it
comes to them. Head-on. Courageously. Without the use of scientific witchcraft.

I've done enough of that already. My very existence is a trick of
nature. My speed, my strength, my vision, they are all weapons
of deception. A way to cheat life . . . and death.

It's time I confront my future like everyone else.

Like a Normate.

Like a human being.

The hours tick by, slow and obstinate. No one comes. No one
delivers food. Somewhere on this compound they are deciding
what to do with me. What my punishment will be.

It makes no difference to me what they decide. The real consequences of my actions—the ones that matter—aren't happening

in here. They're happening out there. Outside the fortified walls of the compound.

My fate may rest in the hands of Diotech.

But Diotech's fate now rests in the hands of everyone else.

I have no idea what time it is as I have no idea how long it's been since I was deactivated by the Modifier. But I estimate four hours before a door materializes in one of the steel walls and opens.

Of all the people I expected to walk through, Kaelen was the last of them. He's also the person I'm least prepared to see.

I swallow and sit very still as he enters the room and the door seals closed behind him. It takes every ounce of my strength not to run to him. I can tell from the fidget in his hands and the hard curve of his jaw that he's fighting the same fight.

But our restraint is built upon very different foundations.

For him, running to me, holding me, kissing me will undermine his strength. His authority. I am the prisoner and he is still the hero. I am the traitor and he is still the dutiful soldier. I am the villain and no matter what his genetic blueprint says, he can't love a villain.

At least not with his arms or his lips or his words.

No doubt there are eyes on the other side of these walls. No doubt they are watching us now. Listening to everything we say. Or, as the case may be, *don't* say.

I, on the other hand, don't restrain myself because he is my enemy. I could never again look at Kaelen and see an enemy. I do it because I gave up my right to run to him, to claim him as my own. I gave it up the moment I betrayed this place and everyone in it. I no longer have the right to love him.

At least not with my arms or my lips or my words.

My heart is another story.

The enhanced DNA running through my veins, building my cells, holding my bones together will always belong to him. But

I've experienced something that Kaelen has not. I've loved deeper than my DNA. Deeper than my skin and blood and marrow.

I've loved Zen.

I feel bad for Kaelen. He has never felt that. He has never known what that's like. How it alters you. How it changes you at the core.

And he probably never will.

"They want you dead." Kaelen is the first to speak. I now understand why it took him so long. The words struggle to come out of his mouth.

I nod. "I assumed as much."

They tried erasing my memories. It didn't work. They tried re-associating my memories. It didn't work either.

They've evidently run out of ways to control me.

Death is the only option they haven't tried.

Kaelen hesitates. "I'm trying to talk them out of it but—"

"You don't have to do that."

"Yes, I do." His answer is hurled back at a thousand miles an hour, instantly exposing his true emotions. He's furious at me. For what I did. For who I am. For regressing to my former, traitorous self. He looks at me and sees weakness where he wants to see his own infallible strength.

He doesn't realize I feel the strongest I've ever felt in my life.

Didn't he hear what I said on the Feed? Doesn't he understand he's working for the enemy? Or does he not care? Since the day I first met him in that abandoned apartment in 2032, he's made it clear to me, he works for Diotech. His allegiance is to Dr. Jans Alixter. And for a while, that was okay. Because for a while, I thought we were on the same side.

Will I ever be able to convince him to cross over with me? Somehow I doubt it. And that deeply saddens me.

"Wouldn't you have done the same for me?" he asks, toxin souring his tone. "If the scenario was reversed?"

Of course, is the answer that shoves its way into my head.

But the answer I give is, "This scenario would never be reversed."

He can't argue with that.

"How does Dr. Alixter want it done?"

Kaelen shakes his head. "Dr. A is no longer in control of this compound. He's currently incapacitated."

"Incapacitated?"

Kaelen sighs and removes a rolled-up Slate from his pocket. He opens it and hands it to me. On the screen is a live capture from the inside of the Health Center. I almost don't recognize the man strapped to one of the hovering beds. He's too frail, too powerless, too small to be Dr. Alixter, the charismatic, short-tempered, tyrannical ruler of this compound.

His body is still but his eyes are open and unfocused. His jaw hangs ajar and moves ever so slightly, as though he's attempting to mouth words but his lips can't keep up.

"After your appearance on the Feed this morning," Kaelen explains, angling himself away so he doesn't have to see what I'm looking at, "he went into a state of shock. He snuck into the memory labs and tried to erase his own memories. The results were . . . damaging, to say the least. The doctors are fairly certain he'll be in a vegetative state for the rest of his life."

My mind is whirling. He did this because of me? Because of the things I said on the Feed?

Or because he was afraid of what might happen to him as punishment for my public treason?

I take one final look at the shadow of a man Dr. Alixter has become and then roll up the Slate and give it back to Kaelen. He returns it to his pocket and stares at the ground, his hands balling into fists at his sides. At first I think it's compassion that's making this difficult for him. He and Dr. A were always close. But I soon recognize the emotion running through him is something else entirely. The slight hunch of his shoulders, the clench of his jaw.

I'm not the only one he's angry at.

"Kaelen?" I ask gently. "Are you okay?"

"He's weak!" he shouts, rage suddenly flashing in his eyes, causing me to flinch. "He's a coward! He tried to bury his head in the sand instead of face what needed to be done. This is the time when we have to be strong. When we should be focused on rebuilding. Relaunching the Objective. Instead he's lying useless in that glitching hospital bed like a warped idiot."

His reaction frightens me. He is so quick to turn on the man who created him, who treated him like a son. Like a protégé. How easily he shames him. There's no empathy there. Only disappointment.

The irony is, it's exactly how Dr. A would react in this very situation.

It's almost as though Kaelen really *were* his son.

The thought unsettles me. The notion that I could fall in love with anyone like Dr. A is not a notion I'd choose to entertain. But as hard as I try, I can't chase the idea away. It clings to the corners of my mind, demanding attention, refusing to be so hastily dismissed.

Then, like a weed, it begins to grow, spread, bloom, until it's more than a thought. More than just an idea. It's a life-changing shift in perspective.

I reflect upon the memory that bombarded me in Dr. Rio's lab. The realization of my true origins. S:E/R:A was only successful because it contained a portion of actual human DNA. Not synthesized.

The only reason I'm here—the only reason I exist—is because Dr. Rio took pieces of his daughter's genetic code and wove them into mine.

But what about Kaelen?

He was created *after* Dr. Rio left the compound. Whose DNA was used to make sure his sequence survived?

Despite our genetic connection, I always suspected Kaelen and I were different at our cores. He is so charming. So easily angered. So comfortable in the spotlight.

I don't know why I didn't see it before. They are so similar in so many ways. Even down to their silky blond hair.

As I sit in my cell, once again a prisoner of Diotech, I peer up at Kaelen's towering, almost menacing figure and another unsettling truth crashes down upon me.

Dr. Alixter wanted to live on in a stronger, faster, more resilient body.

And there's only one way to do that.

74

INHERITED

Suddenly so many things make sense. Their special relationship. Dr. A's favoritism toward him. The secrets he would entrust in Kaelen but not in me. Dr. A always looked at Kaelen like he was the son he never had. He looked at me like I was a traitor.

Because I was. In my own actions and in my very birthright. Dr. Rio betrayed this company. He betrayed Dr. A's ultimate Objective. And I am his daughter. The duplicity runs in my veins.

I wonder how much of this Kaelen knows. I decide it doesn't matter. If he doesn't know the truth about his origins, I'm not going to be the one to tell him. Especially not while he's so riled up about Dr. A's shortcomings.

Kaelen crosses his arms over his chest, reminding me so much of the statuesque boy I first met in 2032. Apparently I'm not the only one who's regressed.

"Director Raze and I are making the decisions now," he tells me with a certain entitled authority that makes me shudder.

"Director Raze and I."

Just like that, Kaelen has maneuvered his way to the top of the chain. Just like that, he's swooped in and taken over this company, fulfilling his duty as Dr. A's unofficial commander-in-training.

If he's anything like the man who made him in his own image, there's no hope for me. No matter what his heart might be telling him, no matter how many kisses we shared within these compound walls, his genetic programming will be stronger.

He'll despise me just as Dr. A despised me for so long.

If he hasn't already started to.

"Okay," I reply. Because there's really nothing else to say. There's nothing else to do. I'm not going to beg. I'm not going to plead for my life. I'm done trying to escape this place. In my mind, I've already escaped. And that's enough.

He stands up straighter and releases his arms. "Okay," he repeats, feeling the same deficiency of words. "I'll let you know what decision we come to."

"Thank you."

It's the most wrong thing to say for so many reasons, but it's the only thing that comes out.

I'm not hopeful of the news he'll bring back here. What else can they do with me besides kill me? Replace my brain? Turn me into an absentminded droid like Rio? I might as well be dead.

Kaelen swipes his finger against the seamless metal, causing the door to reappear. He begins to walk through it but stops just short and turns back around. "I really did love you."

I don't know what compels him to say it. I know it's not Dr. A's genetics that are driving his last-minute confession. It's something else.

I release a soft chuckle. "You have to say that. It's in your DNA."

His smile is strained. "Maybe. But that doesn't make it any less true."

75

FAVORS

Over the course of the day and night, I receive two more visitors.
The first is a med bot to inject me with a fresh new set of nanosensors. I'm not sure what that means. That they plan to keep me
alive? Or maybe they plan to use them to watch me die.

The second visitor is Crest. I haven't seen her since right after
the attack. When she was huddled over that poor man's body,
bawling her eyes out. She doesn't look much better now. Her bubbly, effervescent demeanor is long gone. Replaced by something
tired and murky. Even her nanotats are displaying dark, gloomy
captures of people screaming in agony and crying over lost loves.

When they open the door for her, she's not stoic and statuesque
like Kaelen. She runs to me. She throws herself to the ground,
wraps her arms around me, and sobs into my shoulder.

I try to comfort her but it's never been my strong suit. I end
up silently patting her on the back. I won't tell her everything is
going to be okay because those seem like empty words that have
no meaning.

"Sera," she blubbers. "I'm so lost. I'm so confused. I don't know what to think. Everything is falling apart. They're storming the walls outside. They're trying to get in. I don't know if Raze can hold them back any longer."

Startled, I pull her away and shake her so that she'll focus on me. "What? Crest. Pay attention. What is happening?"

She sniffles, attempting to compose herself. "Your feedcast. It's . . . people are so angry. They're rioting outside the compound. They're trying to climb the walls. They're flying over in hover-copters and dropping people down. I don't want them to be angry at me. I didn't know! I swear I didn't know!"

She starts to cry again.

"No one is angry at you," I assure her. "No one blames you for any of this. You were just doing your job. How many people, Crest?" She shudders, her gaze drifting. I shake her again. "How many?"

"I don't know," she cries. "A thousand. Two thousand. Too many to count. I can't even see them all. Eventually, Raze darkened the VersaScreens so we couldn't see out. How long do you think he can hold them off?"

This is bad. This is very bad. Director Raze is already short on soldiers after the bunker explosion. He already sent the police away. If enough people decide to storm this place, I don't think he can fight them off.

"Listen," I tell Crest. "You need to get out of here. Can you get to a hover?" Her eyes glaze, like she's lost in a daydream. "CREST!" She blinks her attention back to me. "Get to the Transpo Sector. Find a hover. Get as far away from here as you can. Do you hear me?"

She nods vaguely. "What about you?"

"I'll be fine. Don't worry about me. I'm strong. Remember what you said to me? That night in my room? I'm stronger than I give myself credit for."

She nods again, uncertain. I feel myself panicking. She has to get out of here. She *has* to. I can't handle one more innocent person I love dying because of my choices. And Crest is as innocent as they come.

"You look terrible," she says vacantly, reaching out to run a fingertip through my unwashed hair.

A hint of a smile breaks onto my face. "I know."

"You need a bath. And a body scrub. And a hairbrush."

"Can you do me a favor?" I ask her.

"Yes."

"Can you go to my room and get my brush, and my body scrub, and all of the other things you think I might need? Then can you get in a hover and take them somewhere far away from here?"

"Where?" She sounds so small. So traumatized.

"Anywhere. A hotel. An island. Anywhere you want to go. Then you ping me when you get there, okay? You ping me the address and I will meet you there. I will break out of this place and come find you. Do you understand?"

Another nod. I can see a hint of focus returning to her eyes. A purpose filling her sunken cheeks. I've given her a task and, most important, she believes it's real.

I reach out and pull her into a hug. I kiss her cheek, right atop a looping tat of a woman walking through what's left of a bloody battlefield. Then I give her slight push. "Go. Now. I'll see you soon."

She gets to her feet and walks to the door, pounding on it to be let out. "Don't say anything to anyone," I tell her.

"I won't," she whispers as the door opens.

I can deduce from the noise and commotion outside this room that rioters have already gotten inside the walls I once thought were so impenetrable.

The walls that were built to protect me.

As I watch Crest disappear behind the door, I pray that she can make it out of here safely. I pray that she'll find another life that makes her happy.

I pray that someday she'll forgive me for lying.

76

END

The next time the door opens, several hours later, it's not anyone I recognize on the other side. A mob of eight men charge into the room, drag me to my feet, and carry me out.

I don't struggle.

I'm transported down a long corridor that I recognize as a hallway of the Publicity Building. I was right. I was being held in one of the testing cells. The din from outside is growing louder the closer we get to the exit. As soon as we're through the doorway and into the heart of the Administration Sector, I hardly even recognize the compound anymore.

It's been completely overrun.

There are people everywhere. Not just thousands, as Crest speculated, but tens of thousands at least. Every available space has been filled with bodies. Incensed, thrumming, chanting bodies. When they see me hoisted into the air by the arms of the men carrying me, they only get louder. They cheer and applaud my capture.

I could break free in an instant but what would be the point?

I'd never get anywhere. I'd be rushed and squeezed to death by the mob.

As the crowd continues to chant, I'm carried into the Residential Sector. I'm overwhelmed by the smell of sweat and fire.

Right then, a loud booming voice rattles the air and shakes my bones.

"Aha! The second one has been apprehended!" The words are slightly distorted from whatever speaker system they've managed to rig up, but I recognize his chilling voice. His crisp, sharp cadence.

Pastor Peder.

I twist in an effort to see where the voice is coming from, and that's when I catch sight of what's become of the Rec Field.

It's so crammed with people, I can't even see the green surface of the synthograss below. At the far other end, still a hundred yards away, a makeshift stage has been erected. Peder stands atop it, his arms outstretched toward me.

It's hard to get a good view from my awkward position sprawled out above the sea of heads, but behind Peder I can make out two large transparent globes hovering thirty feet in the air. They look almost identical to the ones that were used during our first interview with Mosima Chan.

And to my horror, staring out through the thick synthoglass of the ball on the left, is Kaelen.

That's when I start to struggle. But I quickly discover it's no use. There are too many people. Too many hands. They pass me forward, a progression of rough, eager fingers poking my back and spine and legs until I arrive at the stage.

Kaelen is pounding on the glass, screaming something but I can't hear it. None of us can. The synthoglass is too thick. Even if I could hear him, the sound would be drowned out by the raucous shouts from the horde.

I finally make out what they're saying.

"Ex the Gens! Ex the Gens!"

They want us both dead. I didn't need a chant to figure that out.

The egg on the right is lowered and I'm jostled inside. The clear surface seals around me, locking me in. At least it's quiet in here. At least I no longer have to listen to them.

I spread my legs for balance as I'm hoisted into the air.

From here, I can see almost the entire compound. The glinting domes of the Aerospace Sector. The impressive hangars of the Transportation Sector. The vibrant flowers that line the walkways. Even the gnarled, twisted cottonwood tree. Where Sariana's life ended and mine began.

The sight takes my breath away. So many angry faces, I can't even begin to count them. They must have come from all ends of the earth.

Is Zen out there somewhere?

A breath of fresh air mixed into this madness? A single pinprick of light in the darkness?

Some of the compound buildings have been partially destroyed. Some are being raided now. The Owner's Estate behind us is ablaze. The flames are just starting to break through the VersaScreen windows and lap at the sides of the house. All I can think is that I hope Crest got out in time.

I hope she's not still in there searching for hairbrushes and nanopins.

Panicked, I turn toward the Medical Sector in the distance. It's by far the most impervious sector on the compound. The buildings are reinforced with synthosteel. The labs are secured. But what if they manage to get in? What if they find what I've done? They'll destroy it for sure.

Has Zen looked at the cube drive I left him?

Has he watched the memory I stored in there?

Or is he too angry at me for repressing his transession gene and leaving him behind?

I need him to access the contents of that drive. I need him to protect what's inside Rio's lab.

My globe prison comes to a halt as I reach my position alongside Kaelen. His body is turned to me, his palms flat against the curved surface of the ball.

I match his position, placing my hand against the glass. As if I could reach out and touch him. As if I could feel his skin against mine one last time.

My eyes lock onto his and in that moment, I understand. I know. We both do.

He doesn't hate me. He never could.

Just as I could never hate him.

Maybe Dr. Alixter was right all along. Maybe we really are incapable of hurting each other. Because as our gazes intersect and I feel that warm, familiar magnetism drawing me to him, even through this impenetrable glass, I know that all is forgiven.

And soon all will be forgotten.

Peder is speaking to the crowd now, riling them up even more. He's pointing vehemently toward us as we hover helplessly in the sky.

Part of me wishes I could hear what he's saying.

Part of me is grateful I can't.

Because in the end it doesn't really matter. I wanted to make people see the truth. I wanted to help build a new world. One where corporations like Diotech can't get away with deceiving people. With brainwashing people.

Looking out at this astounding spectacle, I guess I've succeeded.

Even if it wasn't in the way I envisioned.

Synthoglass is known for being airtight. Eventually we will run out of oxygen in here. It will take a long time, though.

But it soon becomes apparent they're not willing to wait.

I watch the silent green vapor seep out of the small canister that's been secured to the top of the sphere. It slithers menacingly toward me. Like a long, crooked finger, outstretched and beckoning.

"If it was deadly it would have been green."

Kaelen holds his breath. I do the same. It doesn't seem to matter, though. As soon as the vapor reaches my skin, I cry out in agony. It burns. It suffocates. And as I watch Kaelen's face, his lips parted wide in a scream, I soon realize it disfigures as well.

As the gas boils and blisters my flesh, I almost have to laugh. I find their weapon of choice so disturbingly fitting.

The two most beautiful specimens of humans, born in artificial chambers not too dissimilar from these, dying an ugly, deforming death.

As I scream and writhe and try in vain to brush the vapor from my skin, through the green poisonous cloud that envelops me, high in the sky, I can just make out a hovercopter in the distance. Followed by a second, a third, and a fourth.

Do they hold more rioters?

Or do they hold help?

I turn to Kaelen to see if he's spotted them, but he's not looking up. He's looking at me. Fighting to peer through the thick green fog. Our eyes connect once again. I place my blistered, rotting hand against the glass. Slowly, agonizingly, I begin to play the chords of our secret language.

Index finger, fourth finger = G.

Index, middle = O.

Index, middle = O.

Thumb, index, fourth finger = D.

My muscles give out before I can finish and my hand falls to my side. As my legs crumple, and I hit the glass bottom of my prison cell in the sky, I can only hope that he was able to infer the rest of the message.

Now that I'm down, the vapor works hard to finish me off quickly. For that, I'm grateful. My damaged body convulses. My bones shrivel up inside my skin. My eyes feel heavy. The last thing I see before they shut forever is Kaelen. He's still standing. Still holding on. Still bracing against the pain. Even though we both know it will eventually take him, too.

His determination makes me smile.

He always was the stronger one.

77

AFTER

THREE HOURS LATER . . .

The captain shouts several orders at once as his hovercopter touches down upon the broken earth. The Neutralizers they sprayed over the compound cleared out most of the rioters, but there are still a few stragglers wandering aimlessly in circles, like zombies lost in their own shadows.

As he disembarks, he takes in the destruction that lies before him. A mansion burnt to the ground. Buildings torn open, like large, bleeding wounds. And two giant orbs, suspended in the air like soap bubbles, each encapsulating an unconscious body and a monstrous cloud of green gas.

"Get those glitching things down from there and get those people out!"

His subordinates run toward the hovering chambers, searching for the controls that are keeping them afloat. When they finally manage to lower them to the ground, the captain notices the boils and blisters on the prisoners' skin.

"Stop!" he calls out. "Don't open those yet. Someone get me a suit."

The area is cleared and the captain, protected by a layer of synthetic rubber, opens the first chamber. He barely recognizes the girl. Her face has been almost completely deformed by the gas. Her flesh is corroded and her hair singed away in places, leaving behind rough and blotchy patches of scalp. It isn't until he lifts her swollen eyelid and sees the luminous purple hue staring back at him that he can start to piece together exactly what happened here.

He pulls a Slate from his pocket and scans for a signal. Two sets of nanosensors appear on his screen. They recount the sad conclusion to a story that started and ended within these walls. An ending he was too late to prevent.

"Dead," he announces into his earplant. "Both of them."

He transmits the orders for the bodies to be retrieved and relocated to a nearby army hospital where the state can decide what's to become of them.

As he places the girl onto the ground and steps away, he feels a hardening in his heart that can't be stopped. And probably won't be thawed for a long time.

"Glitching bastards," he mumbles under his breath.

Then, through his plant, someone shouts so loudly it makes him cringe and press a finger to his ear. "Captain, I think you better get over here!"

The coordinates are transmitted and the captain moves quickly, tearing off his suit as he leaves the area marked on his Slate map as RESIDENTIAL SECTOR and enters the one labeled MEDICAL SECTOR.

He follows the signal of his subordinate until it leads him into a dark, vast lab, lit only by the glowing orange, liquid-filled sphere in the center. Despite his high rank and the fact that he's seen just about everything there is to see in the world, he can't help the gasp that escapes his lips.

"Holy flux," he swears under his breath.

"We were able to hack into the security system and shut down the power grid," the sergeant informs his boss. "It was the only way we could get into this fortress."

The captain just nods, unable to take his eyes off the remarkable sight in front of him. Through the thick, gelatinous orange fluid, he can just make out a hand, an arm, the side of a face.

"Do you know how much longer it has to be in there?"

The sergeant points to a screen fastened to the side of the giant contraption. On it is an active countdown.

35 days, 8 hours, 7 minutes, 9 seconds remaining

"Oh," the sergeant adds, "and we found this." He yanks at the shirt collar of a tall, slender young man huddled behind the incandescent machine and drags him into the captain's line of sight. "He was clearly affected by the Neutralizers because he's mumbling nonsense. But he won't leave the room. We tried to escort him out and put him with the others, but he lost it. Started screaming and kicking and flailing. Landed a punch right in Private Lanster's face."

The captain hides a smirk as he eyes the private, standing off to the side, scowling from behind a pink, swollen nose.

"Can we transport this thing?" the captain wonders aloud. "I mean, without disturbing it?"

The sergeant nods. "I think so. I called in a technician from the base. He's on his way here to check it out. It's still running even after we cut the grid. I think it has its own independent power source. Which means we should be able to simply load it onto a hover and get it out of here."

Just then, an animalistic, primal scream resonates through the lab, startling the captain. The young man who was huddled behind the sphere comes charging toward him, hands outstretched. "NO! Don't you take her away from me! I won't let you take her away!"

Three privates are required to restrain him.

The captain chuckles. "So much for Neutralizers. You better

414

let him come along. He may be our only hope in figuring out what the glitch this is."

THIRTY-FIVE DAYS LATER . . .

The young man sleeping in the lobby of the army hospital snaps awake as the doors to the intensive care unit unseal and a pair of shiny black shoes *click-clack* their way down the synthotile floors.

He looks eagerly and anxiously into the eyes of the doctor, who comes to a halt in front of him.

"She's awake," the doctor says.

The young man leaps to his feet, feeling the sway of the earth beneath him, as he struggles to walk a straight line behind the billowing white coat. This is the moment he's been waiting for ever since he woke up to find that tiny cube tucked in his hand. Ever since he connected the drive to his best friend's Slate and watched the downloaded memory file she had stored there. Ever since he realized what she had done.

She had created a life in the very lab that once created her.

Or rather, she had *returned* a life.

To its rightful owner.

Her words echo hauntingly in his brain.

"Fall in love with me in a different world."

He heard them in the memory, but they felt eerily familiar. Like she'd whispered them right into his ear as well. Somewhere between sleep and dreams and the cold harsh reality of daylight.

He can't undo what she's done. He knows that. Some things simply can't be reversed.

All he can do is live with her decision.

Live with it, try to understand it . . . and wait.

But now, the waiting is over.

The doctor veers left down a hallway and right down another until they reach a section of the hospital that's guarded by a synthosteel door and two men in uniform, holding the kind of weapons the young man has only seen on Feed shows. He doesn't even want to know what they're capable of doing in real life.

They pass into another corridor and the doctor stops in front of a room. The young man can hear his own heart pounding in his ears. He waits for the door to be opened, but instead, the doctor turns to face him, trepidation etched into his old, wrinkled face.

"I should probably warn you, Zen," he says, his voice grave, sending chills down the young man's spine. "She doesn't remember anything. She hasn't spoken. She barely knows the letters of the alphabet. In many ways, she's like a newborn baby."

He nods, understanding.

"But she'll learn. It will just take time. Her brain functionality is normal. Her vitals are all normal. Apart from the mental and speech impediments, she's just a normal eighteen-year-old girl."

He turns and scans his fingerprint against the panel on the wall. The young man captures a breath in his lungs as the door glides open.

The girl lying in the bed looks smaller than he imagined. Then again, he's spent the last thirty-five days building her up in his mind. If she had any hope of matching the vast array of fantasies he concocted while daydreaming about this moment, she'd have to be twenty feet tall.

But it's her beauty that surprises him most.

He honestly wasn't sure what to expect.

Her skin is the same shade of honey, but with a sprinkling of faint freckles. Her hair is the same golden brown. It just doesn't sparkle. A pink birthmark, in the shape of a maple leaf, sits just under her chin.

But the moment he gazes upon her, he knows. Without a shadow of a doubt, he knows.

It's the face of the girl he loves.

Because he understands what lies beneath it. He always has.

"Sariana." He tests out the name from the memory file, saying it aloud for the first time. The *S* is familiar to him, an intimate sound on his tongue. The rest will have to come with time.

She opens her eyes at the sound of his voice. Blinks. Two brilliant chestnut gems—so richly brown they're almost purple—stare back at him, stealing his breath away. She looks him up and down with subtle fascination, as though she's memorizing him for the very first time.

"Do you think she recognizes you?" the doctor asks from the doorway, remarking upon the strange, almost whimsical look on the girl's face.

Yes . . . always yes.

"No," the young man answers quietly. "She's never met me before."

But as he turns back to the girl and allows their eyes to lock again, a faint, lopsided smile finds its way to his lips.

She doesn't know him. She doesn't remember him.

But she will.

ACKNOWLEDGMENTS

Ideas may come from a single spark of inspiration. But ideas don't equal finished books. Ideas don't put stories in the hands of readers. They don't edit, market, hand-hold, support, love, encourage, critique, or make you laugh when all seems lost. You need people for that. Brilliant, funny, supportive, *extraordinary* people.

Thank you to the unparalleled team of *superhumans* at Macmillan Children's Publishing Group: Simon Boughton, Joy Peskin, Allison Verost, Caitlin Sweeny, Kathryn Little, Angus Killick, Molly Brouillette, Lauren Burniac, Jon Yaged, Lucy Del Priore, Katie Halata, Jean Feiwel, Liz Fithian, Courtney Griffin, Holly Hunnicutt, Kate Lied, Ksenia Winnicki, Mark Von Bargen, and Nicole Banholzer. A super-bubbly, jazz-hands thank-you to Janine O'Malley and Angie Chen for pushing me to make these books the best they could be and for always saying "yes!" when I asked for more time. To Stephanie McKinley for being a fangirl, friend, and beta reader! Elizabeth Clark for designing the three best glitching covers ever. And Chandra Wohleber for copyediting the crap out of this beast and for calling the ending "perfect" when I needed to hear it most.

Mary Van Akin, you deserve your own line. Your own paragraph. Your own book. You make being awesome look easy. But you make finding the words to express my gratitude so very hard. Thank you for being my champion, friend, travel buddy, confidante, master strategist, and, oh yeah, publicist.

Thank you to my incredible agents, Bill Contardi and Jim McCarthy, for your never-ending wisdom, enthusiasm, encouragement, and patience (it requires a bold and courageous spirit to undertake a career working with writers). Thank you to Marianne Merola and Lauren Abramo, the queens of foreign rights! Also thanks to my amazing film agent, Dana Spector, and super-savvy entertainment lawyer, Mark Stankevich.

Thank you to Soumya Sundaresh, Deepak Nayar, Tabrez Noorani, and the amazing people at Kintop Pictures and Reliance Entertainment for bringing Sera's story to sparkly Hollywood. And especially to Soumya for holding my hand through this exciting yet scary yet remarkable process.

Across the pond, thank you to Claire Creek and everyone at Macmillan Children's UK for your amazing support and kickarse covers!

No matter what we authors do to perfect our characters, the booksellers, librarians, and teachers are the real heroes of any young adult story. Thank you to every single person who has placed my book in a reader's hand and who has said the magic words "I think you might like this." Especially thanks to Cathy Berner at Blue Willow, Caitlin Ayer at Books Inc., Jade Corn and Cori Ashley at Phoenix Book Company, Carolyn Hutton and Kathleen Caldwell at A Great Good Place for Books, Crystal Perkins, Maryelizabeth Hart, Courtney Saldana, Amy Oelkers, Julie Poling, Heather Hebert, Damon Larson, Mike Bull, Sandy Novak, Dennis Jolley, Sherri Ginsberg, and Allison Tran.

Because of the sheer talent, skill, and awesomeness of Nikki Hart at Multi-Designs, Mel Jolly at Author RX, and Dan Martino and Janey Lee at Haney Designs, I am able to stay sane, organized, and appear relatively on top of things.

I am so grateful for my "tribe"—the people who actually "get" it. My Fierce Reads sisters: Emmy Laybourne, Anna Banks, Leigh Bardugo, Gennifer Albin, Ann Aguirre, Nikki Kelly, Lish McBride, Elizabeth Fama, and Marissa Meyer. My Girls Gone Sci-Fi warriors: Tamara Ireland Stone, Jessica Khoury, Lauren Miller, Melissa Landers, Sophie Jordan, Victoria Scott, Alexandra

Monir, Gretchen McNeil, Beth Revis, Megan Shepherd, Meagan Spooner, Debra Driza, Amy Tintera, and Anna Carey. My Traveling Story stars: Robin Benway, Kevin Emerson, Megan Miranda, and Claudia Gray. My Steamboat Soulmates: Marie Lu, Morgan Matson, Brodi Ashton, Jenn Johansson, and Jennifer Bosworth. My dear friends Brad Gottfred, Robin Reul, Carol Tanzman, Lauren Kate, Alyson Noël, Carolina Munhoz, Raphael Draccon, Nadine Nettman Semerau, Mary E. Pearson, and Joanne Rendell. And a very special thanks to Michelle Levy, who is responsible for pretty much the coolest thing to ever happen to me!

Thank you to my beautiful and supportive family: Laura and Michael Brody (a girl can't ask for better parents. Well, she could, but she'd never find them!); Terra Brody (the founding member of Team Zen); Cathy and Steve Brody, who are always genuinely excited about whatever I do (You wrote a book? Yay! You went to the dry cleaner? Yay!); and my fur-babies: Honey Pants, BooBoo-Shush, Gracie-Kins, and Baby Baby. No matter how long I disappear for, you are always happy to see me. And, of course, Charlie, my rock and my Zen. Thank you for always keeping your feet on the ground so I can fly.

At the risk of sounding completely crazy (too late!), I want to thank Seraphina and Zen. You are as real to me as anyone else on this page. I will miss you.

And now comes the hard part. How do I properly thank *you*? The person responsible for all of this. If you're holding this book right now it means you made it to the end. You took the whole journey with me. There were so many other things you could have done with your time (played Candy Crush, watched *The Mindy Project*, eaten a bagel) and yet you chose to spend it with Sera and Zen. Even though I make a living stringing words into sentences, I'm not sure I'll ever be able to effectively convey how grateful I am that you're here. That you came along for this ride. You might just have to trust me. You might just have to believe.